MW01232375

The Winston & Baum Steampunk Adventures

Winston & Baum and the Secret of the Stone Circle

Winston & Baum and the Seven Mummies of Sekhmet

Winston & Baum and the Disk of Night

Winston & Baum and the Trials of the Baba Yaga

Winston & Baum
And
The Trials of the Baba Yaga

By Seth Tucker

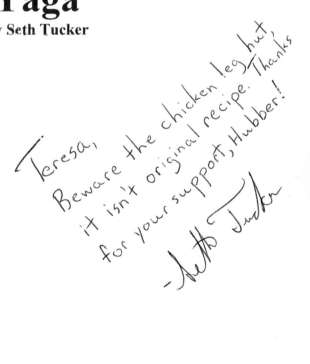

Teresa,
Beware the chicken leg hut,
it isn't original recipe. Thanks
for your support, Hubber!
- Seth Tucker

Text Copyright © 2017 by Seth Tucker
(radioactiverabbitink.com)
All rights reserved. Except as permitted under the U.S. Copyright Act of
1976, no part of this publication may be reproduced, distributed, or transmitted in
any form or by any means, or stored in a database or retrieval system without the
prior written permission of the publisher.

First print edition May 2017
The characters and events portrayed in this book are fictitious. Any
similarity to real persons, living or dead, is coincidental and not intended by the
author.

Cover Image Copyright © 2017 by Caralyn Edwards-Tucker
(www.mysticreflections.com)

To Caralyn for always listening and smiling, even though I know it sounds crazy sometimes.

Intro

The fog lay heavy on the cobblestone streets as the gas lamps struggled to pierce the thick white veil. Lee Baum, Dan Winston, and Brackish walked the lanes of Spitalfields. Dorset Street was not far now. Four women had been murdered, each of them within the crowded, filthy alleys of Whitechapel. Horrible mutilations to the bodies had originally led them to believe a maniac was loose on the streets. The most recent killings had been brought to the attention of the Office of Abnormal Affairs, and Winston and Baum had been handpicked for the case.

Elizabeth Strides and Catherine Eddowes, the latest victims, were also the only two to be killed on the same night. Strides' body was found in a small courtyard nearby where a hansom cab driver had startled the killer and interrupted his task, saving the young woman's body from the mutilation and disfigurement the other victims had suffered. The man had told the constables that he had seen great fangs and red eyes but could say little else. Catherine Eddowes had been found in Mitre Square, the only one found so far from her lodgings at Spitalfields, her throat slashed and her body ripped open. As in the previous killings, the killer kept pieces. For what purpose was yet unknown, but it was clear that they were being taken for a reason.

This, along with the description given by the cab driver and the rhyme found near Eddowes' remains, had forced the authorities to admit that they were not dealing with a human killer. Found on Goulston inside a tenement stairwell were a piece of Catherine Eddowes' bloody apron and a simple statement. While the anti-Semitic statements garnered the most attention, Metropolitan Police Commissioner, Sir Charles Warren, was not so interested in the words as the symbols they found on the wall. Having dealt with dark arts before, he contacted the Office of Abnormal Affairs, or Glorianna's Dungeon as most people knew it.

The killer's exploits had been spread throughout the papers and circulars found on every street corner, overshadowing even the war effort against Prussia. With the bombing of Dublin, the British Empire had found itself thrust into war with the Eastern European juggernaut. The continental power sought to usurp Her Majesty's kingdom for supremacy. Little had the Czar known, the island nation would stand her ground and fight. Troops had been sent and were now engaged in operations against Prussian forces within the very lands of the hostile country. The gruesome and alarming nature of these murders had proven a greater concern, though, especially to those who lived and worked in the crowded streets.

Women, those who chose to sell their companionship, no longer loitered on the streets. Fear of what might happen to them drove them indoors, but the killer would only have to wait. The women would have to work soon or risk being homeless. Either option could prove a death sentence.

"You know, I can't understand why he's picking these women," Dan said.

"Women of abandoned character make an easier target, I would assume," Lee replied.

"Shoot, last time I checked, wasn't nobody interested in their character," Dan retorted with a grin.

"Brackish?" Lee asked.

Pushing through the fog to stand beside the Englishman, the goblin had the collar of his small trench coat pulled tight around his face. One of

Dan's old, worn bowler hats sat on his bald, green-skinned head, and the brass hand attached to his prosthetic arm occasionally glinted in the gas lamps. Lee had designed the limb after Brackish lost his natural arm helping them with a case, and the goblin had been part of their team ever since. His sense of smell had proven a great advantage in previous hunts, so they had sent their small compatriot to scout ahead. "Nothing," Brackish answered, taking a deep breath of the night air, "fog too thick."

"Hell, that's an understatement," Dan stated. "What makes you so sure our boy's going to strike tonight?"

"The signs found on the wall in Goulston; they were astrological symbols, all of which pointed to either tonight or tomorrow," Lee explained. "Since most of the killings have at least been in this area, we may be able to prevent the fiend from doing any further harm."

"Good plan," Brackish admitted.

"Given how empty the streets are, you think he'll find any victims?" Dan asked.

"Hopefully not, but he'll most likely be hunting, whether there is an abundance of prey or not," Lee replied.

With the little information they had, Lee had been unable to tell what manner of creature they were facing. He was hoping it was something simple: a vampire or werewolf. Another creature may require more specialized means to be dispatched. With the threat of Prussian bombs, it was difficult for Lee to concentrate. Dan had admonished him several times that since the war started, only one bomb had fallen near London and then only on the outskirts. The coastal defenses had been holding remarkably well. Large cannons that fired explosive shells, which would detonate in mid-air and shred the canvas of any Prussian dirigible, had been placed along the coastal wall of England. For weeks, great piles of wreckage had been washing ashore, with a few live aeronauts, as the Prussians called them, accompanying the debris. These men had quickly been placed in military brigs until the Office of the Interior could complete an interrogation.

Even with the limited information, both men could protect themselves and, if not able to destroy the creature, at least wound it. Any sound leaving the nearby buildings was quickly swallowed by the fog. Only the noisily sung tunes from pubs could penetrate the gloom. Passing by Dorset Street, a stench of sulfur and rot stung their nostrils. Dan covered his mouth and turned away from the smell. Lee fought back a gag and peered through the thick white cloud that covered the street. Brackish was retching into the gutter. "Not here before," he finally managed to say.

"You're sure?" Dan asked.

Brackish nodded his head. Lee raised the Winchester from underneath his long coat. Dan's shotgun had been hidden within the folds of his trench coat, but the great pneumatic pack attached to it had been on his back for all to see. "Which way?" Lee asked.

The goblin turned his head to all four corners. Gagging once again, he pointed to the right. Turning onto Dorset Street, the hunters took shallow breaths, not wanting to breathe in the rancid scent too deeply. "What's this thing called anyway?" The American asked. "I've seen Ripper, Slicer, and Butcher in the papers."

"So far, it doesn't have an official title," the Englishman explained. "Some of the more dramatic titles for it have been the Whitechapel Horror and Bloody Hand of Propriety."

"Me heard it called Jack," Brackish offered.

12

"Jack?" Dan asked with a snort. "Great name for a monster. Everyone trembles at Jack."

"Just saying, heard it called Jack," Brackish responded with a shrug.

"Well, when we get to it, we'll ask its name," Lee said. "Perhaps it is Jack."

The stench was unbearable. As the trio of hunters progressed down Dorsett Street, the sour smell grew thicker. A small, squat structure stood back in one of the alleys. A sign leaning against the wall announced it as *Miller's Court*. For such an unassuming structure, the smell seemed to emanate from within it. Dan reached behind him and grasped the cord to turn on the pneumatic pack in anticipation. Following down the front of the building, the American saw closed windows and doors. One of the small rooms, *number thirteen* the paint above the door proclaimed, had a closed door with a missing pane from its window. Looking over his shoulder, Dan pointed at the window with the shotgun. Leaning over, Lee peered in as the curtain wafted in the night air. Gasping, Lee pushed himself away from the window as the door to the room burst out into the street. Dan pulled the cord and heard the piston engage. Tracing after the fleeing shape, Dan quickly lost sight of the fiend in the fog and pursued the being, Lee quickly behind him. Brackish ran beside Dan, a pistol clutched in his hand. "Can you smell him?" Dan asked.

"Ahead," Brackish answered.

Briefly in the fog, Dan caught sight of a top hat and cloak flapping as the mysterious murderer distanced himself from the hunters. There was a flapping sound, and Dan no longer heard footsteps ahead of them.

13

Stopping, the American glanced down at Brackish. The goblin's face wore a confused look. "Gone," Brackish stated. "Smell lingers, but he gone."

"Where?" Lee asked, searching the fog.

Brackish shrugged. "What did you see?" Dan asked his partner.

Lee shook his head, trying to force the image from his mind. "There is something on a bed in that hovel," Lee stated. "My fear is that it was once human."

Returning to Number Thirteen, Miller's Court, Dan, Lee, and Brackish glanced inside. The smell had dissipated some, but still the room carried an odor like a butcher's shop. The embers of a fire glowed in a fireplace with a kettle sitting on top, waiting for the heat to reach it. Dan reached for his pocket lantern, another device of Lee's design. Turning the crank to wind the dynamo, Dan flipped the switch, and light shone in the small room. "Dear God," Lee mumbled.

Dan pulled his handkerchief from his back pocket and covered his mouth. Brackish looked within the room but did not understand the men's reaction, until he saw the shape on the bed, and the red hair clinging to the pillow. Realization dawned on the goblin; this had been a woman once, like the other victims. Stepping over the threshold, Dan swept the light around the room. Lee and Brackish followed. The body lying on the bed had been cut open, with all the internal organs either on the table or the floor next to the small cot. The face of the woman had been brutalized as well. Great gashes had rendered it unrecognizable at all.

"Lee," Dan said in a hushed voice. "What are we dealing with?"

"I don't know," his partner answered. "We can't let this go on. The others were bad but nothing like this ferocity."

"Do you think it's because of the room?" The American asked.

14

"I don't know," the English hunter responded. "The killer hasn't attacked anyone indoors before. We should get a constable."

Stepping out into the foggy night again, the men felt better to be free from the gore-drenched room. None of them were strangers to death and violence, but the sheer destruction within was unlike anything they'd ever seen. "I go; constables no like me," Brackish said.

"Okay, but tell Ms. Edwards and Elizabeth that we will be along later," Lee instructed the goblin.

With a nod, Brackish backed into the fog and was lost to sight.

It took several hours for a constable to summon enough men to scour the scene. Several high-ranking officials of the Metropolitan Police Force came down and surveyed the damage. All of them left paler than before. "I'm not talking to another one of you," Dan shouted at a constable, the latest to question the two hunters on the events of the evening.

Aggravated at having to repeat himself, Dan made good on his promise and did not speak to another constable. A man, dressed in a suit that belonged more to a bank manager than a policeman, stepped towards Dan and Lee, his moustache as bushy as Dan's and connected to his large sideburns. "Inspector," Lee greeted.

"Fred," Dan acknowledged.

"It's Inspector Abberline, when I'm on duty," Abberline informed Dan.

"Right, sorry," Dan apologized. "So, why are we getting the third degree?"

"You *did* find the body," Abberline stated. "The boys are just antsy to get this ugly affair concluded, and you two presented an opportunity. What did you see?"

"Looked like a guy in a top hat and cape," Dan admitted. "Fella was fast, I'll say that. He also smelled something fierce."

"If I might interject, Inspector," Lee said, joining the conversation. "I don't know if it was a man, but I would not be so quick to believe so."

"You think it was a woman?" Abberline asked, flabbergasted.

"While I cannot confirm what the attacker was, I can tell you that it did not use a knife," Lee continued. "I saw it through the window, and I know its hand was formed into a razor-clawed caricature of a human's."

"What are you saying?" Abberline insisted.

"I'm saying that whatever this killer is, it is not human. No matter how badly it wishes us to believe it."

"Explains how it got away," Dan interjected. "Ain't many things that can get away from Brackish's nose."

"Speaking of the little devil, where is he?" Abberline asked, looking around.

"Went back to the flat," Dan answered.

"Police constables aren't too accommodating to little green beings at murder scenes," Lee explained.

"Have you heard from any of the other hunters?" Abberline asked. The two men shook their heads. "Do you have a plan to stop this insanity? The people are fit to riot. Between this and the war, something has to give."

"As a matter of fact, if you'll meet us back here tomorrow night around eleven, I believe we can put a stop to this before it gets any worse," Lee said.

Dan looked at his partner, a confused look crossing his features. Abberline did not notice the American's expression, and a hopeful smile emerged from underneath the inspector's moustache. "Good, good," he said. "If you have need of anything, send round to the Whitechapel H Division. I'll be there."

Abberline left the scene, excusing Dan and Lee from further questioning.

"I hope you know what you're doing," Dan said when he was sure they were far enough away from the police.

"I have a plan," Lee admitted. "Besides, have you ever known me to rush into a situation unprepared? If memory serves, that is *your* usual approach."

"I get the job done," Dan retorted.

"I've never insinuated otherwise, but this fiend is clever," Lee observed. "We will need to play this as you would a well-matched game of chess."

"More of a checkers man myself," Dan replied to Lee.

"When playing chess, it usually helps to be three steps ahead of your opponent," the Englishman continued, ignoring his partner's comment. "When tomorrow night arrives, I believe I understand his actions, at least partially, and have deduced his next course of action."

Away from the squalor of Whitechapel, in the countryside within the remains of a small village known as Falls, a hunched figure concealed within a great cloak shifted through the ashes of a building. Once it had been a tavern, but that was before Winston and Baum had passed through. Most of the town had burned, but the figure's withered and gnarled hands searched with purpose through the ash.

Outside the city walls, a small group of soldiers had been stationed to guard the city until it could be completely cleared of all dangers. Private Jameson Rhoads heard something from within the empty city, but rather than raise the alarm, he decided to investigate. It was his turn to work the late guard post, and he was the only soldier on watch. The past few times there had been a disturbance, it had only been rats or the occasional stray dog. Walking away from the warmth of the campfire, Jameson stepped over the few pieces of rubble that now marked the border to Falls.

Clutching onto a gray knob, the cloaked figure let out a joyful cry. Heaving on the piece, a large bone shifted, pulling free of the surrounding rubble. Once free, the intruder raised it high into the sky and danced about like the pagans who had once populated the British Isles. Wrapping a leather cord around the end of the bone, the mysterious being let the grotesque souvenir dangle from a weathered wrist. The figure walked down the remains of the street choked with rampant plant life and turned beside a house with a great garden overgrown behind the building's faded façade. There, jutting from the gutter, were the rotted pieces of wood that had once been a broom. Reaching out a hand, the creature of malice felt for the spark. A warm tingling came over her fingertips, and she knew it was close. At the first glimpse of white within the drain, she dropped to her knees and reached in. The muck and refuse cluttered about were of no concern to her. She grasped her prize, raised another large bone from the drain, and fastened it to the first.

"Halt!" Jameson called as he turned the corner and saw the figure, bones dangling from her wrists.

"Come to stop an old woman from visiting her family?" The figure inquired.

"No one is allowed within the city," Jameson explained. "If you have family that perished here, then a visit can be requested from Her Majesty's government.

"Too kind, too kind," the cloaked creature replied as it took a shambling step towards the young soldier.

Something about the approaching being scared Jameson. The soldier raised his rifle. "Halt, ma'am," he ordered. "My superior will need to come and determine what should be done."

"No need for any of that," the figure said.

A horrible light flared from the old, withered hands and engulfed the soldier, temporarily blinding him. When he could see again, the person he had confronted was gone. He tried to lower his rifle. Nothing happened. Willing his fingers to open, his muscles ignored him. Trying to see what was wrong, his neck also would not respond. His eyes roamed in their sockets, looking for any sign of what had happened to him. It was not until morning that the rest of his squad found him. He was standing stark still and could not move. The men had been forced to tip him over and carry him laying him in the back of a wagon and taking him directly to the nearest military post with a medical facility.

None of his fellow soldiers had found any evidence as to why Jameson had wondered into the ruined city or what evil had befallen him there.

The morning passed with Dan and Brackish sleeping, while Lee was busy about the flat, writing notes and sending messages to Abberline for men and supplies that would be needed for the night. Elizabeth, the only survivor from the village of Falls, and current ward of Ms. Edwards, made her way upstairs. She gently knocked on the door, and when no one answered, she let herself in. She smiled as she saw Brackish on his small cot by the fireplace, snoring loudly. The small goblin had saved her while Lee and Dan had been in America. Going to Lee's quarters, she found the door shut. A short rap on the door brought results as Lee opened it and looked at the little blond girl.

"Good morning, Elizabeth," he said smiling at her.

"Good morning, Mr. Baum," she replied. "Ms. Edwards wanted to know when you'd like lunch served."

Lee thought for a moment. "Around one should be sufficient," he answered.

"Also, sir, I had a vision this morning," Elizabeth informed him.

Lee looked earnestly at the child. Her ability to catch glimpses into the future had been the reason she was spared when the rest of her village was butchered. "Should I wake Dan?" Lee asked.

"No, sir," she replied. "This was just you. I don't know a lot; it was fuzzy, but I see you running from something. I never saw what was chasing you."

"Well, I may be giving chase to something tonight," Lee offered.

20

"No," Elizabeth stated, "you were not in London. There were trees, and in the distance, grass. You were running in muddy fields. I didn't see your rifle, Mr. Winston, or Brackish. It left me before I saw the end, but the shadow that loomed over you was merciless and held a big sword. Then, it was gone."

"Thank you, Elizabeth," Lee said, gently patting the teenage girl on the shoulder. "I will do my best to avoid your premonition."

"Thank you," she responded, visibly relieved. "I'll tell Ms. Edwards that you'll take lunch at one."

With a curtsy, Elizabeth turned and left the flat. Lee stood puzzling over the child's warning. To date, she had not been mistaken. For the time being, Lee had no plans to visit any place outside of the city. He was more intent on explaining his plan to Dan and Brackish over lunch, so he pushed her words of warning from his mind.

Darkness once again enshrouded the great city. Fog still hung on the streets, but it was not the thick miasma it had been the previous evening. Outside of Miller's Court, Inspector Abberline waited. His coat was pulled tight around him to fight off the chill, and he pulled his derby down further onto his head against the wind. In the distance, he could hear approaching footsteps and gripped his revolver inside his coat pocket. "That you?" Dan called.

"Yes, who else would it be?" Abberline asked.

"Good to see you again, Inspector," Lee stated. "I trust everything is in place."

"All just as you asked for it," the inspector stated. "Would you mind explaining your special requests?"

"I feel that if we wait, everything will be made clear," Lee replied.

"No sign," Brackish said as he came upon the three men.

"Give it time. It will come through here," Lee advised.

"What will come through here?" Abberline asked. "I've given you my full cooperation and would appreciate an explanation."

"Very well," Lee said, wanting to calm the irritated inspector. "Our killer approached from the other side of town and made his way here. When he fled, it was in the opposite direction. I believe that in the fog, he made his way past us and retreated the same way he came."

"Then why are we standing here?" Abberline asked still confused.

"The symbols painted on Goulston indicated the celestial configuration found last night and tonight," Lee stated. "I'm sure he'll be back again tonight. Also, he's made a point of staying near Dorset Street, and this gives us the best position to intercept him."

"All sound reasoning," Abberline admitted. "So, what are we dealing with if it's not human?"

"That, I still don't know," Lee confessed. "But with everything in place, I intend to find out."

"Shhh!" Brackish hissed as he took a deep breath. "Smell it."

"Inspector, signal your men," Lee whispered.

Turning away, Abberline lifted and replaced the cover on his bullhorn lantern three times, and a slight rustle came from the rooftops overhead. A dark figure emerged from the fog down the street, the dim silhouette of a man in cloak and top hat. A rapping sound as of a metal-tipped cane hitting the cobblestones echoed off the walls. Coming near Miller's Court, the man stiffened slightly when he saw Abberline and the hunters but continued down the street apparently unperturbed.

Approaching the lights of the Blue Coat Boy pub, the man pushed away from the light onto the opposite side of the street.

Dan reached back for the cord on the pneumatic pack, but Lee held up a hand to stop him. "Brackish?" He asked.

"Not him," Brackish answered. Looking down the street, the goblin pointed. "Him."

Another figure stood watching them. It also appeared to wear a top hat and cloak. "Inspector, perhaps you'd care to make the initial approach," Lee suggested.

"Certainly," Abberline said, stepping towards the figure. "Sir? Scotland Yard. We have a few questions to ask you."

The figure turned back the way it had come. "Stop!" The Inspector called.

Dan, Lee, and Brackish ran past the inspector, giving chase to the retreating figure. Pulling the cord, Dan activated the pneumatic pack and took aim at his prey. As he was putting pressure on the trigger of the shotgun, the man darted down one of the alleyways leading off Dorset Street. Again, they heard a flap, but this time, it was followed by an angry screech.

A dark shape was tangled in the thin lines of a net as it tumbled to the street. The inspector's men stationed on the roofs had managed to ensnare the fiend. Abberline rounded the corner and stopped, staring at the struggling creature before them. Dan took aim and let loose with a two-shot burst. The pellets hit the target and elicited another shriek and an angry hiss. "Back!" Lee ordered as droplets splattered from their wounded quarry and began to sizzle as they struck the cobblestones.

"What…" Abberline started.

"Not now," Dan interrupted.

The creature freed itself from the net and struggled towards the alley's opening. The cloak unfurled, exposing giant wings, and with two great strokes, the creature was airborne. Dan aimed on the rounded edge of a wing and squeezed the trigger, and several gaping holes appeared within the membranous surface. With the loss of the wing, the creature spun out of control and clipped the corner of a building before crashing in the street. As the men approached the fallen monster, it leapt to its feet and ran at an alarming speed away from them. "Abberline!" Lee shouted as he took aim on the retreating figure.

Dan's shotgun was useless at a distance, but Lee's Winchester was perfectly suited to the task. As Abberline pressed his whistle to his mouth and filled the night with a shrill call, Lee fired. The bullet struck the creature in the back of the leg, and Lee watched in amazement as the fiend stumbled, fell, and then rolled back onto its feet and continued fleeing, dragging its crippled leg behind it. At Abberline's whistle blow, constables stationed at one of the major intersections had moved wagons into place to cut off the thing's retreat. Seeing its path blocked, the creature turned toward the men.

"Christ, he's ugly," Dan announced.

Standing in front of them was a large creature that resembled a bat. Raising its ears to the sky and dropping its arms, the men saw how it had appeared as a man in top hat and cape. The creature stood still for a moment, as if listening. A whistling sound was coming from the sky above them. Dan, Lee, and Brackish raised their weapons toward the creature. "Do you understand us?" Lee asked. "Will you take us to your master?"

The creature turned its attention back to the men and pulled back, letting its claws glisten in the light. Above them, the whistling continued to grow louder. Dan raised the shotgun and was going to put the beast down when the world was filled with light and then replaced by a deep darkness.

1

Brackish opened his eyes. His vision was blurred. Something sticky was covering his face. His body ached. A loud ringing filled his ears, and he could not hear anything else. "Dan! Lee!" He shouted.

His vision cleared, but his right eye refused to open. Looking down with his good eye, Brackish saw a fine, white powder coating his skin. Wiping at the sticky spot on his head, he saw his own blood dripping from his hand. The street where they had been had changed drastically. A giant crater stood in the street, the remains of two of the small buildings scattered about them. Other buildings were damaged but seemed to be holding up. Remembering the bat beast, Brackish looked for his revolver but could not find it, so he drew his dagger from its sheath.

Across the street, spread across the front of the building was the fiend they had been facing. Great bits of steaming gore dripped onto the cobblestones. The monster had been standing near where the edge of the crater was now. No sound penetrated the ringing in his ears. Brackish tried to find Dan and Lee's scent, but the air was filled with too much dust and debris. A leg, wearing gray trousers, jutted from a nearby pile of rubble. Stumbling over to it, Brackish began to shift the bricks. After a few minutes, he saw Lee's hair poking through and began throwing the bits of masonry. Uncovering the back of Lee's head, Brackish cleared enough rubble to roll the Englishman over. Several cuts adorned Lee's face, but he was breathing. Satisfied, Brackish turned his attention to finding Dan.

The American had been thrown much farther than Lee. Only a few boards covered him, and Brackish saw that he was breathing. Struggling to lift Dan's bulk, the goblin slid the pneumatic pack from the American's

27

back. Brackish wanted to make sure that it would not explode and released the pressure from the tank. It had only done so once in Egypt, but the blast had almost killed Dan. Satisfied that he and his partners were safe, the goblin sat down on the cobblestones. His mind was working; he was sure that he had forgotten something.

As Brackish sat trying to remember, Inspector Abberline staggered from one of the nearby alleyways. The sideburn and portion of his moustache covering the right side of his face had been scorched off, the skin underneath an angry red. Looking at Abberline, Brackish saw his mouth moving. The inspector gave an annoyed look at the goblin. "Can't hear," Brackish shouted in explanation.

Waiting for a moment, Abberline seemed to understand and stumbled towards the intersection where the constables and wagons had been. Brackish could not tell if they were still there because of the great black smoke that obscured the street and rose into the sky.

When medical workers from the nearby hospitals arrived, Brackish was quick to watch them. He had already collected Dan and Lee's weapons to make sure no one took them. The small, white hospital carts were packed with wounded constables. Dan and Lee had both started to rouse but did not fully awaken as they were carried off to St. Thomas' Hospital.

Due to the lack of space, Brackish could not ride with the men, so he proceeded back to the apartment, uncertain that he could keep up with the cart in his current condition.

As he opened the door to the building, Ms. Edwards emerged from her quarters. "My Heavens!" She exclaimed. "Elizabeth, fetch some water and bandages!"

Brackish was glad that the ringing in his ears had begun to dim; he was never so happy to hear Ms. Edwards' yelling. Sitting the weapons in the hallway, he stood for a second. "Dan, Lee, taken to St. Thomas," he stated.

"Thank the Lord they're alive," Ms. Edwards said, clutching a hand to her heart. "Now, you come in, and we'll get you cleaned up. Were you caught in those explosions?"

"Maybe," Brackish admitted. "Boom, light, nothing else."

"It certainly sounds like an explosion," Elizabeth commented, carrying a pot of water with white bandages draped over her arm.

"Came from sky," Brackish explained.

The color drained from Ms. Edwards' face. "Good Lord!" She exclaimed.

Elizabeth stood beside the landlady, holding the pot out to her. Sitting Brackish down on a footstool, the older woman removed the remains of his bowler, pulled a sponge from the pot, and started to dab at the dried blood on the goblin's face.

Cleaned, bandaged, and wearing new clothes with his old cloth cap, Brackish left with Ms. Edwards and Elizabeth. Ms. Edwards hailed a passing motorized carriage and waited as the driver climbed down and opened the door for them. He was a young man dressed in heavy coat and hat, and thick, soot-smeared goggles adorned his face. "Saint Thomas', please," Ms. Edwards informed the man.

"Right away, ma'am."

As the engine began to push the carriage along, Ms. Edwards held tightly onto the seat, her knuckles white from her grip. "It ok," Brackish stated, trying to comfort the woman.

"I know," she responded. "I've just never trusted to these mechanical devices, not as reliable as a horse."

Elizabeth seemed at ease in the vehicle. Of course, her path to London involved a great deal of travel. Looking across the small aisle at Brackish, Elizabeth smiled even larger. "Do you think they'll let Mr. Winston and Mr. Baum come home?" She asked.

"I have no idea, child," Ms. Edwards responded. "Knowing those two men, Mr. Winston especially, they are probably causing the nursing staff enough grief to be banned from the place forever."

Elizabeth chuckled. Brackish gave a weak smile. He heard the doubt in Ms. Edwards' voice and knew that she had only been trying to keep Elizabeth hopeful. The carriage pulled up to the front gate of Saint Thomas Hospital. Exiting the carriage, Brackish pulled money from his pocket, handed it to the driver, and followed the ladies. The driver lifted his goggles to look at the ten-pound note the goblin had given him. "Thank you, sir!" He called, smiling at the large tip.

The hospital was filled with nurses, mainly women in grey dresses with white aprons, their hair tied back in buns. White-tiled floors and white walls amplified the light. Brackish tried not to breathe too deeply; the thick smell of antiseptic was harsh to his nostrils. Ms. Edwards, being familiar with hospitals, went to the small desk in the corner where one of the nurses sat. "Excuse me?" The landlady inquired.

30

"Yes, ma'am."

"We are seeking two men who came in tonight from Whitechapel."

"Part of the bombing?" The nurse inquired.

"I believe so. Lee Baum and Dan Winston were their names. One of them is an American," Ms. Edwards stated.

The nurse fought the urge to frown. "Yes, I believe I know just the men you are looking for. Halberk!" A fit young man in a gray shirt and pants stepped to the desk. "This is one of our attendants, Halberk. He will escort you to the patients." Turning to the attendant, the nurse explained, "the room with the American."

Halberk did not fight the urge to frown. "Oh," he said by way of explanation. "Right this way, ladies and..." he stood, puzzling over Brackish for a moment. "I don't believe he can..."

"See here," Ms. Edwards snapped, "he is a valued business partner of the two gentlemen -- more importantly, he is family -- and will not be excluded."

Halberk looked to the nurse for some assistance, but she was artificially absorbed in her novel. "Very well," Halberk relented, deciding it was better to not cause any trouble.

Following the attendant down a hallway lined with white doors, Brackish noticed the small windows set near the top of the entrances. This puzzled him until Halberk stopped and looked in through one of the windows. Facing the ladies, he opened the door and allowed them inside, and Brackish followed behind, tipping his hat at the man. Dan was sitting up in bed, taking a big bite out of an apple, while Lee lay in the bed across from Dan staring at the ceiling. "What test could you possibly run now,

Doc..." the word died in Lee's throat when he saw the trio in the room, and his face split into the biggest grin anyone there had ever seen.

Seeing his partner's reaction, Dan looked and saw their company. "What are you three doing here?"

"We came to ensure that your thick skull did not get damaged," Ms. Edwards retorted. "What trouble did you two get into tonight?"

"It was not our doing, or the result of our business," Lee explained. "I believe that more details will be known over the coming days, but something fell from the sky."

"Real bright and real loud," Dan said. "I hear you dug us out," he pointed at Brackish, who slid the cloth hat from his head and blushed slightly.

"You scare me," the goblin admitted. "How you know it me dug you up?"

"Abberline came by not too long ago, told us about it," the American stated. "Appreciate you getting the womenfolk."

"No problem."

"What list of ailments have you collected?" Ms. Edwards asked.

"We are both concussed. I've strained my shoulder, while Dan decided to break several bones in his hand," Lee said.

Dan raised his other hand and showed the cast covering most of his forearm, wrist, and hand. "Not too bad, given what could've happened," the American admitted.

Brackish had seen the remains of the creature and knew that Dan was right. "Hopefully, we will be away from here soon. They have exhausted the tests that they can perform and have found no other damage," Lee stated.

"Lord knows they've tried, though. I've been poked and prodded like a side of beef," Dan simplified.

"Besides, by my calculations, we still have a job to finish."

"If you'll excuse us, Elizabeth and I will leave you to talk business in private," Ms. Edwards said, taking Elizabeth by the hand and leading her from the room. "Mr. Brackish, we will be waiting at the front desk for you."

Once the door was safely closed, Dan looked at the goblin. "I bet you gave them one mighty big shock tonight."

Brackish nodded his head. "They both worry. Think you hurt worse," the goblin stated.

"Yes, Ms. Edwards and Elizabeth both have a tender heart towards our welfare," Lee admitted. "We will have to rest up once this job is finished, which should ease their worries."

"You keep saying 'when this is finished.' Didn't you hear Abberline?" Dan asked. "The bat blew up."

"I realize, but we have yet to deal with the master of the creature," Lee explained. "Whoever created the monster we saw tonight will create another if we do not stop him."

"What are you talking about 'created'?" Dan asked. "Do you know what he's talking about?"

Brackish shook his head. "Remember the sizzling droplets that the creature bled?" Lee asked. Both Dan and Brackish nodded. "That was not blood or any other type of bodily fluid; it was sizzling fat from a candle."

"Witchcraft," Dan stated flatly. "I hate witchcraft."

"Not quite," Lee corrected. "This is alchemy."

"I hate that, too," the American said. "So, how did someone make that thing?"

"A candle made from the fat of hanged men was molded. With the proper tools and knowledge of both science and magic, someone could have created the creature we saw tonight. While the candle burns, the creature lives and obeys its master. When the creature was injured, its blood was the contents of the candle its life force," the Englishman stated, sliding off the bed and stretching.

"This is like that German guy a couple of years back, some Baron or something?"

"No, he used strictly scientific principle," Lee stated. "I suppose, the principle is similar, but as you'll recall, that man's creation killed him. Our fellow will have complete control over his monster."

Dan stood up. "Well, where do we start looking?"

"I might know," Brackish added.

Both men looked at the goblin with smiles.

Lee's shoulder injury prevented him from being able to use the Winchester, so he left it behind at Ms. Edwards' house, and with Dan's hand in a cast, he could not operate the pneumatic pack, which was fine since Lee would need to examine the device to determine if it needed repairing. Dan had refused to leave his old pump-action shotgun behind, though. Standing in their flat, he had been able to work the pump but was aware of how slow he was going to be between shots. Fortunately, Brackish's prosthetic arm had only taken cosmetic damage in the blast, so he brought his short-barreled shotgun and the spare pistol from its case under his bed after his first had failed to turn up. They had tried to reach Abberline, but he had been called to Scotland Yard to make a full report.

The streets were more active than they had been. Several explosions had detonated across the city; the one in Whitechapel was just the first. Most people were afraid that more were to follow. "What happened, Lee?" Dan asked. "It's all a little vague to me."

"Something fell from the sky and blew up," Lee stated plainly. "If it had not hit that building, I fear that we would have all suffered the same fate as the bat creature."

"No much left," Brackish commented.

"Quite," Lee responded. "Now, Brackish, where do you think the master of the creature is?"

Brackish gave a devious smile. "Follow," the goblin instructed as he turned and headed uptown.

An hour later, Brackish stopped in front of a tobacco shop. Lee and Dan looked at each other, then their goblin guide. "He's here?" Dan asked.

"Don't know. It a clue."

Dan raised a questioning eyebrow. Lee stepped up to the darkened building and knocked on the door. A light in the back of the shop came on in response. Waiting a few moments, Lee knocked again when the light did not move. "Well?" Dan asked.

"Someone's coming."

A small, hunched man came through the aisles of the shop, holding a small candle in front of him. Wrapped in his robe with a night cap on his head, the old man looked almost comical. "Can I help you?"

"Morty!" Brackish said, stepping up to the man.

"Brackish, it's a little late for a business call. Besides, your order isn't due for another few days."

"Need help. Bad man bought tobacco here."

"You've been coming here to get cigars?" Dan asked.

Brackish grinned and nodded. Dan and Lee had wondered where the goblin would disappear to. Neither man realized that Brackish had apparently become a regular at this shop. "Oh my," Morty said, looking around. "Well, I suppose you'd better come in."

The shop was rich with the smell of tobacco, which Dan drank in. Lee was less enthused but stepped inside. Following behind, Brackish walked down one of the aisles and pointed to a jar. He glanced at Dan and gave him a wink. Morty locked the door behind them. "Now, what's this about a bad man?" The shopkeeper asked.

"I'm not sure. Brackish, would you please explain yourself?" Lee inquired.

"Okay," Brackish answered, "we fought monster; it smell like..." Brackish searched for a moment before stopping near a small container on one of the shelves. "This! When it burn, smell like this."

Brackish grabbed the container and carried it to Morty. "Oh my, well, that is unfortunate," the shopkeeper stated.

"How many tobacco shops carry that?" Dan asked. "And what is it?"

"It's a very special Peruvian pipe tobacco. I'm the only shop in London that carries it," Morty admitted, puffing up proudly. "I only have two customers that buy it."

"Can you tell us who they are? And where they can be found?" Lee asked.

"Gladly, sir," the small man explained.

While Morty wrote down the names and addresses of the two men, Dan looked around, appraising the shop. It appeared to be no bigger than the tobacco shop on their street, but it had a far wider selection. "Thank you for your assistance, sir," Lee said as he took the slip of paper.

"My pleasure," he answered. "I'll be sending word when your cigars come in, Brackish."

"Thank you," Brackish said, stepping back onto the sidewalk.

As the trio of hunters headed back out into the night, Dan looked down at the goblin. "Next time you come down here, let me know. I wouldn't mind trying some of his stuff."

"Okay," Brackish agreed. "Where we go now?"

Lee looked at the names on the list. "Well, both of these men live nearby," he stated. Stopping, Lee looked around at the street signs and buildings. "Let's visit this second address first."

"Why?" Dan asked.

"He lives to the north of Whitechapel," Lee stated. "If you'll recall, that's the direction that our rending fiend arrived from."

Lee led them through an upscale area of London where large manor houses lined the streets. Stopping outside of a gate, Lee checked the address. "This appears to be the residence."

Opening the gate, Lee walked to the door. Keeping a good grip on their shotguns, Dan and Brackish slid them inside their trench coats. Dan nodded at Lee when they were successfully hidden. Picking up the bronze ring on the front of the door, Lee dropped the heavy knocker twice. A light came on in the upper floor. After several minutes, a middle-aged man opened the door. The man had immaculate posture. His clothes were well pressed, and his hair was perfectly combed. It did not look as if he had been asleep at all. "Can I help you, sir?" The man asked.

"Yes," Lee answered. "We would like to speak to the master of the house."

The butler gave him a dubious look. "That will not be possible, sir. The master has retired for the evening and will not receive any visitors until the morning. If you would like to return at a more decent time, then you are most welcome to do so."

The butler started to push the door closed. Dan stuck his boot in the way. "Sir, please remove your foot," the servant requested.

"No," Dan said flatly. "Somebody's up; we can see the light in their window. Now, if you won't let us speak to the big man, how about answering a question for us? Can you do that?"

"Yes, sir," the butler said, his voice thick with annoyance.

"Can you tell us if Adam Harwood resides here?" Lee asked, reading the name from the paper.

"He does. Adam is one of our coachmen."

"Since your master can't be disturbed, can we see him?" Dan asked.

"If you insist," the butler stated. "Please see yourself to the servant's entrance at the rear of the house, and I will bring Adam to talk with you."

Dan moved his foot and allowed the butler to close the door. "Think he'll actually bring the guy?"

"I believe so."

"We think coachman bad man?" Brackish asked.

"It is possible," the Englishman stated. "Although, I would not have suspected a coachman of such knowledge or talent."

Waiting by the servant's entrance, the trio stood patiently. The sound of the bolt being drawn was loud in the quiet night. Standing in the doorway was the butler, and in front of him stood a young man rubbing his eyes. "Are you Adam Harwood?" Lee asked.

The young man nodded. "I am, sir."

"We need to talk to you," Dan said.

"What for? I ain't done nothin' and don't know you."

"Have any business in Whitechapel recently?" The American asked.

"No, sir," Adam answered. "I've not been to Whitechapel for months."

Dan grabbed the young man by the shirt collar and pulled him out into the yard, his bare feet dragging the ground. "Listen boy, I was almost blown up tonight fighting that thing you made; now you come clean. Why were you doing it?" He demanded.

"Honest, I don't know what you mean," Adam pleaded.

Dan let him go to fall onto the grass. "You buy a rare type of pipe tobacco. Were you aware of this?" Lee asked.

"It's not my pipe tobacco. I buy some fags from a tobacco shop, but the pipe isn't mine," Adam explained.

"Whose?" Brackish asked.

Adam saw the goblin for the first time and drew back quickly. He stopped as he bumped into Dan. "Answer the question." Dan ordered.

"Sue, the kitchen lady," Adam stated. "It's her tobacco and her pipe."

Lee turned back to the butler. "Does she have access to a large room, one that no one else ever enters?"

"She has full access to the cellar and ice house," the butler answered.

"We need to see them now," the English hunter stated.

The butler stood firm in his post and refused to let the hunters enter. "Absolutely not! You may come back at a decent hour."

"You realize your cook may be making monsters that have been killing women in Whitechapel," Dan informed the butler. "We stopped one of them, and you sure as hell better hope that none of them get loose in the house, or you'll all be dead."

"Nigel, let them in," a calm voice said from behind the butler.

Nigel turned and saw the master of the house, dressed in slacks and an evening jacket. "Yes, sir," the butler answered and complied, stepping aside.

"Gentlemen, I am Robert Hawthorne; please come in," the master of the house introduced himself. "What is this all about?"

"Sir, earlier this evening, we encountered a winged beast. It is this creature that has perpetrated the recent murders in Whitechapel," Lee explained.

"Good Lord, I believed those were just stories created to sell papers," Robert gasped.

"They ain't," Dan replied.

"You believe that this creature came from my house?"

"It is a possibility, one that we can quickly rule out," Lee informed the man.

"Then by all means, search where you must," Robert said, turning to go back upstairs.

The hunters took notice of the cane and noticeable limp that Robert exhibited as he left. Nigel led them to the kitchen. "The ice house is through the door at the rear corner. You will find the cellar can be accessed by the doorway underneath the stairs," Nigel said as he stepped back into the hallway.

The kitchen was large with several portly, wood-burning stoves. A brick oven sat in the corner near the stoves, and copper pots and pans hung from the ceiling on black, wrought-iron racks, while knives and other utensils hung on the wall behind a bloody butcher block counter. "What do you think?" Dan asked.

"Cellar," Brackish answered. "Ice house cold."

"Cellar it is," Lee agreed.

Walking down the stairs to the main floor of the kitchen, the men looked underneath the stairs. A wooden door was laid into the tiled wall. With no civilians present, Dan and Brackish pulled their shotguns from inside their coats. Lee reached out to the dilapidated door knob. "Wait," the goblin cautioned. "Lamp."

Dan and Brackish quickly wound their lanterns, turned them on, and clipped them to their coats. Dave gave a nod to Lee, who pulled the door open with a quick jerk, revealing an empty staircase descending to a dirt floor. Brackish went first, and Dan followed behind as Lee brought up the rear.

Once they reached the bottom of the stairs, they could see what they were looking for. Food and other kitchen staples were pressed against the walls. In the center of the room was a candle of yellowish wax that had been partly burned. Several symbols were carved into the ground with several other small idols placed in the center of the symbols. Lee and Dan had seen similar sights before, during other alchemy-related cases. Brackish did not recognize the symbols but knew bad magic when he saw it. A small table stood nearby, chemicals and taxidermy tools arrayed on the scarred wooden top. Five large containers sat beside the table, lids tightly secured to them. "Lee?" Dan asked.

"It appears that she hasn't created a new creature yet," Lee answered. "We need to find her."

Rushing back upstairs, they found Nigel still waiting for them in the hall. "Where's Sue?" Dan asked.

Nigel was taken aback by their urgency. "In her quarters, I would imagine."

"Show us." Lee demanded.

Hurrying down the hallway, Nigel led the trio of hunters to the female servants' quarters. "Second door on the left," he informed them, pointing at the wooden barrier.

"She bunk alone?" Dan asked.

Nigel nodded.

Stopping at the door, Dan turned the handle, and something dark lashed out, sending Dan through the door on the opposite side of the hallway. A woman screamed from the room. Lee drew his pistol and waited. "Thought you'd catch me unprepared?" A crazed voice called. "Always have another, 'just in case' me mama used to say."

Another bat creature stepped from the room. Its broad shoulders filled the hallway. Trying to raise its arms, the creature caught its hand in the smashed-in doorway. A gunshot sounded from the room that Dan had been propelled into, and the creature withdrew a ruined stump, candle wax pouring onto the floor. Turning its back on Lee and Brackish, the creature started to stoop into the room. Brackish's shotgun barked, and wax began to pour from the wound in the creature's side. Not sure which threat to face, the monstrosity turned back towards Lee and Brackish. Raising the revolver, Lee fired all six shots into the upturned nose and grotesque mouth. Dan leaned against the doorframe. Stumbling backwards, the beast sought refuge from the stinging bullets. Brackish continued pumping shots from his shotgun into the creature, with Dan firing at a slower rate until it quit moving. A mass of drying wax pooled underneath it.

As the shooting subsided, the other servants started to come from their rooms with terrified expressions on their faces. "Please remain in your rooms until Nigel has told you it's safe," Lee ordered.

The butler stepped into view, holding his chest, and nodded so the others would obey the strange, armed man. Lee and Brackish started down the hallway towards the monster's hiding spot, doors closing on both sides. Dan stepped fully into the hall from the room he had been put into. "Sorry, ma'am," he said, tipping his hat.

Popping his neck, Dan started to step into Sue's room. "She's not in there," Nigel stated. "In the confusion, she shoved past me."

"Towards the kitchen?" Lee asked, and Nigel nodded. "Dan, we have to go; she's planning something big," the Englishman called.

The trio of hunters ran back to the kitchen; seeing the cellar door standing open, they knew their ultimate destination.

"Don't come in here," the crazed voice called as Dan put his foot on the top step, leading into the cellar. "I've done nada wrong."

"Then no be scared," Brackish responded.

"Stay back. The Daughters of Camazotz do not take kindly to fools who meddle in their affairs."

"Sue," Dan called. "I'm coming down."

"You do so at your own risk," the woman threatened. "I am Soona, Priestess of Camazotz. The great death bat will not tolerate your intrusion."

Dan continued downward. "Stay here," he instructed his associates.

Lee and Brackish heard the sounds of a light scuffle, and a moment later, Dan appeared at the bottom of the stairs, leading a small, haggard woman by the arm. She appeared to be from South America, a bruise forming on her cheek. "That was much easier than anticipated," Lee commented.

"Yeah, normally more fight," Brackish agreed.

"Well, she tried to stab me, but I was able to persuade her not to." Dan stated.

"How?" Brackish asked, surprised that Dan had been able to talk the woman into surrendering.

"Smacked her with the butt of the shotgun."

"Oh."

"Let's get a carriage," Dan suggested, passing the butler in the hallway. "Tell Mr. Hawthorne we're sorry 'bout the mess."

Nigel remained silent as the hunters passed him on their way to leave.

2

Arriving outside of Scotland Yard, Lee led Sue from the motorized carriage. Dan and Brackish followed, stepping into the chill night air. As Lee started up the steps to the looming police building, he noticed that Dan and Brackish were making their way to the smaller building, the home of Glorianna's Dungeon. "Where are you going?" Lee called.

Dan turned towards his partner. "To let Roger know about her tools. Hey! Stay with her; I want to know what she tells the police."

Lee nodded as he started back up the stairs with Sue.

Brackish and Dan entered the foyer of the building where two doors stood opposite them, separated only by wood paneling with a single button set into it. A painting of the Limestone Massacre hung on one side wall. It was a terrible event. Royal Marines had killed a group of battling dwarves and goblins. It was the moment that had led to the realization that the creatures of myth and legend were more realistic than previously believed. Brackish ignored the ghastly painting of the massacre and pressed the single button. The goblin and man waited, expecting the short, bespectacled man, who normally answered, to make his standard appearance.

As the panel slid aside, a lovely young woman with red hair looked out at them instead. "Brackish!" She shouted excitedly.

"Eden!" The goblin responded, matching the woman's exuberance.

Brackish had met the young woman while Dan and Lee had been away in America. He had not seen her since but had been very fond of the nice woman, who was not scared of him. "Don't believe I've had the pleasure," Dan said, extending a hand to the woman. "Dan Winston."

"Eden," she replied, shaking his uninjured hand. "It's so nice to finally get to meet one of Brackish's associates. Here for Roger?"

"Yes," Brackish answered.

"Come right on back," Eden said as she opened the door.

Stepping through, the hunters went through a room full of desks. Roger, their Regent Warden, had his desk situated near the rear of the room. Regent Wardens were government liaisons for bounty hunters, like Dan, Lee, and Brackish. Dan sat down in front of the desk. Brackish looked around before taking the chair beside him. "So, is that the girl from your little romp with the unicorn?" Dan asked.

"Yes," the goblin confirmed. "Eden is nice, not scared."

"Hell, she seemed right fond of you," the American admitted. "See, not all people judge a book by its short, green cover."

Brackish just nodded as Roger stepped from the door at the back of the room. "To what do I owe the honor?" Roger asked sourly.

"You know about that Whitechapel business?" Dan asked.

"Indeed, I do. I also know that the creature was not destroyed by you. Therefore, no bounty can be awarded," Roger smiled smugly. "If there's nothing further..."

"Actually, there is. We killed another one tonight at the house of Robert Hawthorne. Seems his cook was using... what was it Lee called it?"

"Alchemy," the goblin answered.

"Yeah, alchemy. Anyway, the old cook was using it to make and run that critter, and she had a spare. We killed it, and since you boys have special people to clean up after mad men of science and witches, thought maybe they'd clean up since this is both," Dan said, returning Roger's smug look.

"I see," Roger replied, taking a pencil from his desk drawer. "I need the address where this happened, and can you tell me where the practitioner currently is?"

Dan told Roger where the alchemist had been practicing and how Lee had taken her to the police. "Very well," Roger said, finishing his notes. "Once we have confirmed the creature's destruction, any bounty owed will be sent to you. Now, if you'll excuse me, I have to arrange for a retrieval."

"Sure thing," Dan said, standing up. "We can see ourselves out."

Normally, the hunters left from the basement since that was where they collected their money. As they weren't getting paid right now, they headed back towards the foyer to leave by the front, where Eden was waiting by the door. "Good night, gentlemen. Come back any time," she said.

Dan tipped his hat and exited. Brackish smiled at the woman. "Bye, Eden. Take care," he said.

"You first," Eden responded, winking at the goblin.

Dan and Brackish waited outside of Scotland Yard in the cold for an hour before Lee joined them. "Well?" Dan asked.

"Robert Hawthorne is apparently a very large antique dealer, specializing in Mayan and Aztec artifacts," Lee started. "Soona needed a piece that he had collected and managed to land a position on his personnel staff during his last expedition. He enjoyed the cooking so much that he brought her back. She's a high priest for a cult that worships a bat god of some sort. The details were not quite clear, but she was trying to open a portal and resurrect this deity."

Brackish let out a low whistle. "Big idea," he commented.

"Crazy people usually come up with some doozies," Dan agreed. "Why the body parts?"

"She needed them in the ceremony to resurrect Camazotz," the Englishman explained. "Something about organs of life; again, she wasn't quite clear in that regard, though we know that these types of spells are normally only clear on the ingredients and never the reasons why."

"Well, she's safely locked away now. Roger's on his way to clean up the house," the American stated.

"Good," Lee said, rubbing his hands against the cold. "If we hurry, perhaps we can arrive home before dawn."

The three hunters climbed into the rear of the carriage, giving the driver the address of their home.

The figure that Jameson Rhoads encountered in the village of Falls had retreated from the dilapidated village to a small thatch hut outside the ruins of a large manor house. A long-forgotten sign near the overgrown carriage path stood beside the unassuming hut that blended perfectly with the woods around. Sitting before a fire, a split skull in front of her, the figure laid the two bones she had procured beside her, forming a triangle with the fire. A black kettle sat upon it, steam pouring from the spout and soon began to whistle its tune. Removing it from the fire, the hunched figure poured a vile-smelling concoction into the open top of the skull.

Setting aside the black container, the figure lifted the vile cup to her lips and drank deeply of the contents.

Dropping the skull, the figure began coughing and spasming but fought to remain within the three sides of her triangle. Closing her eyes, she opened them and found herself in a dark place. This was the place that she had sought, the meeting place of the great witches. A fierce old woman stood before her. "Who are you to call me?" The woman demanded.

"You know me, as I know you," the figure answered. "If you must have a name, then perhaps Megara will do."

"Aye," the woman agreed. "Megara will do fine, though it is Meg that most call you. Now, why have you called me? What does a fool sister from Britannia have to do with me?"

Megara let out a delighted cackle. "Look closer, fierce mother. Know that I am more powerful than you now."

Closing her eyes, the woman reached out to feel the power coursing from Meg. Quickly, she withdrew her senses. "You seek to contain that power!" The woman shouted. "Foolish sister! You will find naught but pain and death in that path."

"Mayhaps," Meg conceded. "But you will obey, or I'll visit it upon you first."

"You will die before you master such a force."

"And if I do not, before my final breath, I will ruin your land and turn it into a vast stretch of charred bones and dead forests." Megara threatened. A quick flash of light brightened the gathering place.

"What request have you of me?" The woman asked more subdued than before, rubbing a gnarled hand over her eyes, feeling a thickness over them…

"I feel it time you took a greater role in the events that have transpired amongst the men of our countries." Megara cackled, while inside the hut her body lay still before the fire. "There is one that we must draw to your bosom."

Most news from the war had been on the successes of British forces and the destruction of Prussian airships on the coast. In the wake of the explosions of the previous evening, the people of London were much more subdued. Dan and Brackish sat in their apartment, both drinking beer and smoking cigars, celebrating another closed case. Lee had left to see what news he could get regarding the explosion. Opening the door, the inventor shook off the chill from outside and hung his coat on the rack. "It seems that we were fortunate enough to survive a Prussian bombing," he announced.

Dan and Brackish both sat holding their bottles and gravely looked at Lee. "How'd they get past the coastal defenses?" The American asked, blowing out a ring of smoke.

"They didn't," Lee responded. "Setting off from Germany, they took the northern air currents around the tip of Ireland and came at us from the rear."

"Only one?" Brackish asked, crushing out the glowing ember of his cigar in the clay ashtray at his side.

"Yes. This was most likely a test to determine the strength of our defenses. Had they sent a larger force, I fear that the city would be catastrophically damaged," the Englishman explained. "An acquaintance of mine within the Ministry of Defense has assured me that a train left the depot this morning loaded with a detachment of artillery. The coastal defense will be on both sides of the island, now. Irish volunteers will be spotting around the clock for incoming air ships. In three days' time, the Prussians will not be able to breach our defenses and attack us again."

"It was a nasty cheap shot," Dan commented, "almost as bad as Dublin."

"Indeed, it was," Lee agreed.

The bombs that had fallen on Dublin had been the act of aggression that started the war. Germany had fallen easily to the Prussian war machine, but little did they realize that the little island empire had a will of iron. Many of the citizens questioned what had transpired to mitigate such an attack. Queen Victoria's daughter, also named Victoria, was Crown Princess of Prussia married to the Crown Prince Frederick. As much as some supposed, no rift existed between mother and daughter. Instead, Otto von Bismarck, the Minister President of Prussia, had managed to repress the power of the royal family and start a war of his own devising. British forces had made great bounds in pushing the Prussian forces from Germany and were preparing to enter into Prussia itself.

Now, Prussia had managed to drop bombs on the great city. Its citizens were shaken, the war they had been reading about delivered to their very doorsteps. The Office of the Interior was trying to keep the populace calm, while the military was making sure that no troops were dropped into the countryside as part of an invasion. With enlistment offices filled, Lee had experienced a great swelling of national pride and wanted to enlist with the others. Even though he met all the physical requirements to enlist, he was aware that he was over the age for such an action. He had served Queen and Country in India. His experiences there had not been unpleasant, but he had not been serving during wartime either. So, Lee was content to stay home and assist the war effort in other ways, while the heads of state made their plans for victory.

Huddled on a small airship, a battalion of Her Majesty's Marines was being transported behind the Prussian front. They were going to drop down and disrupt the Prussian supply lines. Corporal John Trenton had been extremely successful in his training for this mission. As a child, he had grown up alone on the streets of London. It had not been easy for a child to stay away from the police and keep out of the orphanages and workhouses. Quick wit and daring had served Trenton well, that is until he had reached the age of enlistment. He had received his first taste of combat at Stonehenge a couple of years before. They had not been fighting men with rifles then but hordes of monsters. Now, he would be shedding human blood. It was not an idea that he relished, but the Prussians had made their choices. Now, they would have to answer for them.

The company commander was pacing the deck. To keep the ship as invisible as possible, there were no windows; the captain was steering the ship through a small porthole and using starlight to mark the landing. The airship had seemed a strange sight when the Marines had first beheld it. Black paint coated the metal, and the nylon balloon used to lift the vehicle was also dark. It was unusual to conduct airship maneuvers on moonless nights, but this operation called for it. The bulk of the vessel would show against the silvery light of the moon.

Trenton thought he heard something from outside the ship. "Sir?" He asked the company commander.

"What is it, Corporal?"

"Permission to step outside, sir?" Trenton asked. "I thought I heard something."

"Did you?" The commander stopped for a moment and listened.

There was a slight tap from outside on the walkway. Ignoring Trenton, the commander went to the small tubing set onto the wall. Lifting the rounded mouthpiece, he put a call into the ship's captain.

"I was hoping that was one of your boys smoking," the captain replied. "Send some men out to investigate. If they find an untied cable, tell them to reattach it."

"Corporal, take two men with you," the commander ordered.

Trenton selected two men and went to the exterior hatch. Checking to make sure that his rifle was ready to fire, he pulled back the hatch and felt the cold Prussian air. Looking both ways, Trenton did not see any immediate threats. Stepping out, he waited as the other two men cautiously took position behind him. It seemed unnaturally bright on the catwalk around the cabin of the airship. A strange yellow glow was emanating from the rear of the hydrogen-filled sack that sat on top of the compartments. Going to the stairs, Trenton climbed upwards, noticing that the light seemed to be growing brighter. A large bird was standing on the rail with a crest on its head. The crest glowed red while orange and yellow light radiated from its body and the long, trailing plumage. "What is that?" One of the men asked.

"Shhh!" Trenton hushed him.

The animal did not pay any attention to the men but looked ahead at the thick skin wrapped around the hydrogen bladder, darting its head forward and pulling at the material. Trenton raised his rifle, and the weapon's sling hit the railing with a slight, metallic ring.

The bird looked at the trio and let out a strange, warbling cry. Placing his finger on the trigger, Trenton prepared to squeeze off a shot when he heard a hiss from above them. Something dropped down directly behind the Corporal, and the two men with him gave a startled cry. Trenton shot at the bird, and the bullet struck the strange animal in the side, drawing a second cry from the creature before renewing its efforts to pierce the hydrogen compartment. Where the bullet had wounded the creature, flames licked out into the night. As Trenton stared in amazement, something latched onto the back of his neck and hoisted him off his feet. The two men who had accompanied Trenton fired into the menacing figure that had appeared at the bird's calling. Swinging wildly, Trenton felt his hands connect several times. Each time the flesh gave beneath his fist, but the grip showed no signs of weakening.

Taking the rosary his mother had given him before he had shipped out, Trenton kissed it and started to say the Lord's Prayer. The crucifix dangled as he did so and touched the skin of his attacker. There was a flash of light and the smell of seared flesh, and Trenton was suddenly dropped to his feet as his assailant stumbled back. Turning around, the soldier saw the pale, translucent skin, red eyes, and extended teeth. "Vampire!" Trenton shouted, holding the crucifix in front of him. "Quickly, one of you tell the commander that we have a vampire and some strange bird attacking us."

Stumbling back, one of the soldiers rushed to the compartment to notify his superiors of the invaders onboard. The more stalwart of the two stepped up beside Corporal Trenton to deal with the undead attacker. "Forget about the vampire!" Trenton ordered. "We have to stop that bird."

Turning his attention beyond the pale being, the soldier immediately saw the metal filaments being plucked and snapped. Once they were free, the bladder filled with hydrogen would be simple work. A puncture would send them hurtling out of control. Trenton did not bother to tell the soldier about the flaming insides of the bird, and that they were riding on a giant bomb. Raising up their Winchester rifles, the two men took aim. Stepping in front of the intended target, the vampire absorbed their first few shots. A wicked smile crossed its bloodless lips, and it uttered something in Prussian.

Stepping closer to the monster, Trenton gripped the rosary tightly. Charging at the undead stowaway, the soldier grabbed the monster's shirt and slipped the hoop of prayer beads over the creature's neck. The vampire rushed frantically about as the crucifix set its torso on fire, screaming until it hit the guard rail and plummeted over the side. "Now!" Trenton shouted as he raised his rifle and put several rounds into the unprotected flank of the bird.

The bullets slammed into the brightly colored flesh, and flames burst from the wounds, forcing the two soldiers back. Staggering back to its feet, the bird pressed its wounded side against the giant inflated bladder. The metal had been sheared in several places and the thin rubber would quickly burn away under the flames. Grabbing his fellow soldier by the arm, Trenton dragged him toward the bow of the airship. He knew that what was coming was going to be vicious. "What are we..."

"Run!" Trenton shouted in answer to the unfinished question.

Reaching the bow, Trenton dove over the railing, dragging his compatriot with him. Both men screamed as they plummeted. Their shouts of terror were overpowered as the hydrogen within the dirigible ignited, and an explosion lit up the night sky. The pressure wave slammed against Trenton and his companion, shoving them closer towards the dark landscape of Prussia.

From a nearby field, the old woman stood watching as one of the great creatures of her homeland sacrificed itself against the English invaders. It was not her way to interfere with the wars of men, but she had been persuaded. She realized the pains of her land caused by these invading fools. One of their industrial men especially had to be lured and destroyed for the evils that he had perpetrated. Now, with the first blow struck, others would come. Among them, the ones that she sought. Nearby, the vampire dragged itself across the mud and muck. A holy symbol had disfigured the creature, but it was of no consequence. "I have failed you," the vampire stated.

The old woman dismissed the statement. "The ship is destroyed, and the English will now know that there are greater forces than those of men aligned against them," she commented.

Before the explosion, the captain of the vessel had managed to send a wireless transmission. In England, seated behind a desk at the Home Office, a communications officer read the words as they came in. Even though he was not a high-ranking officer, he knew this was an important message. Transcribing it, he rushed to the courier's office and immediately dispatched a messenger to the home of Prime Minister Robert Gascoyne-Cecil, the third Marquess of Salisbury. While having only been the Prime Minister for a few short months prior to the first Prussian bombing, he had proven himself a stalwart leader. His orders had been very simple: any high priority communiqués were to be directed to him first, and then he would follow-up with Her Majesty.

Woken by his butler, Robert put on a dressing gown and hurried to retrieve this vital message. Sitting at his desk, he tore open the envelope and unfolded the transcription, which read simply: *vampire and strange bird attacking ship*. It was rather abrupt and did not contain the normal sign-off by the ship's captain. That worried Robert more than the context of the message. If the supernatural elements of Prussia were mobilizing with the military, then the war had just entered a very deadly phase.

Shaking his head to clear such thoughts, Robert calmed his nerves. One time was an occurrence, twice was confirmation. Writing out new orders, he folded the commands and sealed them with the signet ring of his office pressed into the fresh silver wax. Waking up his personal runner, he handed the orders to the young boy and gave him express instructions to take them immediately to Queen Victoria's personal attendant at Buckingham Palace and not to give the orders to anyone else.

The Palace Guards, upon seeing the seal, ushered the young man into a waiting room. A well-dressed woman entered and took the message. Queen Victoria found herself sleeping less and less as the war continued. Her brass hand was a marvelous invention, and she was grateful for the opportunity to continue living as a whole person. However, sitting in her chambers, she missed her natural appendage and the sense of touch that it had. She was not normally found to be in such maudlin moods, but with the reports of amputees and wounded coming in daily, she feared more men would be living in a worse state than her, men who were fighting on her behalf.

A knock sounded on her door, signaling that her attendant, Guinevere, had returned with the message. "Enter," Victoria stated, her voice strong and regal carrying all the weight of her position.

"A letter from the Prime Minister, Mum," the attendant set the letter on the edge of the vanity table and retreated from the room.

Breaking the wax seal, the Queen read the alarming message and recommended actions. "Guinevere?" Her Majesty called.

"Yes, Your Highness," Guinevere bowed, entering the room.

"Have the messenger return and inform his Lordship that I will be discussing the matter with our military advisors first thing in the morning."

Guinevere left the room without another word. Robert's recommendations were the most logical step. Send another vessel on a similar mission and see if the same fate befalls it. The Queen's thoughts were troubled as a chill crept up her spine. Something about these circumstances did not sit well with her. After her morning meeting, she would move forward with the best course of action as recommended by her military advisors. It had been a long day, and the night was half over. With a sigh, Queen Victoria – known as the Iron Lady due to her brass and bronze prosthetics, the result of a life-saving operation – laid down on her bed and tried to sleep. What little sleep she could find was plagued by bad dreams.

The next day, another of the stealth air ships was sent on a mission into a different part of Prussia to see if they would fare better than their predecessor.

Lee folded the paper, tired of reading about the losses of life on the front. "How's the war going?" Dan asked.

"Who knows," the Englishman replied. "Every paper is filled with numbers of deceased soldiers, but they tout that we are pressing the offensive."

"If you aren't in the war, you just get to hear what they want you to know," Dan stated. "Besides, they couldn't tell you if they were losing; it's bad for morale."

"If win, we keep land?" Brackish asked.

"Not exactly," Lee replied.

A confused look passed over the goblin's face. "Then what point?"

"I couldn't tell you," Dan answered.

"We would have some concessions from the Prussian people, but we would not usurp their sovereign government," Lee explained. "A people that cannot govern themselves is often ripe for rebellion."

"Yeah, instead you set up a puppet regime that follows the orders they get from the conquerors, and things don't go too well from there either," Dan commented.

"Human war complicated. Goblins go war, we take land or food," Brackish stated.

"That's because on some things, goblins have better sense than people," the American added with a smile.

"I know," the goblin replied.

3

Three days after sending the airship beyond the enemy lines, the vessel returned. It had been battered and beaten, and most of the crew was dead or missing. The tale the survivors told was disconcerting. Like the first attempt, they had been attacked by a strange bird that could produce fire. The bird had been accompanied by a vampire, but strange half-woman, half-bird creatures had also attacked the soldiers as they tried to defend the ship. Once the news reached the Queen, she sent the word out. Every Regent Warden received notice.

As the oncoming Wardens entered Glorianna's Dungeon, none could even sit at their desks and enjoy their morning cups of tea and coffee. Roger read the message waiting for him on his desk, the same message all the other wardens had received. A grimace creased his already lined face. The thick moustache of black hair salted with gray turned down over the corners of his mouth, emphasizing the frown he wore.

Dan was sitting on the sofa, a bottle of beer in his hand, enjoying the fire roaring within the fireplace. His hand still ached, and the doctor told him it would be weeks before he could use it fully again. Brackish sat beside him, a matching bottle of beer in the goblin's prosthetic hand. Lee was in his workroom, tinkering with some new invention or repairing one of those that had been demolished by the bomb when a knock echoed up from the front door of the house. Dan listened to the sound.

It was hollow and low, almost ominous. Hopefully, Ms. Edwards would not hear it, and whoever was knocking would go away. "One moment," the landlady responded, crushing Dan's hopes.

The world outside the windows was gray and showed the lazy drizzle that seemed to frequent London this time of year. Fall was the time of year that Dan missed his original home of Kentucky and his father's house in Tennessee the most. Back home, the leaves would be changing colors, and the deer would be moving about, ripe for hunting. Not here in London, though; the sky would be gray, and the heavens would make it as miserable as possible. Hard-soled shoes echoed the approach to Dan and Lee's door. "She must've let them in," the American muttered to himself.

His hand rested casually on the butt of the pistol by his side. With an immensely powerful witch after you, it didn't pay to let your guard down. The footsteps ceased their booming procession, and a single knock sounded on the door. "I get, I get," Brackish said, sliding off the couch. "It just Roger."

Dan moved his hand off the revolver. It wouldn't do to shoot his Regent Warden. Brackish opened the door and revealed that indeed, Roger was standing there, his cloak covered in a fine mist. "Roger, what brings you out?" Lee asked, stepping from his workshop.

The goggles on his head and smears of grease on his face were a clear indication that he had been in the middle of something. "Lee, Dan, Brackish," Roger replied, nodding at each of the exterminators in turn. "I've come on urgent business. Direct from the Queen herself, this message is only meant for Dan and Lee. I'll have to ask you to step into another room, Brackish."

"If the Queen wants us to do a job for her..." Dan started.

"This message is being distributed by every Regent Warden across the whole of Britain to each of their charges," Roger answered. "Due to Brackish's species, he cannot be considered suitable under the guidelines provided." Brackish didn't like being excluded from a potential job, but he also knew enough about Roger to recognize that his calling on them at home meant serious business was afoot.

"What is this message?" Lee asked, sitting in one of the chairs beside the dinner table once Brackish had excused himself.

Clearing his throat, Roger unrolled a sheet of paper. "By Royal Decree, Her Majesty, Queen Victoria, hereby provides that any English hunters bound by the Treaty of Abnormal Threats are heretofore requested for active duty within Her Majesty's Armed Forces to combat threats by natural and supernatural enemies." Roger rolled the paper back up and waited patiently.

"Can we say no to this?" Dan asked.

"It is a request, not a command," Roger replied, his expression indicating his dislike of the American.

"Why are we being asked to enlist?" Lee asked. "It seems odd."

"Rumor has it that several of our units have been attacked by something other than soldiers," Roger replied. "They are only rumors, but this decree gives it a little more substance."

"What if we were to agree?" Lee asked.

"You would be picked up tomorrow morning and transported to your training barracks," the Regent Warden explained. "After your training is complete, you will receive your orders."

"Weapons?" Lee asked. "I've dealt with those modified rifles our men use; they are not to my liking."

"Each man that accepts is requested to bring his weapon or weapons of choice. Each weapon will be evaluated and then determined if fit for active service," Roger replied. "May I consider your acceptance?"

"Yes," Lee replied.

"Absolutely not," Dan answered.

Lee looked at Dan, his mouth gaping. "But Dan… the Queen…"

"I'm not a citizen, and I told you in America: I've had enough war to last me a lifetime," Dan answered.

"I never thought you a coward," Roger stated.

Dan was on his feet in an instant and had his good hand wrapped around Roger's throat. "Have you ever been in a war?" Dan asked as the Regent Warden's eyes bulged in terror. "You ever shot a man and seen the life drain out of him, not in self-defense but because someone far removed from the danger told you they were bad. I have, and it'll make you sick. You want us to go over there to fight monsters, but when it's over with, you'll have us butchering men, too."

"Dan," Lee stated quietly, placing his hand on Dan's shoulder.

Dan released Roger from the hold. Gasping for air, the government official rolled to the side and tried to get to his feet. Stepping past his partner, Lee helped Roger up. "Terribly sorry about that," the English hunter apologized, "but you should not antagonize him. You know how temperamental Americans can be."

Roger mumbled something and stepped out the door, hurrying to the street. Listening to what had transpired, Brackish opened the door and stepped out, a smirk on his face. "What's so funny?" Dan asked.

"Roger scared bad," the goblin stated, chuckling.

The American chuckled, and some of the tension left his shoulders. "Yeah, I suppose I did come across a little strong."

"Just a little," Lee commented from beside the door. "So, you'll not be joining?"

"I can't do it, Lee. I've seen war, and I won't sign up for another visit," Dan commented. "Are you going?"

"I was once in Her Majesty's service," Lee replied. "It appears that I am destined to do so once again. The country needs us, Dan."

"I know," the American whispered. "It will start with them wanting us to fight ghouls and beasts, but before it is over with, they'll have you lined up shooting men whose only crime is being born somewhere else."

"It is my sincerest hope that you are wrong," Lee responded.

"Mine, too," Dan agreed.

The room had settled into a melancholy mood with the realization that Lee was going to be leaving for an extended period. "If I'm to be going, I need to make sure you are properly equipped," Lee stated, hurrying to his work room.

"Lot of food and beer," Brackish commented, unsure of Lee's meaning.

"You two will always find a way to take care of your stomachs," the Englishman joked. "And with the penchant you have for destroying gear, I'll need to make sure you have several spares waiting around."

Closing the door to his workroom, Lee shut off any further conversation. A heavy burden on his shoulders, Dan sat back down and took a long swig from his bottle. "You know," he said to his goblin drinking companion. "I wouldn't tell Lee this, but I'm worried about him."

Brackish nodded his understanding. "Lee tough. He be fine," the goblin replied to comfort his friend.

Elizabeth stepped into the room carrying a basket of laundry. Her porcelain skin looked drawn and paler than normal. "Everything okay?" Brackish asked.

"I don't know," she answered. "Something feels wrong. Almost like something evil is coming."

They had learned that when she felt something foreboding approaching, things ahead were going to get rough. Dan thought of Lee's decision and tried to push his worry aside. "If you get any visions, you let us know," the American commented.

"Right away, sir," Elizabeth agreed. "Will you need dinner tonight?"

"Stew?" Brackish asked.

Elizabeth giggled at the goblin. "We do indeed have some, just put on. Shall I bring some up later?"

Brackish nodded fervently. "Yeah, bring up some for us," Dan agreed. "Will you and Ms. Edwards join us for dinner this evening?"

"I can ask," the girl replied.

"Please do; Lee has an announcement to make," the American stated.

As the grandfather clock in the corner began to chime seven, Elizabeth returned with Ms. Edwards. Dan helped the ladies with their large stew pot, wrangling the cast-iron beast onto the holder over the fire. The American stepped away and let Ms. Edwards take up her place beside the pot, stirring. "I get Lee," Brackish proclaimed, leaping over the back of the couch and rushing to the door.

The scent of stew was filling the house, and Brackish's mouth was starting to water at the smells of tender beef, mingling with broth and vegetables. He gave a quick rap on the door with his metal hand and turned to rejoin the others. "Can I help you, Brackish?" Lee asked, cracking open the door.

"Dinner," The goblin replied. "Ms. Edwards, Elizabeth here for announcement."

Brackish chewed on the last word for a moment. Finally, satisfied that he had repeated the word Dan had used correctly, he continued back to the sitting area, where he could watch the stew as it bubbled.

"Announcement?" Lee asked, confused.

Taking a moment to clean the grease off his face and set his goggles on his work table, Lee stepped from his room and closed the door behind him. "Ms. Edwards, Elizabeth, it is so nice to see you," Lee stated, greeting the unexpected dinner guests.

"Well, when Mr. Winston said that you had an announcement to make, we knew that we could not miss it," Ms. Edwards responded.

"Wonderful," Lee replied, giving Dan a decidedly unhappy look.

Stepping over to Dan, the Englishman leaned in close. "What is the meaning of this?" He asked.

"If you are leaving to go off to war, don't they deserve to hear it from you?" The American asked calmly. "I admit they may not be blood, but the five of us are the closest thing most of us have to family. You at least owe them the truth."

Lee nodded. He had thought Dan's intention was to shame him into not going into service. Lee had been wrong about his partner. He should have known that Dan would respect his decisions. The American had a sentimental side, despite never showing it. "The stew is ready," Ms. Edwards announced.

Sitting out a few loaves of bread on the table and setting up drinks for everyone, the five individuals who resided within the house gathered around the table. "Before we dine, I suppose I should make my announcement," Lee started. "I have been recalled into Her Majesty's Armed Services. Tomorrow morning, I will be leaving for training."

"When will you be back?" Ms. Edwards asked.

"I don't know," the Englishman answered honestly. "Once I've completed training, I do not know if I'll be able to return home before being given my orders. I trust that you ladies will keep Dan and Brackish out of as much trouble as you can, in my absence."

The improvised family sat eating and talking around the table for some time. Excusing themselves, Ms. Edwards and Elizabeth went downstairs to their quarters. "That was pleasant," Dan stated.

"Thank you," Lee said.

"For what?"

"That. I had not planned on telling them. It was the right thing to do," Lee confessed. "Truth is, I'm going to miss this apartment."

"You'll be fine," Dan stated.

"I won't miss that infernal racket that I hear coming from your room every night though," Lee commented.

"What racket?" The American asked.

"You, sleeping," Lee replied with a smile.

Brackish chuckled at the joke. Dan gave a smile. "You've got a long day tomorrow," the American announced. "Better get some sleep."

"Yes, I do," the Englishman agreed.

68

Going back to his room, Lee closed the door. Rather than go to sleep, the inventor had more work to do, to make sure that his associates did not run through the mechanical instruments they had come to depend on in their work.

The next morning, Lee had packed a small satchel of belongings. His Winchester rifle was leaning against the door. Brackish and Dan stood beside it, waiting. Stepping from his room, Lee gave one last look around. Several of his prototypes were sitting unfinished on his desk, but he told himself that they would be waiting for him when he returned. Closing the door, he stepped towards the stairs and draped the satchel over his shoulder. "Well," he said, not sure what one was supposed to say in these moments.

When he had initially joined and left home, his father had given him a firm handshake and said no further word. His mother had been deceased for several years before then. Dan stuck out his hand. Lee shook it. "I won't be there to help you out," the American said, sounding guilty. "So, keep your head down. You make sure you get back here in one piece."

"I will," the Englishman promised.

"Bye," Brackish said. "I make you food."

The goblin held out a package wrapped in butcher's paper. Lee smiled and thanked Brackish for the gift. Dan mouthed "sausages" to relieve Lee's fears. Walking him to the front door, Dan and Brackish tried to stay out of the way as Elizabeth and Ms. Edwards said their goodbyes to Lee. A knock at the door notified the Englishman that it was time to leave.

"Hopefully, I will be home in several weeks," Lee announced, as he headed to the front door.

Dan patted him on the back. "Write and let us know you're okay," Ms. Edwards requested.

Lee nodded and stepped out into the gray autumn day. A motorized carriage was waiting on him. The driver sat behind the cabin, his goggles pulled down to keep the smoke from the small coal furnace out of his eyes. Roger was standing at the foot of the stairs. "Ready?" The Regent Warden asked.

Adjusting his grip on the rifle, Lee took one last look at the closed door of his home and forced a smile. "Quite."

Boarding the carriage behind Roger, Lee sat across from his government liaison, half-listening as the brick façade of the house grew smaller while the carriage accelerated. Finally, with a turn, it passed from sight, and a slight depression settled in Lee's chest. "Are you all right?" Roger asked. "Not coming down with something, are you?"

"No," Lee answered, "just the weather."

"Yes, it is quite gray, isn't it?" Roger asked rhetorically before going back into his talk of the roaring success the wardens had finding soldiers from the ranks of bounty hunters and exterminators.

Dan stood in the hallway in front of the stairs to the apartment. Brackish had gone up shortly after Lee had left. The American did not know how he felt. Lee had been renting the place when Dan arrived. Due to their assignment from the Queen, it had made sense for them to bunk under the same roof. Now for the first time, Lee was not going to be there for a while. Dan ran a hand through his thick head of brown hair. "He's

70

going to be fine," the American muttered to himself, turned around, and stomped up the stairs to the apartment.

Brackish was in the kitchen, eating the remaining sausages that had not fit into Lee's going away gift. "You sad?" The goblin asked.

Even though he had only been living in human society for a few years, the small creature had quickly learned about human moods and emotions. "Naw," Dan lied, "it's just weird for Lee to be gone."

Brackish nodded his understanding, tossing the last bite of sausage into his mouth. "He fine," Brackish commented. "Come back soon and clan be whole."

It was always about the clan with goblins. Dan smirked at the goblin's optimism. "Yeah," Dan agreed. "One good thing about all those hunters going out of town, though..."

"What?"

"More bounties for us," Dan commented with a smile.

Brackish smiled. The goblin and the American both shared an affinity for the more violent side of the job, and they also tended to spend their money in a similar fashion, beer and cigars. With all the Regent Wardens out collecting soldiers, Dan figured he would wait for a day or so and then see what assignments might be available. Lee wasn't going to be sitting around bored, so there was no reason he and Brackish should. Not to mention, Ms. Edwards would grow very tired of the two bored males hanging around. Their attempts to relieve their boredom often resulted in property damage.

The motorized carriage arrived at the train station. Lee raised an eyebrow at Roger. "You didn't think you'd be staying in the city, did you?"

"No, I suppose not," the hunter replied.

Motorized carriages were dropping the city's hunters out along the platform. Most of the vehicles held five or six hunters. "No one else accepted your offer?" Lee asked.

"The acclaim and popularity that you and your partner have gathered since your debut have forced me to focus solely on maintaining your endeavors," Roger admitted.

"Are we truly so busy?" Lee marveled, not realizing the prestige that Dan and he had amassed.

Making his way to the train station, the Englishman nodded to the hunters that he recognized. The train pulled into the terminal, and Lee was pleased to notice it was a newer model with incorporations of his design. By making a few adjustments to the original concept, he had created an engine that could produce more speed with less fuel consumption. Stepping onboard, he walked down the aisle and chose a seat in an area where few of the hunters had clustered. Sitting by the window and resting the Winchester against his leg, he settled into the seat. It was not overly soft or well-cushioned, but having worked through the night, the British inventor was incredibly tired.

Before the train had left the station, he was asleep.

"Well, well, what have we here?" A thick Scottish accent asked, waking Lee.

He opened his eyes and saw a giant towering over him. Thick red hair and a matching bushy beard covered the scarred face staring down at Lee. "Brogan?" He asked. "Have we already passed Blackmoore?"

"No," the Scotsman answered, sliding the great Claymore from his shoulder to take the seat beside Lee. "I was working nearer Manchester when the call went out, so I picked up the engine there."

Brogan was one of the more eccentric hunters. He was possibly the most well-known hunter outside London. Lee and Dan had fought beside the large man at the Battle of Stonehenge. The horde of orcs there had been sorely pressed to deal with the large Scotsman and his sword. He had ridden into battle on the back of one of the giant orc wargs.

Lee cleared the sleep from his eyes and glanced around. It seemed that most of the other hunters were not willing to get too friendly with the large man in the kilt, or perhaps Lee thought *they wish to stay away from me.*

"Where's your American?" Brogan asked, glancing around the train car.

"He did not sign up."

"I never would've thought that. He's always first one to throw into a fight," Brogan commented, rubbing his jaw.

If memory served, Lee was almost positive it was the same place that Dan had punched the hulking man to clear up a disagreement. "He doesn't mind a fight, but he isn't one for war."

"It's all the same," Brogan said dismissively.

"Not to him," Lee commented. "He served during the American Civil War."

"I've heard nasty stories about that."

"Dan swore he'd never join another army, an oath he plans to keep," Lee explained.

"Well, he'll be sorely missed. At least we've got the brains; I'll have to take up his place as the brawn. You stick by me, and you'll be fine," Brogan said, almost knocking Lee out of his seat with a slap on the shoulder. "Training wasn't too bad in my day."

"Have you served before?" Lee asked.

"Aye, three years in Her Majesty's Marines," Brogan admitted proudly. "Toughest bunch of men I've ever known."

"I was part of the Indian peacekeeping squads," Lee said.

"Good, some of these lads haven't even faced a third of the beasties we've put down," the Scotsman whispered, glancing at some of the fresh faces seated around. "It'll be up to the men like you and me to bring them home in one piece."

"I don't think we'll be seeing that much battle," the Englishman confessed. "It seems to me that they are only having a little trouble and needed our expertise."

"That's what they want you to think," the Scotsman continued whispering. "Friend of mine is still in the marines. He tells me that three airships have been attacked by the Prussian monsters, led by an all-powerful hag. Over half the men on board the ships have been lost. Rumor is that one ship went down, taking all hands with her."

"Wonderful," Lee grimaced.

He was willing to bet that most of the hunters did not have the full breadth of information like Brogan did. The Scotsman was a welcome sight. Lee had only worked with him once before, but Brogan had a similar problem-solving technique like Dan: throw enough fire and bullets at it until it was dead. It was a method that Lee could easily work with. "We should stay close to each other," Brogan said, repeating his earlier conclusion to Lee. "Not many lads on this trip have worked with me before."

"What about your assistants?" Lee asked, remembering several young men that had been assisting Brogan when they had encountered that nasty business with the Council of the Black Forest.

"Good lads all, but Sean was hurt fairly bad by one of those orcs from Germany. After that, James decided to learn a different trade. Matthew settled down as an assistant in his father-in-law's shop. As I said, good lads, but Sean was the only one really cut out for this life. After Matthew left me, I decided to hold off for a while before taking on any other apprentices."

"Wise decision," Lee commented.

"Aye," Brogan responded as he settled his large bulk into the seat and started working it around to make himself comfortable.

With the Scotsman settling in for sleep, Lee closed his eyes and tried to drift back off. His eyes seemed to close for a moment before the train was stopping, and someone was shouting. "On your feet and off the train!"

Lee's eyes sprang open, and he saw Brogan getting up. Standing and retrieving his rifle, Lee could see a Marine Sergeant standing at the front of the train car, bellowing orders. Brogan smiled. "I've missed this, haven't you?"

"Not even slightly," Lee said, remembering why he left the armed services.

He was much too fluid and did not appreciate the rigidity with which they did things. Their methods and results were commendable, but his mind found more success in a slightly more chaotic environment. "Off the train and line up!" The sergeant ordered.

Lee followed Brogan out of the train, where a platform had been built. The hunters were milling around, forming loose lines, and Brogan and Lee fell into one that just started. Several other military officers inspected the men as they came off the train. Apparently, sergeants had been designated to rouse the men from the train cars. Each of these non-commissioned officers descended onto the platform and began berating the hunters in turn, ordering them into straight lines. After the chaos of disembarkation had been settled, a distinguished officer stepped onto a small podium to address the assembled volunteers.

"Welcome. You all know why you are here and what is expected of you. It will be the responsibility of my staff and I to ensure that you are fit soldiers and ready to perform upon the battlefield. Your barracks are down the road several miles. The sergeants who were kind enough to get you off the train will guide you there. Gentlemen?"

"You heard him," the sergeant nearest Lee barked. "Start running."

Looking down at his shoes, Lee realized that he had chosen poorly. While his footwear was perfect for the hard, cobbled streets of London, they had not been designed for running through the countryside. Shaking his head, Lee started jogging behind Brogan, the sergeant remaining nearby throughout their trip.

4

The barracks were crudely constructed buildings, short and squat with just enough room for two-tiered bunks and not much else. A small building would serve as the mess, where meals would be served, and another to serve as a supply depot. Before finding their bunks, each man was sent through the supply depot and given two uniforms and proper footwear. Lee was grateful, as his feet ached from the run they had just endured, and blisters were forming on his heel.

It was night when Lee stumbled into the barracks, and he was pleasantly surprised to find the bunks already had linens on them. "Lee!" Brogan called from the other end of the building.

He had found a set of bunks and was guarding them. His kilt was the only non-regulation piece of clothing he had. "Where's your pants?" Lee asked.

"I'll not be trading in my kilt for some of their finery. I've nothing else to show that a Scotsman fights beside you cods," he laughed.

Most of the other beds had already been claimed, with many of the young men looking as worn out as Lee. In their current profession, some running was expected, but nothing like what they'd done today. "I'm Sergeant Ward," announced the non-commissioned officer, stepping into their barracks. "It's my job to see to it that you men have what it takes once you get to the Prussian front. Get some rest; tomorrow morning is going to come early."

Ward turned and stepped back out. Lee climbed onto the upper bed as Brogan sprawled out across the lower bunk. Before pulling the blankets up, Lee pressed the Winchester in close against him, making sure that the safety was on.

A roar shook the barracks, and Lee sat straight up in bed. A fur-covered silhouette stood in the doorway. The shape was that of a werewolf. Pandemonium erupted all around them as the hunters fought to get out of their bunks and prepared. Reflexively, Lee raised the Winchester, switched off the safety, and sighted on the top of the head. Breathing out, he squeezed the trigger. A moment later, the top of the monster disappeared.

Gas lights blazed to life across the top of the barracks. Ward stood beside the door, his hand on the control lever. The werewolf was just a mannequin that someone had constructed. The head and part of an arm had been severed. Brogan stood with his claymore in hand off to the side, searching for any further targets. Ward started to clap. "Lovely," the sergeant commented. "We've rigged several of these tests for you throughout your training. Out of twenty-four men, only two of you were prepared. Seems one of you was a little trigger happy but missed the shot."

"I believe you are mistaken," Lee replied.

The other hunters were realizing that they had been duped. "Mistaken?" Ward asked, picking up the severed dummy's head. Sitting between the eyes was a bullet hole. "So I was. Good shot. Now, get up and get dressed. Leave your weapons here. You've got five minutes to be out front dressed and ready for drills."

Ward strolled from the barracks as the confused and bleary-eyed hunters started getting dressed. Brogan came back to the bunk and started to slip on his shoes. "Nice shot," he commented.

"I couldn't let the pretend monster keep terrorizing us, could I?" Lee asked. "Why did everyone else have so much trouble?" He asked in a hushed tone.

"I'll show you. How many of you lads have collected more than five bounties?" Brogan asked.

The gathered men looked between one another. "This has to be a joke," Lee commented when no one raised a hand.

"I told you," Brogan replied. "All right, get dressed, lads. It's going to be a long day."

Lee, Brogan, and the others gathered in front of the barracks in white-striped trousers and a white tank top - traditional exercise clothing for the men. Even Brogan had donned the trousers, leaving his kilt on his bunk. It was obvious that the large Scotsman was uncomfortable in the confining clothing. "All right," Ward shouted, stepping from the side of the small wooden building. "I'm going to turn you boys into Marines. Form ranks!"

The men fell into three separate lines as quickly as they could. It was an ugly process with the men bouncing off one another. "Left face!" Ward ordered, telling the men which way to turn. "Now, since this is your first day, we're going to celebrate with a ten-mile run," the sergeant informed the men. "Now, march!"

The three lines of men started off at a jog, Ward staying beside them the entire time. Lee tried to focus on the head of the man in front of him. "Bloody hell," Brogan grumbled.

Ignoring the comment, Lee focused on keeping his breathing steady and stared ahead. Halfway through the march, the man's head in front of Lee was bright red and covered in a sheen of sweat. It was not long before the man was on the side of the track, vomiting into the grass. Lee's legs burned, and he could feel the sweat covering his face. His breathing was still steady, and he felt that he might be able to make it. "Halfway there," Ward informed the men.

Lee's hopes faltered; he had anticipated that they were well past the seven-mile mark. Pushing aside the doubts, Lee continued to take in deep breaths through his nose and out through his mouth. It was a routine that kept him focused more on his breathing and less on the distance. Continuing onwards, Lee was thrilled to see that they had made a loop of the camp, and the barracks were peeking out of the murky light of dawn in the distance.

Bolstered by the finish line, Lee maintained his pace and ignored the burning in his legs and the heated sensation that had just started in his lungs. Onward he jogged, Ward keeping pace the entire way. "Halt!" The sergeant called when they had returned to their starting point.

Lee stopped and looked around, noticing that most of the other men were stumbling along and had not kept up with him or the sergeant. The experienced hunter had focused on his routine and not noticed as the others fell behind. "Impressive," Ward stated. "No recruit has ever kept up with me for the morning march on their first day. I'll have to keep an eye on you."

Cramps were threatening to seize up the muscles in Lee's leg. He began walking in place to keep that from occurring and waited as Brogan came in with the last bunch of men. "Give me a house full of orcs, rather than all this bloody running," Brogan wheezed.

"Now, that we're done with the warm-up, let's get started on the hard work," Ward stated, a smile more savage than gleeful covering his face. "Everyone to the parade grounds."

Ward led them on a short jog onto the large field in the center of the camp. Climbing up on the small stage, Ward glanced over the men. "Down, it's time you ladies learn how to do a proper pushup," the sergeant shouted, dropping into the proper position.

Lee and the others quickly got into position. From his vantage point on the stand, Ward started counting out pushups as he did them. After the fifth pushup, the sergeant stood up and started walking among the men, still counting. Several of the soldiers in training collapsed before the count of ten. Amidst the men, Ward issued orders to correct the method some of the men were using for their pushups. Brogan was proceeding much easier through this exercise. Lee had not done any serious calisthenics since his original enlistment of Her Majesty's Service. Now, he remembered how much he had hated it. "Fifty," Ward shouted, "on your feet."

Most of the men stood; others were curled into balls as their legs and arms spasmed. Those standing looked on with concern for their fellow recruits. "They'll be fine!" Ward informed them. "Just getting used to the job. Now, let's see how you lot can handle some jumping jacks."

As before, Ward started counting and demonstrating then walked about correcting their form as needed. He kept counting until he reached one hundred, then it was back down for more pushups, another fifty. Once this was done, the men ran through several other exercises to loosen up their muscles and get in shape. "You aren't the worst bunch I've seen on their first day, but it's obvious that you aren't Marines. Now, change into your uniforms and get breakfast. I'll meet you there," Ward instructed.

The men moved sluggishly, grumbling as they went. Lee's arms and chest felt like lead weights. All he wanted was to crawl back into bed and sleep. Brogan was beside him, breathing hard. "That was tougher than I remember," he admitted.

"Yes, I don't recall it being so strenuous," Lee agreed.

"You did well. I didn't see you falter once," the Scotsman said, a hint of admiration in his voice.

"Towards the end, I wanted to lie on the grass and pass out," the Englishman confessed.

"You made it through that marathon this morning just fine."

"Don't think about the distance; just focus on your breathing and you'll do better," Lee said, explaining his method.

"We'll see, but when I can't bloody breathe, it's tough to focus on anything else."

"Didn't they teach you anything your first time through? Breathe in through your nose and out through your mouth."

"That'll help?" One of the other recruits asked.

"It keeps you from blowing all the air out of your lungs," Lee explained. "And it gives you something else to focus on."

Assembled in the quickly erected mess hall, the men ate voraciously, going through several pans of eggs and bread. "Do you think we'll be doing more running this afternoon?" Brogan asked.

"Since we are in uniform, I think we may be moving onto a more formalized training," Lee speculated. "I would not be surprised to have rifle training this afternoon."

"Who needs a rifle?" Brogan asked. "I've brought me six-shot, and my family blade has always served me well."

"They're trying to make soldiers out of us if you recall. That means they will all want us cross-trained on the standard weapons."

"Still, I don't see why I need any," Brogan complained.

A smile crossed Lee's face. *In some ways, it's like Dan's here.* He thought.

After the group finished with their meal, Ward met them outside. "Now ladies, it's time to teach you how to shoot," he announced.

Several groans and complaints arose from the gathered unit. "If you maggots can qualify on the range, I'll let you waive your rifle training for the duration," the sergeant offered.

That silenced the men's complaints. Leading the way, Ward took them to the back corner of the compound. A large dirt mound had been thrown up to prevent any bullets from escaping the range. Several dummies hung from wooden frames. Each dummy had a red bullseye painted above the heart and on the face. Another sergeant stood at the edge of the range, a pair of field glasses hanging from his neck. At his feet were two green crates, their tops opened to reveal the Colt B-3 rifles used exclusively by the British military. Lee preferred his Winchester, but the Colt rifle was of a similar design. The main difference was that his Winchester shot a .44 shell, whereas the Colt used the slightly larger .45 caliber round.

It would not add too much undo recoil when fired. "This is going to be bad," Brogan commented.

"Why?" Lee asked.

"I can't use a long gun; why do ye think I carry a pistol and a sword."

Lee shrugged his shoulders at the comment. "This is going to be your best friend," Ward started, lifting one of the rifles into the air. He ran through the proper procedure for loading and firing the weapon. "Any volunteers?"

Each of the hunters looked around at each other. Lee let out an exasperated sigh, annoyed at the trepidation of the other hunters and raised his hand. "Come on up, dead-eye. Show us how it's done."

"What would you like me to aim for?" Lee asked.

"Just do the best that you can," Ward instructed. "Make sure you stand behind the line."

Taking the rifle, Lee felt the difference in the weight between his traditional weapon and this new one. Looking down, he saw the line that Ward had referred to. It was a line that allowed the sergeants to know how far away from the target a shooter was. Loading the shells into the breech, Lee made sure that the safety was off and raised the rifle to his shoulder. Sighting on the nearest target, Lee fired one shot into the heart target, worked the lever to chamber another round, and deposited a bullet into the head. Repeating the process, Lee worked his way through all the targets. When he had shot all the targets in the center of their bullseye, he still had one round left. Smiling, he fired at the rope holding the nearest target and was pleased with himself as the shot split the rope and dropped the target to the ground.

Ejecting the final spent shell, Lee turned around. Ward and the other sergeant stood dumbfounded at the display of marksmanship. It was Ward that recovered first. "Not bad," he stated. "Now, who's next?"

If the hunters had been hesitant before, they were completely cowed after the display they had just witnessed. "Oh, bloody hell," Brogan muttered as he stepped forward out of the crowd.

The Scotsman had not been lying when he said that he did not know how to use a rifle. He at least hit most of the targets, not close to the bullseye, but the bullets landed. It was a poor display, but it ran rings around most of the others. "Well, it seems that most of you can't shoot your way out of a paper sack, so we'll be doing this every day until you can shoot like a Marine," Ward informed the men. "Any grumbling, and you'll be doing a fifteen-mile jog in the morning."

The threat silenced the thought of any complaints. Having finished weapons training for the day, Ward ran the men back to the parade field where they repeated the exercises from that morning. Once they were thoroughly tired and their uniforms soaked with sweat, Ward dismissed them for lunch, all except Lee.

"You wanted to see me?" Lee asked.

"Your display on the range was the best this camp has ever seen, probably will ever see," Ward explained. "It's clear that you don't need any training, but the rest of your companions could use as much help as you can provide them. Do you understand my meaning?"

"I believe so," Lee replied. "If possible, I would like to bring my own rifle to the range."

"What is it?" Ward asked.

"A Winchester, 1863 lever-action rifle."

"I don't think we can supply ammunition for that."

"On the contrary," Lee countered, "the Webley Mk II pistols that the officers are assigned fire a .44 cartridge, the same as my rifle. It's the main reason I have a Webley as my sidearm, cuts back on ammunition."

Ward thought for a moment. "You help your fellow recruits learn how to shoot, and I'll get your rifle cleared."

"Consider it done," the hunter stated.

"Go join the others."

Lee hurried off to the mess hall. He entered, filled a plate with food, and took a seat beside Brogan. "I'm going to teach you how to shoot," he announced.

Brogan's eyebrows rose in shock as he shoveled a forkful of food into his mouth. He chewed for a moment and then swallowed. "I don't need teaching," the Scotsman proclaimed.

"Your results today would seem to indicate otherwise," Lee retorted.

"I always get the job done."

"How do you normally shoot?"

"I point the gun in the right direction and keep pulling the trigger until the monster drops, or I'm out of bullets."

"Dear Lord, you shoot like Dan," Lee proclaimed.

"How's that?"

"You throw enough bullets at it to do the job," Lee explained. "Haven't you ever wondered why he uses a shotgun? While he is proficient at short distances with his pistols, he refuses to take the time to shoot properly with a rifle."

"I still don't see the need," the Scotsman grumbled.

"Unfortunately, I have been tasked with assisting in the rifle training for the group. You will not be the only one that I'm assisting."

"One day here, and you're already at the head of the class."

"Nonsense," Lee replied. "We are all in this together. I feel it is all of our responsibilities to see that everyone has the necessary skills and tools to succeed."

"Fine, if you'll stop giving speeches, I'll let you show me how to shoot," Brogan answered.

After lunch, the men were taken to a small room with tables and chairs. Sitting on the table in front of each seat were pages of paper and a pencil. "Take a seat," Ward ordered from the back of the room.

An older man dressed in a well-worn suit entered and walked to the front of the room. "Good afternoon," he stated. His English was good, but he had a distinct Prussian accent. "My name is Vladimir Abramov. I have been asked here to help prepare you men for the dangers that you may face."

Lee picked up the pencil and waited for the lecture to begin. "Bloody school?" Brogan asked.

"Calm down," Lee whispered. "If we don't have the proper information, then we may find ourselves well over our heads."

"First, it is important to note that the creatures of Prussia are different from those found in your native country. One of the terrible beasts described by those returning on the airships is the Alkonost. There is no counterpart to this creature here in your land. This temptress is a beautiful face and chest of a woman growing from a bird's body, a great bird at that. While their talons are quite fierce, one has much more to fear from the song they sing."

"It is said that they have the power to mesmerize a man and make him forget everything. In such a state, the man will pursue the creature, even going so far as to leap from mountain cliffs. A sister to this beast is the Siren and the Harpy. Only the strongest willed and minded of men can withstand the songs of either creature. How would one expect to dispatch such a creature?" He asked.

"With a bullet," one of the younger hunters offered.

"True a shot will fell the creature, but how does one defeat it before the sounds of its song reach the ears?" Vladimir looked around the room, comfortable that he had provided a valid point of thought. "As you see, much like Odysseus of old, one must stop up the ears."

"How can we hear any oncoming danger if our ears are plugged?" Another recruit asked.

"How will you hear any oncoming danger if you leap from the ship to pursue the flying temptress?" Vladimir countered. "I am not here to provide solutions to all of your problems, but these creatures are working against you, being led by the hand of the motherland itself. Have any of you heard of the Baba Yaga?"

Lee and Brogan both raised their hands.

"Good!" The instructor exclaimed, clapping his hands together. "The Baba Yaga is the living embodiment of the magic throughout Prussia. Some believe her to be a powerful witch and her ability to work magical spells is legendary, but it is the belief of myself and others who have studied that she is closely tied to the land itself. If you encounter her, I urge you to flee. No one has ever found the limits of her power, and all manner of animal, both natural and unnatural, are at her command."

"One tale told around the hearths says that one night an old beggar woman came through the streets of a village, its name now lost, and begged for scraps of food from every house. The last house she came to was owned by a kindly, old widowed man, who lived there with his grandson. They did not have much food, and the winter was close approaching, but he shared the little bit of soup with the old woman. She thanked him and left. Moments later, a giant mortar was seen flying overhead and a curse was laid upon the village. When the sun rose, only the old man and his grandchild remained. All the other homes had been broken into and the families within killed."

"The Baba Yaga, offended at the cold hearts of the people, had commanded the bears of the forest to descend on the people and destroy them, so if ever a beggar comes through a village, they are greeted with bread, wine, and a bed for the night. She is not the villain that most of you English would portray a witch to be, but she is not the Fairy Godmother of the Grimm brothers' tale either. It seems that she will not tolerate the attack on her home by foreigners and has decided to lead the powers at her command against you," Vladimir concluded the story. "Shall we continue?"

For two hours, Vladimir showed drawings of creatures and lectured about the threat and best method to dispose of the beasts. Lee had used most of his paper and several sheets of Brogan's. The Scotsman had found himself hard-pressed to remain conscious through most of the lecture. As the class ended and the men started out into the late afternoon sun, Ward stopped them. "Before supper, we're going to have a quiz on what you maggots should have learned. Any man who doesn't pass it does not get to eat tonight. Do I make myself clear?"

"Yes, sergeant," the men replied half-heartedly.

Ward smiled as he stepped aside and let the men return to the barracks. "Looks like I'll be trimming down," Brogan stated.

"I don't mind going back over the material with you," Lee offered. "It could not hurt, and we need to be prepared to face these beasts."

"Well, I would like to eat," Brogan replied. "Who thinks they'll fail that test?"

Everyone raised their hand. "Looks like I have my work cut out for me," Lee replied. "All right, gather round."

Standing outside the mess hall, Ward handed each of the men a piece of paper, three questions were written on each piece. No two sheets had the exact same questions to prevent them from cheating. Lee was the first to hand in his. Ward glanced at it and motioned him into the mess hall. Each of the men handed in their papers, and each in turn was admitted in for dinner. As the men sat around eating, Ward stood at the head of the table. "Well done," he bellowed. "This will be your routine for the next few weeks, until we have been told that you are fit for duty. As you are not going to be traditional Marines, I am willing to answer a few questions regarding your training."

"Why is a Prussian on the base?" A recruit asked. "How do we know he isn't up to no good?"

"Vladimir Adamov is the top Prussian folklorist and mythologist in the world. He fled shortly after the German-Prussian war began; due to his politics, he was in danger of losing his life. You will need the knowledge he has if you are to be of any service to the Queen. Next?"

"Why are we training on those bloody long guns?" Brogan asked.

"Because while you are not going to be traditional Marines, you will still be in her Majesty's Service and as such expected to perform at a certain standard. That includes competent use of a rifle," Ward responded. "Any other questions?"

No one had further queries. With a curt nod of his head, Ward left the building.

That was how the next few weeks went for Lee: running, calisthenics, breakfast, helping the others learn how to properly shoot, calisthenics, lunch, class, tutoring the others, dinner, and bed to start the whole process against the next day.

5

It had been a few weeks since Lee had left for his military training, and only three days since the cast had come off Dan's hand. Never one to stay still for long, the American was anxious for some action. Brackish had been keeping an eye on possible cases and had found one that he thought would be simple. The goblin hoped it would at least be enough to satiate Dan's desire to get out of the house and do something. Since Lee's departure, the house had settled into a melancholy state. The goblin did not understand everything about it, but he knew that it stemmed from the missing hunter.

A rash of grave robbings had struck the area surrounding Saint Paul's cathedral, and Roger was all too happy to hand the case over to Dan and Brackish. The American drove the velociter into the affluent neighborhood, parking across from the churchyard. The Tin Man, the mechanized, armed transport Lee had created, sat on its trailer behind them. Saint Paul's was a large domed structure renowned for its beauty and design. It also happened to be the seat of the Anglican Church.

Dan stepped from the cab of the vehicle and lifted his shotgun from its rack beside the seat. When Brackish had delivered Roger's notes, the American felt content that they were dealing with ghouls. If he was right, then the Tin Man would be needed to blow up the nest. The old pump-action shotgun that he carried would be better use against the undead carrion feeders than the pneumatic version. Also, these ghouls tended to be quick, and the pack would just slow him down. Unlike the ghouls they had encountered in Egypt, those in England did not travel through the soil, nor were they larger than a man. The only thing that both varieties had in common was the black talons that tipped their fingers, sharp enough to rip a man open in a single swipe.

Brackish walked around the velociter, his shortened shotgun resting across his shoulder. "Guess I should go talk to the vicar," Dan suggested.

The goblin shrugged. "I go smell, see what I find."

"I'll meet you back around front," Dan stated, walking across the street towards the front of the church. The goblin walked around the side, trying to discern some clues through his keen sense of smell.

Stepping through the large doors, Dan took a moment to appreciate the artwork that covered most of the church's walls, a far cry from the humble country churches that dotted the landscape of Dan's home country. A somber-looking man in the traditional vestment of the clergy was standing by the door. The American removed his bowler hat. "Are you the vicar?" Dan asked, lowering his voice as he heard the question echo through the large structure.

The man of faith glanced over Dan, lingering on the pistols at his waist and the shotgun in his hand. "I am the Rector, and this is my flock. Do you mean us harm?"

"Hardly," Dan chuckled. "I heard you've had some problems with grave robbing."

"Are you the man from Glorianna's Dungeon?" The suspicious clergy asked.

"The one and the same," Dan confirmed. "So, what's been happening? I didn't see a cemetery."

"Not here," the rector said as he turned and led Dan into the smaller confines of Saint Dunstan's Chapel, held within the larger cathedral.

As Dan stepped into the room, the Rector closed the doors. "So, what do I call you?" Dan asked. "Seeing as how you don't like the title Vicar, and I'm not going to call you Rector."

"I am the Reverend John Stems," the man replied, drawing himself up to his full height.

"All right, Reverend," Dan stated, "why don't you tell me what all the trouble is?"

"I feel that you have been slightly misinformed," John stated. "We have no cemetery in the style of your colonial churches. Several well-respected individuals are interred here beneath the main level."

"So, no graves have been robbed?" Dan asked, confused. Roger's information was normally dead on.

"None of our tombs have been disturbed. However, several of our members, while not qualifying for interment on the grounds, do conduct small funerary services here before transferring the body to the place of final rest," the reverend explained. "It is customary for the body to be installed the night before with the service taking place early the next morning so as not to disturb our mid-day worship times."

"And?" Dan prodded.

"Some of the bodies have been taken during the night," John stated. "It is quite embarrassing for a body to vanish with nary a clue as to how it happened."

"I can imagine," Dan replied. "Any signs of vampirism?"

"No," the reverend answered quickly. "We check all of them; besides, most of those undead creatures cannot set foot in the church let alone wake within the holy confines."

"Okay. Who has access to the church?" Dan asked.

"Myself, the assistant priest, and the caretaker."

"How long have the assistant and caretaker been here?"

"Hamish Grant has been with us for seven years, serving in his current capacity. Hans Kleve is our caretaker and his tenure is nearly that long."

"How is Grant's background?"

"Sterling," the reverend replied, offended at the question. "I assure you that he would not take part in such goings-on."

"Sounds good, then that means this Hans is responsible. Where does he live?" Dan asked.

"I'm not sure that I can give you that information."

"If he isn't responsible, then I won't be doing anything other than talking with the man," the American replied.

"Very well. I believe he rents space on Peter's Hill. The third dwelling," John replied, reluctantly.

"Thank you very much," Dan said, smiling. The hunter took a step past the reverend and then stopped. "One more question: have you noticed any changes in the man, pallor, mannerisms, anything like that?"

"He's been keeping to himself more than he did and acting rattled, but I'm sure it isn't related to this. He's a good man and has always performed his duties wonderfully."

"Thanks, Reverend," Dan replied as he stepped back out into the gray day.

96

Brackish was standing by the velociter. "Luck?" The goblin asked.

"Yeah, I think I know who we're looking for," Dan replied. "Did you catch anything?"

"No ghoul," Brackish replied.

"After my little talk with the reverend, that doesn't surprise me. The caretaker, Hans Kleve, has been acting strange lately, and the body snatching has just been in the last month," Dan explained. "Let's go have a talk with Mr. Kleve and see what he has to say."

"I come?"

"Yes, but you should stay in the velociter unless it gets crazy," Dan stated.

"I know, I know. Goblin scary, oooooh," the goblin said, indicating his understanding of the way people perceived him.

Leaving the shotgun in the vehicle, Dan walked to the plain-looking wooden door, giving a quick rap on the unpainted surface and listening. From inside, he could hear footsteps and hurried movements, like someone trying to cover something up.

A moment later, the door opened and a nervous middle-aged man was looking out at the hunter. "Yes?" The man inquired.

"Are you Hans Kleve?" Dan asked.

"I am," Hans answered, not giving any further information.

"May I come in? I have some questions for you."

"Now's a terrible time; I'm quite inconvenienced at the moment," Hans explained.

"Okay, one quick question then. Why is an educated man living in a pauper's hovel and caretaking a church?" Dan asked.

Hans' eyebrows shot up in surprise. The American had noticed that the man's speech was not the same as the common working men and women that populated the city. "Perhaps, you should come in," Hans offered, stepping aside.

Dan entered and looked around. Remnants of scientific equipment were scattered about the enclosed space. Turning to face the suspect, Dan placed a hand on the butt of his pistol and smiled at the man. "I'm sure that you've heard about some rather disturbing developments at Saint Paul's Cathedral," the hunter offered, trying to bait the man. "I'm asking to see if anyone knows anything."

"That's nice of you to assist the reverend," Hans stated, his eyes darting around refusing to focus on Dan.

"So, do you know anything about it?" The American asked.

"Just what I've heard."

"Why do you have all of this equipment?" The hunter queried, pointing to the nearby gear.

"I'm performing a few experiments," Hans answered. "I don't really see what concern it might be of yours."

From the next room came a clinking of metal on glass. "What's that?" Dan asked, gripping the pistol tightly.

"I've a guest. An old friend of mine has recently arrived in town."

"Let's go meet this friend."

"Hans?" A well-cultured voice called from the back room. "Do we have company?"

"Yes, Dr. Franken," Hans replied.

"A doctor?" Dan questioned.

98

"Yes," Franken replied as he stepped into the doorway. "I hold several degrees in multiple disciplines."

He was a rail-thin man with a well-groomed appearance whose eyes told of a wild intelligence. Dan glimpsed several crimson spots on his well-pressed, white shirt. "What are you fellas working on?" The American asked, trying not to let his suspicions show.

"I believe you were asking questions about some peculiar happenings at the local church?" Franken replied. "Why don't you come back here and see if our work can shed some light on your dilemma?"

The smile on the doctor's face was the same as that of a wolf snaring a deer. Taking confidence in his two pistols and the Bowie knife in his boot, Dan decided to take the bait. "Lead the way," the American answered.

"Gladly," Franken replied. "Hans?"

Hans stepped to his associate, and they both entered the next room. Dan followed at a safe distance. Upon entering, he saw beakers of multi-colored liquids bubbling away. A confused look crossed Dan's face, and then he heard a chain dragging on the floor. Turning, he saw a horribly scarred figure shambling in the corner. "What have you crackpots done to him?" Dan asked.

"Done?" Franken asked, the offense clear in his voice. "Why, we gave it life! I have not spent my life studying to have a foolish brute like Death stop me."

"I've heard of another man that tried to create life. Things didn't turn out to well for him," Dan stated.

"Oh?" Franken inquired, laughing. "I would wager that the story ended much different than you know."

Hans reached down and pulled a pin free from the floor. The chain fell slack at the scarred figure's feet. "Get him!" Franken yelled.

As the creature stumbled forward, Dan saw that the face and top of the head of his attacker did not match the rest of the head. It had been stitched on. Two mismatched hands reached out to grab the American. Drawing his pistols, Dan put several shells into the malformed body. "Doctor!" Hans exclaimed.

"I told you encasing the organs would ensure greater longevity," Franken replied in a clinical voice.

Fortunately, the lumbering abomination was slow, and Dan could duck away from its grasp. He delivered a kick to the back of its knee, but the creation just turned for another go. "What have you done?" Dan asked, firing more bullets into his attacker.

"I am merely carrying out the previous work that I started years ago," Franken explained. "When you spoke of someone pursuing similar work, I assume you mean the Baron von Frankenstein?"

"Yeah," Dan confirmed, dodging another swipe by the monster.

"I suppose it is no concern now, for you shall soon be dead, but Frankenstein's story did not end at the gallows as some have assumed, nor did it end with his death. The Baron had taken on an assistant, a very skilled young doctor, my good friend Hans. At the end of the Baron's life, his assistant transferred the brilliant mind into another body. You see, I am the Baron von Frankenstein. My life's work is too important to allow a trivial thing like dying to stop me."

"Okay," the American said as the creature lunged for him again.

This time, a hand clasped onto his jacket and pulled him back. The two oddly paired extremities hoisted Dan into the air and sent him sailing across the room. Plaster and wood broke as he bounced off the wall and onto the floor, his pistols falling from his hands. *He shouldn't be that strong.* Dan thought as he searched for his weapons.

His hands closed around the grips, and he rose, firing a round, not at the monster but the two men controlling it. Hans grabbed his shoulder and fell back, while Frankenstein retreated around the door frame. The familiar sound of a shotgun blasted from the front room. "Dan!" Brackish yelled.

"Back here," the American called to his partner.

Putting a bullet right between the creature's eyes did nothing to faze the monstrous child of science. The goblin rushed back and quickly took stock of the situation. Pumping a round into the shotgun's chamber, Brackish unloaded the shot into the monster's flank. The creature spun towards this new threat. Dan's mind raced, trying to clear the daze from his flight across the room. There was some piece of information that he remembered having read at one time about the Baron's creations. *Lee would be handy right about now,* Dan thought, knowing that his partner could have recalled the information almost immediately.

Brackish rushed around the misshapen thing and fired another round. This one went wide and struck several of the beakers sitting on the table. As they shattered and met the exposed flame of the burner below, they lit the table ablaze. Screaming, the creature backed away. "Fire!" Dan yelled, remembering the information. "It's afraid of fire."

Brackish smiled and fired into the rest of the chemicals, adding to the flames licking at the table and up the wall. "You must not aggravate it!" Frankenstein demanded, coming around the corner, a small pistol in his hands.

101

Turning and firing, Dan put a round into the mad scientist's arm, shattering the bone and causing the pistol to fall harmlessly to the floor. In the time it took to disarm the doctor, the creature saw an avenue of escape and rushed towards it. "No, listen to me. I made you!" Frankenstein ordered.

The creation paid no attention as it battered him out of the way to flee the growing flames. Falling limply onto the floor, the man made no move to cause further problems. With the fire licking the ceiling, Dan searched for Hans, who had managed to crawl into a corner. "Brackish, go drag the little man outside," Dan ordered as he grabbed onto Hans' collar.

The goblin rushed out and took hold of the unconscious scientist with his prosthetic arm. Glad to have the mechanical limb, Brackish easily carried the man outside. Even with his slight frame, Frankenstein was taller and heavier than the goblin. Dropping the fiend onto the cold, hard sidewalk, Brackish waited as Dan pulled another man from the quickly burning building.

Spotting a woman peeking from the window of the next house, the American threw up an arm and started shouting at him. She opened the window a moment later. "What do you want?"

"Number three is on fire; you need the fire brigade, and get your neighbors out of here," Dan ordered.

"Lord," the woman exclaimed, vanishing from the window and screaming fire.

"Do you know where he went?" Dan asked, turning back to his partner.

Brackish pointed back in the direction of the church. "These men?" The goblin inquired, pointing to the two wounded scientists.

"We'll come back for them," Dan stated, heading towards the velociter.

Opening the outer storage compartment underneath the operator's seat, Dan started rummaging through the different gear that Lee kept within. "A-ha!" Dan proclaimed, lifting a lantern.

Brackish gave a questioning look to the man. "It light out," the goblin explained.

"I know that," Dan replied. "Just get in."

As the velociter turned around and headed back in the direction of the church, Dan took the time to explain his plan. "The patchwork man doesn't like fire, right?"

"Right," Brackish agreed.

"Before Lee's powered lanterns, we used these old kerosene burners. With the little bit of fuel still in this one, I'm hoping to be able to light up Frankenstein's science project," the American explained. "Are we still on the right track?"

"Church," Brackish stated, pointing ahead.

"Well, I guess the reverend should be happy. The bodies he lost are coming back." A harsh laugh escaped Dan's lips.

Brackish chuckled beside the man. In the heat of the hunt, the humor kept them from becoming too focused and succumbing to the stress of the situation. Several hunters over the years had found themselves within the confines of Bedlam – or Bethlem Royal Hospital as it was officially known, the dreaded sanitarium in London – because their minds snapped. Stopping directly in front of Saint Paul's Cathedral, Dan and Brackish exited the vehicle, looking for any sign of their quarry. Securing the velociter against theft, Dan looked over to the goblin, seeing if his sensitive nose could discern the scent.

Sniffing the air, Brackish tried to find the path the creature had taken. Taking but a moment, the goblin pointed to the door. "Inside?" Dan asked. Brackish nodded.

Keeping their shotguns at the ready, the hunters walked towards the entrance, neither one stepping directly in front of the door but keeping to the side of it. While the front entrance was grand and elegant, the side entrance was almost hidden in the garden, its plain door easy to overlook. Grabbing the handle, Dan pulled it open quickly, and Brackish stepped in, aiming the shotgun around the space and searching for a target. The shouts coming from within the church gave Dan an idea as to where the creature had gone.

With no shots fired, Dan stepped in behind the goblin. "Follow the screams," the American instructed.

Walking beside Brackish, Dan could see the Reverend John Stems standing in the middle of the great domed room that took up most of the middle section of the church. "In the name of God, I command you to stop this sacrilege!" The reverend commanded.

A hand lashed out from behind the wall and struck the holy man in the jaw. He spun around before dropping to the floor like a sack of potatoes. Seeing the attack, the hunters ran the remaining distance into the circular architecture of the dome. It was a beautiful room, but they had little chance to admire it. Standing in the room with them was a creation that could be classified as nothing less than abominable. The creature was looking around at the different sights and weeping.

Stations for votive candles and prayers were located at several of the halls leaving the room, which allowed Dan to formulate a plan, one he hoped would not be needed. "Stay back," the American instructed his partner.

Stepping back into the hallway, Brackish tried to stay near the wall and was alarmed when Dan set the shotgun on the floor. "Hey," the hunter said in a calm voice.

The patchwork man saw the hunter for the first time, and a snarl curled his lip. "No need for that," Dan stated, holding his hands out to show that he was unarmed. "Can you understand me?"

The monster circled Dan. "I'm asking, because if you can understand me, then we don't need for this to get ugly," the hunter explained. "I would rather be able to end this without any further violence. Would you like that?"

The monster seemed to understand the American's words and calmed down. That was when another man, the Reverend's assistant Hamish Grant, Dan assumed based on how the man was dressed, came into the small room. "What have you done?" Grant demanded, seeing Stems' sprawled body.

The creature was slightly agitated by this man's interruption, and Dan could see the calm slipping away. When Grant laid eyes on the reverend's attacker, he stopped in his steps. Pulling a crucifix from his pocket, the assistant priest started shouting at the creature. "In the name of God, I cast thee out. Begone from this Holy place, demon!"

The monster grabbed Hamish's arm and slung the man into a column. A crunching sound accompanied the hit, and Dan was sure that some of Grant's bones were pulverized. Whirling on Dan, the creature lunged forward. Brackish leapt from his hiding place in the hall and landed in front of the creature. Surprised, the monster stopped for a moment. Dan hurled the lantern at the patchwork man, and the glass casing shattered as it struck the odd-shaped brow, kerosene running down onto the face, shoulders, and shirt front of the science experiment.

With the fuel in his eyes, the creature flailed and stumbled back, landing on the votive candles. A moment later, the thing screamed as the kerosene ignited. Flailing about, the monster tried to stifle the flames before dropping to the floor, its movements slowing. Taking off his long coat, Dan attempted to snuff out the fire, but the creature stopped moving before he could. Dropping the coat, Dan pressed down, robbing the flames of oxygen. Lifting his garment, the American saw the burned remains of the creature. It would not pose a problem to anyone else.

Inspecting the Reverend John Stems, Dan found a pulse but could not find any broken bones. With a firm slap, he woke the man. "What?" Stems asked startled.

"It's fine," Dan answered. "My associate and I have taken care of it."

Sitting up, the reverend saw the burned body and the fallen form of Hamish Grant. "What in the name of God?"

"This is what remains of the missing bodies," Dan explained. "See that they get a Christian burial. First, you may want to help Mr. Grant; he's going to need a doctor."

The reverend nodded as he started towards his assistant. Stopping, the man stared at the goblin walking beside the American towards the side entrance. "Let's go back and have a talk with the good doctors, shall we?" Dan asked.

"Yes," Brackish agreed.

Stowing their shotguns, the two hunters drove back to the neighborhood of Peter's Hill where Hans Kleve's house was fully engulfed in flames. The local fire brigade had arrived and was furiously working to prevent the flames from spreading to the neighboring houses while Hans and Frankenstein gave a statement to a constable. Stepping from the vehicle, Dan heard the accusation he was expecting. "That's the man there! He broke in, attacked us, and then set the fire to finish the job," Frankenstein lied.

"Constable," Dan said, tipping his hat to the lawman.

"Mr. Winston," The constable replied. "Mr. Brackish."

The goblin waved. "Would you like to know what really happened?" Dan asked.

"Gladly, sir," the constable said, smiling.

Dan told what had happened from their initial arrival at the cathedral until their return to the blazing home. "If you don't believe us, you can go look at Saint Paul's and see for yourself," Dan finished.

"Quite all right, if you would come down later and make a statement to the captain," the constable requested.

"Glad to," Dan confirmed.

"Yes," Brackish agreed

A smug smile crossed the hunters' faces as Frankenstein and Hans were placed in manacles and marched down the street. "I swear the past two cases have been people building monsters, as if there aren't enough of them naturally," Dan grumbled as he climbed into the velociter.

"People crazy," Brackish responded.

"If we get back to Glorianna's Dungeon and pick up our bounty, we should be able to stop and pick up a few bottles and get home in time for supper," the American stated.

A happy grin spread over Brackish's face. "Hurry," he replied.

Arriving back at the flat after having purchased a few bottles of beer, Dan and Brackish were headed to the steps up to their quarters when Ms. Edwards' door opened. "Mr. Winston, Brackish, we've received a letter from Mr. Baum," Elizabeth informed them; her face lit up the hallway. "He also sent one for you."

The young lady held out the simple envelope to Dan. Smiling, he gladly accepted it. "Dinner will be served at the regular time, if that is acceptable?"

"Completely," Dan replied.

"What we get?" Brackish asked.

"Ms. Edwards and I have prepared a Cornish game hen, potatoes, and some greens that we acquired at market today," Elizabeth informed them.

Brackish licked his lips, mainly for the meat and potatoes. The goblin was not a big fan of vegetables.

Entering the apartment, the two hunters stowed their gear and sat down, each of them popping open a bottle. Dan took a big swallow and sat his drink on the coffee table. Opening the letter, the American began to read the neat script that was Lee's handwriting.

Dan and Brackish,

I hope this letter finds you well. Unfortunately, as our training here has drawn to a close, it has been made known that we are not being granted leaves to return home. While that had been my wish, Her Majesty has other plans for us. The day after our training has completed, we will be split into units and given our assignments. Where we are going has been kept a secret, but it is clear to every man present that we are to be deployed to face the enemy. I trust that you have not burned down our home yet, please continue to not do so.

Sincerely,

Lee

Dan smiled. Even far away, Lee was giving him grief. The American proceeded to tell Brackish about the contents of the letter. "We no burn clan house down," Brackish stated. "How he know about house today?"

Dan almost spit out the mouthful of beer laughing. He got it under control and was able to swallow. "He doesn't," Dan explained. "He's just giving us a hard time."

As the goblin and the American laughed, both of them were worried for their absent partner, but neither would give voice to the concern.

6

Lee was thrilled to finally be done with the training portion of his military service. With a great deal of effort, he had been able to assist in turning his fellow recruits into decent shots. The classes they had been forced to sit through provided a glimpse into the foes that they would face once on foreign soil, but the highlight of the training, for Lee, had been the new Gatling guns. Airships, to better combat threats, had been armed with rail-mounted ones, not possessing the large, barrel-shape constructs on which their predecessors had sat but, thanks to a smaller motor mounted onto the rear, could fire at the same speed. The original trigger crank had been replaced with a pedal, which now connected to two buttons mounted onto the handle, and the original, gravity-fed drum had been exchanged for a long belt of ammunition stored in the airship's structure. It was quite a revolutionary idea and would allow for more ammunition than the traditional magazine.

It was the first time that Lee had ever used a Gatling gun, of any variety. The sheer swath of destruction it had cut was astounding. The day following the display, the recruits had been taken to a tower away from camp. There, they spent several hours learning how to use parachutes. Lee had immediately recognized the adjusted design he had used to drop the Tin Man from an airship and land at Stonehenge. It seemed that the military had found a much more practical use for it and had adapted it into a small pack for men to wear on their backs. Upon leaping from the tower, the men would pull a cord that ripped open the pack and allowed the fabric to catch the wind, slowing their descent so that they could safely reach the ground.

Questioning Sergeant Ward, Lee discovered that the first few missions had been expected to land the airships for a quick disembarkation. Since those ships never had an opportunity to touchdown, it was deemed necessary to have a means that would quickly allow the troops to reach the ground as well as provide safe escape should a ship be damaged beyond flight. After completion of their training, the men had all been assigned to separate units. Lee and Brogan found themselves assigned to the same group. With the sounds and sights of training behind them, they joined their unit on the train.

The train ran for two full days before stopping on the coast of Scotland, facing the channel. Lee admired the large artillery placements that had been keeping the Prussian air fleet from launching the destructive wave that had conquered the Germans so easily. The coastline had been converted to a small rallying point. An airship stood anchored nearby; a transportable ramp led from the beach up to the immense aircraft. "All right, lads!" An officer shouted. "Gather your gear and get on board!"

The men set about gathering their items. All of them had been assigned updated uniforms, not the traditional red coat and black trousers but a green and brown-patterned fabric to allow them to better blend with the environment. It was a solid material that stood up well under most weather conditions, which Lee was grateful for. The thought of going into battle wearing a wool coat made his skin crawl. They had been horrible while he was stationed in India. Brogan was wearing his Claymore across his back and a Webley Mk II in his hip holster. He carried an added burden with the shotgun that had been assigned to him. Lee had made him into a decent shot, but Brogan had never picked up on the finer aspects of marksmanship. Lee's Winchester rested comfortably in his hand, his own

Webley revolver secured in his shoulder holster, and a compact combat knife was secured to his hip.

Climbing aboard the airship, Lee saw it had more in common with the first one that he had ridden in years ago, functional and barren of any comforts. The seats were long wooden benches bolted into the floor. While sitting, he leaned back against the metal walls and tried to get comfortable as the rest of the unit entered. "Where do ye think we'll be going?" Brogan asked.

"Since we are not being given leave and have been outfitted for service, I would surmise that we are headed to the front," Lee answered.

The younger, less-experienced men around them grew nervous with the statement. "The only problem with fighting in Prussia is that the women are as ugly as the men," Brogan proclaimed, slapping the soldier beside him on the back. "I hear it's because of the beards."

The men chuckled at the joke, and some of the tension eased. Lee was the only one not to be surprised by the squealing metal as the cargo door closed. "Hold onto something," the Englishman cautioned, getting a hold of the bench.

The others followed his example, which was fortunate as the ship began to ascend. Shaking like it was going to fall apart, Lee maintained his grip until he felt the engine level out and start their forward progression. "At least, we might get to see Paris," Lee mused optimistically.

"You aren't going to be seeing anything until we reach the forward observation point," one of the ship's officers commented. "I am First Lieutenant Guthrie. The captain has sent me to notify you that meals will be brought to you, and the latrine is aft of this deck. No soldiers will be permitted outside of the hull until we land."

"Why all the bloody secrecy?" One of the soldiers asked.

"Captain's orders, any man disobeying will be shot on sight or transferred to the brig where he will face disciplinary action upon landing," Guthrie informed them. "Do you understand?"

"Yes, sir," most of the soldiers mumbled.

"I can't hear you," Guthrie repeated, not liking the soldiers' attitudes.

"Lad, you best be off," Brogan cautioned. "We aren't your traditional Queen's Marines. You see this lot here, we're monster hunters. While you'll be ferrying men and supplies across the pond, we'll be risking our necks, so why don't you shove off." Guthrie stared in shock at the Scotsman. "Sir!" Brogan added as an afterthought.

Retreating up the stairs, Guthrie hurried and closed the hatch. "I believe you scared him," Lee stated.

"Good," Brogan replied. "Little brat needs to learn to respect his betters."

Several of the soldiers started up the stairs, to test if the hatch was bolted. "Stop!" Lee commanded. "We do not have to like it, but the lieutenant was correct. The captain outranks any soldier, especially on his own ship. He can have us shot for insubordination. While I do not appreciate how we are being treated, I will not have it be said that we are a mutinous lot. Do I make myself clear?"

The men abandoned their notions of following the lieutenant. "Looks like we've got some time," Brogan announced. "Join in, if you know it."

114

With that, the large, kilted Scotsman launched into an old pub song. In minutes, he had all the men singing along.

Two days later, the men in the hold felt the large ship descending. It took an hour before the transport stopped moving, and then Guthrie appeared for the first time since his initial appearance. "If you will gather your things," the lieutenant stated, "we will be opening the ramp in five minutes."

Not waiting for a response, the officer left. True to his word, the mechanical winches controlling the ramp began to move, lowering it to the ground, and a captain from Her Majesty's Marines stood on the ground waiting on the men. "Report to the commander's office," the captain ordered, then turned on his heel to march away.

"Where can we store our gear?" One of the recruits asked.

"You can't," the officer replied. "The commander will explain everything."

Stepping into the sunlight after having been in the hold gave all the men pause. Their eyes took several moments to properly adjust to the bright surroundings. The airship had docked in the center of a large field that had been converted to a stationing area. Trees had been cut down and buildings hastily erected with mobile artillery units stationed in the center of the camp. Groups of soldiers were performing drills or hurrying about on some important errand. A smaller building was situated near the mobile artillery. Lee assumed it was the commander's office. "This way, men," Lee instructed as he started towards the structure.

The others followed him, a few at Brogan's insistence. Other soldiers gave the hunters strange looks. It might have been the variety of weaponry they carried or that their uniforms were slightly different. Brogan and Lee both knew it was because the hunters did not move like soldiers. A hunter needed to be loose and able to adapt at a moment's notice, while soldiers tended to move stiffly and follow orders.

Lee knocked on the door; a small sign at eye-level read *Commander Reynolds*. "Enter!" A harsh voice called from inside.

"Brogan?" Lee asked.

"You boys stay here. We'll be back in a minute," the Scotsman said as he stepped up beside Lee.

Pushing the door open, the Englishman saw a worn and scuffed desk whose items belied the organized mind of its owner. Wearing a pristine uniform, the commander sat staring at the men. He made no attempt to hide his contempt for them. A large, brutish-looking man with Sergeant's stripes on his shoulder stood beside the desk. Judging by the shadow showing on the floor, another such man was waiting behind the door. Sitting his Winchester against the exterior frame of the door, Lee stepped in. Following his lead, Brogan left the shotgun outside.

Once they were inside, the door closed, which served to confirm Lee's suspicions. "Commander Reynolds, the special Marine unit has arrived and is awaiting orders," Lee stated, standing at attention.

"Marine?" Reynolds said, his voice dripping with contempt. "You are not fit to be in Her Majesty's service."

"It seems to me she thought we were," Brogan spoke up.

"You are insolent, undisciplined, and unfit for duty with a true Marine," Reynolds stated. "I, and several of my contemporaries, have voiced this concern. It seems that our comments have fallen on deaf ears."

"What are our orders, sir?" Lee asked again.

"A true Marine is easily a match for you men. Wouldn't you say, sergeants?" Reynolds asked.

The brute from behind the door laid a hand on Brogan's shoulder, and the thug stationed beside the desk stepped towards Lee. Brogan spun around, latching onto his attacker's wrist, and pulling the man in close, the Scotsman planted a knee firmly in his opponent's solar plexus, doubling the man over. Raising him back up, Brogan planted his massive right fist in the man's jaw, sending blood and teeth onto the clean walls as the sergeant collapsed into a heap.

Lee did not have time to appreciate Brogan's fight, being engaged in his own. As the man approached, his hands raised in a traditional boxing stance, Lee delivered an open-handed chop across the man's windpipe, Lee watched as the brute clutched at his throat, trying to force air down. Lashing out with his leg, striking the side of his opponent's knee, Lee watched as the twisted joint refused to support the man's weight, and he landed hard. With their opponents disabled, the two men stood back at attention in front of the commander. They enjoyed the shocked look on the officer's face. "Orders, sir?" Lee asked.

Reynolds sputtered, trying to find a response. "You have orders for us, don't you?" Brogan asked, leaning on the desk.

Fumbling through his organized papers, Reynolds retrieved a sheet and handed it to Brogan, who gave it a quick glance before passing it to his companion. Scanning the paper, Lee smiled. "Let's gather the men. We have a ship waiting for us. We'll get more information once we are in the air," he explained.

Brogan followed Lee to the door and then stopped. "Where are we anyway?" Brogan asked the commander.

"G-g-g-germany." Reynolds stammered.

"Awful close to enemy territory, aren't we?" Brogan asked as he shut the door behind him.

"Not to worry. After they thrashed them, the Prussian's left a fairly autonomous government. The Eastern portion of the country is subject to the Prussians more than here. I imagine that the actual front, if the papers are to be believed, should have been pushed back close to the Prussian border," Lee replied.

Gathering their weapons, the two men informed the unit of their orders. "Are we going to get to eat first?" One of the men asked.

"Doubtful, perhaps they'll feed us on the ship," Lee offered.

"Who put you in charge?" Another man asked.

"I tell you what, when any of you boys have been around as long as we have or killed half as many boogeymen, then we'll talk about letting you lead," Brogan stated, cutting off any further protests.

Having silenced the dissenters, Brogan stepped aside and motioned Lee forward. Nodding his appreciation, the Englishman led the rag tag group towards the indicated docking pylon. "What's the name of the ship?" Brogan asked quietly.

"It is the *H.M.S. Orpheus*," Lee answered.

"Weird name," the Scotsman stated.

"A bit ominous really," the English hunter responded.

"Why?"

"Orpheus went into the underworld seeking to retrieve the spirit of his dead wife."

"I guess it fits. They seem to be sending us into Hell," Brogan countered, laughing.

A wry grin crossed Lee's face. "I suppose they are. Let us hope we fare better than our ship's namesake."

As they passed the large pylons and the supply ships docked beside them, they did not see the *Orpheus* until they were past all the other ships. Comparatively, it was a much smaller ship, its design sleeker, built to reduce wind resistance. Lee was familiar with the theories associated with it but did not know they had been put into practice yet. The large canvas covering the air bladders, along with the gondola, carrier hull, and catwalk were all solid black in color. It appeared that even the windows around the gondola had been tinted to an extremely dark shade. A large turbine engine sat at the rear of the gondola with its twin mounted to the other side out of view. "Looks like a bloody storm cloud," a soldier commented.

Brogan slapped him on the back, almost toppling the smaller man. "It looks like we'll be able to make lots of thunder, eh, lads?" Brogan shouted to make sure all the men heard him.

Indeed, from where he stood, Lee could count four of the modified Gatling guns. If the other side of the catwalk was sporting the same number, this ship outgunned others of its size. Two cannons, much like those he had installed years before in the Tin Man, were supported on the front, but whereas Lee had used a triple-barrel theme, these were single barrels with a gravity-fed magazine set on top. A pneumatic tank and cables snaked up from the floor and connected into the back of the cannon. "Fair assumption that this is something new," Brogan said.

"Indeed, it is. This will be our maiden voyage," a well-dressed naval officer stated.

The man had been standing beside them, quietly watching how awed the soldiers were by his craft. "The captain of the vessel, I presume," Lee smiled, extending his hand.

"Captain Abbott, at your service; may I see your orders?" He asked, shaking the offered hand. Handing over the paper, Abbott gave them a cursory glance. "As I suspected, you lot are the monster hunters. If you'll board, we'll open the next set of orders."

"Can your galley provide the men some food? It's been several days of limited bread and water," Lee explained.

"Certainly," Abbott smiled. "Once their gear is stowed in the bunks, they can sample our hospitality. I take it you lead these men."

"He and I are just the most experienced," Brogan interjected, not wanting to be left out of the decisions.

"Very good. Once you've stowed your gear, come to my quarters," Abbott instructed. "Now, if all of you fine gentlemen will, welcome to the *HMS Orpheus*."

Leading the men around the side, the captain motioned to the much smaller ramp being lowered. Two at a time, the men boarded the vessel. The bunks were small cabinets set into the wall, where the men could lay down, with footlockers built under the bottom bunk. The men picked bunks and stored their gear. As most of them made their way towards the galley, following the signs, Lee and Brogan went in search of the Captain's Quarters.

The sailor's directions led them right to the officer's rooms. Lee gave a quick knock. "Enter," Abbott called from the other side.

Stepping inside, Lee and Brogan were happy to see that even as the ship's captain, his quarters were economical compared to others officer quarters they had seen. Sitting on the slender desk in front of the captain was a sealed envelope. "This was delivered to me directly from the Commodore. His instructions were not to open it until we were safely in the air and on our way to the front," Abbott explained. A bell notified him of a message coming in from the bridge. He lifted the handle and listened. "Proceed. Please, gentlemen, have a seat."

Taking the offered chairs across from the captain's, the two men felt the ship begin to lift. It was much smoother than the previous airship. The three men sat in silence for several minutes until the bell sounded again. Lifting the handle, Abbott gave a few instructions and replaced the instrument into its cradle. "We are now on our way to the Prussian front," the captain explained. "Shall we?"

Removing a stiletto from his desk drawer, the naval officer quickly broke the seal. "So, what level of manure are we stepping into?" Brogan asked.

"A fairly large amount," Abbott replied, reading the orders. "These orders are for us to proceed over the Prussian front as deep as possible. No ship has made it deeper than fifteen miles before being brought down."

"That's it, just see how far we can go?" Lee asked. "Seems odd."

"On the contrary, it isn't. We've lost several ships and had several more put out of service. Our mission is to find any concentration of otherworldly offensive capabilities that the Prussians have and deploy your unit to handle the trouble."

"To what end?" Lee asked, knowing there had to be more to the story.

121

"Some of the returning ships have spoken of a woman flying inside an apothecary's tools. It is believed that she is the one leading the attacks," Abbott explained. "I believe you were trained by one of the men that Her Majesty consulted with on this matter."

"Vladimir Abramov," Brogan and Lee said in unison.

"Along with several other experts on the folklore of the Baltics," a wry smile crossed Abbott's face. "As soon as I was given this ship, the information from those meetings was accessible to me. So, gentlemen, they want us to find the Baba Yaga and put an end to her interference in this war."

"Won't the winter be setting in soon?" Lee asked.

"Not from what we can determine," Abbott replied. "Napoleon choked on the snow, and his armies died in drifts over their heads, but all of our meteorological predictions show that the hard, Prussian winter is not coming. I'm going to tell you men something, but it cannot leave these quarters. Is that understood?"

Lee and Brogan nodded their understanding. Captain Abbott leaned back in his chair before speaking. "Our first ship to infiltrate the Prussian front was going to deploy a contingent of Her Majesty's Marines to hinder enemy supply shipments. Our forces are doing well at pushing the Prussian troops back, but they are fighting bloody hard for every inch. If we can cut off their food and bullets, then our boys can make short work of their defenses and wrap this war up in months. That ship sent a single transmission from its onboard communications; it was a quick warning about the assault they were under. All hands were lost when the ship detonated."

"What were they under attack by?" Lee asked, leaning forward.

Brogan was just as interested in the answer. "A vampire and a strange bird," the captain replied. "We now know the strange bird is the firebird; it ignited the hydrogen and destroyed the ship. The vampire was most likely acting as a guardian so that the creature could accomplish its task"

"Would've been nice if someone would have told us this earlier," Brogan commented.

"This ship was designed to travel quietly and without being seen in the night sky. It is so heavily armed because we anticipate that this will not stop any of the enemies we will meet once the front lines have been crossed."

"Don't worry, Captain; we'll do all we can to see that this ship does not meet a similar fate," Lee replied solemnly.

"I know that you will. Also, ear plugs were issued from the Quartermaster with instructions that each of the soldiers should wear them at all times while on the deck," Abbott opened a drawer and sat the large box of ear plugs on his desk.

"What about the cabin crew?" Brogan asked.

"The cabin is completely soundproof," Abbott responded. "We've heard that strange song, but coming through the line, it does not have the same effect. So, we will still be able to receive calls from anyone manning the guns."

"Captain, thank you for all the information, but I feel that we need to meet the men in the galley so that they can be informed of our orders," Lee stated.

Joining the soldiers in the galley, Lee stood at the front of the assembled men and explained everything. "Why are we doing this?" One of the men near the back shouted.

Several others joined their voice to his. "Because you are licensed bounty hunters and are expected to face all manner of threats. You agreed to join the Royal Marine Corps for this action and as such are subject to orders," Lee responded calmly.

"She's just one witch, boys. They aren't too hard to kill; a bullet, a knife, hell, even a club can put a witch down," Brogan shouted.

"You heard Abramov," another soldier replied. "She's not just some witch."

"And?" Brogan asked. The man did not continue his line of reasoning. "Just because she's Prussia's number one witch doesn't mean she can't be killed just like all the rest."

"As my associate has pointed out, we are here to kill one witch, not every monster in Prussia. Also, I would wager that we are not the only group of hunters on this mission. Prussia is rather large and we may not see any of the beasts that other ships have," Lee offered.

The men seemed to take comfort in his words. Lee had to admit that the stories of the Baba Yaga put her in a class of witch all her own, but the men did not need to know that. It was probably the reason Brogan had not started telling them horror stories. "When are we crossing?" A soldier asked.

"I don't know the exact time, but it'll be after nightfall, at which time, eight men will stand guard on the deck at all times. The border is the point of no return," Lee looked at the assembled group.

Most of them had become hunters because they felt it was an easy pay day. They had not learned the hard lessons that hunting taught. Going into war, Lee knew that not all the men would return. He realized suddenly that he may not return. It had been his intention to sit and dine with the others, but he found his appetite gone. How many times had he chided Dan for being reckless and endangering himself? Once or twice, Lee had gotten fleeting ideals about his mortality, but this was an epiphany that he may never see the apartment, his partners, Ms. Edwards, or Elizabeth ever again.

With no more questions, he excused himself and went back to the bunks. Opening the canvas bag with his other uniforms in it, Lee dug to the bottom and felt the hard surface that he had been looking for. Pulling, he forced the brass chestplate to the top. Once they crossed the Prussian border, he would make sure to wear it underneath his uniform top every moment of every day until he was safely back on English soil.

As night fell, clouds covered the stars and made the sky black as pitch. The ship stayed its course and pierced the border of Prussia as Lee and Brogan both found themselves on watch. Standing guard behind the Gatling gun, Lee's eyes searched the darkened landscape for any sign of a threat. The large Scotsman had volunteered to man one of the cannons near the front. It was not surprising. Lee surmised that Dan would have chosen the same. "What is that?" Rutledge, the hunter to Lee's right shouted, pointing at a shape flying below them.

Staring into the darkness below, Lee could make out the faint outline of a strange bowl. Reaching into his pocket, he retrieved a small, circular glass disk and attached it to the barrel of his Winchester.

Tightening the screw, Lee kept an eye on the strange thing. Raising the rifle, he used the magnifying effects of the glass to discern more of the shape. A hunched figure with white hair wildly flowing in the wind was riding in the object. Lee knew what he was seeing wasn't natural. It was the Baba Yaga.

Steadying himself, Lee took a breath and sighted on the back of the figure's head. One shot and he might be able to accomplish their mission, which would be a first for him. As his finger started to tighten on the trigger, he saw the figure turn. An unholy yellow light shone in the eyes and stared directly into the lens. The hair on the back of Lee's neck rose, and the hunter knew that things were about to get worse.

7

Lee lowered the rifle and started to shout a warning when the cackling laugh below alerted everyone onboard to the danger. The Baba Yaga shouted in her native tongue, and the night erupted with motion around them. "FIRE!" Lee ordered, shouting to be heard above the cacophony of noise.

Grabbing the handles of the Gatling gun, the hunter quickly pressed the trigger buttons, sending a shining line of bullets toward the witch and her carriage. Shadows intercepted the rounds and fell away as quickly as they appeared. Two rounds fired out from the front cannons. The phosphorous tips illuminated the night, revealing a daunting scene. Almost any type of flying creature that Vladimir had spoken of was ascending to greet them. Spotting the giant, wooden mortar with the old hag flying amongst her forces, Lee trained his aim on her. Holding down the trigger, he watched as the rounds chewed through the conglomeration of monsters and struck the witch's transport.

Hammering through the wood, Lee saw a round puncture the old creature's shoulder. As soon as its mistress was wounded, the mortar dropped from the sky. Satisfied that the Baba Yaga was out of the fight, Lee concentrated on the assembled forces. Feathered creatures of all sorts were fluttering about, some of them natural birds of the lands beneath them and others much fiercer supernatural specimens. The dreaded Alkonost flew nearby. A hint of sound infiltrated past Lee's ear plugs. Swiveling the automatic weapon up, he fired and watched the creature's human breasts and neck disintegrate beneath the onslaught.

In the few moments since the aerial battle began, the English hunter had not paid any attention to those around him. Now, the other hunters poured out from below decks. Some were barely in uniform, with outer shirts unbuttoned, while others had not bothered at all. They were all armed with their rifles, firing at targets as they presented themselves. Turning, Lee motioned to the front of the deck. Following his gestures, the men spread out.

Sparing a glance to Brogan in the cannon's seat, Lee saw one of the explosives detonate in the air dazing the monsters with its concussive force. Some of the beasts plummeted to the ground, others merely continued in a daze. These creatures were dealt with by the additional soldiers that had made their way forward. Even with the added protection of the ear plugs, Lee could hear the loud, rapid-fire sounds of the Gatling guns, combined with the cannons, and now all the rifles that had joined the fray. A man, aiming over the rail beside Lee, was pulled from the deck and hurtled away. Lee saw the body fall away into the night, heading towards the ground far below.

A pale figure pulled itself up over the railing. Smiling, the vampire revealed a row of sharp fangs. Removing a hand from the machine gun, Lee drew his revolver and put a round directly into the monster's head. Grabbing at the wound, the vampire stumbled back and fell over the railing. It plummeted out of sight, and Lee resumed his efforts with the Gatling gun. He saw the last of the ammunition belt fall from the feed above him, and a second later, he had expelled the last of the deadly projectiles. He knew from training that it might take three minutes or more before a new belt could be fed down to him, no time at all usually, but right now, it was time he could ill afford to waste.

Sliding the Winchester off his shoulder, Lee started firing at the enemy as they approached. As one of the men near him fell to the deck, Lee saw the ear plug fall from the soldier's ear. A glazed look appeared on his face. Jumping to his feet, the man ran and leapt from the ship into the air. One of the siren-like Alkonost dug its claws deep into the man's flanks and pulled large pieces of flesh and organ from him. At no point did the man's face reveal anything other than complete rapture. Disgusted, Lee worked the lever and put a bullet directly between the hybrid creature's eyes, and down it fell, taking the body of the dead hunter with it.

As the gleam of brass dangled from the feeding station, Lee slid the rifle strap on his shoulder and began to load the belt into the Gatling gun. Before he could close the catch and prepare to fire, great streaking projectiles hurtled towards the vessel. At first sight, they appeared to be great flaming balls, but the shape told Lee that the firebirds had been held back in reserve while the ammunition dwindled. Several of the Gatling guns swung towards the approaching creatures. "Brilliant strategy," Lee mumbled as he managed to shoot two of the birds from the sky.

Undeterred, the other creatures continued their onslaught. Everyone onboard knew that it would only take one firebird to puncture the gondola and turn the ship into a fiery heap of scrap metal. An explosion at the front of the ship caused the deck to buck wildly underneath Lee's feet. Holding onto the trigger handles was the only thing that kept him from falling completely to the floor while something large that smelled like smoke stumbled past him.

Brogan's large hand wrapped around the rail beside the English hunter. With soot covering his face, and his beard singed, the Scotsman

129

was a sight. His eyes seemed to be roaming while he clutched tightly to the shotgun.

Captain Abbott sat in his chair, watching the fierce battle that raged all around him. Damage reports streamed in from all quarters, but they were not as bad as they could have been. The hunters, fighting for their lives on the deck, were the only reason the ship had survived this long. With the flaming streaks closing the distance to his ship, Abbott carefully weighed his options. "What are our choices of evasive maneuvers?" He asked.

The ship's chief engineer cleared his throat. "The engine is strong enough to make some impressive moves, but it's still just an airship. Without ascertaining the damage from our forward compartments, we may split the ship. Even then, I can't guarantee what sort of chances we would have against those flaming beasts."

The cabin crew had seen the explosion from the ship's bow. Having been aboard enough ships, Abbott had known it was a long shot at best. "Very well," he said, removing his hat and running a hand through his short hair. "Helm to full reverse, then bring her about."

"Aye, aye, sir," the helmsman replied, calling down to the engine room to relay the orders.

"Sir?" His navigator asked.

"We have a few more surprises," Abbott said, smiling. "Prepare to deploy countermeasures."

Surging to make the necessary preparations, the cabin crew began to prepare for what the captain called "countermeasures," but the rest of the crew knew it as an antiquated last hope.

Lee felt the engines slowing, and then the ship began to reverse. He had no time to ponder the unexpected change of course while he continued firing the destructive might of the Gatling gun. The heat coming off the barrels was noticeable, and Lee hoped that the weapon would not melt. Brogan had taken a knee beside him and appeared to be gradually coming back to his senses.

The ship had backed several dozen feet away from its previous location when it began to turn. Lee's position shifted so that he was facing the entire onslaught, while the other was granted a reprieve. A massive explosion rocked beneath him. Releasing his grip on the automatic weapon, he leaned over to look down at the side of the ship. A cannon jutted from a concealed panel. Surveying the vessel's flank, the hunter could see several other cannons appearing out of hiding places. "Good show, captain."

Holding onto the rail, Lee tried to hold himself steady as the cannons fired, were reloaded, and fired again. Given the time between shots, he assumed they were outdated cannons retired from Her Majesty's Navy and retrofitted onto the airship. The force of each blast caused the ship to swing slightly. The large metal projectiles were plowing a swath of destruction through the enemy forces, but the remaining firebirds continued undeterred.

Retaking his position behind the Gatling gun, Lee tried to make his shots count. Despite the temptation to churn the enemy into paste, he knew that the firebirds were a priority. He smiled as one of them detonated, setting several of the Alkonost on fire. While their songs had been threatening to overwhelm the ear plugs, their screams were heard clearly, sounds of anguish, suffering, and death. Lining up the weapon on another firebird, Lee felt the heat of the weapon in his hands. Dropping the handles, he saw the white-hot glow of the barrel and knew that the weapon was useless.

Until the battle was over and the barrels could be replaced, he would have to resort to his Winchester. Stumbling away, Brogan entered the ship. One of the marines looked questioningly at Lee. Blood dripped from a wound on the soldier's scalp. "Medic!" Lee shouted.

Turning back to view the field of battle, Lee saw an oncoming Alkonost and was unable to do anything about it. The creature slammed into him, pinning him to the deck, and tried to dig the thick talons into his chest. Tilting its head in a bird-like manner to indicate its confusion, the Alkonost fell off as several other hunters exterminated the creature. The brass chestplate showed through the torn holes in his shirt. Pushing himself to his feet, Lee turned to sight back to the firebird. From the corner of his eye, he saw an orange streak closer than all the others. Swinging around, he put a shot into the creature, which lost momentum and fell on the deck. Squawking, the bird strutted around before a soldier put a round in its head, which caused a small explosion of lava-like blood and fire. Immediately upon hitting the deck, the blood began to burn through the wood and metal.

"Put it out!" Lee ordered.

Brogan emerged from the ship, a canvas sack draped over his shoulder under his parachute. Several of the Alkonost and a few vampires formed a protective barrier in front of the last remaining firebird, providing a shield of bodies. Several other bird women flew under the ship, only to climb towards the covering over the hydrogen bladders once they had passed beneath *Orpheus*. A red light started to flash behind the hunters. It was the signal to abandon the ship. Looking around, Lee saw the panicked look on some of the soldier's faces. In their hurry to battle stations, they had not worn their parachutes. "Go!" Lee shouted. "There's still time."

"Not for us," Brogan stated as he tossed Lee over his shoulder and leaped over the rail.

Several other men had jumped when the order was given. Lee felt the freefall start, and then he was separated from Brogan. Reaching for the cord that would release the canvas sheet that would prevent him from falling to his death, if none of the airborne horrors got to him first, Lee clutched onto the small metal ring and pulled. A moment later, he was jerked up, and his descent began to slow. Closing his eyes, he thought back to the training he had received. Grabbing the draped fabric handles that would allow him to direct his descent, Lee started to head towards what he thought was a clearing.

His boots touched water, and he instinctively lifted his feet and tried to turn more. What he had thought was dry land was actually a lake. Realizing, he was not going to be able to reach the shore, he put his feet down and was quickly rewarded to find that he could easily stand up. The water reached to his knees. Quickly unbuckling the parachute, Lee made his way towards the shore. Above him, the *HMS Orpheus* detonated, giving the hunter plenty of light to see his destination. Hurrying to the shore, he stood trying to find any other survivors from the ship. As he scanned the surrounding landscape, trying to ignore the falling airship, something crashed into Lee and knocked him unconscious.

Abbott sat in the mud; other survivors of the *HMS Orpheus* knelt in the wet soil of a foreign land beside him. When the bladders had exploded, the captain had known for sure that this was the end. The ship had plummeted, coming to rest in a river, and though such a fortuitous turn was not enough to save the ship's hull, it allowed for a great many more survivors than would have been expected otherwise. They had done their best to swim to shore. He remembered watching Chief Engineer John Stouts pulled downstream, sinking beneath the black waters. Watching the panic in the man's eyes, Abbott had tried to reach him, but it was a futile effort. John vanished beneath the waters and never resurfaced. The captain had focused his eyes on the shore and swam for all he was worth. Burning debris from the wreckage provided light for the journey.

They were met by a small force of goblins and what he assumed to be trolls gathered around the flames, but these beasts were no threat for the hunters. The small group of surviving, armed men could defeat the otherworldly forces. The large shapes behind these threats, though, persuaded the men to hold their ground and not attack. They were larger than the trolls and seemed to be more animal-like. Light from the fire hinted that the strange things were covered in fur. Landing in front of the goblins, a wooden mortar set down on the mud with its weight rested gently on the ground. A frail old woman with a bulbous nose and spindly legs climbed from the vessel. She walked with a slight limp, and the cane she clutched in her hands looked suspiciously like a pestle, the same tool that would be used to crush herbs within a mortar. Blood trickled from the bullet wounds in her shoulder.

Abbott knew exactly who he was facing, and the naval officer was terrified. He had heard the stories of how mercilessly she would act if provoked. "Everyone remain calm," the captain ordered in a calm, reassuring tone.

"Wise man," the Baba Yaga replied.

Surprised that she spoke English, Abbott quickly recovered to reply. "One does not wish to cause offense."

"Throw your weapons into the waters of Prussia," the old witch stated in a conversational tone, which downplayed the command it carried.

"Madam, as a military officer, it is improper for me to order my men to surrender without a military officer of the other forces present," Abbott stated.

Looking all around her, as if she had forgotten something, the Baba Yaga grinned at Abbott. "No such men are here. If you do as I say, then I will see most of you safely into the hands of these military men. If not, then my friends will make short work of you."

The hunters raised their weapons. Holding his hand up, the captain stopped them.

"May I ask whom you will not see safely away?" Abbott questioned, realizing that at any moment the witch may show her less generous side.

"There is one that has come with you. He is the reason that I have entered into the affairs of you foolish mortals," she explained. "He pollutes our home and kills the land."

"So, you will let all but one of us leave?" Abbott asked. The brief lessons he had received on supernatural beings told him that he had to clarify any dealings, or they could easily be used to maneuver him into a trap.

"Yes," she nodded.

"May I know which man?" The officer asked.

The Baba Yaga walked among the men, sniffing. Abbott could see the unease on all their faces, but none of them made a move to flee or fight. "Not here," she commented after having smelled all the men. "Man that hit me with his angry metal bee is not among you." Bending over, she cupped a hand in the water and drank. "Not drowned in our waters. Where is he?"

"I don't know whom you're speaking of," Abbott answered honestly.

"The one who sounded the alarm, the one who hurt me," she demanded, a snarl crossing her lips.

Looking around for an explanation, Abbott found one of the men standing stark still, his lips pressed tightly together. "What do you know, soldier?" Abbott asked.

"It was Lee Baum, sir," the soldier answered.

"Yes! Where is he? Where is this man?" The Baba Yaga demanded of the man, laying a hand on his shoulder.

Trying to step away, the man found himself held tight by the bony hand. "I don't know. He jumped overboard with Brogan," the man admitted, whimpering.

"May we still go?" Abbott asked.

"A deal has been struck?" The Baba Yaga questioned.

"Unfortunately, I need a definite agreement," the captain replied.

"Throw away your weapons," she stated.

"Like hell," one of the hunters shouted, raising his rifle and shooting a goblin.

It was a very short fight. The trolls and goblins waded in amongst shots from the hunters. Several of the hunters and beasts fell before the captain realized what was happening. "Stop!" He shouted in as much worry for their lives as his own.

Both sides ceased, staring at the man. A few hunters had been wounded, as had some of his ship's staff. A devious-looking goblin was only a few feet away from the officer with a wicked knife drawn.

"Men, toss your weapons into the river," Abbott ordered, realizing that everyone would be killed if he didn't agree to the witch's terms. He hated to surrender, but his responsibility was to ensure the safety of his crew first and foremost.

Hesitantly, the men looked at the water then slowly they started to discard their last line of defense. Once the last of the weapons struck the surface of the water, the large shadows stepped forth. Giant bears encircled them. Had the men fought their way through the goblins and trolls, they would have quickly been torn to shreds by the waiting animals. The rifle rounds were not strong enough to bring down these massive beasts, and the Baba Yaga knew this. She came prepared. Abbott counted his luck that he had been able to stop the skirmish. "They will lead you to the military men of my land whom you seek," the Baba Yaga explained. "Should you try to run, your men will fill their bellies."

"Thank you for your kindness. I assure you we will not attempt to escape," Abbott stated. "That is an order."

"Sir?" One of the sailors asked.

"You heard me. I will not have the blood of anymore of you on my hands," the captain stated through gritted teeth. "Understand?"

137

The rest of the men did not question it. Unhappy about being forced to surrender, the hunters tried to find some path of escape. One of the young hunters turned to flee, but before he had gone a step, a giant, clawed paw hit him in the head, crushing his skull. The others had seen enough and knew that the witch's threat was not an idle one. If they had still been armed, they would have tried to fight. They would have all been killed, but they would have tried. Without their rifles, they knew their only hope lie in following orders. Lining up beside the men, the bears started to walk. Grabbing anything they could find, the men made improvised torches and followed their fur-covered guards.

"Seems this man is tricky as my sister warned," the Baba Yaga said. "No matter, I have a way to track him. He is still in Prussia. I feel the taint of his foreign blood upon my land."

Whispering into the wind, which came from nowhere but the witch's will, she called forth the weapon that she would need most for this task, one that had never failed her. Hobbling back to her mortar, she climbed in. The goblins and trolls stood watching her, their fear of angering her clearly etched on their faces. "Be about my business and find these men. I do not care about the one they call Brogan, but you will bring me both."

Not waiting to see if they completely understood, the Baba Yaga rose into the air and vanished into the darkness.

Lee awoke to find that it was still night, and he was being carried by something. The weight of his Winchester was still across his back, and he could feel the holster with his Webley Mk. II pistol. Gently, he started to reach for the sidearm, hopeful that he could get a shot off against his captor. "Are you awake?" A familiar voice asked.

It took Lee a moment until the Scottish accent cemented itself in his mind. "Brogan?" He asked.

"Aye, who else will be carrying you through the mud?"

Lee felt himself set down, and his feet sank slightly into the soft ground beneath him. "Where are we? What happened? I remember standing beside a lake, and then something hit me."

"That would be me," Brogan explained.

"What?" Lee demanded.

"I didn't see ye; I was guiding myself down when the blasted thing spun, and I found myself dropping right behind you, didn't think it would be proper to leave you there."

"What about the others?" Lee asked, remembering having seen several other parachutes floating down.

"Scattered all over the countryside is my guess," the Scotsman stated. "The ship landed in a river of some sort. I saw several of the men come ashore."

"How?"

Brogan held up Lee's magnifying lens. Snatching the instrument from the Scotsman, Lee checked the lens and replaced it in his pocket. "So, as I was saying, I saw some of them make it to the shore. Goblins and trolls were there to greet them, and some of the largest bears I've ever heard tell of. The old witch Abramov warned us of was there too."

"What did she do to them?" Lee asked with anxiety weighing in his stomach.

"I heard some of the boys try to fight back, but they wouldn't stood nary a chance," Brogan stated. "That was about two hours ago. So, I kept walking in the other direction. I've heard things, sounds like something is searching."

"Searching for what?"

"Survivors," Brogan guessed. "So, I say we keep moving as best we can."

"Yes, but what are we walking towards. How can you even see in this blasted night?"

"If you look there, you'll see a light," Brogan replied, pointing into the darkness.

Squinting, Lee could make out a light of some sort. "Which means people and buildings that can provide a place for us to hide," Lee finished the thought. "Good thinking."

"Just watch your step, I've found more than a few holes here," Brogan commented.

"This is probably one of the forests that the Prussians ripped up. Great trees reaching high into the sky were cut down, their roots pulled up all for the Prussian war machine to continue onward after they devastated Germany."

"Speaking of Germans, how did a German get to be the leader of Prussia?" Brogan asked; the complexity of politics was far beyond his education.

"If I were to make a guess, he did so through treachery and deceit, and now has somehow usurped the Czar from power," Lee commented.

In the darkness behind them, they heard a goblin's laugh travel over the desolate landscape. A moment later, several shots followed. Lee and Brogan surveyed the darkness, unable to see any signs of the monster or their target. "We can discuss politics later. I think it would be wise to keep moving," Lee stated.

Brogan did not say anything but started walking forward.

Using the light ahead of them for guidance, Lee and Brogan continued making their way through the night. As the sunrise turned the dark sky to a lightened gray, the men could see that they were approaching a small inn with several small outbuildings around it.

Keeping low to the ground, the men made their way towards the nearest building. Lee kept his Winchester in his hands and at the ready. Brogan carried the shotgun in one hand while keeping an eye on the surrounding area. Smoke rose from the chimney in the inn, letting the hunters know that someone was there. Pressing against the outbuilding, Lee and Brogan listened. From the other side came the sound of a door shutting. Waiting a moment, the two men crept around the side of the structure and saw a woman in her early twenties. Shocked at the sight of the two men, she dropped the firewood in her arms but did not call out.

Lee was dumbstruck by the woman. Her fine features could have been carved on a porcelain doll, and there was a smudge of grease on her cheek. Lee was not sure about the source of the smudge but would recognize the substance anywhere. It seemed out of place on such a lovely face but complemented her demeanor. She was shocked but did not panic, and Lee saw the handles of tools jutting from the pockets of her drab olive colored dress. Brogan reached for her arm, and Lee saw her hand clutch one of the tools. "Wait," Lee said, calmly. "Do you speak English?"

"Yes," she answered. "You are English?"

"Yes," Lee replied.

"I'm Scottish," Brogan corrected.

"Close enough," Lee chided his companion.

"From airship?" She asked.

"Yes. Has anyone come through looking for survivors?" Lee asked.

"No. Prussian Army are dogs," she announced and spat onto the ground. "They come here years ago and take down beautiful trees. Once before war, this was large forest. Peoples came from all over to see it. I learned English from missionary that spent summer with us. Are you soldier?"

"Of a sort," Lee commented. "Our ship went down under attack by the Baba Yaga."

The girl gasped and used her finger to make the mark of the cross over her heart. "You have little hope if the Old Mother is about."

"Can you help us?" Lee asked.

"I can try to take you close to the border. A cousin I have lives near," the woman explained.

"What's your name, lass?" Brogan asked.

"Esmeralda Guryev," she said, tying a handkerchief around her blond hair. "I must tell father that I go, or he will worry."

"I don't..." Brogan started.

"All right. Where's the horse and cart?" Lee asked. "We'll start hitching it up."

"Horse and cart are in booth beside inn," Esmeralda stated. "Careful, my work is in there also."

Nodding, Lee and Brogan made their way over to the small booth adjoining the inn. "You shouldn't have done that. What if she tells her da about us?" Brogan asked.

"Who's he going to alert?" Lee asked. "You can see that there isn't anyone around for miles. At worse, he'll come out to defend her from us."

"If he does?"

"Don't hurt him; we'll just let him know that we mean his daughter no harm."

Lee carefully slid open the doors to the adjoined structure. A beautiful horse stared at them, noisily eating oats. An old cart sat behind it. A canvas sheet hung from a beam, bisecting the small structure in half. "You want to start gearing up the horse, and I'll move the cart," Brogan suggested.

Lee went about gathering the harness and bit for the horse and preparing it for the journey. The animal did not mind as Lee affixed all the necessary buckles of the harness. Eyeing the stranger warily, the horse refused to let Lee put the bit in its mouth. Snapping at him, the horse turned back to its oats. "Fine, finish eating," Lee replied, stepping away with the bit in his hand.

Brogan had already pushed the cart into position and was hooking the horse's harness to the rails. Lee heard a small chuff of machinery from the other side of the sheet and turned towards the noise. There it was again. Sliding back the curtain, he saw the small workroom of a fellow engineer and inventor. A small, steam-driven device was turning itself along the desktop. Lee watched fascinated as the device stopped for a moment, and the arms spun around. When they reached the top of their rotation, a small puff of steam blew from the top, and the arms fell, pushing it along again. A smile crossed the Englishman's face.

Looking around at the other inventions, he could see some that had been completed, others in states of progress, and a few that had been discarded. Burns on their metal indicated that these did not work as intended. Removing one of the devices from the pile, Lee examined it closely. "She's been gone a while," Brogan commented.

"It's fine. I didn't see any nearby homes for her to run to," Lee commented.

Taking a screwdriver from the table, he began to disassemble the device. Carefully examining each item as he removed them, he found the problem. One of the springs was too close to the boiler, and probably caused the metal to warp and the machine to not work properly. Examining the different parts arrayed on the scarred tabletop, he selected a few choice pieces and made a few adjustments. As he put the last screw in place and sat the device upright, he heard a familiar sound, the sound of a hammer being drawn on a revolver.

"Hands up," Esmeralda stated.

Turning around, Lee saw the pretty woman pointing an antique revolver, one of the first Prussian models, directly at Brogan. "Had to pack, huh?" The Scotsman asked.

"One never can tell; she might have been packing or searching for an old family pistol," Lee replied, raising his hands.

Brogan followed suit. "Why you think I help you?" She demanded. "You as bad as men that take trees."

"Not quite," Lee commented. "As you can see, we were very kind to your horse."

Her eyes glanced at the curtain; in her anxiety at confronting the two invaders she had not paid any attention to where Lee had been. "What did you do to my work?" Esmeralda demanded, motioning Lee and Brogan out of her way.

After a quick glance around, she noticed the previously discarded device had been moved. "Foolish thing, would not work," she commented.

"Try it now," Lee suggested.

Giving him an angry glare, Esmeralda reached forward and pulled a small lever on the side. Slowly, the device started to spin. The tiny figures on it dancing in a graceful, brass-covered ballet. Steam from the small boiler was bustling up through pipes on the side, simulating organ music. "How you fix?" She asked.

"It wasn't hard. One of your springs was in contact with the boiler and warped as a result. I just made a workaround connection," Lee explained.

Brogan was lost in the conversation and slowly worked his hand towards his revolver. "You are man of machines?" Esmeralda asked Lee.

"Lee Baum, at your service," he answered with a slight bow.

Her face brightened. "I have heard of you. You redesigned engine, and now trains much faster."

"Yes," he stated, blushing at the recognition. "It was a trivial matter, really."

Esmeralda lowered the pistol and tucked it into a pocket on her coat pocket. "I must apologize. If I had known a man of skill was coming, I would have prepared rooms."

"No. Please, I assure you, had I known that I would be meeting a colleague, then I would have dressed in something nicer."

Esmeralda smiled. "Since you have made Alexei ready, it is a waste not to take him out," she stated, removing the bit from the workstation. "Come, Alexei, we take men on trip."

"What about your father?" Brogan asked, loosening his grip on his pistol.

"Father passed winters ago. Is only Alexei and I," she explained. "Sorry is not nicer, but you will need to ride in back, under potato cover."

A worn, rough canvas sheet was draped across the rear of the cart. "It is far better than being seen in foreign uniforms by Prussian troops," Lee commented.

"Or our flying friend," Brogan agreed, grumbling.

Climbing under the canvas, the Scotsman tried to hide his large bulk. After unsuccessfully lying on his back, he laid the claymore down beside him, rolled onto his side, and tucked his knees up. "I feel like a wee baby," he commented.

"You no look like baby," Esmeralda commented. "Close door, please."

Lee waited as she seated herself behind Alexei and directed the horse out into the muddy terrain. With the door closed and barred, Lee climbed into the back of the wagon. "This is probably going to be long trip," Esmeralda commented.

"We'll be fine," Lee replied, catching a glimpse of the woman where the canvas did not quite meet the side. Beside him, Brogan was snoring.

8

As Lee was introducing himself to Esmeralda, Dan and Brackish found themselves in a very different predicament. Ducking behind a tree, Dan waited while Brackish had run off into the woods after the monster. The creature they faced was one known to Dan. Its kind was the reason the American had been summoned to the English Isles. This was not a tortured soul, cursed with an affliction. The thing they hunted tonight was a killer, reveling in the carnage and satiating itself on blood and flesh. All werewolves did so, but the afflicted were led by the lunar cycle. Creating a magic pelt, this werewolf had found a way to turn at a moment's notice. The only problem was that the fool had not realized how great the need to be the wolf would grow within her like a cancer feeding on her soul.

The reasons for their actions were not Dan's concern, though. Buckets of blood had been spilled by this monster, and the hunters were going to put an end to it. A branch snapped from the other side of the clearing. It was far out of the shotgun's limited range, so Dan kept a steady grip on the weapon and waited for his prey to step into the gaslights surrounding Hyde Park; he recalled Brackish's tale of putting down a unicorn in this same place. Dan thought that perhaps the absence of the unicorn had allowed the shapeshifter to set up his hunting grounds.

Something moved beneath the trees across from the hunter. Peering intently at the shadows, Dan watched as Brackish stumbled out of the growth, a twig tangled in the collar of his duster. Letting out a breath, Dan maintained his vigil as the goblin started to make its way to him. When the goblin stopped and stared over the American's shoulder, Dan knew where the creature was. He heard a growl rumble within a thickly muscled chest, and flipping the shotgun over his shoulder, squeezed the trigger. The boom of the rifle competed with the werewolf's roar for dominance. He then threw himself to the ground, rolled, and came up on a knee. The monster had torn great chunks of bark from the tree where the hunter had been standing heartbeats ago.

Dropping onto all fours, the giant wolf creature stalked towards the two hunters. Blood dripped from its shoulder, a good sign that Dan's shot had struck the creature. The silver was not bothering the beast, but that was not unexpected. Only some of the were-beasts displayed that weakness, but all of them died with enough gunfire. Growling, the monster pulled black lips back over its jagged teeth. The two hunters separated, working their way around, trying to encircle the werewolf. Trying to keep both hunters in its sight, the monster knew it had stumbled into a trap.

Backing away, the creature exposed its flank, and Brackish fired a round from his short-barreled shotgun, the pellets tearing into the furry hide. Howling in misery, the werewolf no longer wasted precious energy but turned and rushed back into the thick trees that comprised the forest of Hyde Park. "Damn it," Dan cursed.

"What now?" Brackish asked.

"You caught it pretty good," the American stated as he knelt by the tracks, thinking. "This thing seems smart, but not human-smart. Like all wounded animals, it'll go back to its lair or to water. Do we know where it has been hiding?"

Brackish shook his head. "Human come into park, not stay here," the goblin replied.

"All right, let's see where the nearest body of water is," Dan replied, replacing the spent shell in his shotgun.

Stepping back into the dense forest he had just exited, Dan wound up the flameless torch that Lee had designed. As the mechanism flared to life, Dan clipped it onto his belt and was glad for the illumination. Werewolves were tricky beasts - vicious, cunning, and smarter than your average wolf. They always had the advantage when in the wilderness. With their senses, they could smell, hear, and see better than a human. Dan knew that the device would not betray his position to the monster, because it had always known where the man was. Now, the American could at least see the bloody trail that the creature left.

Smeared on leaves and occasionally forming a puddle on the ground, the sanguine flow led them over a fallen tree, where a small pond had formed from recent rainfall. It should have been a serene setting with the stars reflecting on the calm surface of the water. The only problem was the fierce-looking beast lying beside the pool, trying to lap some of the cool liquid into its mouth. The man and goblin, armed with shotguns, also served to spoil the tranquil setting. Trying to raise up onto its feet, the werewolf fell back down and started to growl at the hunters. It was a weak sound, the sound of a dying creature.

Turning to face its hunters, the werewolf struggled away from the water. Brackish stepped forward, raising his shotgun. Dan put a hand on the goblin's shoulder. "This is a mercy killing," Dan stated. "It requires a gentler touch."

Drawing one of his revolvers, the American sighted right between the wolf's amber eyes. The creature closed them and lowered its head, accepting the death. Squeezing the trigger, Dan ended the creature's existence of death and carnage. A few moments passed as the gunshot echoed in the small clearing, followed by the cracking of bones. When the song of crickets once more reigned in the park, a woman's dead body draped across the ground. No sign of the monster that she had been remained, except for a small fur glove on her hand.

"Bad magic," Brackish commented as he pointed at the glove.

"Yeah, don't touch it," Dan cautioned. "Get a stick to get it off her, and we'll deal with it."

Carefully, the goblin found a sturdy stick and used it to peel the glove away from the deceased woman's hand. With the razor-edged dagger on his belt, Brackish started shearing the pelt. The skin gave easily beneath the blade. A moment later, Dan rolled the body aside, and the goblin maneuvered the glove away to a clear spot on the ground. Grabbing a few pieces of dead lumber, the two hunters built a small pyre. Lighting their cigars, Dan used the match to burn the leaves and wood. Puffing on their cigars, the hunters watched as the fire consumed the glove, leaving only ashes where the evil garment had been.

"Can you find the velociter?" Dan asked.

Brackish raised an eyebrow, amused at the question. "Fine, go sniff it out and hurry back with the blanket."

He sat down on a log that had nestled next to the water, looking over the pool and trying to ignore the dead body by his feet. Brackish ran through the woods, following his nose to track their scent. Ten minutes passed before the goblin returned carrying the heavy canvas material. Helping his partner, the man and the goblin spread the sheet flat on the ground. Brackish grabbed the woman's feet as Dan took her wrists, then the two of them maneuvered her onto the edge of the fabric. Rolling it up and tying the canvas with twine, the American hoisted the burden over his shoulder. "Lead the way," he instructed.

More familiar with the way, Brackish stopped several times and watched as Dan struggled with the load on his shoulder. Reaching the path around the expanse of forest, the American knew where to go. After securing the body on the back of the velociter, Dan opened the door to the vehicle and climbed in. "You okay?" Brackish asked, noticing how fatigued Dan was.

"Yeah, just tired. We've been a little busy lately," Dan explained.

"Lots of monies for beer," the goblin replied happily.

'Yeah, it is. I may need a break. You know we've been on a hunt every day for the last few weeks," Dan stated.

Brackish thought about it. He was still not overly familiar with the concepts of weeks as opposed to the phases of the moon that the goblins used to tell time. It had been almost a whole moon since they had not hunted. "Need break," Brackish concluded.

"First, let's go visit Roger," Dan replied, engaging the vehicle's engine.

Parking right in front of the squat building beside Scotland Yard, Dan stepped out. Glorianna's Dungeon was nothing spectacular and did not command the respect that the halls of Scotland Yard did, but the work going on within was far more interesting. With Brackish's help, Dan maneuvered the body back onto his shoulder, and the goblin hurried ahead to open the door. As soon as Dan was through, his miniscule partner joined him. The oak-paneled room was deathly quiet as they entered.

Jumping onto the small desk front, Brackish wrapped on the wooden divider. He waited for the pudgy man with glasses to move the object while Dan grumbled under his load. Their usual greeter did not appear. In fact, no one opened the divider, but the door on the right swung open. "Hello?" Dan called. "This is heavy; I'm just going back."

Stepping into the door, Dan and Brackish saw their usual greeter standing inside. "No say hello?" Brackish asked, puzzled.

"You two are the only hunters left in London. If someone knocks, we already know who it is. Roger is waiting for you," he informed them, his face looking as soured as ever with his nose redder than usual.

Must've interrupted his nightcap, Dan thought.

The two hunters walked through the area where the Regent Wardens performed their duties. The desks were empty with barely any papers sitting on top of them. Roger sat with his impeccable posture and immaculate suit behind his desk, waiting. Something about him seemed off, but neither Dan nor Brackish could pinpoint the difference. It was something around his eyes. "Is this the Hyde Park Beast?" He asked.

Dan dropped the bloody canvas onto the floor. "Yeah," he confirmed.

"No beast, werewolf," Brackish corrected.

"But the moon…" Roger started.

"This wasn't a curse; it was magic," the American explained.

"Ah, I see. And the magical article?" The warden asked.

"Burned," Brackish answered with a smile. The goblin was almost as big a pyromaniac as Dan.

"Very well, then. Shall we take a look?" Roger asked, pointing to the bundle.

"For modesty's sake, you should just unwrap the head," Dan stated.

"A woman," Roger replied, his eyes wide.

Dan nodded. Removing just enough canvas to inspect the deceased woman's head, the Regent Warden pushed back her lips to show the retracted secondary row of teeth that would burst forth upon transformation. Briskly, Roger went to the door at the back of the room and knocked. Two other wardens stepped out and after a few quick instructions dragged the wrapped body away. Retrieving his ledger from his desk drawer, Roger wrote out the bounty receipt for the two hunters. "Please have a seat," he instructed, before handing them the receipt. A confused look on their faces, Dan and Brackish sat in the chairs across from Roger. Taking a sealed letter from the other side of his desk, he held the letter out to Dan. "It's about Lee."

Dan tore into the envelope, reading it. "What it say?" Brackish asked.

"Lee's ship went down. He's missing," the American stated, lowering the letter. "Roger?"

"I feel that you deserve to hear the entire story. Some of our reconnaissance agents have spotted the crew of the *HMS Orpheus* at a military compound. If our men are to be believed, they were escorted by a pack of bears," Roger explained. "We think the Baba Yaga took down the ship and sent the prisoners to the compound."

"Isn't the army going to do anything?" Dan asked. "Send in more troops or something; you can't leave those men in the Prussian's hands."

"Yeah," Brackish agreed. "Clan no abandon each other."

153

"I'm afraid that information has not been shared with me, although I feel that it is not likely," Roger stated. "We do not want to send more men behind enemy lines to be captured."

"Hell, just send me and Brackish," the American offered.

"Out of the question," Roger replied. "You had your chance to enlist and refused."

Dan seethed at the immediate dismissal. The damned bureaucracy again. They'd sooner open their throats than admit they needed help. "This isn't over," he threatened, standing up and storming from the building with Brackish following after.

Dan drove the velociter recklessly through the pre-dawn streets of London. Brackish rode beside him, each of the hunters silent. Ms. Edwards and Elizabeth needed to know, and then the hunters would have to get ready. Dan had made a demand in the middle of the office, but it had been thoroughly dismissed by Roger. No matter. Dan and Lee had made some friends well above Roger; if need be, he would call in every favor owed to him.

Taking up both of the designated velociter spaces in the shed with his haphazard parking, Dan hopped from the vehicle with Brackish close on his heels. He gave a quick glance to the second space; it had been Brackish's original clan that had dismantled the other vehicle. The hunters had not bothered to purchase another one. It was a fleeting thought as the two pounded up the rear stairs. As he opened the door, Dan saw Ms. Edwards standing in the entryway, concern etched on her face and a frying pan in her hand. "Dear Lord, Mr. Winston," she scolded him. "Must you make such a fuss when entering?" One look at his face, and the rest of her comments died on her tongue. "Is something wrong?" She asked, lowering the frying pan and stepping into the hallway.

"Lee," Dan mumbled.

The frying pan fell from her hand as she covered her mouth in shock. "I am so sorry." Tears fell freely from her face.

Elizabeth came out, her face streaked with tears. "Mr. Winston?" She asked.

"Yeah," he replied.

"I don't want to tell you, but it wouldn't be right if I didn't," the young woman stated.

"Tell me what? Is it about Lee?"

She nodded, her blond hair falling over her face. "He needs your help," Elizabeth said weakly. "I've seen him and a big man in a kilt. They are running through dark country."

"Then he wasn't captured?" The American asked.

"I don't know, but I don't think so."

"We go then," Brackish stated.

"If you go, you may not all make it back here," Elizabeth stated.

"Will some of us?" Dan asked.

She shrugged. "Maybe. I don't know; it's all blurry, but it'll be real bad. Without you, I don't think Mr. Baum will survive."

Dan pressed the girl against him in a hug. "He's alive. If there is a chance that I can bring him home, then I need to."

"But..." She started to protest.

"We've come out of your visions ahead of the game before," the American stated with a smile. Recalling the first time they had met,

Elizabeth had predicted their deaths, only to be proven wrong. "I don't see any reason we can't do it again. What do you think, Brackish?"

"Lee clan, clan fight for each other," the goblin said solemnly.

"Couldn't have put it better myself," Dan agreed as he released Elizabeth and stood up. "Ms. Edwards, don't worry about any lunch for me. I've got some arrangements to make." Leaving Brackish in the hallway, Dan rushed from the house back to the waiting vehicle.

His first stop had been at Glorianna's Dungeon. The Regent Warden had always been skeptical of Elizabeth's gifts, and Dan was unable to convince Roger of Lee's fugitive status. Now, there was only one other place for him to go.

With the country in the midst of a war and the recent attack within the borders, Dan knew that security around the government offices would be extensive, but when he saw the first roadblock, he realized just how much the security had been strengthened. Several sand bag barricades were positioned on the sides of the street, and large rows of barb and razor wire had been stretched down the alleys to prevent anyone from circumventing the checkpoints. Behind each of the sandbag barricades were the mechanical Gatling guns. These were not the newly designed versions that had been mounted on the *HMS Orpheus* but the classic mechanisms housed within a barrel that also served as a stand. They did not hold the same amount of ammunition as their modernized relative either, but the damage they could wreak on an approaching vehicle or body was still disastrous. Stopping before the lowered arm of the blockade, Dan waited as an armed soldier stepped forward, never knocking on the window but waiting. Pushing the glass back, Dan waited for the soldier's directions. "Will you please step from the vehicle, sir?" He asked.

"Okay," Dan replied as the soldier stepped back. "I'm armed."

Dan saw the immediate tension in the men surrounding the sandbags. "I have no intention of using the weapons, but I thought the statement should be made. I'm a bounty hunter with the Office of Abnormal Affairs, and I've come directly from a successful hunt. You have my apologies for not leaving my irons at home."

"Remove the weapons before exiting the velociter," the soldier ordered.

Slowly, Dan reached down and undid the gun belt at his waist. Careful to not give the wrong idea, he untied the tongs keeping the holsters tight against his legs and stepped out, leaving the guns draped on the seat. Raising his hands, he waited as the soldier stepped forward and patted him down for any other weapons. Satisfied that the American was not armed further, the soldier turned him around. "What is your business?"

"I need to speak with Victoria," Dan stated.

A mocking smile started to creep over the soldier's face. "The Queen?" He asked, barely holding in his laughter.

"I tell you what. Call back to your men inside Buckingham Palace and tell them that Dan Winston is here to call in a favor," the American said, his voice almost a growl.

"Give the call. Let's see if this one will be bound for Bedlam like the rest," the soldier said, his mocking attitude still firmly in place.

One of his fellow soldiers lifted a small device from behind the barrier. Dan did not pay any attention to it. He waited several minutes.

"Someone's coming out for him," the soldier replied, putting away the device.

The soldier did not attempt to mask his shock or concern at having offended the American. "Why don't you go back to pretending you're important," Dan commented.

The American did not have a high tolerance for authority to begin with, but the pompous air about the younger soldier had really irritated him. A new-styled velociter made its way through the barricades. Dan was impressed at the four-door vehicle coming towards him. The short, squat vehicle had been armored up and elongated to allow for a nearly doubled in size front compartment, and the boiler was now in a smaller hatched rear. As the vehicle pulled up beside his own, Dan noticed that all the glass had been covered with a layer of armor, except for a small rectangle, which he assumed was so the operator could see. One of the rear doors opened, and a man's gloved hand motioned Dan to enter. Stepping into the rear of the vehicle, Dan waited as the door closed and the vehicle started forward.

"So, who the hell are you?" Dan asked, staring at the man beside him.

"Robert Gascoyne-Cecil, Prime Minister," the man identified himself.

"Oh, yeah, I've seen you in the paper," Dan commented. "So, we going to see the queen?"

"Unfortunately, Her Majesty is currently indisposed and cannot be bothered," Robert answered.

"Then, why am I wasting my time. I need to get to Prussia," the hunter stated.

158

"I am here to act in Her Majesty's stead, but you make a most peculiar request. Were you not able to volunteer with the rest of your compatriots?" The Prime Minister asked.

"I don't fight in the army anymore. I'd already had my fill of war before I came over here."

"Then, why do you wish to go into a war zone?"

"It ain't for the war. My friend is over there. If I correctly read between the lines of the lovely worded letter I received, he wasn't in a war zone. You fellas were trying to get men behind it and succeeded," Dan explained, his stare hard and accusing.

"Well, you are most well-informed," Robert replied, refusing to meet the American's glare. "For months, we have tried to insert troops into the rear of the front lines, but supernatural forces have been attempting to stop us."

"So, you sent in a bunch of hunters to get the job done right."

"In a manner of speaking. Mr. Baum's ship was one of three that had been dispatched to different parts of the country. It was the only one that came under attack. You realize that we cannot confirm if your friend survived the wreckage. If you were to go in, it might be for a lost cause. Also, you are not a trained soldier, and we can hardly spare the room onboard our ships for non-essential personnel," the Prime Minister explained, smiling.

"Yeah, you put me and my remaining partner on an airship and get us over there. We'll be more than happy to drop from the ship and pick up the trail from the wreck," Dan replied.

"And why would we do this?"

"Because, this country owes me and Lee a whole lot more than this," Dan answered, leaning over and getting into the Prime Minister's face. "Also, I can be a might more persuasive if I have to."

"There will be no need for that," Robert replied. "A ship is preparing to leave this afternoon. Gather your gear, no more than a duffel each, and a carriage will pick you up. By tomorrow afternoon, you will be boarding a ship to take you after your friend."

"Why are you making this so easy?" The hunter asked, wary of the politician's motives.

"Her Majesty does not forget her debts," Robert replied. "I'm afraid that I cannot give you any further assistance beyond this."

"Bobby, I intend to make the best of it. You give me a chance, and I'll make it work," Dan explained, vigorously shaking Robert's hand.

"Please call me Robert."

Just as the Prime Minister had promised, shortly after two o'clock, a motorized carriage arrived, and Dan and Brackish said their farewells to Ms. Edwards and Elizabeth and climbed aboard. Each of the hunters carried a duffel bag, the pneumatic pack on Dan's back, and his spare magazines fastened to his leg in their holder. The goblin and the human were dressed in similar manner with loose work trousers, white shirts made of rough cotton, trench coats, and bowler hats. The only difference, apart from their size, was Dan's boots. His goblin counterpart was more comfortable barefoot with strips of leather across the top of his foot and a pair of goggles on his hat brim.

Climbing into the passenger compartment of the carriage, the duo was surprised to see Roger waiting on them. "Dan, you know that if Lee

160

did not arrive with the other prisoners, then he may be dead. Best case scenario, he's lost in the Prussian wilderness with no supplies, which makes his chances bleak."

"Roger, I appreciate the effort, but Elizabeth has seen him. If we go, there is a chance that we'll bring him home," the American explained.

Rubbing his bottom lip thoughtfully, the Regent Warden considered the information. "Very well, if you cannot be persuaded, then I will wish you Godspeed and good fortune."

Roger extended his hand, and Dan shook it but was shocked when Roger offered his hand to Brackish in turn. It was the first sign of respect that the warden had paid to either of the hunters. Stepping from the carriage, Roger closed the door, and the vehicle rolled forward. "He think we no coming back," Brackish stated.

"Maybe he's right," Dan replied.

"Nah, half bottle of beer in kitchen," the goblin replied.

The American half-snorted his laughter at the goblin's logic. "You raise a good point," he conceded. "I think some sausages are still cooling off in that big cold box Lee bought, too."

Arriving at the airship depot, the carriage took the hunters directly to the side of the ship. Their accommodations were not the commercial travel ships that they had taken before, plush and comfortable, but they would suffice. Climbing aboard, the two were shown to a small closet, converted to a cabin, where they could sit away from any other personnel onboard. The ensign who came to alert them of their imminent landing the next day was shocked to hear the cacophony of sounds coming from the room. Expecting to find a mechanical error of some sort, he was surprised that the sound was just the combined snoring of the American and the goblin.

"Excuse me, sirs?" The sailor said.

Dan snapped to, his pistol half drawn from its holster. "Sorry," he apologized with a sleepy smile.

"We are coming in for a landing. You will be able to disembark within the hour." With that, he turned on his heel and returned to his duties.

Dan gave Brackish a shake on the shoulder. The goblin opened his eyes, his hand reaching for the dagger in his belt. "We'll be off this boat in an hour and into another one."

"Next ship land near Lee?" Brackish asked, stretching.

"I'm not sure, but they are supposed to put us down close to where his last ship crashed," the American replied. "I can't imagine that he could get too far on foot."

The military ship that they had been ushered onto was of a similar design as the *HMS Orpheus*. Built for stealth operations and crossing enemy positions at night, the ship was loaded with supplies and Marines, waiting only for the last two members of its force. As Dan and Brackish climbed the ramp into the belly of the ship, they were greeted by the First Lieutenant. "Gentle..." he paused not sure what to call Brackish.

"Yeah, thanks for taking us with you," Dan replied, saving the officer from further embarrassment.

"Of course. I'm Lieutenant Anderson. The task of making sure that you understand the proper use of the parachutes that you will be using has been given to me."

"What?" Brackish asked confused.

"Isn't the ship taking us to the crash site?" Dan asked, as confused as his shorter counterpart.

"Yes, sir. At that point, you will disembark and utilize the parachutes to safely land," Anderson explained, covering what a parachute was and how they would be used in their current mission.

"You want me to jump off this thing?" Dan asked, still not believing the man.

"Yes, sir. It is far too dangerous for the ship to attempt to land. We would simply be too exposed."

"It fine," Brackish replied. "Lee take Tin Man off ship same way."

Dan took a calming breath, remembering the rescue that Lee and Brackish had mounted to save his hide from some unpleasant German creatures years ago. "When should we be at the site?" Dan asked, resigning any arguments he had about leaping from a perfectly good airship.

"We have begun preparations to lift. With no obstacles and favorable winds, the captain thinks that we can make the location as early as midnight," Anderson replied cheerily. "May I show you to your quarters?"

"Might as well," Dan answered, as he and Brackish followed the young man.

Having rested fitfully for a few hours, Brackish and Dan stood at the rear of the ship as the ramp closed behind them, the parachutes strapped on, though Dan's pneumatic pack made a snug fit. "I hope these things can support us," the American commented.

163

His duffel bag was strapped across his stomach. Brackish's bag was fastened in a similar fashion on his small figure. "We fine," the goblin commented.

"Once the ramp starts to descend, you need only walk off the end of it," Anderson said, standing beside the controls. Dan still thought it sounded ludicrous. *Just walk off a perfectly good airship into nothing but air. Sure, why not.*

The officer lowered the ramp, and the two hunters started walked towards the dark abyss behind them. With a shout, the goblin jumped into the air and plummeted. Closing his eyes, Dan stepped off and tumbled into the night sky above Prussia.

9

As Dan dealt with his first parachuting experience, Lee and Brogan continued their journey in the back of Esmeralda's wagon. This was their second night lying on the wood planks, and the trio decided that they would stop well into the night and sleep for a few hours before resuming their travel, which gave Lee and Brogan a break from their uncomfortable accommodations, and allowed Alexei to rest from pulling his heavy load.

Something was shining ahead of them. The light filtered through the rough canvas over the hunters. "Something ahead," Esmeralda informed them. "Little men."

Brogan and Lee laid their hands on their rifles. In their line of work, several creatures could be described as little men, and most of them were not friendly. "What do we do?" Brogan whispered.

"Follow my lead," Lee replied. "We'll see what they want."

The wagon slowed and pulled to a stop. The two men sat listening in the back as Esmeralda carried on a conversation with something in her native language. A hole in the wood gave Lee a small vantage point. He looked out and caught a glimpse of a stone-tipped spear and green skin. "Goblins," he whispered to Brogan in the quietest voice he could.

"Both sides of road," their driver stated before continuing in the Prussian tongue.

Checking their weapons, the two hunters made sure their rifles were loaded and ready. The conversation stopped abruptly, and a growl started to rise from the goblins, making it clear that their vehicle was surrounded. "If do something, now is being the time," Esmeralda said, anxiety heavy in her voice.

With a shout, Brogan pushed up into a sitting position, threw the canvas sheet off him and Lee, and opened fire with his shotgun. Rising beside him, Lee made quick work of two goblins before the small monsters could attack. Watching several of the creatures draw back their spears, Lee grabbed Esmeralda's collar and pulled her back into the cart with them. "Get down," he instructed as the first weapon sailed through the space where she had been.

Brogan's shotgun had done a good job of thinning out the little, green-skinned beasts on his side, but it was empty, and reloading didn't seem to be the best option. Drawing his revolver, he poured the six shots into the last remaining clustered group. The forces aligned on Lee's side quickly spread out, providing a greater challenge for the marksman. Something slammed into his chest, and the English hunter fell back onto Esmeralda. "Terribly sorry about this," he apologized.

The stone-tipped spear had broken on the brass chestplate, but the impact had been enough to knock him over. Rolling off the woman, Lee started to stand up when Brogan dropped down beside him. "I've got to reload," he stated.

"With what?" Lee asked.

Smiling, the Scotsman opened his pouch and pulled out a box of ammunition for his shotgun and Lee's Winchester. Raising back up, Lee put down three more of the creatures with three shots. From behind the wagon, a lasso lazily sailed through the sky, dropped around Lee's throat, and began to tighten. Trying to free himself from the constricting rope, Lee felt himself being pulled towards the end of the wagon. The attacking monsters were shouting something in their language. Too preoccupied with surviving at the moment, Lee ignored the words and continued his struggle. His index finger was the only thing preventing his airway from being completely closed off.

He might be able to free himself, but to do so, he would have to drop his rifle and retrieve his dagger. As his fingers started to lessen on the wooden stock, Brogan's claymore cut through the air, severing the noose. Dropping back to the cart, Lee quickly worked the rough fibers over his head and rubbed his throat. Taking deep breaths, the Englishman was happy to relieve the burning that had started in his lungs. Standing in the center of the wagon, Brogan was firing and turning in all directions, trying to convince the goblins to flee. Spears flew, barely missing the imposing figure. Kneeling beside the Scotsman, Lee dropped the three figures trying to form a new lasso. Turning about, he dealt another two deadly blows while Brogan's shotgun boomed into the dwindling forces.

When only a handful of the goblins remained, the creatures fled into the darkness, dropping their torches onto the barren land as they ran. "What was that about?" Brogan asked. "I know goblins are mean little buggers, but I never picked them for highwaymen."

"Traditionally, they aren't," Lee agreed. "What were you talking about?"

"He asked what I carry. When I tell him radishes, he call me liar, claimed to smell man flesh. Tell me that Baba Yaga seeks the flesh of the foreign dogs that have invaded our land," she stopped, looking at Lee.

"What were they shouting when they tried to strangle me?" The English inventor asked.

"They say, 'found him, the old mother's treat,'" Esmeralda pushed herself back onto the driver's bench.

"The horse did good. Most animals get spooked by them little beasts," Brogan stated, praising the animal.

"Alexei?" Esmeralda asked, raising an eyebrow. "No, he too dumb to know run away."

Looking at the decimated bodies of the goblins, Lee felt sorry for them. They had never had much of a chance. They seemed almost frail now, and Lee found himself wondering where his goblin friend was. "So, the old mother is the Baba Yaga?" Brogan asked.

Lee nodded. "What makes you so special?" The Scotsman asked. "I mean, of all the hunters on that ship, why you?"

"I wish I knew," Lee answered. "Whatever it is, it can't be good."

"If she want you, all of Prussia will be looking," Esmeralda stated. The ominous nature of the statement was not lost on either hunter.

"Where did you get the shells?" Lee asked, changing the subject and picking up the box of .44 cartridges.

"On the ship, when I went back in," Brogan confessed. "I couldn't really see well enough to fight, but I knew we weren't going to be staying in the air for long."

"So, you took it upon yourself to…"

"Ensure our survival," Brogan proclaimed. "If not for me, you would've still been on the ship when it went down."

"Possibly, although you didn't really give me an opportunity to evacuate on my own," Lee pointed out.

"Bloody ingrate."

The wagon suddenly lurched to the side. Both hunters spun and aimed their weapons at the problematic corner. "Is wheel." Esmeralda stated. "Either of you know how to replace?"

168

Brogan and Lee exchanged a look. "Come, I tell you how. Is not too bad," the Prussian woman hopped from the seat, a smile on her face.

Two hours later, and sweating fiercely, the two men wrestled the wheel in place and secured it. "See, not too bad," Esmeralda said, confirming her previous statement.

The hunters would have argued, but they were too tired. "We should think about resting for the night," Lee stated.

Brogan looked around. "We're still too close to those goblins," he replied. "I'm surprised they haven't come back around and attacked again."

"Unless they went to tell someone about us," Lee grimaced.

"The air will carry words quickly. We ride until morning, then find a place to stop," Esmeralda said. "Should be near trees soon, is not great forest as before, but enough to hide."

As planned, the trio rode until the sun peeked above the mountains in the east. Lee and Brogan rode in the back, not bothering to cover up in case further dangers presented themselves. The area around them was not as desolate as it had been around the inn. Views of empty mud gave way to thinning grass, and trees formed a forest that hedged the road. Esmeralda was having trouble keeping her eyes open. The rhythmic movement of the seat combined with the sound of Alexei's steps lulled her into a peaceful state. As she drifted off to sleep, Lee reached over and grabbed the reins.

Gently, Brogan eased the sleeping woman back with him and laid her down in the cart. She did not stir from her slumber. "I'll stop at the first place that seems inviting," Lee explained.

"That's fine. I could do with a stretch of me legs," the Scotsman replied.

Passing by the trees and rocks that threatened to break another wheel, if the wagon were to leave the road, Lee found a spot that seemed perfect for their needs. Guiding Alexei off the rough road, the wagon passed between two trees and continued until the road was hidden from view. Stepping down, Lee unharnessed the horse and walked him to the impromptu corral that had formed between the wagon and the trees. Removing the bridle from the animal's head, the Englishman dropped a rope over the horse's neck and tethered it to the wheel of the wagon.

Brogan dropped down onto the soft ground. "I was expecting much worse weather given the stories I heard told of the Prussian winters. Isn't that what kept Napoleon out?"

"Yes. They were so bitingly cold that the soldiers were freezing to death on the field of battle," Lee answered. "There is a chill in the air, but nothing that one would expect given the time of year."

"I'm going to take a walk and see if there's anything that we need to be aware of," Brogan stated as he stood up and began to walk off into the trees.

Lee stood watch, his revolver in hand, with his rifle laying in the rear of the wagon within reach. The animal sounds that usually filled a forest were absent. It gave the landscape a more somber quality, almost ominous. Remaining on alert, Lee heard a snapping twig. Pistol raised, he turned towards the sound. A moment later, Brogan appeared through the brush. Seeing the revolver, the man raised his hands.

Embarrassed, Lee lowered the weapon. "Anything?" He asked.

"An old abandoned cottage not too far, but I feel it might be smarter for us to stay in the open. Be able to see anything tries to come for us."

"I'll take first watch," Lee offered.

While Esmeralda had been sleeping the entire time that they stopped, Lee and Brogan would spend four of the next eight hours on guard duty. It was easier for them to do, partly because of the demands of their profession, but also because they could usually drift to sleep while riding in the cart.

Looking at his pocket watch, Brogan confirmed that four hours had passed. He gently reached into the rear of the wagon and tapped Lee's boot. The hunter sprang awake, rifle in hand. Raising a hand, Brogan allayed Lee's concern. Lee's other hand was intertwined with Esmeralda's. With a smirk, the Scotsman walked away. Blushing, Lee freed his hand and gently shook the woman. "Esmeralda?" He said in a soothing voice. "We need to start moving."

Sluggishly, she opened her eyes and sat up. "How you do these things and wake bright-eyed, I do not know," she stated.

"Part of the job," Lee replied. "I'll get Alexei situated."

At the mention of his name, the horse lowered his head over the side of the wagon. "Stupid horse! Must be English, is also bright-eyed."

"How much longer do you think the trip will be before we reach your cousin?" Brogan asked.

"Perhaps day and half, two days most," Esmeralda answered. "She will be glad to see me, possibly you, too." The woman pointed to Brogan. A confused look crossed the Scotsman's face.

"Me?"

"Ja, she like big man, strong, like bear."

A smile crossed his face. "Well, I look forward to meeting her now," Brogan confessed.

"Alexei is ready, if we are," Lee stated, having listened to the banter of his traveling companions.

"Should we cover back up?" Brogan asked. "The goblins saw us last night, and they've probably already spread the word."

"That is true, but in case we pass any soldiers, it might be beneficial for us to stay hidden," the Englishman offered.

"Old mother's creatures will take you to her, and soldiers will not be nice. Shoot us all on sight," Esmeralda replied.

"Hiding it is," Brogan said, as he laid down.

After they had been on the road for an hour or so, a distinct sound could be heard approaching them. "Is troops, stay quiet," their escort instructed.

Someone shouted in a foreign language, and Esmeralda pulled the wagon off the road. For almost an hour, they sat there as the music of marching feet played. Waiting as the sound passed them and then began to fade, Esmeralda put the cart back on the path and continued forward. "Did they suspect anything?" Lee asked her.

"Ni," she replied. "They are heading to front and think they come home big heroes... fools."

"Well, once they get there, we'll have to keep a watch out for the soldiers they're relieving," Brogan commented.

"They not relieving anyone," Esmeralda said. "Men do not come home from front."

Lee and Brogan exchanged a look, both understanding what their escort meant. The goblins from the night before would most likely regroup and continue their pursuit with reinforcements, but no soldiers would be crossing their path ahead. "Something in trees," Esmeralda commented.

She began to sing a song in her native tongue. Lee did not understand the words, but it was a haunting melody, and Esmeralda's voice was lovely. Brogan tapped Lee's leg. "Don't go drifting off on me," the Scotsman said. "I want to know what's in the trees."

Lee tried to see through the small hole in the cart, but he could not angle himself to see anything high up in the trees. "Let us know if it follows us," Lee whispered.

Through the small gap between the canvas and the wagon, he saw her give an imperceptible nod. "Well?" Brogan asked.

"She'll keep us informed," Lee said.

They did not hear anything as something watched them from the woods. After several minutes, the Englishman posed a question. "Is it still with us?" Esmeralda nodded once again. "We're being trailed," Lee told Brogan.

"Should we take care of it now?" Brogan asked.

"Ni," Esmeralda stated, continuing with her song.

Brogan gave Lee a confused look. The Englishman shrugged in response. "We don't know what it is or how many there are," he surmised.

"Is Drek, only one," Esmeralda replied. "If can get away, is better; it is very dangerous."

A growl came from the woods by Lee's side of the wagon. Esmeralda began to sing once more, and the growling quickly faded.

"Drek?" Lee whispered, trying to remember the creatures presented to them during their training.

"Drekavac," Brogan replied, "unbaptized baby that wanders after death."

Lee's astounded look made Brogan look away. "I remembered it because no one knows what they look like," the Scotsman explained, embarrassed.

"Apparently, someone knows," Lee commented, raising his eyes towards their driver.

"Her singing seems to keep it calm," Brogan noticed.

Lee listened closely to the melody and did not recognize the song, but given the simplistic nature of the melody, he was almost positive that Esmeralda was singing a lullaby. "Did Vladimir cover how to destroy them?" Lee asked. He remembered a few vague statements but nothing concrete about the creature.

Brogan shook his head. "All he said was that some had been burned to stop them. I'm surprised that it's stalking us during the day."

"Me, too," Lee agreed. His memory was clear that their instructor had stated plainly, "the Drekavac roams at night, seeking victims to lure from their homes."

"Keep going like normal and keep singing," Lee instructed Esmeralda. "Stop after dark, and we'll build a fire. If that doesn't keep it away, then we'll take care of it."

The woman gave no indication that she had heard Lee's instructions, but she continued singing and steering the cart.

Stopping only to take a drink of water, Esmeralda had continued singing the same lullaby for hours. Now with the sun set, and a guiding lantern hanging on the side of the wagon, she sought a place to pull Alexei off the road and rest for the night. The gangly form in the trees continued following them. She could see its glowing eyes perched in the trees, watching her. Forcing her gaze onto the side of the road, the Prussian tried hard to keep her mind off the nightmare creature nearby.

Seeing a perfect spot to camp for the night, she pulled on Alexei's reins. The night was colder than its predecessors had been, which meant winter was finally arriving. As soon as the cart made the transition off the road, Lee and Brogan dropped off the back and looked around. The Scotsman saw the monster first and pointed it out to his companions. Nodding, Lee took up watching the creature, his rifle held at the ready. Brogan started to gather firewood so they could have some warmth and something to deter the monster.

They had foregone fires previously, for fear it would give away their position. With the Drek watching them from the shadows, it seemed safer to betray their position with a fire. Brogan gathered as much brush and kindling as he could from the surrounding area. A few moments later, Lee heard flint strike steel and knew that Brogan was getting the fire started. A warm glow started to brighten the area. Watching the glowing eyes, the Englishman saw them blink. After the third blink, the eyes were gone. As the flames continued to illuminate the area, Lee saw the tree was completely empty now, but claw marks on the upper branches showed where something had been.

The Baba Yaga sat in her house amongst the trees, the giant chicken legs at the corners acting as stilts. Her shoulder ached from the wound, but it was not the first or last injury that she would receive. It paled in comparison to the continuous agitation in her leg and itch in her eyes. Packed into the bullet wound was earth and stone from the forest floor. Her forces were searching, no longer concerned with the foreigners flying into their homeland. Men were men; they would all squander the riches of Prussia, but the Baba Yaga would remain and see that the land remained as well. Her weapon was now on the trail and seeking the Englishman. He had caused the damage to her land. There was much that she did not remember, but after meeting with the English witch, the Old Mother perfectly understood how Lee Baum had caused all this suffering. It was a crime that he would pay for.

It was only a matter of time before her weapon would have them. The goblins had reported his presence the night before. They would replenish their forces from other clans and take back up the hunt. The Drekavac had sent her the vision of the two foreigners being helped by a Prussian girl. Men with their pretty words and trinkets had defiled a daughter of the land, but no matter. She was not the first girl to go astray, nor would she be the last. The Drek wanted the woman. She had sung to the tormented soul of the unbaptized. It was no concern to the Baba Yaga. If the Drekavac failed to claim the woman, because of the men's interference, it was no matter. Or perhaps the spirit would succeed in destroying both men.

It was unlikely but not impossible. The Baba Yaga sat and waited. A crow flew overhead, guided to the woods where the foreigners slept for the night. Using the bird's eyes as her own, the Old Mother guided the creature to the best perch to observe the evening's events.

Brogan and Lee did their usual, each man taking a four-hour watch. Esmeralda laid down, wrapped in her blanket. The warmth of the fire kept her cozy, and Lee was happy that it kept the Drek away. At least, he assumed as such. Brogan had not seen any sign of the creature, and neither had he. The campfire was making it hard for the Englishman to keep his guard up. Shaking his head to keep from dozing, the hunter stood up and walked closer to the darkness. The chill in the air was enough to keep him awake.

From the other side of the campsite, Lee thought he saw something move. It was a quick gray flash, darting just close enough to the fire to stand out. Whatever, he had seen was gone as quickly as it appeared with the shadows of the forest providing cover. "Brogan," Lee whispered, his eyes roaming over the darkened woods. The Scotsman did not wake. Moving across the campsite towards the specter that he had seen, Lee tried to find any sign of the being that he glimpsed. A slight breeze rippled through the trees, pulling leaves from their perches and scattering them about. The fire whipped up slightly. A crow sat in a nearby branch, watching the hunter intently. Something about the way the animal stared at him made Lee feel uneasy.

Esmeralda was curled tightly in her blanket, dreaming of running through the replenished Prussian fields with Lee Baum. The man had come as an invading fiend, but he was intelligent and resourceful, both

177

traits that Esmeralda admired. Something caught on her blanket. Not waking from her sleep, the woman kicked at the snagged cloth. Then something wrapped tightly around her ankle. Realizing that this was no dream, the woman screamed as she was pulled from the fireside. Brogan rolled out of his blanket and came up shotgun in one hand, the hilt of his sword in the other.

Lee spun around and saw the gangly monster dragging Esmeralda towards the forest. Raising his Winchester, the hunter put a round right between the protruding shoulder blades. The emaciated form collapsed forward. Esmeralda clawed at the dirt and began to pull herself back towards the safety of the fire.

Pushing itself up from the ground, the Drekavac turned and faced the Englishman. Lee saw the horrible gray skin and the overly long, thin legs and arms connected to a withered torso, the ribs clearly protruding underneath the husk. Sitting on top of this strange physique was an overly large head. It was amazing that the thin neck could support the weight of such an orb. Long, matted hair draped down, half covering the hideous face that stared with such hatred at Lee. Opening a mouth of rotten teeth, the monster wailed, the sound of a baby in fear and suffering. It was a heart-wrenching scream.

Lee and Brogan froze, both taken aback by the sound emanating from the nightmare before them. With Esmeralda still crawling towards the fire, she had placed herself between Brogan and the Drek. Dropping the shotgun onto his blankets, Brogan adjusted his grip on the claymore's handle and stepped towards the monster. It raked one long arm towards the Scotsman, but with a downward strike, the sword separated the arm at the elbow.

The wound did not bleed. It seemed to Lee that the monster did not even notice that it had lost a limb. With the creature focusing on Brogan, it gave Lee a full view of the hideous profile. Taking careful aim, Lee put a round directly through the Drekavac's throat. His bullet shattered vertebrae as it passed through the monster. Its head dropping to the side, the creature struggled to maintain its balance while continuing to swing at Brogan with its remaining arm.

Ducking under the latest swing, the Scotsman ran his sword through the creature's chest and lifted the blade over his shoulder. The Drek fell behind Brogan, struggling to stand. Lee raised the rifle to take another shot, this time in the center of the forehead. Brogan saved him the bullet by placing a powerful kick directly into the protruding sternum of the monster. Collapsing under the force of the blow, the strange creature lay there for a moment before pushing itself backwards. The broken vertebrae had healed, and a new arm had replaced the severed limb.

Rushing forward, Brogan swung his claymore in great sweeping arcs. The Drek dodged the blows. As the Scotsman missed with a swing, the creature took the opportunity to attack while the hunter was trying to recover. Slashing at Brogan with its clawed hands, the monster drove the hunter back. Lee shot the beast twice in the face. It stumbled back with each impact but quickly recovered to resume its attack. Standing by the fire, Esmeralda began to sing her lullaby.

With one hand upraised for another strike, the Drekavac stopped, staring at the woman. The mouth turned up in a smile of pure rapture, and Brogan rushed forward, slamming his shoulder into the monster's unprotected midsection. Driving it back, the Scotsman shoved the beast off his shoulder, propelling the creature onto the flames. It screamed and struggled to get off the fire. Plunging his claymore through the Drek, Brogan pinned it in place where it continued to scream as the flames devoured the dead flesh. Within moments, the sound faded away, and only ashes remained of the damned being.

"It was horrible, that scream," she stated.

Lee nodded in agreement. Placing an arm across her shoulders, the Englishman pulled her close. From her perch, the Baba Yaga watched through the crow's eyes. The death of the Drekavac was of no concern to her, but the men that had been able to so easily defeat such a foe were quite a wonder. Never had she seen anyone defeat a Drek so easily. They made it seem like a common feat. Perhaps her English sister had been correct about this man. Noticing how he doted upon the woman, the Baba Yaga formed a plan in her mind. The foolish girl could be of use, but only if the pawns were in place.

A loud explosion and searing pain broke the Baba Yaga's connection to the bird. It could only mean that the animal was dead.

Lee stared at Brogan, holding his smoking shotgun. "Why did you do that?" Lee asked.

"Something about that bird did not sit right with me," Brogan explained. "It was staring at you. Don't seem right, a bird staying calm in all that noise and then taking an interest in you. I don't know what, but something was wrong with that creature."

Lee looked over and saw the shredded remains of the crow. "I saw that bird earlier, right before the attack. I'll agree with you on that point. Something was wrong with it," Lee stated. "We should get moving."

10

Dan and Brackish stood on the side of the road, following the signs of Lee and Brogan's path. The goblin had been able to pick up the familiar scent of the Scotsman when they found where Lee had landed. Dan was relieved that at least Brogan was with him. Alone in the hostile country, a single man did not have much hope. Stealing horses from a farm that they passed, the duo set out after Lee. Arriving at a vacant inn, Brackish had informed Dan that he smelled traces of Lee, Brogan, someone else, and a horse. Currently, they were looking at the remains of several goblins. The duo had been fortunate that no one had seen them since they landed. The horizon was barren behind them with a small forest growing ahead of them. Brackish and Dan dismounted from their horses, the animals needing a rest, and examined the carcasses.

Adjusting the straps on the pneumatic pack, Dan felt the chafed skin underneath. Setting the equipment on the mud, the American stretched; it felt good to be off the horse. They had been pushing the animals hard for the past day and a half. Being unfamiliar with these horses, Dan did not know how long the animals could maintain their speed, given the load they carried. Brackish went about inspecting the dead with no sign of agitation. "Are you okay to look at these?" Dan asked as he rolled one of the small bodies over.

"Not my clan," Brackish replied as he sniffed the air.

Apart from the hoof prints and wheel marks in the road, Dan noticed another type of track running beside the road but cutting through the goblins. Examining the bodies closely, it was easy to find the puncture wound where a bullet had punched through the crude leather armor. The ripping and tearing had been done later. Whatever left the tracks had stopped to make a quick snack of some of the dead. "Any idea what might've left that?" The American asked, pointing at the large paw mark.

Sniffing it, Brackish turned and spit. "Bad magic," he stated.

Walking around the carnage, Dan noticed that several small goblin tracks led away from the battle. It could only mean one thing: some of the goblins fled. "This land bad," Brackish commented.

"Plant some trees and a few bushes, and it wouldn't be so bad," Dan replied.

"No, land bad, not dead," the goblin explained patiently. "Magic run deep, connect to someone powerful."

Dan remembered the brief Baba Yaga write up that he had been given while on the military airship. "I think I know who," he replied. "Any sign of anyone else being hurt?"

Walking about the scene, his nose inches above the mud, Brackish tried to pick up any traces of blood. "No," the goblin replied.

"We need to ride on. Might be able to find cover up ahead and take a rest," Dan said, shouldering the pack once more.

"Rest?" Brackish asked.

"Yeah, won't be any good to Lee if we're worn out when we get to him," the American explained.

"We eat?" The goblin asked, licking his lips.

"We don't have anything to cook."

"I find."

Riding into the forest, Dan hitched the horses to a stout tree and removed their packs from the animals' backs. Brackish disappeared into the woods without a comment. The hunter figured his diminutive partner was going to try his hand at hunting. Thankfully, they had been able to fill their canteens at the inn. The American laid out a blanket and rested on it. The browning grass beneath him was softer than the military bunk had been. With his bowler hat covering his eyes, Dan drifted into a dreamless sleep.

A nudge against his foot woke him. Two dead rabbits stared at the man as he opened his eyes. Rolling to the side, Dan drew a revolver. Brackish was standing beside his blanket, holding the two rabbits with a large smile on his face. "I find," the goblin commented, shaking the rabbits.

"Indeed, you did," Dan replied as he tried to slow his heart rate.

Gathering sticks from the nearby forest, Dan arranged the wood and started a fire. After skinning the small animals, Brackish handed their meals to the man and watched as the meat was spitted and placed over the fire to roast. Licking his lips, the goblin sat down and watched as their food cooked. "Was there any larger game?" Dan asked.

"Something scare animals, most flee," Brackish replied, his gaze never leaving the rabbits.

"And Lee's scent?"

"Not fresh, not old."

Dan should have expected such an answer. Brackish did not have a great grasp of time. "A day?" Dan asked.

"Close," the goblin replied.

Given how long it had taken them to get to Prussia, it was good to know that they had at least made up some time. Drawing his Bowie knife, Dan cut a sliver off the rabbit. Tasting the meat and ensuring that it was fully cooked, he withdrew the animals and handed one to Brackish. "After this, get some sleep. I'll keep watch and wake you so I can get some shut-eye," Dan instructed.

With Brackish snoring by the remains of the fire, Dan was keeping an eye on the brightly lit woods. It was not likely that they would have any trouble, but one could never tell. He had not thought that Lee would have been accosted by goblins, but the evidence lay in the road behind them. Another thought nagging at him was the strange tracks that he had seen following his partner. Whatever it had been was big and heavy. The long claws jutting from powerful paws made Dan think of a bear, but this bear would have to be bigger than a grizzly.

Dan also could not surmise why a bear would be tracking them, but given how the survivors of the ship had been escorted, it was most likely the old witch's doing. No matter, Lee was still alive. Dan and Brackish may be able to catch up to whatever was tracking his partner before it found the Englishman. A twig snapped in the forest. Reaching back for the cord on the pack, Dan watched and waited when a wolf emerged from the woods and stood across from the American. Glancing around, the man was glad to see no more of the pack animals approaching.

Maintaining eye contact, Dan circled the animal. A strange bird call echoed through the trees, and the wolf gave a canine yawn and trotted back into the forest. It was a strange encounter, one that prompted Dan to return to their small campsite and check on Brackish.

Stepping into the small area, the hunter was glad to see the goblin sitting up, sniffing the air. "Something wrong?" The American asked.

"Not sure," Brackish replied.

"Well, that's not good." Keeping an eye on the woods, Dan stomped out the last few embers of the fire. "We should go ahead and get back on the road."

With no argument, Brackish rolled up the blanket and grabbed the equipment. The diminutive hunter stood guard as Dan saddled the horses. The animals were unnaturally skittish. Blowing through the trees, the wind shifted, bringing with it the scent from the portion of road they had arrived on. Brackish grew more agitated. "Bad things coming," the goblin urged. "Not know how many."

"What are they?" Dan asked, trying to see any oncoming enemies.

"Dangerous," Brackish commented as he took another deep breath. "No know what they are."

"I guess we should get a move on then," Dan offered, giving the goblin a hand onto his horse.

Cautiously emerging from the trees, Dan and Brackish looked toward the way they had come. Five lone figures walked in their direction, but they were at least an hour behind them. "Is that them?"

The goblin nodded. Turning the horses, the two hunters continued onward following the unknown tracks and Lee's scent.

After riding for an hour, Dan glanced behind him. The figures that he had seen before appeared closer. How five men on foot could gain on a horse, the hunter did not know, but it was certainly not through natural means. Dan squinted to try and get a sharper look. "Are they running?" He asked Brackish.

Peering at the figures, the goblin was not sure. He reached into his pack and withdrew a spyglass. Dan recognized the device but knew they didn't bring theirs. "Where did you get that?" Dan asked.

Brackish smiled. "Captain no need it."

"You stole from the captain?"

"Borrow, I return," the goblin replied.

Putting the instrument to his eye, Brackish was amazed by the invention's ability to make distant things appear near. Then, his eye fell on the figures following after them. Indeed, they were running, but it was not their motion that concerned the goblin so much as the fact that he could not clearly see them. Whenever the glass would fall on them, they shimmered and became hazy, even while the world around them was still crisp and clear. "We go fast," Brackish said, his voice panicked.

Putting the spyglass back into his pack, the goblin urged his horse forward. Dan did the same, wanting to find out what the goblin had seen. "What are they?" Dan asked, holding his bowler hat down on his head.

"No know," Brackish answered. "Magic make them tough to see. I see shape only."

"It was probably the spyglass," Dan commented.

"No," Brackish said definitively. "All else clear, but not them."

"Something's masking them?" Dan asked.

Brackish shrugged. "No know, makes smell funny."

That explained why the goblin had been unable to identify them by scent, a first since Dan and Lee had met their assistant. Pushing the horses to a gallop, the hunters tried to put as much distance between themselves and the mysterious figures following them.

After a couple of hours of hard riding, the horses were spent. With a lather worked up on their skin, Dan reined in the animals. "We keep pushing them like this, and we're going to have to go on foot," he told Brackish.

The goblin turned the horse around. "Where they?" He asked.

Dan looked over his shoulder; the figures that had been following them were gone from sight. "Maybe we lost them," Dan offered.

A rustling through the brush beside the road alerted the hunters that they were not alone. Dismounting from the horse, Dan reached for the shotgun. The things had flanked them. Two emerged from each side of the road. They appeared as hazy images of people. Dan could not believe his eyes. He had never seen anything like it. Something shifted around them, and the figures melted; standing before the hunters were bears on two feet, towering above them and their mounts.

Pulling the cord on the pack, Dan heard the piston engage and squeezed the trigger. The first four shots stitched a line of gore up the nearest of the monstrous ursines. Falling back to all fours, the creature staggered away, leaving its comrades to the task at hand. Aiming on the second animal, Dan unleashed the remaining four shots. The bullets tore a hole in the giant's abdomen. Stumbling back, the bear clutched at its destroyed stomach with the slippery rope of its intestine falling from between its claws to land on the ground. Tumbling over, the bear tried to right itself only to have more organs fall out through the exposed wound.

Ejecting the spent magazine, the hunter reached for a replacement and was immediately sent flying over his horse. Squelching down in the fallen bear's guts, Dan saw one of the towering beasts threatening his horse.

While Dan struggled to stand amongst the internal organs, Brackish fired into the nearest of his attackers. The pellets opened a small wound on the bear's shoulder. Dropping onto all fours, the bear rushed closer. Pumping another shell into the chamber, Brackish started to squeeze the trigger, but his opponent lashed out with a claw-tipped paw and ripped the shotgun from his grasp. The animal bellowed in the goblin's face. A smell of rotted meat hit the hunter. Drawing his dagger, Brackish stabbed the blade into the bottom of the bear's mouth. Slamming shut, the bear looked confused as the dagger punched through the roof of his mouth. Holding onto the hilt, Brackish punched the bear in the snout twice with his brass-plated, prosthetic arm. With the immense pain of its mouth combined with the massive shock of being hit in the nose, the animal pulled itself free. Brackish's blade did not come loose but cut through the front of the bear's face. Screaming in pain, the animal retreated.

A whinny of fear from Dan's horse caused Brackish to turn. The last of their attackers was lumbering towards the mount. Fearful, the horse had nowhere to run but was raising back, kicking at the bear with its front legs. His shotgun lost somewhere in the bushes, Brackish rushed up and leapt onto the beast's back. Driving his dagger into the thick pelt of the giant creature, the goblin used the weapon to cement his hold and then drew his revolver, firing all six shots into the bear while the animal tried to dislodge him.

Having found his footing, Dan stood with his hind end soaked in the fluids from the dead bear. Drawing a fresh magazine, having lost the initial one among the remains, and listening for a moment, the American made sure that the pneumatic pack was not making any odd sounds.

Satisfied that it was still functioning properly, the American took his horse by the reins and pulled it out of his way. "Brackish, get off!" Dan shouted.

The goblin withdrew the dagger and jumped clear. As the bear continued spinning, Dan emptied the entire magazine into its body. Still spinning with the force of the shots, the animal collapsed, dead. "What were they?" Dan asked. "Werebears?"

"No," Brackish answered. "No shifter."

The human was used to Brackish's unique terminology for certain types of creatures. If these were not shape-shifters, then Dan did not know what to make of them. The human shapes that had covered them were nothing more than puddles on the ground. Sniffing them, Brackish could only detect the smell of magic and dirt. "Weren't there five of them?" Dan asked, sure that he was right.

Hurriedly, the hunters reloaded their weapons. Anticipating another attack, the two stood motionless, waiting for a sound to betray their enemy. After several minutes passed, Dan and Brackish hoped that the bears had learned from the example of its traveling companions and had fled. "Get shotgun," Brackish announced as he carefully approached the bushes.

"Speaking of which," Dan mumbled as he turned off the piston and took off the pack for a quick inspection.

The tank was dented but did not appear to have any damage to the connecting pipes. While not being an engineer, Dan knew how the pack worked well enough. The damage might impact the output of the pack, but the device would still function without exploding. After his near-death experience in Egypt, he was wary of just such an occurrence. Preoccupied

189

with cleaning off the gore from the disemboweled bear, Dan did not hear the figure approaching from the road behind him. As the façade melted away, the last of the giant ursine creatures stood behind him, large, dagger-like claws poised to strike the American down. "Dan!" Brackish yelled as he emerged from the bushes.

Looking over his shoulder, the American saw the beast. Diving forward, the hunter felt the dangerous strike pass by, inches from his back. Rolling over, Dan pushed to his feet and hurried over to Brackish. Stepping towards the horses, the creature made its intention clear: kill the mounts and the hunters. Drawing his revolvers, Dan started firing at the lumbering behemoth. Rushing closer, Brackish slid under his horse and fired two shots into the bear's exposed stomach. Stumbling back, the bear fell forward, trying to smash Brackish into the mud with its front paws.

The goblin rolled aside, so that the animal did not land on him, but his coat was pinned underneath one of the monstrous paws. Pulling at the trapped fabric, the goblin fought harder as the giant bear turned its short muzzle in his direction. Rushing into a flanking position, Dan put two rounds from his pistol into the side of the large skull, and the third shot directly into the creature's muzzle. As the pain ripped through the beast, it roared and started to flee. Grabbing the pack, Dan pulled the cord, engaging the piston. Setting the pack back on the ground, he raised the shotgun and fired several rounds into the bear's rear legs. The giant creature slumped into the mud, still pulling itself along with only its forepaws. Stepping closer to the retreating fiend, Dan put two more shots into its skull directly behind the ear. Tumbling down onto the soil, the creature lay still. Satisfied, that all five of the beings had been dealt with,

Dan turned his attention back to Brackish. "Are you all right?" He asked as he scanned the woods for any further threats.

"Fine," Brackish replied, inspecting the rips in his coat.

His disappointment clear on his face, Dan fought back the urge to remind his partner that the jacket would be a lot messier if the monster had landed on the goblin. The horses were restless, thoroughly spooked by the transforming creatures that they had seen. "We're going to have to lead them," Dan announced. "We might be able to get something out of those bodies though."

Looking at the carcasses, Dan and Brackish saw only large mounds of earth before them, old worn skulls where the heads of the monsters had been. "Magic," Brackish whispered.

Dan never liked dealing with magic, but this was something he had never seen. First, the liquid shells that hid the creatures were new, but now the creatures had transformed into common-looking soil.

Baba Yaga ranted and raved. She threw sorcerous items about her humble house and uttered curses in languages no longer known to man, but it was for nothing. The bears had been gone before man started to build his villages and cities. The five skulls were the last completed bones of the great beasts.

Pulling from the power of Prussia herself, the old witch had formed bodies of the dust and earth and used the skulls to return the creatures to the world of the living. After watching the two men deal with the Drekavac, she had feared that they might prove a match for her great weapon, the tool that had never failed her. As an added guarantee, she had sent the five reborn animals after the Englishman. With their disguises, none would look for long upon them as they passed, but the new hunters in the path had destroyed them.

This one was the other that her sister had spoken of, a great warrior. His accomplice in the destruction of her creations was a goblin, and she found it most peculiar to see the man and creature working in conjunction. His scent was strange to her; it was the blood of a foreigner, but not the ones that she had encountered before. He was something new. If this new foreigner and his traitorous ally were determined to set themselves in her path and protect the Englishman she sought, so be it; they would meet the fate deserving of interlopers. The Baba Yaga sent her power out wordlessly. It reached into the deep places, under the rocks of Prussia where great forces lay dormant, forces that could only be called by a force greater than themselves. Baba Yaga was just such a force.

Dan and Brackish led their horses through the forest, their eyes and ears alert for any disturbance betraying an enemy's presence. The encounter with the bears had made them wary of the very ground beneath their feet. Brackish stopped, his hand tightening on his shotgun. "What is it?" Dan whispered.

"Lee and old fire," the goblin explained.

Taking the reins from his partner, Dan tethered the horses to a tree and pulled his shotgun from its holder on the pneumatic pack. Stepping off the road, Brackish guided Dan to the source of the scent. Cart tracks showed them where a wagon had been parked and a temporary stall created for a horse. The embers of a dead fire lay about them. Something had been thrown in the fire but not to build the flames. The strange mutilated shape was wrong, an unnatural tangle of long arms and legs with a spindly torso and large head. "Lee did this?" Dan asked.

"With help," Brackish commented. It meant that Brogan was still with him, which was fine by Dan. "Bad magic stop here," Brackish continued.

Bad magic could only mean the thing tracking after Lee and Brogan. "How long ago?"

"No know. Not long behind Lee," the goblin stated.

"The horses have had enough of a rest; we need to get a move on to catch up to it before it catches up to Lee."

As the two hunters climbed onto their horses, Dan hoped the animals would last long enough to make the trip and get him to Lee before something worse happened. Brackish hesitated before following. The wind shifted for a moment, and the goblin smelled something very familiar, but it was a weak scent and dissipated as quickly as it had arrived. Examining the surrounding forest quickly, the goblin sought what had left the scent, but seeing no clues, he hurried the horse after Dan.

Several hundred feet away, through thick bushes with heavy-scented flowers, large, powerfully built wolves stood watching with their masters, a hand calming the animals. They set their golden eyes on Brackish, noticing the human weapons he carried, and had seen what they needed to see. The goblin had fought back against the strange creatures and destroyed them. Baba Yaga had given her orders, but the goblin that rode with the man was more important than orders. Green, mottled skin adorned the figures who climbed onto their wolf mounts and gently marched through the forest, staying off the road to avoid being seen. It would be a tough feat to sneak undetected upon the hunters in the night, but the man was only human and his eyes not built to see in the dark. Plans would need to be made, so the wolf riders whispered amongst themselves, hatching their plot as they paced behind their target.

11

Lee rode up front with Esmeralda, a rough cloak draped across his shoulders and covering his head. "What do we say if we meet any patrols?" The Englishman asked.

Brogan's snores drifted up from the rear of the cart. "You say nothing. I tell them you my deaf, mute brother," the Prussian woman explained. "Is boring riding alone; I like company."

Looking at the vastly different lands around them, Lee was impressed by the differing environments that the Prussian countryside could offer. They left the forest hours ago and were now heading through a grassy plateau, with mountains peaking in the distance. "What should we talk about?" The hunter asked. "Or would you rather admire the scenery."

"Is beautiful, no?" She replied. "Even with winter coming late, the world has not given in yet."

This was not the first time that Esmeralda and others had made mention of winter's late arrival. Napoleon's men had lost in Prussia because of the intense winter, which had created almost a natural defense. While the trees in the forest had mostly been evergreens, the few deciduous trees that Lee had seen had almost no green leaves upon their branches. Even here, the grass was more yellow and brown than green but was still a more welcoming sight than the muddied fields, where Esmeralda's forest had once stood. "Given in?" Lee asked, just processing the comment.

"Ja, we rage and burn and kill, but the world, it keeps growing and changing," she explained. "Is miracle."

Lee thought for a moment, retrospective about the statement. "Yes, I suppose it is a miracle. I've never thought of it like that before," he admitted.

"Father taught me there is world beyond mechanics," she stated.

"I was aware, but it has been a while since I've taken part in that less-complicated world," he confessed.

"Now is grand opportunity."

"Yes, I believe it is," Lee confirmed, smiling. "Thank you for showing me."

Esmeralda blushed at the gratitude. She was appreciative of Lee for his company on the bench and was glad that he had been the one to accept the invitation. The large one was pleasant enough, but he did not stir the same feelings within her as Lee did. Something moved at the edge of the grass. Esmeralda squinted, trying to determine if it was a threat. Lee started to raise his rifle, having spotted the object as well.

A moment later, a brown hare bolted across the road before them. As the animal vanished into the sanctuary of the grass, Lee breathed a sigh of relief. Smiling, he looked over at Esmeralda and became concerned. The woman was stiff with tension. "What's wrong?"

"Is bad, what you call... omen," she replied.

"What was?" Lee asked. "The hare?"

Esmeralda nodded. "Something bad is coming."

Her ominous tone put Lee more on edge. The wind picked up and rushed across the field and over them. As it died down, Esmeralda was even tenser. Her shoulders were knotted tight, and her knuckles were white as she clutched Alexei's reins. Lee knew something about the Prussian folklore concerning nature. The Prussians believed that the wind was the deliverer of evil things, such as curses and evil news. "I'm sure it was just a breeze," Lee assured his companion.

Esmeralda shook her head. "You do not understand."

"No, I do. I understand the beliefs you hold about the elements, but not all winds bring evil with them."

"Do not mock me, Englishman," she stated, her demeanor turning as cold as the rumored Prussian winter.

"I'm not mocking you," Lee replied, apologetically. "I am…"

"A stranger in this land, and one unaccustomed to the evils that live alongside us," she spat at him and then mumbled to herself in her native tongue.

"Lad, if you can't keep from arguing, you'll be back here with me," Brogan stated from underneath the canvas.

Not wanting to do more damage, Lee decided to just apologize for his assumption. "Esmeralda, I am sorry. You are right; I do not know your culture or your customs, and I am sorry that I have offended you," he said in all sincerity.

"Is not that," the woman replied. "Evil is coming this night; I can feel it in my bones."

"Evil is something Lee and I can deal with; tell her, lad."

"He's right. We deal with evil often," Lee confirmed. "You saw that last night."

"Ja, and grateful I am," Esmeralda stated. "Worse things than the Drekavac lurk in this land."

Lee glanced over his shoulder and saw something on the horizon behind them. It looked like a rider, but the shape of the mount was all wrong. Convincing himself that he was seeing a wagon far behind them,

Lee decided to try and lighten the mood. He started to discuss engineering designs for a modified wagon that would not require the horse. Esmeralda brightened at the discussion. She could never talk openly of mechanics and engineering design with anyone; it was a thrilling new experience for her. Brogan listened for a minute before becoming completely lost and falling back asleep.

The cart jostled along over stony ground, jarring Brogan awake. Beneath them, the uneven ground was rattling the wagon terribly. Very little sunlight shone through the canvas and the Scotsman decided that he could sit up. As he sat up, he saw a shadow in the fading light of dusk, but it was far off and of no consequence at that time. Had it been a flying mortar and pestle, the hunter would have taken great notice and been highly concerned. The plateau was past them, and now they were in a barren patch of ground littered with great stones.

"Glad to see that you're awake," Lee offered.

"With all this jumping, it'll be a wonder that we don't break an axle," Brogan replied sourly.

"Axles are metal. Put them on myself," Esmeralda stated proudly.

"Should we stop for the night?" Lee asked. "The closer we come to the front, the worse the patrols will be."

"Did you encounter anyone while I was asleep?" The Scotsman inquired.

"A small squad of soldiers," Lee responded.

"And?"

"He was deaf, mute brother," Esmeralda answered.

"They did hear your snoring, though," Lee stated.

198

Brogan's eyes grew wide. "Is fine. Told them you were drunk cousin."

Brogan looked at Lee, who nodded confirmation. "They didn't bother to check me?"

"No need, they could hear you snoring and figured that no foreign soldiers would be traveling with a fine Prussian woman and her disabled brother."

"So, we can stop for the night then," the Scotsman proclaimed.

"Not here," Esmeralda stated. "This ground is dead, very bad to stop here."

"Why?" Brogan asked.

"Things live here. Things that make garments of men," she replied.

"Given our status as outsiders, I say we trust to her judgment and continue onwards," Lee replied as he clicked Alexei's reins to urge the horse forward.

Brogan agreed as he leaned back against the side of the wagon and saw the large boulders that seemed to sprout up from within the earth itself. Something struck the Scotsman as odd. "Lee, how did those boulders get here?" He asked.

The Englishman looked around. Brogan was right; there were no mountains or high lands nearby that would allow for rolling rocks to make it this far. "I do not know. Esmeralda?"

"The land provides for its children, even the evil ones," she replied, taking the reins from Lee and giving Alexei some harsh, Prussian words of encouragement.

Lee and Brogan traded looks, but both men kept quiet as the horse trundled over the rough terrain. "Is that cart still behind us?" Lee inquired.

"Yes," Brogan confirmed. "It's a ways off, though. They'll be stopping for the night soon."

"Few more hours and we come to another inn," Esmeralda informed them. "We stop there."

"Won't we draw some unwanted attention?" The Englishman asked.

"If you come in. I get room; you climb through window," she explained.

"We'll see if I can fit," Brogan commented. "It'll have to be a big window."

The Scotsman was much broader than Lee's lithe form. Without further comment, the trio continued along the road towards the inn.

As the ground became hospitable again, fields began to dot the landscape with humble farmhouses at their centers. From within the field, tall, pointed, black hats moved through the dead plants. "Awfully short farmers," Brogan commented.

Esmeralda glanced at the small moving figures in the waning sunlight. "Little men of the field," she swore and urged Alexei to move faster.

"What's wrong?" Lee asked.

"Polevik," she replied, her eyes begging him to understand.

"Dwarves," Lee told Brogan, "deformed little creatures with different colored eyes. They grow grass instead of hair, so fire might be a valuable weapon against them."

"Are they dangerous?" Brogan asked, checking his shotgun and handing Lee's rifle up to him.

"If you sleep in the field, they will ride over you on small ponies, or if the sun still shines they will kill you," Esmeralda explained.

"Right. That's why they told us not to sleep near the farms," Brogan replied.

"Exactly," Lee agreed.

"Why don't we set fire to the fields?" Brogan asked.

"Burn half the countryside," Esmeralda replied angrily.

"It isn't the farmers' fault that these little beasts are after us," Lee stated. The Englishman was having trouble distinguishing the black hats from the long shadows in the field

The first of the Polevik emerged from the dead stalks along the road, a hunchbacked man-shape with long arms dragging a rusted sickle along the ground and a great bushy beard of straw with matching hair on its head. Even if its spine had been straight, the creature would have needed a step to reach the back of the cart. More creatures emerged, carrying old, disused farm tools. "If we can keep ahead of them, we shouldn't have any problems," Brogan said.

Watching the short-legged beings chase after the cart, the Scotsman chuckled to himself. One of the monsters whistled and horses the size of large dogs appeared out of the fields. Climbing onto their mounts, the Polevik began to gain on the wagon. "Do we have need to be concerned with more of these creatures while we're in the fields?" Lee asked.

He turned around on the driver's bench and sighted on the lead rider. Squeezing the trigger, he watched as the dwarf was hurtled off his ride and thrown into the field. "More can come at any time," Esmeralda answered, having waited for the shot to finish. "I see them."

Lee saw the black caps moving through the fields, harder to see with the light almost gone. Well ahead of the cart, those creatures would be able to cut off their path. "We can't get surrounded," Lee commented.

Shooting another rider from its horse, Lee turned back around and started to focus on the beings still in the fields. Focusing on the tip of the hat and making sure it was not a dark spot in the field, Lee lowered his sights until they were directly below the black peak. His first shot dropped a hat out of sight. The six Poleviks crossing the field stopped their march following the death of their leader. "How brave are these things?" The British hunter asked.

"Like man, each one is different," Esmeralda replied, snapping the reins faster.

Brogan's shotgun boomed from the rear as his shot decimated both a rider and his mount, sending both down to stop in the dirt road. Pumping another round into the chamber, the Scotsman waited until the next rider was close. Firing again, Brogan was satisfied to see the horse slow its pursuit. Its rider was missing, but the saddle was soaked in gore. Seeing the fate of their brothers, the dwarves rode into the fields. "Not too brave," Brogan proclaimed. "Look at how they've run."

"Where?" Esmeralda asked.

"The fields," the Scotsman replied.

"Is no good," Esmeralda said, her eyes darting amongst the decaying crops at their sides.

Flying from the field as if propelled by supernatural assistance, a Polevik soared towards Brogan, an old butcher's knife at the ready. Spotting the glint in the dying sunlight with his peripherals, Lee spun, aimed, and fired. The creature's flight path did not alter when the bullet hit center mass but rolled along the floor, dead when it landed in the wagon. Throwing the small corpse over the side, Brogan put away his shotgun and pulled his great Claymore from its scabbard. Standing in the back of the cart, he was ready for more attackers.

As two more of the creatures hurtled from the fields on both sides of the road, the large Scotsman dealt with them in a single stroke. Spinning in almost a full circle, he bisected both creatures as they sailed harmlessly over the wagon to land on the dirt. Satisfied that Brogan did not need his assistance, Lee focused back to the beings still ahead of them. They had since regained their courage and were making their way to the road. With two well-placed shots, Lee diminished their numbers again. This time, they did not stop but vanished completely. "Where did they go?" Lee asked, puzzled.

"Took off hats or are crawling," Esmeralda replied, guessing.

Brogan gave another shout as his swing took the head off one of the attacking beasts. "This is almost too easy," the Scotsman bragged.

"Don't speak just yet," Lee replied. "Stop!"

Esmeralda pulled back on the reins, causing Alexei to stand on his hind legs. Brogan stumbled, fighting to stay upright. Before the wagon had stopped, Lee hopped to the ground and ran forward. It was tough to see, but his sharp eyes had spotted the wire running across the road.

Removing his dagger from its sheath, the Englishman cut the trap. He quickly returned to the wagon and started to climb aboard when something grabbed his foot and jerked him back down. Lee's other leg was pulled out from underneath him, and he was dragged away. He could see the dead stalks move back into position, obscuring his view of his friends.

Spinning over onto his back, the hunter broke free of his captors. Drawing his revolver, he put a shot into the first Polevik. Before he could shoot the other, it slashed across his chest with the vicious sickle in its hand, sparking as the blade glinted off the brass chestplate, which then jumped onto the dry, brittle plant leaves and started to smoke. Staring at the rising plume, the dwarf ignored Lee, who took the opportunity to shoot the creature and return to the cart.

"Lee," Brogan shouted, waving the Englishman towards him.

Black hats raced past him, headed in the direction he was coming from. Glancing over his shoulder, Lee saw them congregating around the plume of smoke where a small fire had started to take root. Throwing himself over the side of the cart into the back with Brogan, Lee was glad to feel Alexei start forward again. Running, the horse carried them away from the dangerous fields. "What happened?" Lee asked.

"They go to save their home," Esmeralda stated.

"So, we should have set fire to the fields," Brogan replied.

"This was a small fire, and they should be able to contain it," Lee commented. "If we had started a much larger conflagration, it would have been much harder for them to control it."

"Ja," Esmeralda agreed. "I will not hurt my people just to hurt my people. Polevik normally only go after men in their fields. Never come to the road."

"It is safe to assume that we are clearly a high-priority target," Lee replied.

"Let's hope the fire keeps them busy," Brogan commented as he watched the black hats making quick work of the flames.

Passing by the remainder of the fields with no interruptions, the trio was glad to see the lights of the inn ahead of them. "Cover up," Esmeralda told Lee.

Taking the hint, the two men covered up with the canvas as Esmeralda laid out her plan. "I go, rent room, and open window for you. You secure wagon and Alexei."

"Sounds simple enough," Brogan said.

Pulling around to the small stable beside the inn, Esmeralda stepped down and walked around to the front of the building. Lee found a stall for the wagon. Backing the cart into its resting place, he unhitched the horse and handed the reins to Brogan, who secured the animal in a neighboring stall. Petting the steed's muzzle, he fed Alexei some of the hay from a nearby trough. "Let's move before someone comes to feed their horse," Brogan said, gesturing to the other mounts in the stable. The markings on the saddles and blankets, placed them as belonging to Prussian soldiers.

"Be careful," Lee warned. "We don't need any trouble."

"I know," Brogan replied. "Do you nag Dan this badly?"

"I do not nag, but I do tend to caution Dan, as needed. Also, I do not share an apartment with you and have not yet commented on your hygiene," Lee retorted.

"I have a whole new respect for your partner," Brogan stated.

Not wanting to drag the conversation out further, the Englishman turned and led the way into the night.

Esmeralda stood in a common dining room and tavern. A plump man in an apron stood behind the bar. "Welcome, room for the night?" He asked in Prussian.

"Da."

After procuring a key for her, the innkeeper looked her up and down with an unwelcoming leer in his eyes. Sitting in the tavern, Esmeralda saw several soldiers laughing and enjoying a meal and, judging by the empty cups, several drinks. Taking the key, she climbed the stairs to the second floor of the structure and entered the sparse room. To ensure that she would not be interrupted, she locked the door and then tipped a chair underneath the handle. It would not stop a determined attacker, but it would provide plenty of warning. The heavy Prussian pistol was still tucked into a pocket on her skirt. She had never fired it, but the weight of it gave her comfort.

Opening the window, she looked out. It would be a substantial act for the two foreign hunters to scale the wall. Grabbing the linens from the bed, she quickly tied them together, anchored them to the bedframe, and tossed the makeshift rope out the window.

Lee saw the white line flutter into the darkness and fall against the wall. "That must be our room," he said, wrapping his hand around the makeshift rope.

Giving three hard pulls, the Englishman was satisfied that it would hold. "Do you want to go up first?" Lee asked.

"I'm in a kilt, and I'll probably need help getting in with all this gear."

"Ok. Once I'm in, you can start up."

"Right. I'll just keep watch until then."

Watching as Lee easily climbed the obstacle and slid into the window, Brogan gave one last look around and began his own ascent. It was not as graceful as Lee's, and the hunter was worried that he would not be able to get into the window once he reached his target. Throwing an arm in through the opening, he began pulling himself in when he felt something catch.

Lee and Esmeralda grabbed the Scotsman. "Your sword's hitting," Lee whispered, reaching behind Brogan.

Feeling the weapon shift on his back, he tried once again. This time, his shoulders slid through the window. It was a tight fit, but one that he could make. Sitting down on the floor, the Scotsman stretched his burning arms. "Harder than it looks," he stated.

"I could not agree with you more," Lee said, exhausted.

Esmeralda quickly pulled the sheets back into the window and closed it. "You take the bed. We'll be fine on the floor," Brogan offered.

"When you pay for room, you can have bed," she replied, as if any other arrangement would be reached.

Lee stifled a chuckle. Esmeralda left the sheets piled on the floor beneath the window. Climbing into the bed, she pulled her coat tightly around her and settled down. Riding all day on the wagon and sleeping in the fields and forests had proven to tire her more than she suspected. It only took a moment before she was breathing heavily and giving a slight snore, and then the hunters knew she was asleep. "You take first watch," Brogan stated as he lay down on the pile of tied together blankets.

Lee felt fairly well-rested, and the snoring of Brogan was enough to keep anyone awake.

As it was approaching time for Lee to wake Brogan, the Englishman noticed the sounds of drunken humor rising from the first floor. While these noises continued, he also detected the faint sound of a stair creaking. Someone was coming upstairs, but Lee could not hear any difference in the voices downstairs. Watching closely, he saw the door knob start to turn. It was clear that someone was working to pick the tumblers on the lock.

Watching, Lee maneuvered his Winchester into position. He had honestly expected something to try and come through the window. Very few of the creatures that they faced had the patience to pick a lock. Kicking Brogan's boot, Lee roused the sleeping hunter, who looked at Lee. Pointing towards the door, the Englishman told his compatriot everything he needed to know. Getting up from the sheets, the Scotsman drew his revolver and stepped closer to the entryway. Moving the chair out of the way, Brogan stood behind the door, waiting.

As the last tumbler fell into place, the lock gave way, and the door swung inward. The innkeeper stopped when he saw Lee waiting for him with a rifle. Grabbing the man by the back of the neck, Brogan pushed him further into the room, shutting his only means of escape. Keeping his hand firmly locked on the cowering man's neck, Brogan guided him to the window. Replacing the chair underneath the door knob, Lee then went and roused Esmeralda from her sleep. Rubbing the grit from her eyes, she saw the innkeeper and his predicament. "We need to know if he said anything about where he was going to the soldiers downstairs," Lee stated.

Esmeralda translated the question to the pudgy little man. "Ni," he responded.

Brogan shook him. "Ask again," the Scotsman said, growling at the intruder.

The man looked as if he was on the verge of hysterics. Esmeralda repeated the question. Terrified, the innkeeper rattled off a much longer answer this time. "What'd he say?" Lee asked.

"He claims that he was coming to see if I needed anything more," she responded. Her tone of voice indicated how much trust she put in the man's explanation. "How did he get in?"

"Picked the lock," the Scotsman answered, shaking the man more viciously.

Finally breaking down into tears, the man fell on his knees and started pleading with Brogan. Wrapping his arms around the Scotsman's bare knees and wailing into his kilt, the man continued in his native tongue. "What's he saying?" Brogan asked.

"He's begging you to spare his life," Esmeralda answered. "Apparently, he was going to do more than check on my needs. He wanted to fulfill a few of his own."

"Horrid little man," Lee stated, giving the innkeeper a look of disgust.

Not knowing the words but understanding the tone, the man fell on his face, weeping on Brogan's boots. "We can't leave him up here; the soldiers will start to wonder where he is and may come looking," Brogan commented on their predicament.

"It would seem odd for Esmeralda to leave right now. By the sounds coming from downstairs, I do not know that they would not be more inclined to follow the example set by this repulsive man."

The door to the inn banged open from downstairs. Both hunters shared a confused look. It was late for travelers to still be out. After a few confused shouts from the soldiers, followed by what the foreigners took to be challenges at the latest unknown guest, they heard screaming a moment later. "We need to leave through the window," Lee proclaimed. "Brogan, you go first, Esmeralda will follow, and I'll come last."

Throwing the sheets out the window, the Scotsman shoved the innkeeper off his foot and started to lower himself down the improvised rope. A few more shouts echoed from below, followed by gunshots and ringing sabers. Esmeralda was starting her descent when the sounds from the first floor went silent. She froze for a moment, listening. The only sound was the wind outside and the crying of the innkeeper. Lee heard the faint creak from the stairs. "Hurry," he urged Esmeralda.

She did her best to quickly descend the sheets, trying not to slip and fall. Brogan wrapped his hands around her waist and sat her on the ground. "Lee!" He shouted up.

Grabbing the linens, Lee started to push himself out the window when the innkeeper grabbed his arm. Punching the man in the jaw, the Englishman watched the older man crumple to the floor. "Terribly sorry," Lee apologized.

Something slammed into the door. With just his head above the windowsill, Lee watched as great gashes appeared in the door. Something was chopping its way through with a sword that would rival Brogan's claymore. Not wanting to meet their uninvited guest, Lee scrambled to the ground as fast as possible. Landing on the soft soil, the Englishman ran to the stable. Brogan and Esmeralda already had Alexei hooked up to the cart and were starting to pull it out. Jumping over the side into the rear, Lee raised up as their vehicle passed the front of the inn. The door had been knocked down, and Lee could see the inside of the building was coated with gore. One of the soldiers was sprawled on the front step, a saber in his hand. The arm that the hand belonged to was lying several feet away from the body.

Pulling past the inn, a large bear scratched at the wooden wall of the building. "Shoot that bear," Brogan shouted. "We don't need it following us, too."

Aiming, Lee put a round into its flank and another into its hind leg. As they slipped into the night, Lee saw a large figure emerge from the inn.

12

Dan and Brackish road their horses well beyond sunset. The prairie around them did not provide an inviting place to sleep, and eventually, the prairie gave way to a more barren section of land, so the pair of hunters had to make do. The large rocks and boulders gathered here would provide the man and goblin with shelter and concealment for the night. Brackish sniffed the air. "Something wrong," he stated.

"What is it?" Dan asked, his hand coming to rest on one of his pistols.

"Place of suffering and death," Brackish replied.

"Should we keep going?"

"Good land not near," the goblin explained.

"So, it's this or nothing?"

Brackish nodded. The horses had been carrying on a rapid pace and were wearier than those riding them. "We'll have to rest here tonight. I don't think the horses can go any further," Dan stated.

Dropping down, Brackish stopped and sniffed the prairie that they had crossed. A faint scent caught his nostril. "Wolves," he stated.

"Werewolves or normal wolves?"

"Normal," Brackish confirmed.

"We'll build a fire; that'll keep them away."

Something about the wolves was different; they had a smell of gunpowder and other animals about them. It perplexed the goblin, but he didn't know how to tell Dan. They were not magical or monstrous, just regular wolves, and yet they were also something more. Not wanting to cause problems, the goblin decided to keep his observation to himself until he had something further to add. Gathering what kindling and wood he could find, Dan set up the fire. There was an abundance of rocks to place in a ring to keep the flames contained. Striking a match, Dan set some of the dead grass on fire, and the white smoke rose into the sky. Burning quickly, the grass provided enough of a start for some of the smaller pieces to catch, and in moments the fire was burning nicely.

Taking a piece of meat from last night's meal from his saddlebag, Dan ripped the it in half. Putting his piece in his mouth, the American tossed the remainder to Brackish. Catching the strip of rabbit, Brackish tore a piece off and started to chew. "We should keep watch," Dan offered. "Do you want first or second?"

"First."

Dan looked at his pocket watch. "All right, give me three or four hours," he instructed his partner.

Nodding, Brackish hefted his shotgun over his shoulder and stepped away among the larger rocks, so that the fire would not prevent him from seeing any approaching enemies or give any attackers a tempting shadow. Close enough to hear the crackle of the flames and Dan settling down in a blanket, the goblin listened as his partner started to snore. The goblin marveled at Dan's ability to stay awake for long periods of time, or fall asleep easily when he wanted to.

Knowing that he had some time before Dan's watch, Brackish walked a quick perimeter around the camp they had set up. The horses were tethered near the fire, in hopes that the wolves would leave them alone. The animals were nervous in the area, but they had not attempted to run. Something was wrong with this place. Brackish had smelled many strange scents ever since they arrived in this new country, and he could not identify them all. Keeping his eyes open for anything strange, the goblin continued his nighttime vigil.

The wolves and their masters stayed hidden within the high grass of the plateau. From their vantage point, they could spy on Brackish. Their eyes had been designed for seeing in the dark, and the telescopic lens they had stolen from a Prussian officer allowed them to watch from a distance. The area where they had chosen to sleep was cursed. The screams of men and animals often echoed across the plains. Crossing through the stone field at night, one might survive, but none that slept there ever survived, at least not in the same condition that they arrived.

They sought the warrior, but they would wait to see if he passed beyond the cursed stone field and then take him. For tonight, they would wait until dawn and see what was left of him. Lying down in the fields with the wolves, the watchers wrapped themselves tightly in animal pelts to help mask their scent from the goblin.

In the middle of Brackish's watch, something leapt across the tops of the large boulders. The goblin's sensitive nose caught the smell of old, rotting meat, but he could not see anything. It was approaching the campfire, which had begun to burn low. Rushing back to Dan, the goblin grabbed a few logs and tossed onto the flames.

Feeding off the fresh fuel, the fire blazed up. Brackish looked around for any signs of the oncoming creature. "Dan," the goblin hissed.

Instantly, the American was awake with a hand on his pistol and reaching for his pneumatic pack with the other. Something scrambled on the large boulder behind the man, and Brackish turned to see what manner of fiend was approaching. Before his eyes could find it, the thing leapt onto Dan's back, driving the hunter to the ground. A scrawny man, with giant horns like an elk rising from the crown of his head, was sitting on the American's back, jumping up and down slamming him into the ground. Brackish noticed the goat-like feet and talon-tipped fingers before he saw the strange contraptions hooked around the animal-like legs. The devices were giving off the rotten meat odor.

The creature was saying something as it bounced Dan on the ground. Trying to turn over, the American was unable to dislodge his attacker. Brackish could not risk the shotgun and drew his revolver. Firing a round, the goblin was glad to see that his shot struck the creature's shoulder. It hissed at Brackish and jumped up onto the top of the nearest boulder again. Using the shadows, the monster vanished. Rolling over, Dan aimed at the top of the rock. "What the hell was that?" He demanded.

"No know. Goat feet man," the goblin answered.

"Great," Dan replied. "That could be a lot of different things."

"You hurt?" Brackish asked.

"No," the American replied, knocking on his chest with a clanging sound. "I wore that blasted plate that Lee likes."

"It still here," Brackish cautioned, taking deep breaths to pinpoint the location.

"Cover me," Dan instructed as he shrugged on the pack and engaged the piston. "Let's see what he can do now."

From out of the darkness, a stone sailed at Dan. Ducking, the hunter barely missed the formidable missile. More stones followed, some of them tiny pebbles while others were large enough to brain a man if necessary. The onslaught seemed to be ignoring Brackish. Dan had been

216

struck by several of the pebbles but was able to avoid any serious injury. Grabbing a piece of burning wood, Brackish tossed the torch onto the barren ground. He saw the beast flee from the light. The goblin fired a shot while Dan chased after the shadow with an entire magazine. Ejecting the spent magazine, Dan looked all around, expecting more stones. "Anything?" He asked Brackish while reloading.

The smell of rotted meat was still lurking close by, but the strange winds were keeping Brackish from being able to pinpoint the scent. Leaping from the darkness the horned beast slammed into Dan knocking the stocky hunter onto his back. Punching the creature's face, Dan quickly loosened it. "Ain't so tough when I can see ya, are ya?" The hunter shouted as he squeezed off several shots.

Bounding away into the shadows once more, Dan felt himself getting angry at the elusive monster. Kneeling, he retrieved his Bowie knife from his boot. Shotgun in one hand and his blade in the other, the hunter waited. The creature could not move as silently as it appeared to be doing. Anything with those hooves would make a noise. Listening, Dan could hear the crackle of the fire alone. No other sounds reached his ears. "Brackish?" The American asked.

The goblin shrugged, which meant that he could not pinpoint a location based on smell. *Wonderful,* Dan thought.

He heard the scrape of something sharp on stone behind him. Spinning around, he saw the monster leaping towards him. As its hooved feet dug furrows in the ground upon landing, Dan slammed his knife into the creature's shoulder and twisted the blade, drawing back for another strike. Arterial blood sprayed onto the surrounding rocks, but before Dan could continue his attack, Brackish jumped onto the beast's back, latching

217

onto a horn for stability. Emptying his revolver into the back of its head, the goblin continued to hold on as the dead body fell beneath him.

"Good job," Dan commended his partner. "Reload. There might be more of them."

Grabbing the thick, curled hair between the horns, Dan dragged the beast over and dropped it onto the fire. Brackish looked at the American. "I don't know what kills it," Dan replied. "Although shooting it in the head seems to slow it down, at least."

Brackish continued reloading. It was true that some of their foes had specific methods by which they had to be dispatched, but fire traditionally worked on all of them. As the flames ate at the tissue of the monster, Dan examined the gory trophies adorning its legs and feet. "This is human," he announced, pointing at one section. He moved his finger to a different part. "This is horse."

"It wear people?" Brackish asked.

"These look like ligaments," Dan replied. "If I didn't know any better, I'd say it makes a pair of garters and shoes...well, some kind of coverings for its feet out of them."

Both hunters shuddered at the concept. "Can you smell anything else?"

"Magic here, but less," Brackish replied. "No rotted meat but that." Indicating the fire, Brackish was satisfied that no further monsters were awaiting them among the rocks.

"Well, let me get some rest and wake me when it's time for me to relieve you," Dan stated.

"It time," the goblin smiled.

218

Dan checked his pocket watch. "Damn," he muttered to himself. Brackish watched him expectantly. "Fine, a deal's a deal. I'll watch for a few more hours, and then we need to get moving."

The goblin nodded and curled up in a blanket by the fire. With the carcass adding fuel to it, the flames rose higher, a green tint flickering amongst the edges.

The masters of the wolves sat in the grass watching. They had never seen anyone best the creature before. Most who survived did so leaving blood on their trails. These two beings had thoroughly destroyed the lord of the stone field. Amazed, the riders conferred amongst themselves. The warrior was truly the prize they had sought. His prowess in battle had proven that. Even though the creature was destroyed, the riders refused to venture onto the rock field in the night. They would wait and formulate a plan at a better moment, one that would favor them.

Baba Yaga stared at the wall of her hut, absently scratching at the red agitation on her leg. She was shocked. The eyes of the crow had not lied. The Stuhac had been bested completely. No man had ever managed to defeat the Stuhac without finding his life greatly endangered.

At least, the summoning she had cast worked. From deep within the ground, the force had been called; it required time before it would come to fruition, though. This power might well destroy the Englishman if her weapon did not first catch them and the American that followed him.

Her weapon had never failed in all the millennia that she had used him, but these men and their goblin were proving to be more troublesome than any she had ever encountered. With their blood needed to heal the land, she could not take any chances, and any power at her disposal was worth using.

Dan let his partner sleep for four hours. The sun was just starting to crest the hill when he woke Brackish. The goblin stretched and groaned as he started the day. "The horses seem to be rested," Dan announced. "You ready?"

Wiping sleep from his eyes, Brackish nodded, and Dan handed the goblin some more of the leftover meat. Turning back, he saw movement in the tall grass of the plateau. The man squinted to make out the gray shapes better. "Wolves," Brackish stated.

"They've waited this whole time?" Dan asked.

"Guess so."

"That's not normal," the American commented. "You think Baba Yaga is using them to spy on us?"

"Maybe."

"We'll see if we can't put some distance between us with today's ride," the American announced. "Think we'll catch Lee today?"

Brackish shrugged. "Not too far ahead, but bad things between us."

Dan patted his shotgun. "I came prepared for bad things."

Riding through the barren patch of stony ground, the two hunters made quick time as they came to the farmlands that Lee had passed through the previous evening. A small burn patch marked the field to their right. It was an unremarkable mar on the field. The Polevik had learned their lesson from the previous night, as they did not approach with their pointed black hats showing above the tall stalks within the fields. "Something in field," Brackish whispered to Dan.

Engaging the piston, Dan sat the shotgun across his saddle, keeping a grip near the trigger. "Where?"

"Everywhere."

Farmers were working in the fields and seemed oblivious to any dangers that might be present. A few cast furtive glances at the pair riding through their lands, but the American could not see any dangers, nor did he want to start doubting Brackish's highly tuned sense of smell.

There was only one thing for it, Dan decided, and the duo rode right into the trap. Rushing out in front and behind them, the misshapen dwarf creatures surrounded the duo. As they started to emerge from the fields and flank the hunters, Dan aimed and squeezed the trigger. All eight shots of the shotgun tore through the field and shredded several of the creatures. The others quickly retreated, leaving Dan's side free from threat.

Noticing the crude weapons that the creatures held, Dan was not worried about any type of ranged attack. "Don't let them get close," he told Brackish.

Firing at the nearest creature, the goblin was pleased to see it fall dead, the green blood soaking into the soil. Pumping another round into the shotgun, Brackish looked to see if any of the beasts would challenge them further. Dan reloaded his shotgun and aimed at the roadblock before them. "Move or else," he warned.

The creatures did not flinch at the ultimatum, nor did they show fear of the weapon. Dan hated to wipe the creatures out; they did not seem overly aggressive, but he could not allow them to keep him from finding Lee.

Nudging his horse forward, Dan approached the line. Brackish hesitantly followed. The little figures adjusted their grips on their weapons. Dan lowered the shotgun towards the creatures. The center member of the roadblock turned to look at those on both sides. He gave a shout and the tiny beings swarmed forward. Dan squeezed the trigger and laid waste to the attackers directly in his sight. Drawing his revolver, Brackish cleared a path before his horse. "Ride!" Dan shouted as he felt something cut through his pants and into his leg.

Kicking their horses, the two hunters broke away from their attackers. Several of the small figures clutched onto Dan's saddle but were easily thrown off. Brackish felt the shifting of his saddle. Glancing down, he saw one of the figures trying to climb onto the leather seat behind him. Squeezing the trigger on his revolver, the goblin heard the hammer fall on an empty chamber. Holstering the weapon, Brackish kicked back at the hitchhiker and missed. Almost in the saddle, a mirthless grin spread over the Polevik's face. It was the perfect expression to lose teeth as the goblin swung around with a backhand. The brass prosthetic arm collided with the smiling beast. Blood and teeth spewed forward as the diminutive threat spun off the mount and onto the road.

"Dan!" The goblin shouted.

Turning to look at his partner, the American was confused why the goblin was pointing. Looking around, he could see no further attackers. Raising a questioning eyebrow, Dan received a response. "Pack!"

Slowing the horse down, Dan started unbuckling the straps on the pack. The piston was making a strange sound, like something had blocked it. Peeling off the device, he inspected it, and his suspicions were confirmed. Something had struck the piston and bent the arm. "Damn thing's useless."

A strange sound came from behind them, and they looked to see the creatures now pursuing them on small horses. "This'll fix 'em," Dan stated.

He pulled the cord from the stock of the shotgun and then slammed the rifle stock onto the pressure-regulating pipe between the two tanks and watched the gauge start to creep into the red. As soon as the pack was dropped onto the dirt path, the two hunters returned their animals to a gallop. Dan had to admit, it felt better being on horseback without the contraption, but it also left his back completely exposed. The hunters put as much distance between themselves and the malfunctioning device, listening for the telltale sound. When the explosion sounded behind them, they slowed their mounts.

Glancing back, the goblin and the American saw the great crater blown into the road and fires catching in the dry fields. Most of their enemies were now stains on the soil. A few that had been beyond the initial blast had been killed by shrapnel from the exploding pack. "Lee going be angry," Brackish commented.

"They broke it. I just made sure it wouldn't be making the rest of the trip," Dan replied. "Besides, he'd rather have us get to him in one piece without the pack than die on the way."

"Maybe," Brackish responded with a grin.

"Yeah, I'm going to hear about it," Dan conceded.

Elizabeth stood outside a forest not too far outside London. Her visions predicted more dire consequences for Lee, Dan, and Brackish. In the most recent visions, a blind old woman was standing over their bodies. The girl knew they needed help and could think of only one individual to turn to. Contacting her friend, Kate McKendrick, a girl whom she had met shortly after being rescued by Dan and Lee and also a member of the Seelie Court, Elizabeth had gotten the necessary information to find the being she needed. Ms. Edwards had accompanied the young girl to the nearby inn and stood waiting beside her now. They would have to enter the forest at the right hour or wait another day.

"Are you sure about this?" The older woman asked.

"Positive," Elizabeth answered. "Something's wrong with the old woman in my visions. She's blind, but she shouldn't be. I think something is keeping her from seeing the truth."

Ms. Edwards did not understand but knew to trust the girl. The older woman also trusted who they were coming to visit. Glancing at the sun over her shoulder, Elizabeth nodded, and together the two ladies entered the forest.

Shortly after noon, the duo came upon the scene at the inn. The body of the dead man at the door had been ravaged, his severed arm now missing, dragged away by a scavenger. Seeing the carnage, Dan and Brackish stopped their horses and dismounted. Each hunter holding close to their shotgun, they flanked the empty doorframe. Brackish was the first to move, sweeping low across the room. Dan quickly followed, ensuring that nothing came from the stairs.

224

Several bodies were scattered around the room. Even with the carnage and segmented corpses, Dan recognized the military uniforms that the men had been wearing. "Lee here," Brackish stated, sniffing the air. "Not now, last night."

"Anything else?" Dan asked, keeping his eyes on the different possible hiding places.

Brackish took in another deep breath, trying to pick up any scents above the iron tang of the blood. "Old magic, gone," the goblin replied.

Something fell over upstairs. Pressing the shotgun firmly against his shoulder, Dan started up the stairs. The door to the second room on the next floor had been beaten in, and something whimpered within. Brackish patted Dan on the back, their sign to proceed. Hurrying around the doorframe, Dan searched the room, finally finding the source of the noise. It was the innkeeper, hunched in the corner with fear etched into his face. "What happened to you?" Dan asked.

The man muttered something in Prussian and then moaned again. "He okay?" Brackish asked.

"I don't think so," the American responded. "Whatever happened last night, he must have had a front row seat."

Reaching down to shake the man, Dan managed to place his hand on the shocked innkeeper's shoulder when the man flailed and began shouting. Backing away, Dan shared a confused look with Brackish. "We leave?" The goblin suggested. "Lee go through window."

Seeing the sheets tied together, he inspected the window. There were tracks in the mud around back. The flailing man in the corner was clearly going to be of no help. The American agreed with Brackish, and the duo made their way back out to the front of the inn. "What happened after they escaped?" Dan inquired.

Brackish sniffed the ground and recognized the familiar scents that he had been tracking. "This way," he pointed.

Gathering the horses, Dan and Brackish rode after their friend, but Brackish stopped his horse only moments later. A new scent had just appeared on the wind, close and dangerous. Realizing his traveling companion wasn't with him, Dan turned around in his saddle to see what the issue was. "What…" Dan started.

The question fell away as his horse was swatted. A wounded bear had rounded the inn and rushed Dan's horse. The mount's neck snapped as the large paw connected with the horse's muzzle. With his mount lying on his leg, Dan tried to work the shotgun around to fire, but the weapon was violently jerked from his hands as the bear lashed out again.

Realizing the peril his partner was in, Brackish kicked his horse forward, but the animal refused to budge, and the goblin had to fight to keep it steady. The goblin fired his shotgun, but the buckshot missed the animal; now, the creature knew the dangers and backed away. Drawing his revolvers, Dan fired into the retreating creature's shoulders, taking notice of its lame leg and the bloody wound in the limb, and continued shooting into the exposed hindquarters until his pistols were empty. The beast vanished back around the side of the inn. Without the bear right on top of him, Dan worked his leg free and flexed the muscles and joints. "You okay?" The goblin asked, rotating his view to see both possible corners of the inn.

"I'll be all right, bruised but not broken," Dan commented.

Grabbing his shotgun, he saw that the magazine had broken loose and tried to fix it back into place when he saw the pieces that held it had broken free as well. Dan tossed the useless weapon away after emptying the shells from the magazine. Freeing his gear from the dead horse, the American retrieved his backup pump-action shogun along with any necessary gear and started to load it onto Brackish's horse. "This is going to be a bit awkward," Dan stated.

"What?" The goblin asked.

Dan mounted behind his smaller partner. "This."

"Wait," Brackish instructed.

The goblin crawled under Dan's arm and stood on the rear of the horse. A moment later, rope worked its way around Dan. Brackish was safely secured to the American. With the goblin facing the rear and the American looking ahead, they would be harder to surprise. "Did you see the bullet wound in that bear's leg?" Dan asked.

The goblin nodded.

"It looked about the right size for a shot from Lee's Winchester," Dan commented. "I'd be willing to bet he had a run in with that creature."

"It not near," Brackish stated.

Walking the horse across the field, and keeping a wide berth of the inn, the hunters continued on their path. The bear had lain down near the rear corner of the building, barely visible to the hunters, ripping at some meat. Neither hunter voiced the question that came to mind.

Dan noticed tracks following the hoof prints, a man's footprints. "What do you make of it?"

"Old magic," Brackish warned.

Dan kept his eyes on the path, hoping to track the enigmatic individual. A few miles from the inn, the footprints met up with more bear tracks, and from there, the bear tracks led the way. "Hold on," Dan instructed.

Brackish wasn't sure what he was supposed to hold onto; he was already tied to the other hunter. A moment later, Dan spurred the horse, and the goblin found himself being jostled violently.

Staying to the trees and fields, the wolves and their riders watched the hunters battle the monstrous bear, a creature of the old ways. The wolves rode silently after the American and the goblin, remaining out of sight but never far away.

13

While Dan and Brackish camped among the rock, Esmeralda, Brogan, and Lee continued away from the inn guided by a kerosene lantern's light.

"What do you make of the bear back there?" Brogan asked.

"I saw a saddle on it," Lee commented, "so it is a safe assumption that whatever caused the carnage at the inn was riding it."

"Is good you shot bear, means rider need new mount," Esmeralda added. "If it rides bear, Old Mother sent it."

"That is a comforting thought," Lee replied. "How much further must we travel?"

"Another day, perhaps," Esmeralda answered. "We be with my cousin soon. Then you go to battle."

"Can your cousin cook?" Brogan asked.

"Men, always think with stomach," their Prussian escort commented.

"I'm getting tired of dried meat," Brogan added.

"A home-cooked meal will be nice, especially given our rushed exodus from the inn," Lee stated.

"Once safe distance from inn, you can hunt if you like," Esmeralda offered.

Brogan shrugged. "I don't mind snaring a rabbit or two."

"Food can wait. I agree with Esmeralda that our priority should be distancing ourselves from our attacker."

Brogan opened his mouth to protest when a barb-tipped arrow shot out of the darkness and thudded into the wooden wagon. "Goblins!" The Scotsman yelled, raising his shotgun.

Esmeralda pushed Alexei into a gallop. As the horse sped up, the cart became harder to stand in. Lee sat up quickly, his Winchester pressed tightly to his shoulder. "Anything?" He asked.

"No," Brogan repeated.

"Is too dark," Esmeralda stated. "The eyes watching us are better suited to the night."

"Times like these, I wish Brackish was here. His eyes and nose would serve us well," Lee commented.

"Sorry, Lee. You're stuck with me and my standard human senses," Brogan replied, firing two rounds into the darkness.

The only thing that the Scotsman could discern by the little illumination from the blasts was a bit of dirt road and trees. "How long does this bloody forest go?" He asked.

"Long enough," Esmeralda replied.

Something whistled between the two hunters in the rear of the cart, and Esmeralda grunted. "Esmeralda?" Lee questioned.

"Is fine," she replied. "Keep watch."

"This is foolish," Brogan stated as he took one of the kerosene lanterns that he had procured from the inn's stable and lit the wick.

Unscrewing the top, the hunter tossed the instrument into the middle of their path. The kerosene connected with the flame and blazed to life, sending several dark forms retreating from the light. Lee opened fire on the fleeing shadows, and two of the shapes dropped. The Englishman sent bullets after other figures retreating into the darkness and hoped that his shots found their marks. Looking ahead, he saw something protruding from Esmeralda's shoulder. He reached for the object but stopped when he saw the feathers jutting from the stick. "Brogan," Lee called.

The Scotsman turned his eyes from the road. "Lass, you've been shot," he announced.

"Is nothing," she replied, her voice weaker than it had been.

"Goblin arrows are most definitely not nothing," Lee stated.

The Englishman reached around her and took the reins from her hands. Pulling back, he slowed Alexei to a stop. "Must keep going," she tried to protest.

"We've got to get that arrow out of you first," Lee replied firmly. "Goblins live in less than ideal conditions, and the longer that bolt is in your shoulder, the more likely that it will become infected, which may prove deadly."

Guiding the horse off the road, Lee tethered the animal and helped Brogan get Esmeralda down from the driver's bench. Her face was pale, and she was sweating. Supporting the wounded woman, Lee looked at their surroundings. "We need a fire, a big one to keep those goblins away," Lee instructed.

Hurrying into the darkness, Brogan went in search of the necessary materials. "Is foolish. Need to keep going," Esmeralda protested.

"Not just yet, we don't," Lee replied. "Once the arrow is out of your shoulder, and you've been patched up, then we'll continue."

"Is fine," she repeated.

"No, it is not," Lee stated, his resolve solid as granite. "It will only take a moment to remove the arrow. A few more to stitch it closed and bandage it properly. Besides, Alexei could use the rest."

"Fool horse, should have butchered for meat long ago," the Prussian complained.

"Why did you name him Alexei?" Lee asked, trying to keep her mind off the projectile lodged in her back.

"Was boy in school, cute and like horse, very dumb."

Lee chuckled. "I do believe you would get along very well with my traditional partner, Dan Winston."

"You take me to England, I be pleased to meet him," Esmeralda commented. "With Old Mother after us, the sooner away from this cursed land, the better."

"Why do you think the land is cursed?" The Englishman inquired.

"Snow should be up to ankle by now," Esmeralda commented. "Look about, nothing. Is no snow, no howling winds, the land has forsaken us."

"At least it's still giving up wood," Brogan replied, returning with enough wood for the fire. "No sign of the goblins. I think we may have ridden far enough away from them."

"Let's hope," Lee replied as he assisted Brogan in setting up the wood to burn.

With a roaring fire going, the two hunters set about the tools they would need to remove the arrow from Esmeralda's shoulder. Using an old cooking pot from the rear of the wagon, Brogan collected water from a nearby lake and put it on the fire to boil. "My sword isn't good for this business," the Scotsman stated.

"Don't worry," Lee replied, drawing his dagger. "I will take care of the delicate work."

"Good," Esmeralda commented. "Big man is brute - all muscle like bear."

"You people love bears," the Scotsman retorted.

"Bears no do surgery in Prussia," she responded.

"Comforting thought," Lee said.

Placing the edge of his dagger in the flames, the Englishman waited for the fire to heat the blade to kill any bacteria. Satisfied that it was hot enough, Lee tore Esmeralda's shawl to free it from the arrow. Revealing her slender, pale shoulder, he took a deep breath to steady his hand. With Brogan holding tightly to the dark, wooden shaft, and Esmeralda biting down on the hem of her shawl, Lee made two slits alongside the arrow head. His Prussian patient's blood ran rich and red, which let Lee know the wound wasn't poisoned. Gently pulling, the hunters freed the cruel weapon from Esmeralda's shoulder. The forged metal tip had several cruel barbs that dripped crimson.

Dropping his handkerchief in the boiling water, Lee used his knife to remove it and gently laid it across the fresh wound. Drawing in a hiss of breath, Esmeralda bit down on the rough cloth and waited for the pain to subside. Satisfied that the bleeding had slowed down and the wound was cleaned, Lee stepped aside. "Go pull a hair from the horse's tail," Brogan instructed.

Lee gave a confused look and then realized that he had not been thinking of how they were going to stitch the wound closed. Alexei was less than willing to provide the needed equipment, but Lee managed to retrieve the hair. Brogan stood by the fire, the pot of water in his hands. Taking the hair, the Scotsman drug it through the bubbling liquid and shook it out. "I saw some mint leaves growing over there. Go pick as many as you can find," the Scotsman instructed.

Taking a larger piece of flaming wood from the fire, Lee went in search of the plant. It took him a few moments to locate the trove of strong-smelling leaves. Picking as many as he could find, Lee returned with several handfuls of the herb to find Brogan almost finished stitching the wound. Esmeralda would have a scar, but it was better than dealing with a goblin arrow in her shoulder. With silent fascination, the Englishman watched his Scottish counterpart finish his work. "Did you get that mint?" Brogan asked.

"Right here," Lee answered, handing some to Brogan.

Crushing the leaves, Brogan smeared them on the freshly closed cut. Admiring his handiwork, he stepped back. Having re-boiled Lee's handkerchief, the Scotsman took the wrung-out cloth and used it as a bandage. Lee tore the sleeves off his shirt and handed them to the kilted hunter. Nodding, Brogan used the re-purposed fabric to hold the bandage in place. "It's not the prettiest work you'll ever see, but it should get us to your cousin," the Scotsman proclaimed.

A moment later, shots rang out through the night. Dropping to the ground, the two hunters pulled Esmeralda down with them, careful to keep her shoulder out of the dirt. Crawling forward, Lee peered over a downed tree. The muzzle flash of the weapons gave away the positions of the shooters. A lone goblin cry carried across the difference before a final gunshot sounded. Silence set in around them, the sounds of the crackling fire the only noise. "Help me douse the fire," Brogan whispered.

Hurriedly, the two men went about throwing dirt and water onto the flames that had provided them with much-needed light. Once they

234

were satisfied it was out, they set about loading Esmeralda into the rear of the wagon. "You stay with her," Lee instructed.

Climbing up beside the Prussian, Brogan had his shotgun at the ready. Lee climbed up on the driver's bench and guided Alexei back onto the road. With a single lantern to guide them, the Englishman had to take the road slowly or risk breaking the wheel on an obstacle that might lie ahead. "What do you think that was all about?" Brogan asked, his voice just soft enough to be heard over the sounds of the wagon.

"I would guess that some soldiers found our goblin adversaries and dealt with them," Lee replied.

"That's good," the Scotsman said. "Less for us to worry about."

"Unless the Prussian soldiers find us," Lee stated. "I do not think they would view foreign troops kindly, nor do I think that they would have mercy on Esmeralda for assisting us."

"Do you think they saw the fire?" The Scotsman continued.

"Most likely, but I'm hoping that they have more pressing concerns."

"Prussian troops have many worries," Esmeralda replied. "I have heard tales of sabotage."

"Maybe, some of our boys are out there," Brogan offered.

Esmeralda drifted into unconsciousness and dropped against Brogan. "Either way, we need to get her to her cousin's home as soon as possible," Lee said. "Besides, if it is our boys, we can't guarantee they won't shoot us thinking we're Prussian troops."

"You've made your point," the Scotsman agreed. "Do we have any of that dried meat left?"

Digging through the satchel under the bench, Lee felt the rough texture of the field rations and passed it over his shoulder. "We're going to have to get some more supplies soon," the Englishman added.

"I would love something fresh, but it doesn't seem like we've had much opportunity to find anything. Best chance we had was passing through those farms," the Scotsman grumbled.

"Perhaps we'll find some more farms," Lee suggested.

Brogan did not reply, but Lee could hear him chewing on the tough beef.

From within the confines of her hut held aloft on the oversized legs of chickens, the Baba Yaga laughed, a sound of cruelty to rival a goblin's cackle. Boulders crumbled and rolled down onto houses, rivers flooded beyond their banks, all because the Baba Yaga laughed. She was powerful, more powerful than most would ever assume, powerful enough to wake a great, sleeping evil that had lain dormant for many generations. But now, it was in place, and the trap had been set. It was simple, but with the circumstances of her enemies, she knew it would work.

Long ago, great civilizations were lain to waste by great beasts that existed long before Baba Yaga. Some even found the remains of these beasts and became tainted. These tainted became the creatures, living in small pockets, always staying near the source of their curse. One such place the hunters must pass through. The Old Mother had woken sleeping devils, summoning them from the history before man had built cities, and they would take the English hunter to Hell for her.

The sun crested the horizon and revealed a small village nearby, smoke pouring from the stone chimneys. Short, squat stone and mortar buildings populated the landscape. "What do you think?" Brogan asked, wiping the sleep from his eyes.

"I think you need to cover up, and Esmeralda should wake up. I'm going to be her mute brother again," Lee explained.

Rousing Esmeralda, Brogan explained the plan. Lee slid the rough canvas cloak over his shoulders to cover his uniform. "Do you know anyone here?" Lee asked as Esmeralda sat on the bench beside him.

"Ni," she replied. "Never seen village. Before you become mute, I am wanting to say thank you."

"I'm just glad that you weren't hurt too bad," Lee stated, feeling the heat in his cheeks.

The Prussian woman leaned across the bench and kissed Lee. It was warm and welcome, and though the Englishman did not know how to react, he knew that this was a moment that would be forever seared on his memory. He blushed harder as she pulled away. "Cute when you blush," she commented, winking at the hunter.

Lee chose to focus his attention on the road in front of them. "When's the last time you visited your cousin?" The Englishman asked, his discomfort forgotten by Esmeralda's comment about the village.

"Year, year and half, why?" She replied.

"Look at the village; it is much older than that. I would say it has been here for a long time, given the distress on the cabins," he commented. "I don't think we should stop. You'll need to keep going, fast."

"Trouble?" Brogan asked from underneath his canvas cover.

"Maybe," Lee stated. "If you hear me, pop up ready for the worst."

"Gladly."

Alexei worked up to a good pace, not so fast they would draw unwanted attention but fast enough to indicate their intentions to pass through. The small fountain in the center of town was empty. Lee quickly noted not a single soul about; even though dawn had broken, the village was eerily quiet. Retrieving his Winchester from behind the bench, Lee laid the weapon across his knees with his hand resting near the trigger. "If anyone sees, many questions will be asked," Esmeralda cautioned.

"I'm more concerned with being unprepared," Lee replied.

Esmeralda shrugged as she guided Alexei along the street through the center of the village. The doors to the cottages opened simultaneously, and Lee started to raise his rifle. When the occupants of the village rushed forward, he was amazed and terrified at what he saw. Strange humanoids loped towards them, crude weapons of wood and stone raised. The most shocking point was their luminescent green skin. "Devil's Blight," Lee mumbled. The Englishman had encountered similar creatures with Dan in America. They were persistent, never straying too far from their territory, and would kidnap people for food or to create more of their number. Rousing himself and taking aim, Lee squeezed the trigger, shooting the nearest of the damned creatures. "Brogan!"

The Scotsman tossed off his cover and sat up. His shotgun began to roar, striking the rushing hordes. "GO, WOMAN!" Brogan shouted.

Esmeralda, shocked by their attackers, came to her senses and urged Alexei on. The horse, terrified by the unnatural creatures attacking, galloped down the road. Lee took careful aim and put bullets directly between the creatures' eyes. "Why aren't they staying down?" Brogan asked as he reloaded his shotgun.

"Long story," Lee replied. "We have to put enough distance between us, and they'll give up, but they won't die."

"Don't seem right," the Scotsman commented as he tried to thin out the approaching attackers.

"It's not," Lee replied. "Just keep shooting until we're far enough away that they can't reach us."

The first of the creatures grabbed for Alexei's reins. Sensing the danger, the horse moved away. "Not so dumb," Esmeralda praised the animal as the wheel slammed over the misshaped body.

Lee took careful note of the sloping brow and large, bulging jaws of the creatures. He recognized them as Cro-Magnons, a group of early humans long extinct. There was no doubt in Lee's mind that the Baba Yaga was behind this latest threat. Alexei halted and reared back, kicking out with his front legs. The hoofs met the obstruction with wet, thumping sounds. Lee almost lost his footing and saw the circle of green men surrounding them. "We'll run out of bullets before long," Brogan commented.

Dropping to the road, Lee made a hasty, poorly thought out plan. "Once I clear the path, go," he instructed.

"Are you bloody mad?!"

Lee shrugged and started towards the monsters in their path. It was quick work to shoot several of them; they fell and writhed about as their unnatural bodies healed. When the Winchester clicked empty, he drew his revolver and utilized the remaining six shots he had. Counting off the shots, a wry smile crossed Lee's face. *It seems that Dan has rubbed off on me.* He thought as he prepared to find out what the beasts planned for him.

As Lee's last shot fired into his enemies, Brogan rushed past. The great claymore held aloft. With the warrior spirit of his Celtic ancestors, Brogan waded into the poorly armed beasts. His sword cleaved his enemies and separated arms and heads from bodies. The evil beings took longer to recover from these grievous wounds. "Get on the wagon," Brogan ordered.

Reloading, Lee climbed into the rear of the cart and took up Brogan's shotgun. The rear flank of the approaching beasts was too close for comfort. Unloading the rifle, Lee dropped his companion's weapon and raised his own. Something slammed into his arm, and it went numb, making him drop his own rifle. Glancing over the side, he saw one of the Cro-Magnons wielding an ancient sling. The slope-browed brute was twirling the leather above his head again, looking to take another shot at the hunter. "Go!" Brogan shouted.

The Scotsman had seen what Lee was trying to do and had cleared the path before them. Esmeralda slapped the reins, and Alexei rushed into the gap. Stepping over the strange blood and severed body parts, the horse cleared the villains. Brogan hopped onto the rear of the wagon, wiping his stained blade on the canvas. "Look out!" Lee warned as he stretched his hand out behind Brogan.

Lee gave a sharp cry and something struck solidly behind Brogan. Turning around, he saw a bloody stone fall to the dirt road. Lee cradled his injured hand. "What the bloody hell was that?" the Scotsman asked.

"Sling," Lee stated through gritted teeth. "It was aimed at your head."

Esmeralda was glancing over her shoulder. "You, big oaf, come take reins," she demanded.

Not one to argue with a woman, Brogan took over Alexei and switched positions with the Prussian. "Sit." Lee did as he was instructed. "Let me see."

Not looking at the injury, Lee put his hand out to her, keeping his eyes on the world behind them. The Devil's Blight he had encountered in America had continued their pursuit for several miles. Lee could not see any sign of that here, which bothered him more than if they had been rushing to catch them. His attention was drawn back to his hand as a sharp pain erupted within it, and his vision swam. He tried to draw back, but Esmeralda held tightly. "Hurt?" She inquired.

"Yes," he wheezed.

"Bones broken," she replied calmly. "Can stabilize, but you need doctor."

"So... do... you," Lee countered, his vision clearing.

"Hush," Esmeralda whispered, patting Lee on the shoulder. "Will take only a minute."

Cutting two strips of wood as wide as Lee's hand from the side of the wagon, she shoved these down into his sleeve and pressed his injury between them. "Is going to hurt," she warned.

Lee nodded, not trusting himself to speak. Cutting a strip from the canvas, she wrapped the wood. When the cloth was tightened, and his hand was immobilized between the wood, Lee thought he would pass out. A moment later, the pressure was still there, but the pain was now just a dull throbbing. As his stomach threatened to expel what little contents it had, the hunter tried to remember what he had been thinking before Esmeralda had caused the eruption of pain.

Re-grasping the threads of his thoughts, Lee realized what was driving his concern. "Why aren't they coming after us?" He asked.

Brogan shrugged his shoulders and kept Alexei at a gallop. "Perhaps they do not leave their village," Esmeralda offered.

"Stop the wagon," Lee replied.

"Are you bloody mad?!"

"Stop the wagon!"

Pulling back on the reins, Brogan brought the wagon to a halt. "Why are we stopping?" The Scotsman demanded.

"Something about this doesn't seem right to me," Lee explained. "The creatures that we encountered should be after us. The fact that they are not makes me curious as to what lies ahead."

With a raised eyebrow, Brogan turned back to the road ahead of them. Handing the Scotsman his shotgun, Lee climbed off the wagon and took Alexei's reins. Brogan stepped down and stood on the other side of the horse. The Englishman began walking forward, with the horse following closely. "What are we looking for?" Brogan asked.

Esmeralda started to climb back onto the driver's bench. "Stay in the back and keep your head down," Lee ordered. The Prussian woman complied. "Anything out of the ordinary? A tripwire, an oddly laying branch, anything. The ones I encountered managed to stop a steam engine. Even though these creatures are ancient, I imagine a horse-pulled wagon does not provide them with a great challenge."

"What about that?" Brogan asked, pointing to a strange disk lying on the side of the path.

"Maybe," Lee replied as he dropped the reins and carefully approached the object.

It was a small metal disk. The composition appeared to be bronze or copper, but the hunter was hesitant to get too close. As he procured a stone from the path, he had to awkwardly shift his Winchester underneath his arm. If a trap was sprung, it would take him longer than he'd like to ready the weapon. Stepping back, he tossed the rock onto the disk with a ringing clang. Nothing happened. "It appears that…" Lee was interrupted by thudding into the road ahead of them.

Turning towards the noise, he saw crude, barbaric arrows landing into the path in front of them. "Bloody clever," Brogan commented.

"I knew this was too easy," Lee stated.

"What now?" The Scotsman asked.

"Wait until they finish shooting and continue on."

"We need to hurry," Esmeralda added, pointing behind them.

The club-wielding monsters had held back, waiting until the hunters sprung the trap. Expecting to find wounded or dead opponents, the creatures were grunting their excitement. They were organized and intelligent to a startling degree, which gave Lee no small amount of discomfort. "Esmeralda, you're going to have to get up here on Alexei. Brogan, guide them ahead and keep an eye out for any other traps."

Esmeralda hurried and climbed onto the broad back of the horse. "Try to keep step, lad," Brogan commented as he started to hurry the horse down the road, wary of any further disks in their path.

Waiting as the wooden vehicle passed by, Lee stood watching the approaching crowd. He knew once he started shooting that the creatures would hurry towards him, and his brass chestplate would do little to protect

243

him from the rain of arrows once the calm was breached. Still, a plan was formulating. An incredibly dangerous plan, but this was an incredibly dangerous situation. The beasts could see that their prey had not been incapacitated, but they still did not rush after them, which told Lee that more traps awaited them. The Englishman would have to trust his Scottish counterpart to notice and avoid the deadly snares. Judging the expanse of broken arrow shafts and the distance that Brogan had covered, Lee began to feel comfortable with his plan. Stepping beside the disk, Lee took aim on the first of the creatures.

He put a round directly through the monster's eye, and it fell. The other abominations screeched and rushed towards the hunter. He shot those that he could and waited as they gained ground on him. Satisfied that their headlong charge could not be stopped, Lee raised his foot and firmly slammed it on top of the disk. Turning and running after Brogan, Lee watched as the first of the dark shapes flew into the air. As they approached him, he slowed and waited, luring them forward and only diving into the tall grass to the side of the road at the last minute. Shouts of shock and surprise rose from the path. This time, the arrows did not make their dull thumping sound but a rich, wet, ripping noise. One arrow fell short of its brethren – a solitary arrow that missed the path and buried itself into Lee's forearm. The wood from the makeshift splint parted for the arrow head, and the projectile cleanly passed through his appendage.

Biting back the scream of pain and shock, Lee waited as he heard the last of the arrows fall. Quickly standing, the hunter waved to his companions and urged them to remain silent. The tainted Cro-Magnons had been pierced multiple times and were effectively pinned to the road. From the far end of the fields, something was thrashing through the dying vegetation. Holding his wounded arm against his side, Lee ran to his friends. "We should be safe for the moment. We need to ride quickly and carefully. They may have more traps ahead," Lee cautioned.

"Good Lord," Brogan exclaimed in a whisper, when he saw the wooden shaft protruding from Lee's arm.

"Oaf, you drive," Esmeralda instructed. "I tend to him."

Lee climbed into the back with assistance from Brogan. The Scotsman wasted no time in driving Alexei further down the road after helping Lee up. Esmeralda examined the latest wound. "You are not very good at this," she stated, matter of factly.

"Traditionally, my partner is the one that does the most dangerous work," Lee replied.

"Next time, send him to war," she retorted.

"I just might."

"Is going to hurt," the Prussian offered.

"I never had any doubts," the Englishman responded.

As Esmeralda started to remove the weapon from Lee's forearm, the Englishman realized just how right she was. The pain of his latest injury with the dull throb of his hand and the exhaustion from the past few days caused Lee to pass out.

14

Dan and Brackish continued on their surviving horse, trying to draw as close as possible to Lee. "Blood," Brackish declared.

Slowing the horse, Dan drew one of his revolvers. "Where?"

"Ahead," the goblin answered. "Human and goblin, not old."

Carefully moving forward, Dan kept a keen eye on the landscape around them. Brackish would have warned if he had smelled more goblins, but that did not mean that the little monsters weren't about. A spot in the road had several of their cruel weapons scattered around. Wheel tracks told Dan that the wagon with Lee in it had kept moving. A small, dried puddle of red blood sat in the dirt. "Is it Lee's?" Dan asked his partner.

Brackish shook his head. "Other human, not Lee."

Several darker pools of goblin blood were spattered in the dirt as well. Untying Brackish, the American dropped to the ground and waded into the dying plants that bordered the roadway where he found the remains of a few goblins. Scavengers had been at them. A familiar, dangerous-looking print sat nearby, the same that they had been following – the thing that was stalking Lee. Brackish sniffed the air, a confused look on his face. "What's wrong?" The American asked.

"Englishmen over there," he pointed. "Not Lee. Blood and battle happen in field."

"We need to keep after Lee."

"I know," Brackish agreed. "Is odd."

"I won't argue that, but what about this whole blasted mess isn't?" The man replied. "Why in blazes is an old witch in Prussia going so hard after Lee, when there are clearly other British forces here? It puts a bad taste in my mouth."

The goblin nodded, even though he did not understand the expression. He had not seen Dan eat anything recently.

The Baba Yaga threw a centuries-old pot across the crowded interior of her hut. Devils pulled from the very ground had failed her. They were to have killed the hunters and the traitorous woman helping them, but the men had managed to elude them. She tried to console herself. Even in their failure, the green beast men had managed to slow the hunters down, and her truest weapon was oh so close. Soon, it would no longer matter.

The wolves refused to eat the little meat that remained on the goblin corpses, but their riders pulled ribs from the carnage and gave to the woodland predators. As the animals crunched into the bone to drain the marrow, the riders watched the human and the goblin heading onwards. Keeping watchful eyes, the masters of the wolves kept their animal pelts pulled close. This was no place for any living creature. Stories had begun to spread of the things that had taken up residence nearby, great beasts that killed all they encountered. Man and beast alike were shown no mercy. Wanting to be done with the place, the riders climbed back onto their canine mounts and followed the hunters at a safe distance.

Brackish was still following the scent of human blood when he and Dan came to a small clearing. A fire had been hastily extinguished and a bloody goblin arrow carelessly thrown among the weeds. Brackish sniffed the ground. "It not Lee blood," the goblin answered the unasked question; sniffing the arrow, he continued. "It woman. They go.," He paused, sniffing the air. "Something bad that way."

"What?" Dan inquired, adjusting his grip on the shotgun.

"Don't know," the goblin confessed. "New scent."

"Is it magic?"

"Don't know," Brackish repeated.

"I hate surprises," Dan complained.

Brackish rolled his eyes; Dan was always hating one thing or another. "Lee not far ahead," the goblin commented, returning to the horse.

The wind shifted, and Brackish caught a different scent. It was the wolves and another scent: animal musk mixed with black powder. Squinting, the goblin could make out movement behind them. It was faint. Since the creatures posed no danger, the short hunter did not inform his partner of their continuing shadows.

As the hunters continued their journey, Dan could feel the horse slowing down. It was not only slowing but acting as if it didn't want to continue ahead. "Stay in the saddle," Dan instructed as he handed the reins over to his partner and took his shotgun with him.

Taking hold of the bridle, he began moving forward, guiding the animal beside him. As the horse tried to pull free, the American felt a twinge of pain in his recently mended arm. *Well, the doctor did tell you to not take it too hard,* Dan reminded himself. Promptly ignoring his thoughts, the American pulled the horse forward. It looked like a village lay ahead of them. It wasn't anything special, at least not by what Dan could see, but something was off about it, because the horse suddenly stopped walking altogether. Looking at the animal, Dan could see the whites of its eye; the horse was terrified. "Brackish?" The American asked.

Dan heard the familiar sound of Brackish's shotgun as the goblin readied the weapon. Not forcing the animal forward, the man tested which way the animal passed easiest. Heading off the road to pass around the village, the mount was still cautious but did not show the terror that it previously had. "Did Lee go through there?" Dan asked.

"Yes," Brackish confirmed.

"If we came out the other side, we should be able to pick his trail up," Dan commented, mainly to himself. "We don't have too long before it'll be dark."

"No stay here," the goblin replied. "New thing bad, smell blood, spoiled."

"Comforting," Dan mumbled as he led the horse into the woods.

The forest was serene as they walked under the boughs of the trees and continued on through the sanctuary of the woods and into a field. Sections of the plant life looked like they had been trampled recently. "Keep alert," the American instructed.

The goblin kept his head moving around, scanning their surroundings with the shotgun held loosely against his shoulder. The village to their left appeared to be deserted except for the smoke rising from the chimneys of the quaint, stone cottages... with no signs of life around them. It was enough to give Dan pause. Something was wrong, and all the better if he could avoid it. Cutting around the side of the village, the American kept an eye on the hauntingly quiet village. "Something past village," Brackish announced in a whisper.

Dan stopped beyond the edge of the eerie homes. Rising from the roadway out of the village was a green-glowing figure that could not be mistaken. Twice before, Dan had encountered a similar monster made of modern man. The prehistoric throwback was clearly afflicted in the same manner. A multitude of crude stone arrows pierced the creature as it gurgled, poisonous blood spilling onto the soil. Dan had heard the blood of the Devil's Blight would permanently kill soil, but the American had never tried to test the theory and did not plan on starting now. "Brackish, if anything like that gets close, we have to run," the American explained.

So far, they were safe. None of the creatures had seen them, but more of them were rising from the roadway, arrows protruding from their bodies. Dan knew it was a safe bet that he and Brackish would eventually be seen. A large group of them was just cresting the short rise ahead, bows slung over their shoulders. "Any sign of Lee?"

Brackish sniffed the air, his senses trying to find his clanmate amidst the strange odors. "He left here, still going," Brackish replied.

"Sounds like a great idea," Dan stated. "We're going to have to push the horse onward and circle around their territory."

Brackish slid back so that Dan could climb onto the mount. Tying themselves together, Dan kicked the horse in the sides. As soon as the hooves started their frantic gallop, the strange pre-men gave chase, rushing into the field seeking fresh meat. Dan pressed hard upon the horse's flanks, trying to hold on. The animal responded to the threat by running even faster, a thick lather building on its sides. A boom from Brackish's shotgun alerted the American that their pursuers were too close for comfort.

One of the heavy ammunition bags would have to be dropped. Retrieving a stick of dynamite from his boot, Dan struggled to strike a match, light the fuse, and guide their mount all at the same time. Finally, he saw the sparks fly as the fuse ignited. Reaching back, he stuffed the explosive into the canvas sack. "Cut the bag free," he shouted over his shoulder to Brackish.

Not knowing why, the goblin reached for his dagger. "Which one?" He asked.

"The smoking one!". Slicing through the leather strap, Brackish watched as the bag fell from the horse. Freed from its burden, the horse gained speed. "They stop," Brackish informed Dan.

"Keep your head down!" The American shouted.

He thought the monsters might be curious, but even if not, the surprise he packed for them would put a dent in their pursuit. Crouching low in the saddle, Dan heard the echoing explosion and felt the pressure wave beat on his back. With theirs ears ringing, the hunters pushed on. Dan knew they had to be off Lee's trail now, but if those big-browed beasts were infected with Devil's Blight, then the danger they still posed to him and Brackish was very real. The goblin looked through the smoky haze and debris, searching for a sign of their attackers. With all the irritants in the air, his nose was useless. Nothing seemed to move from within the zone of destruction. "Clear!" Brackish shouted.

Dan gave a small thumbs-up but kept the horse running, and then something struck the dirt ahead of them. Squinting, Dan recognized the crude wooden shaft. The creatures they were trying to flee had started to fire at them. Turning the horse, the hunter entered thicker brush, heading in a line directly away from the village and the road that Lee had taken. Angry at having to put more distance between himself and his absent partner, the American gritted his teeth and continued on his current path. Once they had put enough ground between themselves and their pursuers, he would guide them back towards the road. Hopefully, this would not put too much distance between them and Lee. With the hunters having returned empty-handed, it meant that Lee could not have been too far ahead. Pushing these thoughts aside, Dan concentrated on surviving this encounter.

The riders and wolves watched from a safe place as the strange creatures chased after the hunters. It would do no good for the watchers to attack; they would surely be destroyed by these monsters. Mounting their wolves, they rode in a wide arc, keeping the man and goblin on their left.

Riding for several miles, Dan's hearing had returned, and he could hear the shrieks of his enemies. As the calls diminished, Brackish tapped Dan's shoulder. "What?"

"They go back," Brackish informed his partner.

Pulling back on the horse's reins, Dan slowed the animal and turned to look the way they had ridden. The sick, green glow that marked the horde was fading away, headed back towards the "harmless," quaint village. Finding his bearings, Dan tried to calculate the best direction for them to travel so that they would avoid the monsters and rejoin the road. Unhooking Brackish, the American was in the process of dismounting when the horse gave a weak whinny and collapsed. Glad to have landed on top of the collapsed animal rather than underneath, he tried to get the saddle off the mount so that it could rest. Stroking its neck, Dan could not feel the familiar pump of blood beneath the skin. "Damn it!" The horse was dead, which meant that they would have to travel on foot, wasting more time. He knew that the animal had died because of the extreme terror and riding that had been forced upon it. "Sorry, fella," Dan apologized. "Help me get the gear."

Trudging forward, Brackish started to remove the spare ammunition and weapons they had brought. Dan lifted the remaining bag of spare ammunition. It was a heavier load than he had realized. The burden would only slow them down more. "New plan," he informed his goblin companion. "Carry as much ammunition as you can; we'll have to leave the rest."

Loading bandoliers of shells, and making sure that the loops on their pistol belts were completely full, Dan stuffed a few sticks of dynamite into his coat pockets and replaced the one in his boot. The two hunters quickly dug a hole, placed the remainder of the weapons and explosives in the ground and covered it. "We ready?"

"Ready," Brackish grinned.

Dan adjusted his old pump-action shotgun across his back. Brackish was carrying a spare revolver in addition to his traditional pistol. The two were quite a sight, and they looked as if they were starting a war all their own. In some regards, they were.

As the two hunters gathered their weapons and began trudging back towards the road, the wolves and their riders remained nearby.

Tonight, they would strike. The hunter was everything that they needed, and they would not let him escape them.

Night fell quick in the shadows of the mountains. With forests dotting the landscape and fields laid out between, there were no wonderful places to provide cover, but by the same token, few places to set an ambush. Dan set about clearing a small space for them, cutting back the brush as best he could and setting a fire. The flames provided plenty of light but no comfort, as both hunters realized that anyone could see the fire. Dan settled down on his back, shotgun held across his chest. Brackish was restless, refusing to sit still and continually prowling the small perimeter of their fire. "What's got you all squirrelly?"

"Not squirrel, goblin," Brackish replied.

"It's an ex... you know what, don't worry about it. What's bothering you?" The American rephrased his question.

"Wolves still follow us." The goblin informed his partner. "Near, just outside fire."

Dan sat up. "Just wolves, or something else?"

"Something else," Brackish confirmed. "No can tell what. Smell like animal and black powder."

Dan tried to think what creature would give off such a smell. Standing up, the American walked to the opposite side of the fire. He could not see any eye shine from the creatures or any stirring of the plant life around him. Brackish screamed, and Dan spun around and saw the goblin vanish into the brush. "Brackish!" The man shouted as he leapt over the fire and ran through the plants, chasing after the sounds the goblin made. "Don't worry, I'm coming."

"Go!" Brackish shouted his voice fading. "Find Lee; I be fine."

The goblin's voice disappeared, as did the sounds of the wolves running through the tall grass. "Brackish!" Dan shouted into the empty night.

For several more minutes, the American continued his search, trying to find any sign of his missing partner. With vivid detail, he recalled Elizabeth's warning that not all of them may return. Had his need to save Lee cost Brackish his life? Something cold and metallic pressed into the back of Dan's head, knocking his bowler hat onto the ground. "Drop the..." were the only words that the man spoke before Dan turned around and laid him out with a solid punch to the jaw.

Looking around, the American himself surrounded by men dressed in Prussian uniforms. In his frantic search for Brackish, Dan had let himself get captured. He dropped the shotgun and raised his hands. He knew that he could not help Lee or Brackish if he was dead.

"Who are you?" One of the soldiers asked, speaking perfect Queen's English.

"Dan Winston," he answered. "Who are you fellas?"

"What brings an American here?"

"Looking for my partner," Dan replied. "His ship crashed, and he's stuck over here."

"Does this partner have a name?"

"Lee Baum."

"Traveling alone?" The soldier asked.

"Don't know; he might be with a Scottish exterminator and a woman," Dan answered, searching for a way out of his current predicament.

256

"Exterminator?" One of the other soldiers asked. His voice thick with a version of the language heard in Whitechapel.

"Yeah," Dan confirmed. "Lee and I are exterminators of the strange and weird. Maybe you know us better as bounty hunters."

"You're some of those fools what hunt monsters." A general round of muted laughter echoed into the night.

"Well, how did you boys get here?" Dan asked.

The laughter died down. "Our ships crashed as well. If hunters have started coming over, they must have got our message. I'm Corporal John Trenton."

"Corporal," Dan said with a nod. "Can I collect my gear?"

"Not just yet," Trenton cautioned. "Will one of you help Mitchell up?"

Mitchell was the man Dan had punched, still sprawled out among the plants. "Sorry about that," Dan offered. "Bad time to ambush me."

"Clearly. What were you looking for?" Trenton questioned.

"Brackish Thumtum," the American replied. Once he saw the confused looks on the faces around him, he told of his and Lee's goblin partner and how Brackish had been abducted.

"If you wouldn't mind coming back to camp with us, I'd love to hear more of your story," Trenton requested.

"Can't see that I have a lot of choice," Dan replied.

A small smile played on Trenton's features. "Not really, no."

The small contingent of Royal Marines led Dan through the surrounding area until they came to a great canopy of evergreen trees. Within the natural cover, the men had cleared a nice camp. The dense needles and branches prevented anyone from being able to spot the fire burning in the center with several canvas tents spread about. Sitting down on a log by the fire, Dan proceeded to tell the men his story, noticing the other soldiers manning the perimeter. "So, how did you boys meet up?" Dan asked.

"I was on the first infiltration ship. Our mission was simple: get behind enemy lines and raise havoc," the Corporal explained. "When I fell from the ship, I landed in a tangle of trees similar to these. It bruised me up, but nothing was broken. I was headed back towards the front when I saw the explosion from the second ship. Finding more survivors, I decided to continue with my original mission. With every crash, our numbers grew."

"How did you get the weapons and uniforms?" Dan asked, noticing the Prussian rifles.

"I shouldn't tell you this, but if you aren't who you claim to be, you'll never tell anyone else, so I suppose there isn't really any harm. We've only seen two major formations of troops come through. For the most part, we ambush the smaller units, and we've taken a few of the patrols that maintain the front." Trenton explained. "Two trains have been destroyed, keeping supplies for the front lines limited. With the tracks ruined, the Prussians have started using wagons. We were looking for one last night when we stumbled onto a goblin force."

"What happened?" The American asked, leaning forward.

"We dealt with the problem."

"This wagon, did your men get a good look at it?" Dan asked.

"We just saw from the descriptions of our lookout it wasn't heavily loaded. Something followed after it, riding a big bear."

"That's Lee," Dan replied, glad to know that his partner was still safe. "What can you tell me about that village?"

"What village?" Trenton asked confused.

"There's a road running through the countryside back there, the same road the wagon was on. A village is on that road, at least a dozen miles from where you found me."

"No, sir, there is not. The only village is a few miles behind the front, and it isn't much of a village – a blacksmith, tavern, and a few houses for people that work the fields."

The hair on the back of Dan's neck rose. "You're sure."

Trenton nodded.

"There was one earlier today. If any of your men get close to it, they need to high tail it back here," Dan stated.

"Why?" Trenton asked.

"It looks like a normal village, but I can assure you the beasts dwelling there are not human, and they do not die," the American said, telling the men about the Devil's Blight that he had encountered twice before in his home country.

"Right, we'll be sure to give that a wide berth. So, you were responsible for that explosion we heard?" Trenton asked.

"Yeah," Dan confirmed. "It was the only thing that would slow those monsters down. Do you boys have a horse you can loan me? I need to get back out there and grab Lee."

"At the moment, you aren't going anywhere," the soldier stated. "Not until we've confirmed your identity."

It only took an hour before a soldier approached Trenton. After a few whispered sentences, the corporal stood up and offered his hand to Dan. "My apologies, but we can't be too careful."

"So, I guess I'm not going to be executed?" The hunter asked, smiling.

"Not based off anything that we were able to find in your things," Trenton said. "Although, Mitchell might want to."

"Yeah, tell him sorry about that."

"We do have a horse that you can use, but you need to wait until morning," Trenton stated. "A lot of strange things are out here, and they've been getting worse over the last few days, not to mention the Prussian patrols."

"Fair enough; I'll wait until first light, but then I'll need to be off."

Brackish was thankful for the tough leather of the trench coat. It was the only thing that had kept him safe during his abduction. He had been looking at the field when a lasso had sailed over his shoulders and pulled him off his feet. The wolves had been too quick for Dan keep pace with. Confident that he could get himself out of the predicament, he told Dan to continue after Lee. Even though the goblin did not know what he was facing, it was obvious they were not a substantial threat, or they wouldn't have run from Dan.

With the lasso tightly pinning his elbows to his sides, the goblin could not reach any of the weapons on his belt, and the shotgun was staying firmly against his back. The wolves entered a hidden passage within the tall grass, still dragging Brackish. They were in complete darkness, and despite his wonderful eyesight, even a goblin needed some

260

light to see by. The smell of rich earth filled his nostrils and served to block out most of the scents from his captors. The wolves would have to rest eventually, and Brackish would try to free himself then.

The walls grew lighter, and the sounds of a crackling fire reached his ears. It seemed that they would be stopping sooner rather than later. Testing the rope, Brackish tried to find the weak spot. Suddenly, the walls around him rose and curved away. Astonished, Brackish saw the earthen dome above him. In the center, a great fire roared, the smoke flowing up through a series of holes in the roof. Stone huts had been built into the sides of the subterranean dwelling, with barrels of gunpowder sitting against the walls. If Brackish could not escape, then he could most likely collapse the dome.

Brackish rolled along the hard-packed dirt as the rope was untied from the wolf's saddle. A short creature, wearing skins of badgers and deer, jumped from the back of the canine mount. The others did likewise and attempted to surround their captive. Getting to his feet, Brackish started pushing against the rope with his arms. It stretched slightly, but not far enough for the goblin to slip the lasso over his head. However, it did allow him to draw his dagger. Carefully, he angled the blade and cut through the rough rope. The circling beings, all covered in animal furs with yellow eyes the only visible characteristic, stopped and stared amazed.

Knowing that it would take him too long to bring the shotgun around, Brackish drew his revolver and aimed it at the closest figure, and all the creatures stepped back. Taking a quick glance over his shoulder to make sure nothing was sneaking up on him, the goblin returned his attention to the beings before him. The nearest one reached up and pushed back the animal skin from its face. Brackish's face showed his amazement, and the pistol lowered back towards the ground.

15

Lee came to with an intense pain in his arm. Brogan was pressing the heated blade of Lee's dagger against the underside of his forearm where a crude arrow had punched through. The Englishman bit back a scream. "Sorry," Brogan apologized. "I was hoping you'd stay out for this. At least, I finished the top."

"What happened?" Lee asked through gritted teeth. Sweat covered his forehead, and his face was pale as ivory. The English hunter thought that he was going to vomit. "Where are the men?"

"No sign for almost a day," Esmeralda replied from the driver's bench of the wagon.

She was standing in the seat, keeping an eye on the way they had come. "They turned back after several miles," Brogan explained. "We kept riding and stopped when we were convinced they weren't coming back."

Brogan removed the blade from Lee's skin, and Lee immediately felt better. "They don't seem too interested in hunting far beyond their borders," Lee commented. "How far are we from your cousin?"

"Is not far, few miles," Esmeralda answered.

"How long was I unconscious?" Lee asked.

"It hasn't quite been a day," the Scotsman answered.

The Prussian woman squinted against the sun starting to climb into the sky. With the pace the trio was keeping, they could reach her cousin Dasha well before nightfall. "You good enough to travel?" Brogan asked his injured friend. Lee nodded, standing on his unsure legs. "What did you say Dan called those green men?"

"The Devil's Blight," the Englishman replied. "He and his mentor are the only known people to have survived an encounter, until he and I trekked to their village."

"Well, I guess you can add us to the list now," the Scotsman bragged. "Can't say I'm surprised; those lads didn't seem like much."

"No, they didn't," Lee agreed. "They were completely different from their American counterparts. I don't believe that Dan and I could have escaped so easily from the continental village. Where did *that* village come from?"

"What do you mean?" Brogan asked.

"Esmeralda?"

"Is true, village was not there. Only thing there was old chimney and a few stones. Cannot say how village was built," she replied.

"Baba Yaga," Lee mumbled, "that devious witch, she actually called up those monsters from history along with a village to hide in."

"Are you feeling okay?" Brogan asked. "You aren't sounding like yourself."

"I'm fine," the Englishman replied. "Did you get a look at those things? They are several steps down the evolutionary ladder and extinct. Not only do we encounter them, they just happen to be living in a newly built village that stands upon the remains of an old one. She has the power to pull from the history of this country."

"No," Esmeralda corrected. "Not history, the land. Prussia holds many secrets; the soil is rich. Old Mother is tied to the land, and she knows all its secrets."

Lee climbed up into the back of the cart with Brogan's help. The Scotsman stepped up beside the Englishman and handed him back his dagger. "Something is coming," Esmeralda stated, pointing to a lone figure in the distance.

"It looks like a single man on a cart or something," Brogan replied, squinting. "We can take him and see if he has any supplies that we can use."

"It was a single man at the inn," Lee reminded his associate, "riding on a bear."

The Scotsman thought on the sentence for a moment. "You should get a move on," Brogan stated.

"Ja," Esmeralda agreed as she urged Alexei forward.

Baba Yaga smiled, a mirthless gesture with no warmth in it. Her eyes were filled with a mania. The man she sought had come so close to his death, only to have that traitorous whore betray the Old Mother and give away her minion following them. It did not matter; she would suffer for her betrayal, but first, the man would have to be killed. Her weapon was much closer now. Soon, the time would come when the unstoppable would crush the hunters. They were weak and unworthy of the term, but her weapon, it was the truest form of a weapon: ceaseless, relentless, deadly, and above all other things, unstoppable. Baba Yaga had seen to it. Her chicken leg hut sat in the darkness of the woods; when Lee Baum was at the point of destruction, she would move her house to place his skull atop one of her fence posts.

At first, this quest had begun at the behest of her sister from the hunter's land, yet every time that the Englishman and his sword-bearing companion defeated her forces, it was an insult to her, a blatant slap in her face, and she would not allow her power to be questioned. The pain in her leg grew worse; something was wrong with the land. The witch knew it was the English invader that continued to taint Prussia with his presence. She would fix the land by watering it with his blood.

Leaving her house, she climbed into the mortar and took to the air. She would call her house when the time was right, but the witch would not miss the death of the hunter.

"Something is wrong," Esmeralda stated.

"What?" Brogan asked, scanning the horizon for signs of danger, the shotgun held at the ready.

Lee was braced against the side of the wagon, his Winchester cradled in his arms. "We are not moving as fast as we should," the Prussian woman proclaimed.

Brogan rolled his eyes. "Then motivate your old mule."

The wounded Englishman closed his eyes and felt the progress of the cart. "She's right," Lee confirmed, his first words since they had started back on the path.

Brogan turned to the wounded hunter. "Am I missing something, lad, or have you lost too much blood?" The Scotsman asked.

"Feel how slow we're going; look at our tracks," Lee instructed, pointing.

Indeed, they were leaving great tracks in the ground. Stepping off the rear, Brogan landed on solid, hard-packed earth. He turned and gave a questioning look at his traveling companions. Sliding off the back, Lee was surprised to find that the ground did not give as his heels touched the soil. "If it isn't the ground…" Brogan started.

A startled expression crossed his and Lee's face at the same time. "Esmeralda!" Lee called.

It was too late. The metal from the axles groaned and then shot through the bottom of the wagon. The woman screamed and pitched forward, landing on Alexei. Feeling the wagon collapse and become dead weight, the horse stopped moving. "What happened?" Esmeralda asked, her hands fumbling with the mount's ties to the vehicle.

"Hurry up and get out of there!" Brogan shouted, raising his shotgun.

Ignoring the men, the woman went back to the immediate task at hand. Behind her, Esmeralda could hear the wooden remains of the wagon shifting. Something underneath it was breathing heavily. Closing her eyes to keep from seeing what fresh horror awaited her, she continued to unbuckle the snaps. Brogan and Lee were shouting at the thing that destroyed the wagon. Feeling the final strap fall away, she dug her heels in and kicked Alexei. The horse responded and trotted away. A bellowing cry hurt her ears, and she knew that something was very angry.

The two hunters stood dumbfounded as a large, hairy, bipedal shape rose from the wreckage of their ride. "Troll," Lee mumbled, remembering the small bridge that they had crossed not a mile ago.

The Englishman could not believe that such a creature had been residing under the rickety structure over the creek. Shouting taunts at the monstrosity, the hunters kept it occupied until Esmeralda rode away. The creature loosed a howl when it saw its intended target escaping, and a reply came moments later from behind them. "You get this one," Lee stated, turning on his heel and raising his rifle.

"Yeah, yeah," Brogan grumbled as he started walking towards the very angry troll. "Why is it that in every country I visit, you blighters smell like a week-old chamber pot?"

The beast snarled and charged the Scotsman. Smiling, Brogan put two rounds into the rushing behemoth. Each hit slowed the monster but did not stop it. A third shot peeled back the top of its scalp, but the troll refused to fall. Dropping the rifle, Brogan drew his sword and waited for the creature. The troll ran onto the tip of the blade and continued until the hilt was pressed firmly against its breastbone. Brogan's boots had dug two great furrows in the soil of the road, and the hunter was amazed that he had managed to stay upright when two great hands circled his neck. The troll was still alive and trying to snap the large man's neck. Pushing his blade down, Brogan opened the monster's stomach, spilling entrails onto the road.

With the new wound, the troll forgot its plan and tried to stagger back. Drawing his revolver, Brogan put two rounds into the thick, matted hair at the beast's throat. Falling back, the monster clutched at its throat as the blood furiously pumped out. After struggling to staunch the blood flow, the troll finally died. The Scotsman quietly cleaned his blade before sheathing it. "Smelly and stupid," he commented as he kicked the dead troll's foot.

While Brogan fought against the troll, Lee maintained his watch to the rear, trying to find the other monster. Another howl rose from a fast-approaching figure, rising from a nearby ditch and sounding angrier than the previous one. "I think it knows that we've killed one of them," Lee stated.

"Hurry up and make it two," Brogan suggested. "I'll go get Esmeralda."

As the Scotsman jogged after the slowing Alexei, Lee maintained his watch. When the beast was within range, he sighted down the barrel of the Winchester, and letting out a breath slowly, squeezed the trigger. The being flinched but did not fall. Another round slowed the approaching beast, but the third round did the most good. A moment after, Lee watched as the creature not only slowed but fell to its knees before slumping down in the road.

"Took you long enough," Brogan called, holding Alexei's reins.

"Sorry," Lee replied, turning to join them.

"It's still coming," Esmeralda stated, pointing.

Lee could see the solitary rider still pursuing. With only the horse, it would not take long for the lone figure to catch them. "We'll keep moving and deal with any problems when they arrive," Lee stated.

"Is still several miles to Dasha's house," the Prussian informed them.

"Then, we should hurry along," Brogan suggested

Their pursuer smiled. Hearing the cry of the trolls, he knew what it meant. His prey was now on foot, making them much easier to catch. Baba Yaga was going to be most pleased. The ancient monsters that populated the village had stayed clear of his path. Soon, he would finish what he had started and return to his fortress.

Lee knew that Brogan and Esmeralda could make much better time without him slowing them down. His injuries had taken a toll and were forcing him to move slower than he would have liked. "Brogan," Lee said. "Ride with Esmeralda to her cousins. Then you can return for me."

"No," Esmeralda stated firmly, "will not leave you here alone."

"She's right," the Scotsman agreed. "You would be easy pickings for anything coming along. Why don't you two ride on? I'll find it as long as she's off this road. Can you call this a road? It's mainly dirt," the Scotsman replied.

"You need help; come with me," Esmeralda offered the Englishman, ignoring Brogan's comment.

"I would, but unfortunately, in my current state, I don't know that I could offer any protection if we were attacked," Lee answered.

As if to answer his assumption, a wild howl drew their attention, and one remaining troll bolted from the woods, standing well above them. Lee and Brogan unloaded their rifles into the creature, and it fell to the ground. "Any more?" Brogan asked, reaching into his pack for more ammunition.

Lee scanned for any more of the monsters as Brogan shoved the final three shells into the breech. The troll rose on a knee, surged forward, and grabbed Lee. Strong fingers wrapped against the side of his torso and squeezed. Gritting his teeth, Lee tried to raise his rifle. A rib popped, and the hunter's hand seized. Brogan put the three shots right into the malformed face of the troll. This time, it was dead, and Lee collapsed to the road. Esmeralda was off her horse and kneeling beside the Englishman a moment later. "Ribs, at least one broke," he told her.

"Is okay," she offered. "We can bandage."

Brogan stood over the two of them, ever vigilant in case anymore monsters were thinking of ambushing them. He fiddled through the pack for ammunition, finding only two boxes, both shells for Lee's rifle and their pistols. Disgusted, he tossed the shotgun away. "What is it?" Lee asked.

"Ammunition's getting low," the Scotsman replied. "We've got two half-full boxes for your rifle."

"Here," Lee offered, extending the weapon to the other hunter.

"I'm utter shite with that thing," Brogan replied, pushing the rifle aside.

"With my ribs, I can't handle it."

"Give gun to me," Esmeralda stated, taking it from Lee.

"Do you know how to use it?" The Englishman asked.

She examined the Winchester in response. After working the lever, she took aim on the wagon wreckage. It was not a great distance, but it was far enough. She squeezed off a shot and hit center of a board. Smiling, she turned back to the hunters. "Is not so different from rifle my father had," Esmeralda stated.

"Is that where you were aiming?" Lee asked.

"Same place," she replied, firing another round and hitting her target.

"She's a might better shot than I am," Brogan offered.

"Having seen you shoot, I can attest to that," Lee joked. "I don't think any further demonstration will be needed; we need to conserve our ammunition and keep moving."

"You ride horse," Esmeralda stated. "Is better for you."

"I may require some assistance," Lee grimaced.

Brogan formed a step with his hands and helped his wounded friend up onto Alexei's back. Groaning, Lee held on as the Scotsman took

271

the horse by the reins and began to walk on the road. "Why haven't we seen anymore soldiers?" Brogan asked.

Esmeralda shrugged in response.

"Something might be keeping them preoccupied elsewhere," Lee offered. "Perhaps, the Baba Yaga does not want anyone interfering with her prize."

The trio continued in silence.

Prussian troops riding in the back of motorized wagons made their way on the road past the devastated inn. Their wagons were much bulkier than their British counterparts and gave off a thick, noxious, black smoke. As the troops rode along, they did not notice the figure hovering nearby. The Baba Yaga watched as the arrogant men rode towards the front, where the lives of men were traded without thought. It would take them time before they caught up to the men that she was after, but they may cause her more trouble than they were worth.

Lowering her mortar to the soil, she landed in front of the lead wagon. With a groan of gears, it ground to a halt with the others in line following. "What is the meaning of this?" Demanded the man in front.

His hair was gray, and his chest wore great pieces of metal to show his courage. The old woman stepped from her vehicle, the pain in her leg worse, forcing her to limp. Baba Yaga scoffed at the pompous man dressed as a peacock. The man beside him, younger and smarter, dropped to the soil and bowed to the old witch. "Old Mother," he entreated. "What may we do for you?"

"Do not bow to this old woman," the older man ordered. "Clear yourself from our path."

272

The old woman ignored the ranting commander and stepped towards the younger man. "I urge you to turn back. You are venturing into my affairs. If you do not leave, I will take it as an insult," she replied.

"I don't care how you take it," the commander shouted with his face turning bright red.

"I will take those that will listen with me," the younger man offered.

Baba Yaga watched as he went wagon by wagon gathering one or two soldiers with each stop. The decorated soldier in the front blustered and raged, making idle threats to the men. With the obedient man leading his comrades away, the old witch turned her attention back to the commander. "You are a fool," she stated.

With a shocked look on his face, the man reached for his sidearm, and the ground parted, dropping the motorized vehicles into a great trench. The commander, sitting upon his vehicle, was the last to fall into the vent, and with a movement of her hands, the Baba Yaga closed the soil, entombing the men. The sight of the commander shouting and begging for mercy gave the old witch such pleasure. As the muffled screams ceased, Baba Yaga watched the fleeing men. Her mercy towards them would further the stories of her vengeance at those that would not listen. Now, she would begin her journey, which would bring her to her weapon as it completed its task.

Perhaps then, the pain in her leg would cease, and the land would be healed.

Lee tried hard to not let his discomfort show, but each step the horse took grated on his broken rib. "How are you?" Esmeralda asked.

"Managing," Lee offered.

"You are terrible liar," she replied, smiling.

"Once we are back in London, I'm going to get a nice, thick steak," Brogan mused. "What about you, Lee?"

"Sleep in a bed," he replied.

"I just want to be away from this place," their Prussian escort commented. "Winter's so cold that you huddle and hope for enough wood for fire."

Lee could not help but notice again that the Prussian winter had not proven too hostile in their experiences. "How close is the rider?" Lee asked.

"Too close," Esmeralda replied.

"What is he riding on?" Brogan asked. "That's not a horse."

"He's probably riding on a bear," Lee offered without looking back. "I'm going to assume that this is our strange visitor at the inn."

"Shoot him," Brogan instructed Esmeralda.

"No," Lee replied. "You have to make sure he's in range. Let's keep moving; if we can reach Dasha's house, we might be able to formulate a plan of offense."

"Right," Brogan replied. "You busted up, and us with hardly any bullets; it'll be a marvelous offensive."

"Oaf, shut up," Esmeralda said harshly. "Is best plan we have."

The Prussian woman knew that they would not reach Dasha's before the rider had caught up to them. Every step closer brought them hope at least.

Another mile passed before they heard the shouts from their pursuer. "He's in range," Lee offered.

Esmeralda took careful aim, following Lee's instructions: take a deep breath, let it out, and squeeze the trigger. The bullet struck the bear in the head. Groaning, the animal stepped to the side of the road and shook its head. The rider was a large man, easily as large as Brogan, wearing old-fashioned armor with a curved Prussian saber hanging at his belt and a dark blue shield glinting in the afternoon sunlight.

Esmeralda kept the rifle trained on the armored figure, who discarded his helmet, allowing his thick, dark hair to fall about his shoulders and spoke loudly in Prussian. The rifle wavered. "What did he say?" Lee asked.

"He is Koschei, also known as the Deathless; he cannot be killed," she translated.

"All men can die," Brogan responded.

"His spirit is within an egg, inside a duck, within a hare, locked in a chest, and buried under a green oak tree on an island in the middle of a lake," Esmeralda explained. "Without that, he cannot be killed."

Koschei continued speaking, pointing at Lee with a gauntlet-covered hand. "Baba Yaga has sent him," Esmeralda stated. "She seeks you."

Brogan stepped between Alexei and Koschei and drew his revolver. "He can't have him," the Scotsman stated.

Koschei laughed and continued speaking. "What's he saying, lass?"

"He says that you wear a real weapon on your back; do you know how to use it, or are you afraid to face him in true combat?"

275

"Shoot him, Brogan," Lee ordered.

"I'll not back down from a challenge," the Scotsman replied. "I've been using this sword ever since I was big enough to lift it. This man will be short work."

Brogan holstered the pistol and dropped his gun belt to the ground, then gripped the leather-wrapped handle of his claymore, and the Prussian warrior drew his saber. Stepping towards each other, the two combatants crossed the distance, and the sound of clashing metal rang out. Esmeralda pushed against Lee. "You must ride away. The big oaf may be able to hold off Koschei, but he is a wizard as well as warrior," she explained. "Ride, he will not hurt me. It is you he seeks."

"I have to help Brogan," Lee replied, drawing his revolver.

Esmeralda slapped Alexei's rump, making the horse bolt away, and Lee hold on before trying to regain control of the animal.

Koschei stood with the long steel blade in his hands. The Prussian warrior was impressed with the Scotsman. Brogan had proven himself an admirable swordsman. The hunter had heard Alexei's hooves pounding away and hoped Lee was riding to safety. Brogan did his best to keep between the Prussian and the animal.

Koschei made a comment in Prussian and motioned for Brogan to attack him. Happy to oblige, the large Scotsman rushed forward and buried his sword into the metal of his opponents shield. The blade split the wood and leather, keeping the item held together by a few iron studs and a single metal band down the center. Backing away, Brogan narrowly avoided a swipe from his enemy's saber. Shaking the destroyed shield from his forearm, Koschei kicked the useless article away. Adjusting to a two-handed grip on his weapon, the Prussian rushed forward.

Sparks flew as the two weapons clashed. Brogan's large blade was not meant for quick fighting, but he was strong enough to wield it effectively against the lighter blade of the Prussian. Turning aside the last thrust from Koschei, Brogan slammed his shoulder into the immortal's armored back and sent the man sprawling onto the ground. Koschei quickly rolled over and deflected the downward stroke from the Scotsman. A well-placed kick from the Prussian threw Brogan off balance and allowed Koschei to get to his feet.

Both combatants were breathing hard and waiting before rushing back into the fight. Koschei said something to Esmeralda.

"He says that you are a great swordsman, and if you had the centuries of practice, you could be the best, but he must finish this now," she translated with fear deeply etched on her face.

"He hasn't been able to yet; what makes him think that he can now?" Brogan called, never taking his eyes off Koschei.

The Prussian rushed forward, his saber spinning in his hands. Brogan watched the blade closely, preparing to parry the strike. He did not see his opponent reach into a small pouch and throw the powder, which flashed into life, blinding Brogan. The Scotsman followed through with his intended block and felt the satisfaction as the metal blades met and rang across the field. He spun to face where he expected the Prussian to be. His eyesight was blurry, and he could only make out hazy outlines. "What did you do?" Brogan demanded. "Coward!"

Careful of his movements, Koschei approached his opponent. Esmeralda called directions to the Scotsman. Annoyed at the interference,

277

the immortal Prussian warrior took a stone and threw it at the girl. It struck her stomach and doubled her over. As Esmeralda collapsed to the field, retching up the little food that she had consumed, Koschei continued his approach. Brogan was trying to keep his blade out to meet his attacker. It was a simple matter to disarm the blinded Scotsman.

Picking up the dropped blade, Koschei sheathed his sword as he felt the weight of the strange weapon. With a cruel grin on his face, the Prussian wizard drove the point into Brogan's chest. Once the pommel was pressed against the Scotsman's flesh, Koschei stepped back and allowed his opponent to collapse. With blood frothing between his teeth, Brogan struggled to try and withdraw the blade. Too weak from the trauma, the Scotsman collapsed back onto the unforgiving foreign soil.

Lee regained control of his mount and watched as the Prussian callously impaled Brogan. "NO!" He screamed across the expanse between them.

Koschei looked at Lee, a wicked smile on his face, and turned to head back to his mount. "Go!" Esmeralda called after Lee.

Koschei veered to Esmeralda and gave her a hard blow on the head, knocking her back to the soil. "Koschei, come and get me," Lee called as he kicked Alexei back into a gallop.

16

Dan climbed into the saddle. Trenton had been good to his word, and as soon as the sun started shining through the trees, he provided the American with a horse. Taking the reins, Dan was about to head in the direction of the road when Trenton raised a hand and stopped him. "You'll need this," the Marine stated, handing Dan a map with multiple markings on it.

"What in blazes is it?" Dan asked.

"It's a map of our scouts," Trenton stated. "We've salvaged enough carrier pigeons so that we can have long-distance scouts."

"So?"

"Keep your eyes peeled for pigeons. They aren't native to Prussia; if you see one, you can trace it back to the scout. We sent out orders last night for them to keep us apprised of the wagon's movements. They always fly in a straight line," Trenton informed him. "You can't let that list fall into enemy hands."

"I won't."

The Marine pointed the hunter in the right direction and stepped back as the man rode off to try and save his friend. His idea about riding towards the front to cross back over had given Trenton an idea, but the soldier was far from willing to place all his men in harm's way. "Sir, what are your orders?" A young private asked.

"We need a unit for a scouting mission. Our mission to disrupt the Prussian supply train has been accomplished. I want to see if we can break a gap in their front lines," Trenton explained.

Dan rode through the forest and emerged onto a field. The road was nowhere in sight, but he had the heading he needed to reach it, the last known sighting of Lee's wagon. He hated to leave with Brackish in God only knows what kind of danger, but the goblin had told him to go on. The hunter also knew that he did not have enough information about the goblin's whereabouts to search for him. Dan had learned one thing over the years – Brackish Thumtum could take care of himself. The American hoped his goblin partner would be okay.

Glancing up, Dan spotted a gray and white bird flying towards the Marines base camp. Seeing the direction that the pigeon came from, the American changed his horse's course and rode out.

Retrieving the map from his pocket, Dan found a scouting at that heading and determined that Lee and the others would continue on the road, coming by it. Estimating an intercept course, the American kicked the horse's flanks and hurried towards his partner.

Brackish heard whispered tones and welcomed the familiar language. He sat beside a fire, and one of the wolf riders sat down across from him. The animal hides pulled back to reveal an aged goblin face. "What you want?" Brackish asked when he untied himself.

"We are black powder clan," the elder answered.

"I know. I am more than black powder now," Brackish replied.

"We are forsaken. Need new blood."

Brackish did not respond but waited for the elder to continue. "I will bring new blood to the clan. This fool cannot lead us," a younger goblin shouted to his clanmates. Brackish had never seen a goblin so tall or muscular. Even so, the hunter was waiting to see what this newcomer wanted.

A young female goblin sat beside the old goblin. "Our elder wants you to lead the clan," she explained.

"I have a clan," Brackish answered. "Why me?"

"It does not matter," the tall goblin shouted. "I challenge this fool. He is no clanmate of ours."

Brackish pushed himself up to a standing position. Enough of the clan had heard the younger male and come to watch. The hunter could tell that most of the others gathered here wanted to see Brackish lose. Pulling a knife from his belt, the young goblin held it up. "To the death," he stated, taking a step towards Brackish.

Stepping forward to meet the challenger, Brackish waited. When his foe drew back to attempt an overhead swing, the British goblin used his prosthetic arm to punch his younger counterpart in the jaw. Spinning around, the goblin dropped his knife and spewed several teeth onto the dirt floor. Kneeling, the Prussian creature tried to stand. Shaking his head, Brackish stepped forward and knocked the goblin out with another punch to the jaw. When they saw their champion bested in combat, the others shirked back from the foreign goblin. "Are there any others to challenge?" He called, watching as the gathered goblins lowered their heads, refusing to meet his stare.

When no one answered his call, he returned to his seat by the fire.

"You didn't kill him," the elder pointed out.

"I don't kill goblins unless I have to," Brackish answered. "Why do you want me to lead your clan?"

"Your arm is a mighty tinker," the elder responded. "Your weapons are greater than ours. Also, we want to leave this cursed land where the Baba Yaga controls all of us but does not care for our ways. We were going to capture the man you were with so that Old Mother would reward us and look more favorably upon us. Then, we saw you and how you fought. I knew you could lead us to freedom from the witch."

"I have a clan," Brackish stated definitively.

"You clan with men," the female replied, wrinkling her nose. "Not your kind."

"Dan and Lee give me a clan, home, and beer," Brackish answered.

The elder kneeled before Brackish. "May we join your clan?" He asked.

Thinking, Brackish wanted to do what Lee and Dan would do. Neither of the men wanted to hurt creatures that were not dangerous. These goblins were clearly lost and needed help. Brackish determined that as an exterminator of the strange and weird, it would be in the best interest to help this Prussian clan so that they did not become a danger to others. "My clanmates must decide," Brackish stated. "If you help us, they might let you in."

"What do we have to do?" The female asked.

Brackish smiled. "Hunt and fight."

The female returned the smile. "We can do that."

It was only an hour later when another pigeon approached across the horizon. Dan further adjusted his approach, trying to properly gauge how to best intercept them. The American urged the horse faster, trying to

282

gain precious time and said a quiet prayer, hoping that he would be quick enough to get to his partner before the creature tracking him. With luck on his side, he might just make it to Lee before the strange pursuer.

The Baba Yaga knew the man in the rounded hat was trying to rescue the Englishman from her weapon. Koschei was close, but these two mortals were different from his normal conquests. No one had ever been able to withstand her will so effectively. Summoning her minions, she laid her plans for the American. As he struggled through his torments, his friend would be dying at the end of Koschei's blade. Scratching at her leg, the old woman felt the first strips of flesh peel back.

Dan rode hard through most of the morning. As he passed through another quick burst of trees over the primary plains of the countryside, something caught him in the chest and knocked him from his mount. The American plummeted to the ground, the shotgun across his back, digging into his skin. Rolling onto his side, the hunter tried to catch his breath. His horse had stopped galloping and made several steps back towards him.

Something caught the animal's attention, and it stopped its progress. Turning to flee, the mount stopped and backed away, a frenzied look on its features. Realizing that the horse was going to bolt if he didn't get up, Dan pushed his way to his feet. His body was hurting, hot flashes of pain flowing from his spine, but he didn't think he had broken any bones, so he would push onward. Staggering forward, he grabbed the reins and tried to sooth the animal.

The pump-action shotgun in his hand, Dan surveyed his surroundings, trying to determine what had spooked the animal and if he had ridden into a trap. Ear-piercing laughter rang through the trees, and Dan knew what he was facing: goblins. "It's not my first rodeo, come on!"

The tall grass of the fields provided them cover while the thin layer of trees gave Dan a reprieve from the yellow stalks. A small, green figure rushed from cover, animal furs and leather wrapped around it, clutching tightly to a crude axe. "At least it isn't black powder," the American mumbled.

Tying the horse's reins to a tree, the hunter watched as the goblin darted behind a fir tree. Glancing over his shoulder, the hunter saw the stone glint of a spearhead. As soon as he heard the rustle of the grass, he rolled to the side, and the spear landed harmlessly in a tree trunk. Dan came up, shotgun at the ready, aiming behind the goblin's cover, but the creature was gone. Puzzled, the American gave a quick look to make sure none of the other monsters were rushing him. A few needles fell from the evergreen's branches. Throwing himself back, Dan narrowly avoided the blade, and the axe buried into the soft soil in between his legs. The goblin snarled, and Dan delivered a punch that sent the smaller creature flying. "Tricky little..." the hunter's words were interrupted by the eruption of goblins from the field.

With his back to the horse, Dan kept switching from side to side, firing the shotgun into the approaching green masses swarming out of the fields. When the gun ran dry, he took a magazine from the holder at his leg, emptied the shells into his hand, and quickly reloaded with expert precision. The few seconds that cost him gave his attackers an opportunity to get close enough to use their primitive weapons. Using the barrel of the shotgun to block an axe, he quickly kicked out, planting the hard sole of his boot onto the goblin's head, driving the creature to the ground with a satisfying crunch of bone. Spinning, the hunter knocked another leaping beast from the air with the butt of the shotgun. Turning the weapon around, he ran through the eight shots quickly and tried to reload.

One of the goblin's blades cut through the canvas wrapped around his leg where the spare magazines for his discarded shotgun had been held. A quick downward swing with the stock of the shotgun dealt with that threat. Dan was grateful that Lee had used such a thick material or the blade would be buried in his leg; as it was, the American could feel the blood running down his pants' leg. The strap tying the magazines to his thigh did not prevent the rip in the fabric from expanding as it drooped around his knee. Fumbling for another magazine, Dan was forced to bring the shotgun up as several more of the beasts leapt at him, their weapons scratching the wood and metal of the rifle. One of them with a stone club almost knocked the weapon from Dan's hand.

Cursing, Dan swung the rifle like a sling blade, scattering the nearest of the goblins. The sun swept into midday, and the goblins rushed back to the fields. Cuts along his forearms, one on his shoulder – a lucky strike by a goblin – and the gash in his leg dripped blood as the hunter stood confused at his retreating enemy. Something latched onto his ankle, and the American realized there were others monsters about. Dan knew that Prussia had vampires, but had he dug deeper, he might have discovered the Upyr, a rather nasty vampire only active from noon until midnight.

Trying to pull his leg free, he realized that the goblins had purposely kept him here so that if they didn't kill him, their colleague would. Aiming the pump-action shotgun, Dan put a shot through the wrist. With the joint destroyed, the hunter stepped away from the resting area of the fiend while the horse kept trying to pull itself free from the tree. The American was glad that he had tied the reins so tightly, or the animal would have fled right into the goblins. Pulling itself free from the soil, the Upyr stood before Dan. An emaciated figure, ribs threatening to break through paper-thin skin, and a hairless skull, but what surprised Dan were the teeth. It appeared that the creature had teeth made of iron.

"Alktwei," the vampire hissed.

While Dan did not understand the language, he knew the monster most likely only had one thought on its mind. "Not today," Dan responded, firing a round of blessed buckshot into the monster's stomach.

The Upyr stumbled back but did not fall. For Dan, the more alarming fact was that the blessed rounds did not seem to have any effect on the creature. "Feed," it repeated.

Clicking its teeth together, the undead being lunged forward; thin skeletal fingers grabbed Dan by the shoulders and pushed him to the ground. Struggling to break the vice like grip, Dan brought his knees up to keep the abomination from clapping onto his throat. Lunging forward, the vampire snapped its jaws, seeking prey. The clap of the teeth connecting was sharp and loud, but it meant that the beast had not caught Dan's flesh. "Get off," the American grunted, slamming his head into the fiend's nose.

Cartilage crunched, but the Upyr did not budge. "I hate fighting dead men," the hunter commented. "You damn fools just don't feel pain like you should."

Working his legs, Dan pushed the Upyr over his head. The creature's shoulders both dislocated, and its grip faltered. Rolling to his feet, the American drew his Bowie knife and slammed a knee onto the monster's chest, pressing it onto the ground. Quickly, Dan drove the blade straight down into the emaciated throat of his opponent. Piercing cartilage and shattering vertebrae, the Bowie sunk into the soil. Pushing on the handle, Dan watched as the edge of his knife split the Upyr's throat slicing through the thin skin. Being sure to fully sever all the skin, the hunter stood up, cleaning off his knife before replacing it in his boot. With a powerful kick, he sent the head soaring out into the field. "Ain't many things that are still too spry without a head," Dan commented.

He could hear the goblins regrouping; assuming the vampire would finish him off, they had not prepared for his survival. Smiling, Dan reached into the pocket of his trench coat, and removed one of the remaining sticks of dynamite. Striking a match, he lit the fuse and held the red cylinder. Untying the horse, he quickly mounted his ride as the fuse continued to burn. Seeing movement in the field, he lobbed the explosive in the direction he needed to ride and waited, lowering himself as close as he could to the horse's back. The explosion was loud and caused the horse to rear up on its hind legs. As soon as the forelegs met the ground again, the American kicked the horse forward. Goblin pieces were still raining down as the hunter rode into the field.

Something pulled at his leg and tried throwing him off balance. Looking down, Dan saw a small, green monster holding onto the magazine sleeve attached to his thigh. Even with the fabric frayed and drooping, it was enough of a hold to make riding the horse difficult. Reaching down, Dan undid the buckle, and the holder was only tied at his ankle. The goblin dropped to the ground where it was dragged for a few feet before letting go. Reining the horse to a stop, Dan dropped down and used his revolver to dispatch the hitchhiker. Completely removing the holder, he saw only three magazines remained. Dropping them into his pockets, Dan rode off towards Lee with a small goblin force regrouping behind him.

Seeing another pigeon, Dan knew that he was definitely on the right course to meet up with Lee. Another scout was reporting in. Lee was making better time now. The American estimated that his partner was moving like the devil was after him.

Brackish stood in the open air. It felt good after being cramped in the underground dwelling of the wolf riders. They were a different type of black powder clan than the ones from Brackish's past. With their use of animal mounts and furs, they seemed a good mixture of claw clan and black powder; at least they used firearms. Old, outdated guns that would take time to reload after each shot. "Scouts found men," the female goblin, Rommela Wormwood, stated.

"Soldiers?" Brackish asked. "Prussian?"

She responded with a nod.

Brackish smiled and climbed onto the small saddle situated on the back of a wolf. It was not much different than riding a horse, only smaller. Turning the animal in the direction Rommela pointed, Brackish cleared his throat. "We'll go fast, surprise them, and take their guns. I'll show you how to use them, and then we find my clan."

Understanding clear on their faces, Brackish gave the command and rode at the head of the pack as the wolf riders rushed towards their targets. It was a matter of minutes, and the soldiers could be seen milling around a disabled wagon. There were not many men, but a few stragglers that had been hurrying to meet up with the caravan that the Baba Yaga had

288

destroyed, but their wagon had busted a wheel. The men were not prepared for any type of attack.

Bursting from the surrounding area, the goblins quickly surrounded them. With his shotgun leveled at the nearest soldier, Brackish let the other goblins speak to these humans. A few moments later, the goblins rode away, ecstatic and holding the larger rifles of the soldiers and their sidearms. Brackish remembered the feeling when he had first held a modern, human firearm. As black powder goblins, they used old, percussion pistols and single-shot flintlocks, but with the contributions of the Prussian army, they were ready for the fight that Brackish was leading them towards.

Dan was glad to be away from the goblins; he would have liked to have more ammunition, but that could not be helped. Riding hard over the varying landscape, the American learned over his days in this foreign place that dangers were everywhere, especially with an old witch hunting you. He was not sure if the Baba Yaga was after him as well, or strictly Lee, but Dan did not intend to let her succeed on either count.

As Dan's horse thundered within a nearby field, a man stood beside a tree. The blade of his copper knife reflected the sun's rays. As the hunter drew near, he followed the voice in his head, the voice of the Old Mother. With a fluid motion, the man stabbed the copper knife into the tree and began reciting the ancient rhyme. Upon completion of the chant, his flesh melted away, and he stood in his strong wolf form, a Bodark, the fierce werewolf of Prussia.

The American had caught the reflection of light and had been watching the man carefully. It took a moment before he realized that the man had vanished, being replaced by a bipedal shape that the American was only too familiar with. As one of the foremost exterminators of werewolves, Dan knew that there were as many ways to become a shape-shifter as there were types of them. The sight of the man-wolf hybrid in broad daylight did not alarm him like daylight vampire had. Readying his shotgun, Dan continued riding towards the monster.

Climbing into the tree, his opponent jumped in a formidable pounce. Quickly adjusting his aim, Dan squeezed the trigger. As the pellets grazed the beast, it was enough to alter its course. Instead of landing directly on the horse, it struck Dan in the shoulder and knocked him to the ground. Landing hard, the hunter lost feeling in his arm and fumbled to bring the shotgun up. The hunter did not think his arm had been broken, but the way he landed had caused everything below his elbow to go numb.

The Bodark recovered more quickly, the flesh wound it had received barely hurting. In two bounds, it crashed into Dan, sending the shotgun flying from his grasp, strands of saliva dropping onto his face. Gritting his teeth, Dan landed a punch on the snout of the creature. Its head rocked to the side, and blood flew from its split lips into the surrounding grass. With the weight of the beast shifted, the hunter rolled his hips and tossed the monster off of him. Drawing a revolver as he waited for the feeling to return to his other hand, the American put three shots into the creature's back and flank, which sent the werewolf rushing away from the hunter in a whimper.

Squeezing his hand into a fist, Dan was glad to feel the pins and needles playing along his skin. Another minute and he would have full feeling again. The monster had vanished into the tall, yellow grass of the surrounding field, and Dan did not want to chase it down with only one good arm. Walking backwards, trying to catch sight of the fiend, the American found his shotgun. Bending down, he saw the grass by his head part. Raising his arm, he felt the strong swipe strike him, and the bones in his wrist, recently healed, broke again.

Cursing, Dan rolled onto his side and raised the shotgun. The singular boom was deafening as the creature took a shot directly to the chest, and it vanished once again into the grass. Clutching his wounded arm to his chest, the hunter braced the shotgun against the ground and worked the pump. A small pool of blood had formed where the creature had been hit. Knowing he'd wounded it, Dan stayed crouched. Emptying two of the shotgun magazines in his pocket, he used them to brace his wrist. Using the belt from his trench coat, he cinched the brace tight and made sure that it would keep his injury from getting worse.

Satisfied that he would be able to continue, Dan walked through the grass, following the trail of blood. The hunter knew he could effectively get off one shot from the shotgun, before he'd have to draw a revolver. The trail was easy to follow, and it was obvious that the beast was either not trying or unable to cover its tracks. Despite the blood loss, the American was impressed at how far the creature had made it. When he came upon it, the monster was laying on its back, blood frothing between its teeth. It made a low, growling noise but was too weak to move.

"Sorry," Dan told the Bodark.

The gunshot echoed across the open area, scattering crows from their hiding places. Working the pump in the crook of his elbow, Dan reloaded his revolver and the shotgun. Looking across the field, he saw the horse waiting. At least the werewolf had not scared the animal enough for it to bolt. Careful to not spook his mount further, Dan slowly approached, enticing the animal with a soft voice. Catching the reins, he hauled himself back into the saddle. Coming to a small, worn path, Dan plotted his course by the path of the sun and was relieved to find that the route would take him in the right direction.

The hunter had not been riding long when he passed a young woman. She had a staff across her shoulders with a water pot balanced on each end. Dan tipped his hat to the dark-haired native. She gave him a smile and continued. The American noticed that the water pots were empty. Assuming she was going to gather water from a well or nearby spring, the hunter continued on his path, taking a small sip from his canteen. He could feel the horse growing weaker. It had been a long, hard ride. Not wanting to waste the animal, Dan stepped down and walked beside his mount.

A dark shadow passed over the sun, and the hunter looked up, thankful for the shade, but the sky was empty. Glancing around, he did not see anything but the woman with the pots, and she was far in the distance now. The American walked almost a mile before the shadow returned, this time accompanied by the beating of wings. Raising the shotgun, Dan saw a dark shape spiraling out of the sky towards him. Dropping down, he narrowly missed the strike of sharp claws.

The horse was not as fortunate. The thick muscles in the animal's neck were severed. As the horse went limp, Dan continued tracking the

292

attacking beast. It was fast and had flown outside of his range quickly. Watching as it circled back into the air, he decided to push onward while keeping an eye on this new evil. He took several steps when his adversary dived straight for him. Jumping aside, Dan felt the ground tremble as his foe struck.

The thing was a solid shadow: black skin showed no musculature, with horns of equal darkness and two red eyes; it reminded Dan of a gargoyle. Firing a blast from the shotgun, the American watched as the creature absorbed the blast and took a step near him. "Not good," he said to himself.

A moment later, those clawed hands lifted him into the air and threw him. Landing in a deep puddle, Dan took a moment to assess any new wounds. He had thin lacerations bleeding from his sides, but nothing too severe, as the monster's claws had come down to the sides of the chestplate. Since the shotgun had proven ineffective, Dan was forced to utilize the only thing he had that was stronger. Reaching into his coat pocket, he felt the wet stick of dynamite. Dropping the useless red stick, he rolled out of the puddle and reached into his boot. The last stick was still there and dry. Fishing the box of matches from his pants, he flipped open the soggy carton. "Just one dry match," Dan asked of the universe.

Reaching in, he found several had avoided the water. The grass around the field was wilting as the winged monstrosity stalked towards the hunter, a growl rumbling from its throat. Dan saw the red outline of a mouth as the creature grew closer. The flint from the box was too wet to light the match, and his boots were coated in mud and dust. Reaching up, he flicked the match against his teeth. The tip flared to life, and he touched it to the fuse. When the creature reached him, he shouted a challenge. In reply, the monster bellowed at him, a great red maw opening on its otherwise featureless face. Thrusting his hand inside it, he dropped the explosive within the monster's mouth and ran, his bowler hat blowing off his head.

Confused, the child of Chernobog swallowed and watched the man. A moment later, the shadow was dispelled as the dynamite exploded. Pieces of solid dark evaporated quickly in the sunlight, the malevolence keeping them active having been dispelled. Dan checked his weapons. One of his pistols was missing as was his shotgun, the other revolver had gotten soaked along with the bullets on his belt and the shotgun shells in his pocket. Dumping the worthless ammunition, he holstered his pistol and searched for the missing firearms. The shotgun was easy to find. It had been crushed when the obsidian gargoyle had stepped on it. Leaving the twisted piece of metal, he continued looking for his other pistol and found it near the spot where the monster had picked him up, fallen from his holster.

Checking the weapon, Dan came to a stark realization. He only had six shots and a Bowie knife. It would have to be enough. Going to the dead horse, Dan took the map Trenton had given him from the saddle. Picking up his bowler, he dusted it off, sat it on his head, and forced himself onward towards Lee.

The mortar flying above the land of Prussia dropped sharply from the sky. It had taken so much of her power to maintain the shadow being. Great Chernobog was too powerful of an old god for the witch to control, but his spawn could only be used with great effort. The man had defeated it, and the Baba Yaga felt the wrenching pain as the shadowy flesh dissolved in the light. She regained control shortly before reaching the ground. Koschei was close; the hag could sense it. She was also aware of the thick liquid flowing from her putrefying leg. Once the Englishman was dead, her problems would be solved. The witch and the land would be healed.

Dan had lost count of the miles that he had walked, when he saw the familiar figure of Lee Baum running towards him. A thick forest dotted the landscape. Behind Lee was a large armored man, riding a bear. Dan did not come this far to let Lee die. With a boost of adrenaline, the American began running towards his partner.

17

While Brogan lay bleeding on the ground with Esmeralda taking care of him, Alexei hurried across the road. The Prussian wizard mounted his bear to continue after Lee. The Englishman wished he still had his Winchester, but Esmerelda still held it. She was a fascinating woman, but Lee realized that he might never see her again. In fact, the odds were strongly against their reunion. Pushing the thoughts aside, he knew that he only had a revolver with six shots and a dagger at his side. It was the first time in a long time that he had been so unarmed outside the walls of his home. With the Baba Yaga's constant attacks, he wished that he had much more weaponry, and a few sticks of dynamite. He could still not understand the Prussian witch's motivations. She had no previous contact with Lee, but with everything they had discovered, he was definitely her target. The sharp pain in his cracked ribs pushed all thoughts of the witch and her minions from Lee's mind. Instead, the Englishman decided to focus on getting to the front lines. He did not know how he would get across to the British forces, but he would try to work out a plan once he reached them.

Koschei shouted at the fleeing man. Even though Lee was unfamiliar with the language, he could tell that the warrior was not calling after him out of friendship. Lee was relieved to hear the voice growing distant. With any luck, Alexei was not as dumb as Esmeralda thought and would get him to safety.

Koschei kicked viciously into the bear's sides. The animal refused to pursue the man and horse. Examining the creature, the Prussian wizard felt the soft give in his mount's head and saw the blood running for its ears. The woman had dealt this creature a mortal blow. No matter, Koschei would beseech the Old Mother for more power. Closing his eyes, the warrior was instantly in touch with the old hag and made his request to her, which she gladly granted.

Drawing his saber, Koschei slit the thick neck of his mount. Collapsing onto the ground, the bear laid there. Using the power given to him by Baba Yaga, Koschei watched as the animal's eyes glowed green, and the reanimated creature stood up. Now, no mortal weapon would stop the beast. Baba Yaga cautioned Koschei that the spell would only hold the bear together for a few hours. *It will be enough,* he thought.

Lee's mount was going as quickly as possible. His ribs ached with every step the animal took. The English hunter did not know how much of the pain he could endure, but he would persevere as long as possible. He knew stopping would mean his death. The day was still young enough that he felt sure he could reach the front by nightfall. Glancing over his shoulder, he saw Koschei was starting to gain ground. Lee urged his horse onward.

Riding for several miles, the Englishman stayed ahead of his pursuer, and now a bridge stood in the path before him. Either the river was swollen, or the bridge was not meant to sit high above it. Relieved that no trolls could live in the cramped confines under the bridge, Lee dismounted and cautiously led Alexei onto the wooden platform. The water did not look too deep. His pistol gripped loosely in his hand, Lee stopped in the middle of the bridge when he heard a strange sound. It was water splashing as something slid under the surface. "We should hurry," he said as he pulled harder on Alexei's reins.

Something broke the surface of the water and collided with Lee. The Englishman only caught a brief glimpse of his attacker: brown, slime-covered skin and a face that reminded him of a giant toad. As he was tackled from the bridge and into the water below, Lee found the river was deeper than he had previously thought. His opponent wrapped strong arms around his chest and squeezed. With pain erupting from his broken ribs, Lee tried to scream but only succeeded in letting out his air. As water rushed into his mouth, he saw the precious bubbles of oxygen climbing to the surface. With darkness crowding the edges of his vision, the hunter realized that his opponent was trying to drown him.

Raising his hand, Lee noticed that his pistol was missing. Pushing this latest problem aside, he reached for his belt and pulled free the dagger. Underwater his opponent's vision was much better, but the creature did not think the man would be a threat. As the murky sunlight shone off the metal, it was too late: Lee plunged the blade into the monster's side. Twisting the dagger, he pulled it free and stabbed back into the slick flesh. Releasing Lee, the aquatic fiend rushed away, ripping the weapon from Lee's weakened grasp. Pushing towards the light, the hunter broke the surface of the water and took a great breath. His lungs burned at having been deprived of the sweet oxygen, and his chest screamed with the assault on his battered body. Climbing onto the bank, Lee stumbled away from the water and collapsed, wrapping an arm over his ribs.

Alexei had wondered off the bridge and was munching on the hay beside the road. Lying on the bridge where he had been tackled was Lee's pistol. With his dagger gone, the revolver was his only chance at

299

defending himself. Crawling towards it, he pushed it into the holster at his waist. The creature leapt onto the bridge and collapsed. Two gaping wounds were clear on its flank, but Lee's dagger was gone, lost to the Prussian waters. Examining it, Lee recognized the Vodnik, one of the native water spirits.

Legend told how the beasts would drown swimmers. Lee had no doubts of just how malicious the creature could be. Its round eyes were situated on top of its face, and a long, blue tongue hung from its thin, slime-covered lips. Reaching out a strange, three-fingered hand, the creature emanated a gurgling sound and died.

Koschei was close enough for Lee to hear his shouts again. Pushing himself to his feet, the Englishman returned to Alexei, his ribs aching with every movement he made. The horse shook its head and reared back as Lee took the reins. His mount was refusing to go until he had eaten his fill of the hay. "You really are a dumb animal," the Englishman stated.

With more bubbling noises emanating from the river, Lee stumbled away, leaving the horse to its own fate. He could hear the pounding rhythm of Koschei's mount. If he stayed on the road, the Prussian warrior would be able to catch him much sooner. Seeing a forest beyond the field, Lee ventured from the path and headed towards the dense woods.

Koschei laughed when he saw his target running towards the trees. If the foreign dog had learned anything, it should have been that no place was safe for him. Running as fast as possible, the reanimated bear continued, crushing the Vodnik corpse beneath its feet. As the Prussian warlock crossed the bridge, Lee reached the concealment of the forest.

The woods were much darker than the road and field had been, and Lee's eyes adjusted to the new lighting. Glancing back, he saw his pursuer cross the bridge and turn his ride into the field. Running as fast as he could, Lee felt like his lungs were going to burst and could feel his broken ribs grating. The throbbing in his injured hand and forearm were the least of his pains currently. Stepping over a downed log, Lee saw a figure dressed in a shirt made of green moss and pants of tree bark, a great beard that appeared to be made of reeds clung tightly to his face and a bird's nest was sitting atop his head.

The man of the woods winked at the Englishman and waved him towards him. Lee quickly ran through the inventory of information in his head and came across a creature that matched just such a description, the Leshy – a forest spirit with a penchant for leading travelers astray. "No, thank you," Lee replied and turned to go in the other direction.

A cluck of disapproval from over his shoulder caused Lee to turn. The figure had vanished. If the Leshy wanted him to go in a certain direction, it could not be the correct way. Delving deeper into the woods, Lee slowed his pace to conserve some strength. Once again, the Leshy appeared and tried to lead him in another direction. Again, Lee turned and proceeded in the opposite way. Several more times did the man of the woods try to guide the Englishman's steps. At each chance, the hunter turned and took a different course.

Finally, Lee saw the end of the forest and stepped into a field with sunlight. Searching, he could not find the road and assumed that he had emerged into a different field. Hurrying away from the woodland, Lee saw a figure in the distance. A triumphant shout arose from the forest, and Koschei charged out from the woods. "Damn," Lee muttered.

The Leshy must have known that Lee would not follow it and led him right into the path of his pursuer, or more accurately, the Baba Yaga had known and set the creature in his path. Running across the field, Lee tried to escape the lumbering beast and its rider, even though the Englishman knew it was an unlikely prospect. "Lee!" The figure ahead shouted as he ran towards the Englishman.

The Englishman recognized the voice instantly: Dan. It had to be another trick; Dan was safe in England. The hunter turned and cut a route across the field, away from both beings approaching him. "Damn it, Lee, would you stop?" The illusion of his partner called.

"No," Lee mumbled in response. His chest was on fire, and he was having trouble breathing.

He only had six shots in his revolver. Koschei could not be killed, and the bear was most likely strong enough to survive the bullets. The other being headed his way was an unknown, but Lee trusted that he could kill it and continue. With a plan in mind, Lee altered his course back towards the fake Dan. Hurrying, he rushed at the illusion. It looked realistic, even the bowler hat was present, tipped slightly in the fashion that Dan wore it. Pulling back the hammer on his revolver, Lee started to raise the weapon when something knocked his leg out from underneath him.

Dan had been confused by Lee's quick change of course. The American had assumed that his partner had not heard him, but then, Lee had turned back towards him. Trying to reach his partner, Dan had not

302

been close enough when the bear reached out and knocked Lee to the ground. With a shout, Dan drew his revolver and put a round into the beast's muzzle. The creature did not show any sign of pain but raised its head and stared at the American.

"Not what I expected," Dan admitted.

"Dan?" Lee called. "Is that really you?"

"Who else are you expecting to be this handsome?" The American called back.

"It is you," Lee said, his voice filling with emotion.

Dan stepped forward as Lee crawled to him. Gripping his friend's boot, Lee pulled himself up. Koschei slid off the bear and drew his saber. Lee recognized the posture and words that the Prussian was saying. "He's challenging you," Lee informed Dan. "It's the same thing he did to Brogan. He challenged him to a sword fight and then used trickery to win."

"Well, I don't have a sword," the American replied.

Dan pulled the hammer back on his pistol. "You can't," Lee urged. "He can't be killed."

"I don't have to kill him. Can he be hurt?" Dan asked.

"I don't know," Lee remarked as the first shot fired.

The Prussian stumbled back, his saber falling to the ground. Dan had shot directly through the joint at his shoulder. With three more shots, Dan had destroyed his remaining shoulder and both knees. Koschei the Deathless, great Prussian wizard and warrior, lay in the field screaming. "Can't be killed, doesn't mean he can't be hurt," the American commented with a smile. "What about that thing?"

Lee looked at the bear. The ragged wound at its throat and white cataracts covering its eyes indicated it was no longer living. "I don't know," Lee said just as the animal collapsed.

With Koschei's concentration broken, the magic holding the animal to life was erased.

The Baba Yaga's mortar touched the ground and dug a deep furrow. Spilling over, the old hag stumbled onto the soil and took deep, ragged breaths. Koschei's pain was flowing through the connection that she had established. Concentrating, the witch severed the ties. Her heart was thundering in her chest. No one had ever been able to deal Koschei such a blow. During his first lifetime, he had only sustained minor cuts. These wounds, they would heal, but it would take ages for him to mend completely. Cursing, the Baba Yaga stood in the field. All about her, the plant life withered and crumbled into black dust as she drew in its power to strengthen herself.

Calming down, the witch hobbled back to her transport. The pain in her leg was growing worse. Black fluid spilled from the putrefaction, which seemed to increase with this latest insult. She would be there very soon, and then these men would feel her wrath.

"What are you doing here?" Lee asked as he wrapped his partner in an embrace, tears spilling over his eyes.

"Came here to get you back home," Dan announced, returning the hug and choking back the tears of joy he felt building. "Looks like I got here just in the nick of time."

"I'm not sure which way the front is anymore. I had to get off the road to avoid him," Lee admitted, pointing at the still-screaming Koschei. "Dan, Brogan and Esmeralda, I left them back there. I don't know if Brogan survived."

"We can't worry about that now," the American replied. "We've got to get back to the front, then we can tell the troops where he is. And if HE doesn't shut up, I'll cut out his tongue," Dan threatened over Koschei's continued screams. "Border's that way."

Lee looked in the direction his friend had indicated and saw the familiar mountain range. As the two friends continued on their way, they exchanged their tales of the harrowing circumstances that had reunited them. "So, how many bullets do you have?" Dan asked finally.

"Six," Lee replied. "You?"

"Two, now," Dan commented. "Maybe the Prussian army will just let us walk through."

"Dan," Lee gurgled as he started to fall.

The American caught his fellow hunter. "What's wrong?"

"Ribs, and thirsty," Lee whispered.

Dan took his canteen and unscrewed the lid. Tipping up the container, he let Lee take several small sips. "Rest up," the American said. "The front isn't going anywhere. Hopefully, Brogan and that Prussian lady were able to get to her cousin's like you planned."

Lee's eyes were closed, and his breathing was shallow. Dan just shook his head; his friend had fallen asleep. It was a shame, because Dan knew he could not let his partner sleep long. They were in the open and needed to at least find some form of cover before nightfall.

305

A knock sounded on the cottage door. Surprised to have anyone arriving, the Prussian woman went to her door. She opened it and saw Esmeralda standing before her, a great bruise forming on the side of her face. "Dasha," Esmeralda greeted in her native tongue. "We need help."

"We?" Dasha asked, looking outside.

Brogan was propped against the side of the cottage, his shirt stained with blood from the wound in his midsection. "How..."

"I dragged him," Esmeralda answered. "Please help me."

Dasha came out and helped bring the wounded Scotsman into her cottage. Esmeralda sat in a nearby chair while her cousin put on a kettle of water to boil and brought out several rags. Looking back to Esmeralda, Dasha saw her asleep in the chair. Exhaustion had overcome the woman. No matter, Dasha had tended to many injuries in her time. Her father had once been the local veterinarian, and she had learned much by watching and helping him. It was true that humans were not like cows or goats, but they weren't so far-removed that she could not work on one.

Ripping open Brogan's shirt, she saw the wound and decided on her best course of action to save the man's life.

Lee's eyes snapped opened. Dan was kneeling beside the Englishman, a hand on his shoulder. "We need to move," Dan stated. "At least back to the forest."

"Not that forest," Lee cautioned.

"Fine."

The American helped his partner walk across the field towards a small structure in the distance. "Do you think Brackish is okay?" Lee asked.

"I expect he's doing just fine," Dan commented. "He'll probably be across the border before we are."

The hunters chuckled as they walked. Both tried to keep a close eye on their surroundings. "Just how far does the Baba Yaga's reach go?" Dan asked.

"Once we get out of Prussia, we should be free of that witch," the Englishman confirmed. "The problem is going to be getting there. She wants me badly."

"Yeah, she put plenty in the way to try and stop me from reaching you, which I don't understand," the American commented. "You haven't ever been here or done anything to her, so how does she know about you?"

"I've been asking myself that very same question," the Englishman replied. "All I can assume is that she is angry that I shot her."

Before they could continue their conversation, Dan heard a familiar sound. Glancing over his shoulder, he saw the goblins he had previously evaded rushing towards them. "We've got company," he informed Lee as the duo quickened their pace.

"If we can make that shed, we might be able to hold out," Lee offered.

"Let's worry about getting their first," the American suggested, forcing Lee to move even quicker.

The pain in Lee's chest was immense, but he knew that the goblins would do far worse to him if they caught them. Goblin war cries followed them across the field until the small, stone building came into view. There were several abandoned buildings around, but they had been left long ago. Signs of disrepair showed on every roof and window. Only the small shed seemed to be intact. Stepping inside, Dan shoved the door closed as Lee leaned against the wall.

A smell of mold and decay populated the small area along with a sour odor of something spoiled. Looking about, Dan grabbed a length of wood and slotted it through the door, effectively barring the entrance. "Okay, now what do we do?" He asked.

"I'm not sure," Lee answered as a beam of sunlight shone through the roof. "I don't see any other openings, do you?"

"Just that one," Dan said, pointing up.

A ladder was bolted to the post, allowing for someone to climb to the roof. "I think we might have found a smuggler's shed," the American commented. "I bet people would hide out on the roof until it was safe to move on."

"That is all well and good, but what are we going to do about the murderous creatures outside?"

A steady knocking continued from the front of the structure. "We aren't going to shoot our way out."

"Maybe something in here can serve as a weapon," Lee offered as he started searching the small space.

"What's in those barrels?" Dan asked, pointing to the three small wooden constructs stacked in the corner."

"I don't know, but it reeks horribly," the Englishman replied.

Hurrying over, Dan knelt, pulled the cork from a barrel, and took a deep breath. Dipping a finger in, he tasted the contents and made a grimace. "It's well past good, but it still ought to pack a wallop," he announced with a smile.

"This is going to be bad, isn't it?"

Dan shrugged. "We found someone making homemade whiskey. You're gonna want to go up the ladder and stay low. Find the side with the least number of goblins."

Lee started his climb while his partner went to work moving the barrels. He set the two side by side, directly in front of the door. Tipping the final barrel over, the hunter left a trail over to the other containers. Climbing the ladder, Dan saw Lee observing the area. "Which way?" He asked.

Lee pointed towards the rear. Nodding, the American gave a cursory glance to the abandoned hut that sat in their path. It would provide plenty of cover. Opening the matchbox, which had finally dried, Dan dropped most of the contents. He wanted to scream; this was so much harder to do with a busted hand. Taking one of the remaining sticks, he held the box in his mouth and struck the tip to flint. Dropping the lit match, he grabbed Lee's arm and jumped off the shed.

The goblins gave a short cry of alarm as the two hunters rushed for the hut behind them. Once inside, Lee tried to stop. "We need to get further," Dan stated as he continued dragging his partner. The Englishman could barely breathe with his ribs causing blinding pain.

The fire ate at the old hay and climbed the trail into the barrel. When it detonated, rock and timber hurtled in all directions. The goblins nearest were instantly killed with many others felled by shrapnel and shockwave. Those with minor injuries ran in terror.

Lee and Dan were on the other side of the hut and hurrying away from the deserted village. The explosion echoed across the flat expanse. "Wouldn't those buildings have been better for us to use?" Lee asked with a wheeze, shocked that they were fleeing from the safety of the stone walls.

"If we were armed, yeah, but this is a losing battle. We can't hold out against a siege," Dan explained, glancing over his shoulder. "We need to stay ahead of anything so we can reach the border."

Lee accepted the reasoning and found himself agreeing with it. Hurrying away from the buildings, the duo continued on, hoping they could avoid any further enemies.

The earth around them grew barren and pockmarked with craters. Wood from some long-destroyed structure littered the ground. The hunters slowed their pace, allowing Lee to take several deep breaths. "What happened here?" Dan asked.

"Bombs," the Englishman replied. "We must be getting close."

Something shifted ahead of them. Beings were pushing up from the soil. Dan squinted and could make out the skeletal frames and incredibly pale skin. "Vampires," he commented. "Look like the one I tangled with earlier."

"Upyrs," the Englishman confirmed. "Very nasty creatures."

"I know. We can't fight our way through them," Dan commented.

The hunters turned and stopped. Upyrs rose behind them as well. "It appears that we may not have much choice," Lee stated.

"We need to find some place that is at least defensible," the American said, scanning the landscape. "There." Dan pulled Lee along as he climbed into a large crater. The impact in the ground provided a sensible view around them but would force their opponents to come down to them. Lee drew his revolver and pulled back the hammer. "We have to make every shot count," he informed his partner.

"Aim for the head," Dan instructed.

Lee nodded as the vampires waited. It was eerie to watch the creatures standing so perfectly still. Howls echoed across the land. As the wail faded, the Upyrs started a slow approach. "I'm counting nine," Dan said.

"If all goes well, we'll only have to deal with one the hard way," Lee replied.

Bracing his hand over his injured forearm, Lee squeezed the trigger. The shot went spiraling through the head of the nearest monster. Falling in a heap of gray matter, the Upyr spasmed and died. Demonstrating his skill as a marksman, Lee buried six bullets into six Upyrs. "I'm out," he proclaimed, holstering the revolver.

"Take mine," Dan ordered and handed his weapon to Lee. "You are the better shot."

Lee finished off two more of the creatures and returned the pistol. The last remaining monster maintained a steady pace towards the hunters. Dan grabbed two stray pieces of wood. Bracing the wood between his broken wrist and his body, he used his Bowie knife to cut the ends into points. Tossing one to Lee, the American held tight to the other wooden shaft. Stepping into the crater, the Upyr bared its iron teeth. The hunters rushed forward, both piercing the monster in the abdomen and forcing the vampire down, but the creature knocked Dan away with a backhand, busting his lip.

Lee put all his weight into keeping the Upyr on the ground, but the monster was too much for him. Inch by inch, the vampire raised itself. In a single swing, Dan buried his knife to the hilt in the fiend's throat. The vertebrae snapped, and Dan made short work of the rest of the flesh. Spitting a bloody mess onto the ground, the American wiped his mouth with the back of his hand and smiled at his partner. "That wasn't too bad," Lee stated, wondering if his chest would ever stop hurting.

The howl that had signaled the advance of the Upyr echoed once again. Looking across the field, Dan and Lee saw a goblin horde stalking towards them. Rising above the small, hunched green shapes were hairy bipeds with misshapen heads. "Trolls," Dan stated. "I hate trolls."

Turning towards the border, the men saw a small force blocked any chance at retreat that they might have. Dan sat down and leaned against the crater wall. "This does not bode well," he admitted.

Lee joined his friend. "No, it does not. So, what are we going to do? We have no bullets and no weapons between us but your knife."

18

Dan took off his bowler hat and wiped the sweat from his brow. He looked at his trench coat. It had been shredded during his time in Prussia. Shrugging out of the garment, he wished for a cigar. "Any ideas?" Lee asked, straightening his disheveled clothes.

"Can't say I do," Dan confessed.

Overhead, the sky darkened and threatened to let loose a torrent of rain. Great gusts of wind whipped over the field. The first of the goblin scouts reached the crater wall and rushed ahead, a stone tipped club held in its hand. Dan threw his knife, and the blade buried itself to the hilt and dropped the monster. "But I ain't giving up without a fight," the American announced, taking his knife from the corpse and sheathing it. Hefting the club to get a feel for its weight, Dan tilted his head and cracked his neck. "You with me?"

Lee brandished the spear that he had used to pin the Upyr. "We started our exterminator business together, and I see no reason to not finish it together," he commented.

The next few goblin scouts, wearing their tree bark armor slid down into the crater. Lee dispatched a few of them before one managed to break his spear with a well-placed strike by a hatchet. Kicking the monster in the face, Lee took an axe from one of his dead opponents and finished off the dazed goblin. Dan let loose a shout and waded into the scouts, who fell before the might of his blows. One scout with a flimsy bark shield was rewarded with a shattered arm as Dan's club obliterated the protective instrument and bone beneath it.

The injured scout retreated. "That was simple," the British hunter stated, looking at the approaching horde.

"Yeah, only a few hundred more to go," Dan replied.

"Seems like nothing on a fine day like today."

"Yeah, we'll finish this and have a few cold beers."

Sharing a smile and a laugh at their own gallows humor, the hunters prepared themselves for the onslaught nearly upon them. The goblin horde swept over the crater with Dan and Lee standing their ground. Swinging their newly acquired weapons, the two humans cut a gap in the attacking force, receiving minor cuts in return. The first of the trolls reached the crater rim, shouting its challenge as it descended, the goblins parting around the larger beast. Knocking a goblin off its feet, Dan smiled as the troll stomped on the helpless fiend. Ducking under the swatting arm, the American planted the club across the side of the troll's jaw. With a sharp crack, the top of the club shattered, and Dan was left holding the remains of the wooden handle.

Dropping the remnants, he tried to find another weapon. As he ducked under the troll's second swing, he saw the leather-wrapped handle of a crude iron sword. The weapon was short but would suffice. Swinging under the troll's attacks, the American buried the blade into the creature's hide. It bellowed and smacked Dan across the crater.

Burying his hatchet in the head of a goblin, Lee saw his partner's predicament. Pulling the gore-encrusted weapon from the skull, Lee kicked the corpse aside and rushed ahead. Swinging in great arcs, he cleared a path, and while something stung in his calf, he ignored the pain and hurried to his friend's aid. Sensing the oncoming attack, the troll turned to face its new opponent. When the broad face looked at him, Lee slammed the hatchet into one dull eye. The troll screamed and covered its wounded face, flailing within the crater as it fell. The large body provided a shield, which allowed Lee to hurry to Dan.

The American had been piled upon by the goblins. Unable to retrieve his knife, he had taken to pummeling the fiends with his fists. His broken wrist screamed at him, but he continued his assault. Lee was shocked when he saw the wild-eyed Dan. He had never seen such a fierce look in his partner's eyes. Dan's bowler hat was crushed flat but still sat on his head, and his damaged hand was swollen. Lee was sure that his partner had broken a few more bones in the assault. Picking up a discarded goblin spear, Lee began skewering his partner's enemies. Gunfire rang out over the sounds of the attacking goblin horde.

As the enemy forces trained their attention on the shots being fired, Dan and Lee pulled away from the immediate threats and stood with their backs against the fallen troll. "Who's shooting?" Lee asked, drawing in a deep breath.

"No idea," Dan replied, trying to find the source of the gunfire.

A pack of wolves with riders on their backs broke through the goblin ranks. Each of the riders was cloaked in animal skin and brandishing a rifle. At the head of the pack rode Brackish, leading the charge. His rifle pulled tight, he squeezed the trigger, dropping an attacking goblin. Keeping a tight grip around the wolf with his legs, the goblin hunter worked the bolt on the rifle and chambered another round. "Is that…?" Lee asked.

"Yes," Dan replied. "Apparently, he's much better off than I thought."

Seeing his clanmates, Brackish waved before shooting another of the attacking goblins. The wolves crested the crater wall and landed on a small group of wounded foes. Powerful jaws ended the creatures' suffering. Jumping from his mount, Brackish rushed to Dan and Lee. "Who are these guys?" Dan asked, pointing at the wolf riders.

The riders dismounted and pulled the animal skins from their heads, revealing them all as goblins. Brackish said something to them in a deep guttural language comprised of harsh syllables. When he turned around, Dan and Lee were staring at him in confusion. "What?"

"What was that?" Lee asked.

"Goblin tongue," Brackish responded, tossing his rifle to Dan.

The American caught the weapon and checked to make sure it was loaded. "You guys have your own language?" Dan asked.

Brackish nodded. "Learn some of man tongue for our homes," the goblin explained.

"Learn something new every day," Dan commented as he fired at a troll rising out of the crowd.

All the goblins that Lee or Dan had even encountered spoke English. The hunters had assumed that they adapted the language of their homeland. Neither of them had no idea that the creatures had their own language.

Brackish's squad of goblins spread out and took up positions around the crater. "They want be part of clan," Brackish explained. "Think we help them?"

"What did you tell them?" Lee asked.

"I say if they help, we might," the goblin gave a large smile, handing Dan his rifle.

Brackish took another rifle from his wolf's back and handed it to Lee as the diminutive hunter took his shotgun from his back. Giving the weapon a quick inspection, Lee smiled. "Do we have any ammunition?" The Englishman inquired.

Each of the men had a disabled hand, which would make working the bolt-action rifles difficult. Calling to one of his companions, Brackish pointed as one of his fur clad associates brought a crate of rounds and sat it amid the combatants. Brackish hefted his shotgun in one hand and a stone axe in the other. "This be over soon," the goblin commented as he sniffed the air. "Something coming."

As Brackish scrambled over to a section of the crater, the two human hunters exchanged a look. "That was ominous," Lee commented.

"Seems this whole trip has been," Dan replied.

"It does us some good to get outside of London and take in the country air," the Englishman replied.

"Yeah, I feel so much better," Dan retorted, aiming on a goblin.

The interruption of the wolf riders had broken the concentration of the horde, but they were slowly regaining their courage. Even with the advantage of the firearms, they were outnumbered. "Perhaps if we kill enough of them, they will scatter," Lee suggested.

"Sounds good to me," the American stated. "Brackish! Have your new friends open fire."

Brackish gave the order in the guttural goblin tongue, and smoke bloomed from the edge of the crater as the lead bullets shot into the forces gathered against them. Lee and Dan concentrated their fire on the trolls that towered above the other monsters. Dan hit the looming beings, but each of Lee's shots felled a troll like a woodcutter in a forest. "Why don't you concentrate on the closer targets," Lee aggravated his friend.

"Fine," Dan agreed. "Miss my shotgun."

Dan saw a goblin decorated with multiple skulls shouting. "Trying to rally the troops, huh?" the American noted as he squeezed the trigger.

The bullet struck center mass and threw the goblin into the other creatures it had been shouting at. Seeing no other targets warranting high priority, Dan began firing into the gathered forces. With shouts of anger, the horde rushed towards the crater. The attacking goblins wore varying types of armor: wood bark, leather, and even a few with metal, though they did little to stop the bullets punching through them and continuing into another body beyond. Working the bolt, Dan saw the empty chamber staring at him and rushed to the crate to grab two boxes of shells. "Here," he said, placing one beside Lee's arm.

"Thank you," the Englishman replied as another troll was killed. "Do you see anymore?"

The American turned, surveying all the forces about them. "If they are out there, they're keeping low."

Despite the dying monsters, those in back continued to press forward. "They getting close," Brackish called.

"Keep firing," Dan shouted.

Brackish relayed the order. With their teeth bared, the wolves stood near their riders, prepared to join the fight if necessary. The first leather-wrapped goblin foot landed on the rim of the crater, and Lee's bullet took the top of the beast's head off, and it rolled down into the depression. Dozens more were right behind it and started to spill over the ledge. Rushing from behind the dead troll, Dan crushed the first of the goblin's skulls with the butt of the rifle before turning the weapon and shooting another of the creatures.

Lee joined his partner and bashed goblins with the wooden stock while trying to maintain suppressing fire on the reinforcements. Falling back, the black powder goblins retreated step by step to the center of the crater, continuing to fire into the encroaching enemies. Their wolves lunged at the forces within striking distance now, and several foes went down beneath the powerful jaws of the goblin mounts. A group of claw clan goblins rushed Brackish, and the buckshot from his shotgun caught several of them in the face, dropping them wailing to the ground. Meeting his attackers, he utilized the stone axe while still working the shotgun. When his last shot rang out, he dropped the rifle, letting its strap keep it close, and drew his revolver.

Putting a bullet in the face of the nearest attacking beast, Brackish planted his axe in a goblin's chest. The crude blade punched through the green flesh and held tight. Letting go, Brackish spun and landed a punch with his prosthetic arm. The brass connected with a sickening thump as the thin neck of the attacker broke. Picking up a dropped sword, Brackish continued firing his revolver and hacking at those around him. As his last shot rang from the revolver, he spun the weapon and began clubbing his opponents with the wood grips.

Dan saw Brackish's small hat surrounded by angry Prussian goblins. "Lee!" Dan shouted pointing.

"On it," Lee replied, rushing towards their diminutive partner.

Dan grabbed the hot barrel of the rifle and swung the weapon around in a wide arc, keeping the goblins back. Spinning the weapon, he snaked his finger through the guard and squeezed the trigger, destroying the face of a nearby enemy. Falling back, the American dropped to a knee and kept firing at his enemies.

Brackish felt a crude blade split the skin on his cheek, rewarding the blade-wielding fiend by dropping his brass fist onto its head. The skull collapsed under the blow, and another monster filled the hole left by the dead. Something wrapped around Brackish and pulled him above the ground. Drawing back, Brackish was prepared to smash the offending limb with his pistol until he caught the familiar smell. "Lee?" He asked.

"Things were looking a little hairy," the Englishman commented.

A moment later, Lee and Brackish were kneeling around the ammunition crate, the wolf-riding goblins forming a perimeter around them. "Dan?" Brackish asked.

As if in answer, they both heard a "Yee-haw!" Then Dan leapt over the perimeter, rolled, and came up in a crouch.

His arms and legs were bleeding from dozens of shallow cuts. "Keep it up," the American shouted.

The goblins, while not understanding the language, did not need to be told. Brackish took a box of pistol shells and reloaded his revolver. Grinning, Dan scooped the shells and started loading his pistols as well. "Bout time," Dan almost cursed in frustration; with his broken hand, it was taking longer to load his revolvers. "Been feeling naked without my pistols."

"Thankfully, you weren't." Lee retorted.

"Who knows? Maybe they'd have been too intimidated to attack if I had been," Dan offered.

"Or scared," Brackish joked.

The trio laughed as all about them, the goblins continued to press forward. Standing from their brief respite, the hunters began to thin out their attackers. They and their allies knew it was a losing game; even with all the dead around them, they were still hopelessly outnumbered. Still, onward they pressed, refusing to accept the inevitable.

From the rear of the ranks, an explosion blossomed, and another, and another. They were consistently tracking closer to the hunters' position. Terrified, the attacking goblin horde wailed and began to break. "What in the hell is that?" Dan asked.

Brackish shrugged.

Then, a figure dropped to the ground, her white hair crackling with electricity. A brown cloak folded around her, and her breathtaking porcelain skin left no doubt to Lee, Dan, or Brackish who this could be. "Freyja!" Dan shouted, running past the wolf riders and snatching her up in a giant embrace.

"It is so good to see you, too," she responded, placing a kiss on his forehead. "We have business to attend to first, my love."

"Right," the American responded, setting the fey back on her feet.

Other figures landed amongst them, each of them, like Freyja, from the German fey transplanted to England with Dan and Lee's assistance.

With the Prussian goblin forces regrouping, Lee and Brackish joined their partner. "Do we have a plan?" Lee asked.

"We are here to stand with you," Freyja stated. "Once this rabble is dealt with, we will get you back to England."

The forces of the transplanted fey formed ranks with the black powder goblins. It was the most unlikely of alliances.

Baba Yaga could sense that more foreign forces had set foot on her land, seeking to save the object of her vengeance. "Fools," she said into the wind.

The smoke from the battlefield was within sight. Soon, she would be there and would solve the problem with her own hands, baptizing herself and the soil with the blood of Lee Baum, Dan Winston, and all of their allies.

The goblins rushed towards the foreign invaders. Bears had come from the forests to reinforce them. Several Alkonost flew overhead, singing their hypnotic song. "Is it me or do you get the feeling they don't like us?" Dan asked.

"You do get a rise out of people," Lee stated.

"What can I say? I have a way."

"You may want to consider changing it, if this is the response you get," Freyja teased. "Someone deal with those harpies."

The song of the Alkonost had reached them. While it was still too far off to ensnare their minds, none of them wanted to find out how close they had to be. Arrows shot from the German fey, and the woman-bird hybrids shrieked as they crashed to the earth and were silenced.

"What about bears?" Brackish asked, pointing at the large fur-covered shapes approaching with the goblins.

"Shoot them in the head," Lee offered.

"A lot," Dan added.

The British goblin relayed the advice to his Prussian counterparts. "He's right," the Englishman stated. "If those bears get too close, we are done for."

"Then we won't let them get close," Freyja offered.

Lightning leapt from her hands, electrocuting the nearest bear and leaving a smoking carcass. The archers with her maintained their aim, waiting for the animals to come within range. "Brackish," Dan shouted. "Those goblins are in range; we need to start thinning them out."

Nodding, Brackish gave the order to the wolf riders. Shots fired, and their enemies fell. "Lee, hold back and deal with the bears," the American said as he raised his rifle and took aim.

The Prussian goblins refused to be deterred, no matter how many of them died trying to reach the crater. Bolstered by the appearance of the bears and the knowledge that Old Mother was nearby, they all wanted the chance to kill her enemy and gain favor with her. Arrows flew from the German fey, burying deep into the backs of the approaching bears. The animals raised up, screaming at the pain, and more arrows pelted into their upraised midsections. Lee added his bullets to the cause. Of the approaching bears, the projectiles only managed to kill two of them. Most of the other wounded animals continued their approach. The archers at the hunters' side were impressive. Several more of the bears fell, their backs sprouting multitudes of arrows.

"I'm out," one of the fey stated.

Even though each of the archers brought a great deal of arrows, the bears absorbed the damage easily. Down the line, fey ammunition was dwindling. Lee saw the last arrow rise into the sky and plant itself in the head of a bear. The animal stood up, the projectile lodged in its skull, and tried to shake the weapon loose. A shot from Lee broke the bear's muzzle, causing it to fall over onto its back and drive the arrows deeper before the shafts broke. Wailing in pain, the poor beast had only served to make its suffering worse. The English hunter felt certain that its wounds would eventually kill it, hopefully sooner rather than later.

"If they reach us, we are done for," Dan stated.

The goblins broke into a run as they came closer to the crater that had become the foreigners' refuge. "Here they come," Lee shouted.

Arrows spent, the archers drew long knives from their boots and waited on the enemy. Brackish stood beside Dan and Lee. "We clan," he said, placing a hand on their shoulders.

"Yeah, we are," the American agreed.

"Indeed," Lee concurred.

"If this is it, I want them to know they've been in a fight," Dan stated as he reloaded the rifle.

Chaos erupted as the forces charged into the firing lines of the hunters and black powder goblins. The fey used their knives to kill any of the adversaries that came within reach. Lightning flew from Freyja's hand, passing through multiple goblins at once. One of the bears started to crest the hill, an arrow protruding from its head. Lee watched as the creature stumbled and fell, dead. Its body rolled down the slight incline, crushing Prussian goblins beneath it. With the large groups of their dead, the approaching Prussian goblins began to lose their courage. Baba Yaga could feel the cowardice eating through her minions and knew that they would flee if she did not intervene.

"Enough!" Shouted a voice from the sky.

324

An explosion erupted within the crater directly behind Dan and Lee. The hunters were thrown further than any of their allies. Brackish landed at the edge of the crater, while Freyja was tossed in the opposite direction of the men. The other fey and black powder goblins had been shoved about violently by the detonation, but they suffered the least of the disorienting effect.

The American and his English counterpart tried to stand, both unsteady after their flight. Lee noticed that the other creatures had encircled them but were not attacking. "Dan, something's wrong."

"Yeah, her," the American pointed towards an object in the sky.

Above them, the cracked mortar descended. Baba Yaga stood within it, cradling the giant pestle in her arms. Once the wooden instrument touched the ground, the witch stepped from it and stood before the men. The hunters could hear the others fighting within the crater, but they were too far away to get back to them. "You have hurt my land," she stated, pointing the pestle at Lee. "It is only your blood that can heal it."

"Too bad, lady," Dan replied. "You can't have it."

Drawing a pistol with his good hand, Dan pulled back the hammer and squeezed the trigger with amazing speed. The bullet flew towards the witch. Faster than they could see, she adjusted her wooden cane and caught the piece of lead. "Your friend used such a device to wound me, but I am facing you and will not be taken by surprise again," the witch informed them. "Since you insist, I will deal with you first."

With a motion from her hands, vines sprung from the ground and wrapped around Lee, holding him firmly in place. Dan continued to work the pistol as the Baba Yaga approached him. She deflected, dodged, or blocked each of the shots. Holstering the pistol, he tried to draw the twin

325

on his other side, but with his hand on that side disabled, it was not the quick motion that his first draw had been. As his hands wrapped around the pistol grips, the witch lashed out with the pestle and struck Dan in the chestplate, knocking him onto his back. He was having trouble breathing immediately. Trying to get the brass armor off, he backed away from his opponent. "Finally," she said, "you see how futile your attempts to fight me are."

Undoing the chestplate, Dan tossed it aside, noticing the large indention where the wooden cudgel had struck him. He could breathe easier, but at least one of his ribs had broken under the witch's assault. "Like Hell," the American stated, rolling over and getting to his feet. "You can't have Lee."

"You can't stop me," Baba Yaga said as she struck again.

This time, Dan was ready for her speed. He barely managed to avoid the attack, and drawing his Bowie knife from his boot, swung at the hag. She deftly blocked the strike with her free hand, bringing the pestle down on his shoulder. His whole arm went numb as the knife fell from his unfeeling fingers. Placing two of her fingers against his forehead, the witch said something in Prussian.

Dan screamed, falling to the ground, clutching at his head. "What did you do to him?" Lee demanded.

"He will be fine, once he dies," she answered. "The pain will build until his brain leaks from his ears."

"No," the Englishman said, staring at his friend writhing on the ground in intense pain.

"You should be more concerned with yourself," the witch informed him.

326

"Why do you want me so badly?" Lee asked, seeing that physical force could not stop the witch, but perhaps logic could.

"You have hurt my land," she answered simply.

"How?"

"The machines that you have built polluted my land, and she suffers."

"I don't have any machines here," Lee stated. "Everything that I have built has been for England. I've never set foot in Prussia before."

"You are lying. All men will tell such stories to save their lives," the Baba Yaga answered. "I have been shown a great many things; this was how I came to understand your role in the pain of my home." The vines dropped away from Lee. "Come, great hunter, defend yourself. I have seen how well you dealt with those that serve me; shall we see how you do against their master?"

"If I must," Lee stated, quickly raising the rifle and firing.

The witch caught the bullet with her wooden cane. Swinging the rifle, the English hunter knocked the pestle away from her face and tried to punch her. A tiny, gnarled hand with age spots and wrinkled skin caught the young man's punch easily. "You are more foolish than your friend," she stated, forcing Lee back.

His feet became tangled in something, and he fell. Laughing, the witch drew a curved knife from a small pouch at her side. The blade was three times larger than the place that she had drawn it from. Lee did not have time to process the information as the Baba Yaga raised the weapon above her head, determined to bury it in Lee's heart.

"Stay your hand, witch!" Freyja shouted.

The goblin forces had parted for the German fey as electricity crackled around her, forcing the goblins back further.

"Do not be so quick to think you are a match for me, child," the Baba Yaga warned. "I am more formidable than you know."

The offspring of a human Jotun servant and a wind nymph, Freyja was incredibly powerful, but Baba Yaga was legendary. "You will free these men and heal the American," Freyja ordered, making a fist.

"If you wish to die so young, then so be it," the Baba Yaga said and flew across the ground towards her challenger.

Freyja threw up her arm and received the blow from the witch's pestle cane. Two deep furrows dug into the ground as Freyja reeled several feet from the blow. Lee pulled Dan away from the fight. "Stay with me," Lee begged, cradling his friend.

Dan's face was contorted in pain, as the American could not register anything going on outside of his own misery-wracked body.

Freyja continued to block the mighty blows thrown by the Baba Yaga. Breathing heavily, the witch stopped her attack. "You are stronger than I thought, but you are still no match for me, child," the witch stated.

"We are closer to my land than yours," Freyja offered with a smile.

A gust of wind blew in from the east, and the winds began to concentrate themselves around the two fighters. Building in ferocity, the winds listened as their mistress commanded. A moment later, and large pieces of debris spun about them. Guided by expert hands, the weapons pulled themselves from the goblins' hand and hurled at the Baba Yaga. Despite her old crone-like appearance, the witch was spry. She dodged all the incoming weapons and blocked the last with her cane. Throwing her hands flat, she dissipated the wind. Freyja gave a respectful nod to the old witch as giant boulders rose from underneath the soil and flew at her. "So, tell me, why do you feel that the Englishman's blood will heal your land?" Freyja asked.

"My leg has begun to fester. It did not start until he set foot upon my soil," the witch explained as she sent the boulders to crush Freyja.

The German hybrid reduced the stones to dust with lightning from her hands. "I feel that you are mistaken," the porcelain-skinned beauty responded. "How can a lone Englishman defile your land so heartily?"

The old witch stumbled over a goblin carcass. It was the opening that Freyja had anticipated. Sprinting the distance and buffeted by the wind to allow no time for counter or dodge, the warrior wrapped her hands around the Baba Yaga's head and unleashed a torrent of lightning. Grasping at the hands, the witch screamed, and the sound rose in pitch until those nearby covered their ears and collapsed to their knees. Still, Freyja held on. Without warning, she stopped her attack and stepped away from the old woman. The Baba Yaga fell to her knees, great white scales falling from her eyes. No other mark showed on the old crone's face. "She tricked me," the Baba Yaga snarled, lifting the scales from the ground and examining them. "Enchanted me!"

"I am sorry, Old Mother," Freyja apologized.

"No worries, child," the witch replied as Dan immediately sat up all trace of pain gone. "Take your humans and be gone. With the enchantment ended, I have much to deal with. I see now that these foreign fools are not to blame, but those within my own borders have brought this disease to me."

Hobbling back to her mortar, the Baba Yaga climbed in. Lee hurried towards the vessel with Dan following, a confused look on the

American's face. "Before you go," Lee started, "who enchanted you? Why did they want you to catch me?"

"A sister witch from your native lands," the hag replied. "She fears you and rightly so."

Without a further word, the Baba Yaga rose into the air and sped away back into the heart of the Prussian empire. "A sister witch, huh?" Dan said. "I'll tell you who I'd wager on."

"I wouldn't disagree with you," Lee replied. "She must have something rather spectacular planned, if she went to this much trouble to deal with us."

With the Baba Yaga leaving, the forces gathered against them also began to dissipate. The Prussian goblins no longer wanted to wade into the bloody battle they had found themselves in, while the bears merely roamed back to their forests.

Watching as their foes scattered all around them, a question crossed Dan's mind. "What are you doing here?" He asked Freyja.

"Your Queen implored Glorianna to assist in the combat. She refused, but Elizabeth found our forest. Her visions showed a very grim fate for you, caused by a blinded witch. When I learned of the danger, I volunteered to come, and these who joined me did not forget the debt that we owed you."

Before anyone could ask what others, the first of the paratroopers appeared. The white of their parachutes stood out against the overcast sky. "The Prussian front is broken," Freyja stated.

"What?" Dan asked.

"Our ship received word that a group of British soldiers had gathered behind the enemy lines," she explained. "They attacked from the rear and created a gap in the Prussian lines. Now, your countrymen flood into this land."

Brackish joined his partners. "We still alive," he stated.

"Good thing we left some beer back home," Dan stated.

"What about them?" The goblin asked.

Turning back, the two humans saw the black powder goblins and their wolves. They were milling around, trying to avoid the soldiers that had landed, and the fey with them. It seemed that there were fewer goblins and fey than when the battle had started. A few of the uniformed men started to encircle the goblins. "Just one moment," Lee started as he walked towards the nervous creatures, explaining the situation to the ranking officer.

Freyja stepped up beside Dan and wrapped her hand in his. "It is good to see you," she stated.

"You took the words right out of my mouth," Dan smiled. "We should try and get back to the friendly forces."

"Hey," Brackish waved at Freyja.

"Hello, Brackish," she greeted.

"Brackish, give us a minute," Dan instructed. As the goblin went back to the black powder clan, the American turned to Freyja. "I have a favor to ask you."

"And what would that be?"

"Those goblins did a huge favor for us, saved our lives," Dan replied. "Do you think…?"

Freyja silenced the rest of the question with a kiss. "Anything for you, you foolish man."

Dan smiled. "We have to find Brogan and Esmeralda," Lee said, remembering his former traveling companions.

The officer took down the pertinent information. "We should be able to escort them soon."

"What?" Lee asked.

"Friendly forces are in that area now," the officer explained.

"Wonderful," Lee asked. "Can you please let me know as soon as they find them."

"We'll do our best," the officer said, stepping away to attend to matters elsewhere.

"What about them?" Brackish asked.

"They're coming with us," Lee answered. "I don't see why we can't have a larger clan. Dan?"

"I don't see anything wrong with it," Dan answered, tossing the destroyed remains of his bowler onto the ground. "Freyja thinks that they can settle in their forest. She's going to speak to the fey elders about it. I get the feeling that she can convince them."

Epilogue

Dan and Freyja stood at the door to his and Lee's home, Dan's arm in a cast. His more severe cuts were bandaged, while the minor wounds had healed up nicely. It had been several weeks since they had returned to England. "So?" Dan asked.

"I will be back, but someone has to go and help your new associates settle in," Freyja smiled.

Behind the strikingly beautiful woman was an old-fashioned horse drawn wagon, the rear of it loaded down with squirming piles that kept moving beneath their canvas confines. "Alright," Dan agreed. "I suppose they will take some introducing around the group."

"I will see you soon," Freyja promised, her lips brushing Dan's.

"I'm holding you to that," the American replied.

"Just don't go back off to war." And with that, she took her leave.

Dan stood there, watching as Freyja climbed onto the driver's bench and got the wagon moving, taking it away from the city and towards the enchanted forest where Freyja and her people resided. Coming up the street with a paper tucked under his arm, Lee gave a wave as the wagon passed him. His complexion was much better now, and he also had a cast around his arm. His shirt covered the heavy bandages around his ribs. "How's Esmeralda?" Dan asked as his partner climbed the steps.

"She's doing wonderful," the Englishman proclaimed. "The engineering firm that I set her up with is extremely pleased with her skills. Esmeralda is an amazing woman with such a sharp mind," the Englishman explained. "I imagine that she will adapt to life here in England quite quickly."

"Speaking of amazing women, what about her cousin?"

"She's still nursing Brogan back to health up in his cottage."

The two men entered and went up the steps to their apartment. Brackish was sitting on the sofa, a bottle of beer in his hand. "Is good be home," the goblin announced.

"Couldn't have put it better myself," Dan agreed.

"I almost forgot to tell you," Lee started. "I read it in the evening paper before coming home. The war is over. It seems that the Czar was only too happy to make peace with the Queen."

"Then why did he start the war in the first place?" Dan asked.

"He didn't," Lee explained. "It seems that his Minister President had been keeping the Crown Prince and Princess hostage so he could start *his* war."

"Where is bad man now?" Brackish asked.

"A funny thing happened. After Freyja fought the Baba Yaga, the minister vanished from his locked room with only an open window."

"I heard that the troops on the border are getting snowed on," Dan commented.

"It seems that a lot of the Prussian industrial plants that had been working to fuel the war machine have been closed," Lee added. "I suppose the air is clearing up, and the weather patterns will be returning to normal."

"Witch better?" The goblin asked.

"I would imagine so," the Englishman stated.

"What about our witch?" Dan asked.

"I spoke with Roger before my visit with Esmeralda. No one has had any encounters with a witch in the whole of England since we left," the Englishman stated.

"If I've learned one thing, that woman doesn't keep her head down for long," the American replied. "She'll slip up, and when she does, we'll have her."

"Any work to do?" Brackish asked, changing the subject.

"There are a few cases that we could take on," Lee replied, "given our lowered capacities."

"Why are you in a hurry to get back to work?" Dan asked.

"Last bottle of beer," the goblin replied solemnly.

"Well, guess we'll need to take a case," the American stated.

THE END

Winston & Baum and the Secret of the Stone Circle

Winston & Baum are two men who are no strangers to danger and the mythical creatures that plague the English countryside. Now Queen Victoria, a cyborg of brass and bolts, has charged them with an important mission. Representatives from the fairy world have warned that dark forces are gathering to conquer the British Isles and rid it of man and good fey alike. In an unholy bond between the dark races of the English fey and German monsters, a child has been ordered dead. If the girl dies, then the evil forces will be unstoppable. Traveling the English countryside in search of the child, led only by dreams, Winston & Baum must confront overwhelming odds to rescue the girl and keep her safe. The German forces are not willing to surrender so easily, and it is discovered that everything is not as it seems. Winston & Baum will have to unravel the Secret of the Stone Circle to save God, Queen, and country.

Winston & Baum and the Seven Mummies of Sekhmet

Dan Winston & Lee Baum, two adventurers who hunt monsters for a living, find themselves pitted against unimaginable forces. Seven mummies have recently been discovered, the Priests of Sekhmet. On the unveiling of one of these mummies, a madman, with supernatural powers, steals the headdress of the priest. In their search for the thief, they discover a startling truth: when the headdresses of the seven priests are brought together, they have the power to awaken the sleeping goddess, Sekhmet. Now Dan, Lee, and their goblin assistant, Brackish, must travel to the sands of Egypt, where they will battle foes not seen in our world for centuries. In a race against time, Winston & Baum will have to stop a nearly invincible madman, prevent an ancient evil from being reawakened, and save the world from an age of darkness. Just another day on the job for the exterminators of the strange and weird.

Winston & Baum and the Disk of Night

Dan Winston & Lee Baum, the premier monster-exterminating duo of England, find themselves called to America. Billy Hoffster Johnson, a Texas cattle baron and former client of Dan's, arrives with news that a group of skinwalkers, long dead, are once again menacing his ranch and have murdered famed monster hunter and Dan's friend, Pecos Slim. The medicine man that revived these villains seems to be after more than their blood. When a strange black disk is uncovered, bringing with it unholy magic, Dan and Lee are all that stand between the evil man and the chaos surrounding the dark artifact. With their very souls on the line, can the exterminators of the strange and weird rise to the challenge?

Also included in this volume, Brackish Thumtum, everyone's favorite goblin, stars in his own solo adventure: Brackish & the Sleeping Maidens.

Other novels by Seth Tucker

Friedkin's Curse: A Werewolf Tale of Terror

Four friends; Jack, Emera, Ameth, and Owen go to the Friedkin School for Girls. It's supposed to be simple, go pick up Emera and Ameth's sister Ruby, but the students have been seeing something in the woods; something monstrous; something not human. On the first night, Jack is able to hold it at bay. Now the army has arrived, but protecting the people at the school does not seem to be their top priority. Jack will have to rise to the task as the soldiers seem to be unable to stop the beast. His only hope of understanding the creature's origin and motives rests in the two old journals belonging to the house's former owners. Soldiers and civilians alike are dying. The monster seems unstoppable driven by an unholy desire. Jack and the survivors will have to last the night and destroy the beast or die trying. Now what started as an overnight trip has turned into a fight for survival. The horror in the woods wants something that only it knows. In the dark of the night, evil stalks the halls.

Terror Beneath Cactus Flats (A Weird Western)

Jed, the fresh faced deputy Marshall of Cactus Flats, finds himself put to the test as an unknown evil besieges the small town. In order to save the townsfolk, Jed will have to venture into the old abandoned mines and confront the evil awaiting within.

Friends Don't Let Friends be Undead

Three days after her husband dies, Lily is shocked to see him staring at her from outside her home. Calling on the four men he trusted most, Lily relies on them to place Steve back into his eternal rest. Guided by his journal, his friends will find that the man they loved has been replaced by a vicious fiend that will stop at nothing to sate its thirst for blood.

Richard Rex and the Succubus of Whitechapel

A murder in Whitechapel is not uncommon, but the state of the body requires someone more adept at unusual crime than Scotland Yard. Richard Rex, agent of the Queen, must track down this supernatural killer. Can he find it before it claims more victims?

Acknowledgement

This book would not have been half this good without the advice from my wife and cover artist, Caralyn Tucker and the editing talent of Mac Elmore. I owe you all a great deal of thanks for the insight and help.

Author's Note

Thank you so much for taking the time to read the fourth Winston & Baum adventure. These guys are a blast to write and, hopefully, a blast to read. I've tried to do something different with each book and maintain the fun, fast-pace that I established in Winston & Baum and the Secret of the Stone Circle. I knew that I wanted them to go to Prussia and face the Baba Yaga and the horde of monsters found there but initially, the thought of having Lee drafted into the military with Dan and Brackish working to rescue him was far from my mind. I realized that I had never separated the duo for any long period of time; I felt like the third book was a good buildup of Dan's past, and I wanted to showcase Lee in a similar fashion. Rather than have his past come up, I thought it would be interesting to shake things up and have them not fighting for a bounty or to save the world but for each other.

If you enjoyed this book, please leave a review. Your opinion counts and can help others find fun reads.

About the Author

Born on a dark, dreary, winter day, Seth Tucker came to realize that just because things aren't bright and happy doesn't mean they can't be fun. Fascinated with monsters, ghosts, mythology, and folklore, he is always interested in learning something new about these things. Seth Tucker has never seen a hut with chicken legs. If he did, he would most likely wonder how hard it would be to fry them.